Crime Time

The Journal of Crime Fiction
Issue 3.2   June 2000

contents

ARTICLES
literary guilty pleasures
the great and good — 7
george pelecanos
eddie duggan — 52
sarah cauldwell: an appreciation:
hrf keating — 64
living with crowner john
bernard knight — 71
crime from canongate
brian ritterspak — 75
dark detectives
jones, russell & newman — 80
mileniall movies
mike carlson — 249
john barry:
charles waring — 265

HAMMETT, CHANDLER AND CAIN: NEW APPROACHES
ray and dash
kim newman — 96
dashiell hammett, detective writer
eddie duggan — 101
twisted hopes and crooked dreams: james m. cain's double indemnity
steve holland — 117

FICTION
candleland
martin waites — 144
murder on wheels
mary scott — 157
the puppet show
patrick redmond — 275

PEOPLE
peter lovesey — 24
michael palmer — 37
d w buffa — 40
michael cordy — 42
joyce holmes — 45
stuart pawson — 48
david baldacci — 58
max allan collins — 65
phillip friedman — 78
toby litt — 88
jose latour — 91

REGULAR FEATURES
tirade — 4
news — 5
back issues — 288

COLUMNS

flying the flag
mike ripley — 126
collecting crime:
mike ashley — 132
writing crime:
natasha cooper — 244
crime and history:
gwendoline butler — 275
a personal view:
mark timlin — 276
the view from murder one:
maxim jakubowski — 278
...and finally:
john kennedy melling — 280
new crime fiction:
adrian muller — 283

THE VERDICT

books — 200
audio — 242
film — 257
tv: the cops — 260
music — 269

---

publisher
CT Publishing
PO Box 5880
Birmingham B16 8JF
Phone/fax: 01582 712244,
e-mail: editor@crimetime.co.uk
distribution
Turnaround
printing
Omnia Books Glasgow
editor:
Barry Forshaw
design:
Peter Dillon-Parkin
film editor:
Michael Carlson
tv and music editor:
Charles Waring
advertising
Please phone for rates, or write to the editorial address.
subscriptions:
£20 for four issues to
Crime Time Subscriptions, 18 Coleswood Rd, Harpenden, Herts AL5 1EQ
legal stuff
Crime Time is © 2000
CT Publishing
ISBN 1-902002-22-2

All rights reserved. no part of this book may be reproduced, stored in or introduced into a retrieval system, or transmitted, in any form, or by any means (electronic, mechanical, photocopying, recording or otherwise) without the written permission of the publisher. Hidden here where no one can see it is the last goodbye of Peter Dillon-Parkin, last of the last. Remember the old days when *all* issues had hidden messages in stuff? Send him an email at pdillonp@bigfoot.com or check out www.mysterymile.com towards the end of this year. Goodbye!!!

stuff

tirade

WHY DO I DO IT? Putting together a magazine like CT is enough of a Sisyphean task without making things more difficult for myself, but I still like to add those little extras which can guarantee a king-sized editorial headache. This time, it was my masterstroke of inaugurating an authors forum: I'd ask a goodly selection of crime practitioners to come up with a couple of hundred words or so on a given subject. But what to choose as the first topic? I discounted politics and sex (we've got politicians for those subjects) and hit on the idea of winkling out the literary guilty pleasures authors had been keeping an embarrassed secret. We've all got them, haven't we? Who among us doesn't descend from the slopes of Mount Parnassus occasionally? But as soon as I began my phone calls and e-mails, I realised that my biggest problem would not be recalcitrant authors (Michael Dibdin was the only writer who point-blank refused to participate); it was the fact that (in this postmodern age) there is almost no such thing left as a literary guilty pleasure. Micky Spillane? Already celebrated by this magazine, the commie-bashing old brutalist is now everybody's favourite uncle, and the once prevalent concept that he debased the crime genre now seems a touch quaint. Well, how about comic strips? I'd stump up the fact that I'm a consumer of everything from Superman to the original EC crime comics—but so, it seems, were many of our authors. And apart from the difficulty of coming up with suitably unacceptable subjects, several writers were reluctant to name living writers as their guilty pleasures for fear of giving offence—I was amazed at how well-mannered so many crime scribes are. Also, I asked every contributor to mention their current book as part of the reply (I know I could have filled this in myself, but I reasoned that authors would be able to choose a book from a particular publisher, if they were represented in different lists). Not a problem, you may think, as every crime author is constantly whinging about the fact that the publicity departments have not raised public awareness of their books. But I found that a good 80% of the contributors skipped this strapline, and I was obliged to do the filling in myself. As to the answers: well, you can judge for yourself, but I must say that I had great fun finding out just what so many authors considered to be the kind book they would only read behind closed doors. I was hoping Mark Timlin would pick vicarage mysteries—but he had an even darker secret...

In the last issue, we ran a piece by Michael Carlson on the loss to the genre of the great George V Higgins. An intelligent, well-written piece, well up to Mike's impeccable standards. Except, he tells me, that he only wrote half of it. But who wrote the rest? Even *Crime Time* can come up with an insoluble mystery...

barry forshaw

bullets

adrian muller

THE CRIME WRITERS' ASSOCIATION DAGGER WINNERS

The Gold & Silver Dagger for Crime Fiction: (Sponsored by The Macallan) Gold: Robert Wilson, for *A Small Death In Lisbon* (HarperCollins) Sliver: Adrian Matthews, for *Vienna Blood* (Cape)

The Gold Dagger for Non-Fiction: (Sponsored by The Macallan) Winner: Brian Cathcart, for *The Case Of Stephen Lawrence* (Viking)

The Short Story Dagger (Sponsored by The Macallan) Winner: Anthony Mann, for *Taking Care Of Frank*, from *Crimewave 2*, ed Mat Coward (TTA Press)

The John Creasey Memorial Dagger (Sponsored by Chivers Press) Winner: Dan Fesperman for *Lie In The Dark* (No Exit Press)

The Diamond Dagger Award (Sponsored by Cartier; for a significant contribution to crime-writing) Winner: Margaret Yorke

Ellis Peters Historical Dagger (Sponsored by the Estate of Ellis Peters, Headline, and Little, Brown & Co) Winner: Lindsey Davis, for *Two For The Lions* (Century)

ST. HILDA'S CRIME AND MYSTERY WEEKEND

The intimate Oxford convention will take place on the weekend of 18-20 August. Titled 'Mind Games' the theme this year will be psychological suspense in crime fiction. To date no speakers are confirmed, but look out for more details in the next issue of *Crime Time*. For registration details contact: St. Hilda's Crime and Mystery Weekend 2000, please contact: Eileen Roberts, Development Office, St. Hilda's College, Oxford OX4 1DY, United Kingdom.

HOLMES & WATSON

June Thompson is probably best known for her Sherlock Holmes pastiches. However, in 1995 Constable published her extensively researched biography of the Bakerstreet detective and side-kick. Allison & Busby are reissuing the *Holmes & Watson* biography as a paperback in July.

MYSTERY WOMEN

Mystery Women, an organisation promoting female crime writers hosted a drinks party at last year's St. Hilda's weekend, as well as setting up a superb event at London's Crime in Store earlier this year. Chairing the event was Val McDermid, and participating authors were Andrea Badenoch, Mo Hayder, Denise Mina, and Laura Wilson. The next event at Crime in Store will be the 11th of June at 2pm and will feature Alison Joseph. Mystery Women organise events througout the UK and for more details contact: Mystery Women, 34 The Wranglands, Fleckney, Leicester LE8 8TW.

DEAD ON DEANSGATE

The dates for the third annual Waterstone's/CWA organised convention are October 27-29. Confirmed Guest Authors are Ruth Rendell and Reginald Hill. Details of the American Guest Author will follow. Also attending will be this year's Diamond

Dagger Award winner Peter Lovesey. The conference hotel will again be the Ramada, with the adjacent Travellodge as an alternative. For Dead on Deansgate registration forms please send a stamped and self-addressed envelope to: Waterstone's, 91 Deansgate, Manchester M3 2BW. A Dead on Deansgate registration form, together with convention details, can also be obtained from the Waterstone's website: www.waterstones-manchester-deansgate.co.uk See the next issue of Crime Time for a *Dead on Deansgate* update

PETER ROBINSON

The Yorkshireman now living in Canada will be making some rare appearances in Britain to promote his Edgar nominated (see below) *In A Dry Season*, the latest in his Inspector Banks series. Published by Macmillan in April, Robinson will be reading extracts at Leeds Library on Friday the 28th of that month, as well as other unconfirmed dates (including Crime in Store).

THE EDGAR AWARDS
(MYSTERY WRITERS OF AMERICA'S EDGAR ALLAN POE AWARD NOMINATIONS 2000)

Best Novel:
River Of Darkness by Rennie Airth (Viking Press), *Bones* by Jan Burke (Simon & Schuster), *L. A. Requiem* by Robert Crais (Doubleday), *Strawberry Sunday* by Stephen Greenleaf (Scribner & Sons), *In A Dry Season* by Peter Robinson (Avon)

Best First Novel By An American Author:
Certifiably Insane by Arthur W. Bahr (Simon & Schuster), *Big Trouble* by Dave Barry (Putnam), *The Skull Mantra* by Eliot Pattison (St. Martin's Minotaur), *God Is A Bullet* by Boston Teran (Knopf), *Inner City Blues* by Paula L. Woods (W. W. Norton & Co.)

Best Paperback Original:
Fulton County Blues by Ruth Birmingham (Berkley Prime Crime), *Lucky Man* by Tony Dunbar (Dell), *The Resurrectionist* by Mark Graham (Avon Books), *The Outcast* by Jose Latour (Akashic Books), *In Big Trouble* by Laura Lippman (Avon)

Best Fact Crime:
The Ghosts Of Hopewell by *Jim Fisher (Southern Illinois University Press)*, *Mean Justice* by *Edward Hume (Simon & Schuster)*, *And Never Let Her Go* by *Ann Rule (Simon & Schuster)*, *Disco Bloodbath* by *James St. James (Simon & Schuster)*, *Blind Eye* by *James B. Stewart (Simon & Schuster)*

Best Critical/Biographical Work:
Oxford Companion To Crime & Mystery Writing edited by *Rosemary Herbert (Oxford University Press)*, *A Suitable Job For A Woman* by *Val McDermid (Poisoned Pen Press)*, *The Web Of Iniquity: Early Detective Fiction By American Women* by *Catherine Ross Nickerson (Duke University Press)*, *Ross Macdonald* by *Tom Nolan (Scribner)*, *Teller Of Tales: The Life Of Arthur Conan Doyle* by *Daniel Stashower (Henry Holt & Sons)*

Best Short Story:
Triangle by *Jeffrey Deaver*- Ellery Queen Mystery Magazine/*March,* *Snow* by *Stuart M. Kaminsky* -First Cases,Vol. III, edited By *Robert J. Randisi (Signet)*, *Paleta Man* by *Laurie R. King*—Irreconcilable Differences, edited by *Lea Matera (HarperCollins)*, *Crack* by *James W. Hall*—Murder and Obsession, edited by *Otto Penzler, (Delacorte Press)*, *Heroes* by *Anne Perry*— Murder and Obsession, edited by *Otto Penzler (Delacorte Press)*

Grand Master:
Mary Higgins Clark

literary guilty pleasures...

In the first of an occasional series of author forums, a clutch of our top crime fiction practitioners were asked to come up with something that they enjoyed reading – but wouldn't feel too comfortable admitting to (the less acceptable the better)...

IAN RANKIN

Does Jilly Cooper count as literary? Every summer on holiday I seem to end up reaching out a shaking, addict's hand for her novel *Rivals*. I must have read it a dozen times. And Christmas 1999, stuck in rural France with no electricity (thanks to the worst storms in over a century) I reread Jilly's *Polo*. It was pretty good, too, but not as good as *Rivals*. I also read a lot of comic books, but they're treated as a respectable form these days, aren't they? More serious than Jilly Cooper, I mean. What else? Oh, I know: Garfield books. I've read nearly all of them, and reread them now and then, still chuckling at the best strips. I'm also a Simpsons historian (as in the cartoon series, not the defunct London department store), and I read things like *Maltin's Film Guide* from cover to cover (it's an A-Z of every English language film ever made).

Sad old muso that I am, I'm also addicted to discographies, especially the vast encyclopedic tomes written by Martin Strong (*The Great Rock Discography*, for example). These are really just exhaustive lists of recordings by artists (singles, albums, album tracks). I read every damned word... and tuck away the best titles for use in future Rebus novels.

Just a sad bastard then.

Ian Rankin's latest novel is Set In Darkness *(Orion).*

H R F KEATING

My literary guilty pleasure? Oh well, of course, it's erotica. But it isn't. Fierce old moralist that I am, even with myself, I can never quite manage actually to indulge in the pleasure. It's partly, too, timidity, for I expect that (if I did) the eventual outcome would not be any sort of pleasure at all. I was taught Latin at school (though I can never translate even the simplest sentence), but I've been left with a mouthful of miscellaneous tags, many of which I can even understand. So, poised in front of a rack of well-filled shelves of erotica in Waterstones, I'm dismayed, shocked perhaps, I murmur *facile decensus in avernus*, then go home, look it up and re-think *facilis decensus averno*. So if I were to pluck out one thin-looking volume, won't I end up in heaven knows what trouble? Blackmailed? In the police court? In hospital with some awful disease? Anyhow, in some sort of highly unpleasant *avernus*, or hell. So I – here's a nice word - eschew.

Harry Keating's latest book is The Hard Detective *(Macmillan).*

DENISE DANKS

My guilty literary pleasure has to be the *Confessions* series. My particular favourite was *Confessions from a Clink* which included that wonderful line from the ever priapic hero: "*...her breasts hit my chest like two suitcases hitting a custom officer's desk.*" Laugh? I thought my socks would never dry.

Denise Danks' latest books are Torso *and* Phreak *(Orion)*

RUSSELL JAMES

Like many men, I'm an inveterate hoarder - a thousand 78s in the cellar, hundreds of LPs, books of old postcards, scrap albums, articles from newspapers, old glasses, Goss china, football programmes, beer mats and several thousand books. For a while back in the Eighties I legitimised this by running a "collectors" stall at travelling antique fairs. But this gave me permission to buy as well as sell, and before a year was out I had more "stock" than when I'd started. I still rummage through mounds of old stock stacked in my cellar, and I occasionally mount a defence against my wife's demands that I chuck it out, but among the various sub-categories of ephemera - as we dealers call disposables not disposed of - the one that brings me the greatest warmth on winter evenings is the collection I put together from the darkest, dampest corners of second-hand bookshops: bound copies of Victorian magazines.

These densely printed tomes (typically 800 pages, mock leather bound), preferably illustrated with hackwork wood engravings or, in later decades, steel plates, tell you everything you want to know - or everything the publishers wanted you to know - about that Victorian world. You'll find encyclopaedic studies on work houses, factories, industrial practices, housing conditions, missionary work here and abroad - mixed in with recipes, remedies, agony columns, improving articles, fashions, excruciating poems and extraordinary fiction. Aimed at a varied readership, these tales tell of hopeless romance, moral failure, drink, death and love - or alternatively, of cute kittens and wise words from winsome children. Much of this stuff is dreadful - great wodges of pious hackwork - but scattered amongst it and easy to find are fascinating snippets from the history of real people: working conditions in the potteries, a night with the rivermen, the ragged schools, London's hidden rivers, How St Marylebone Got Its Name.

These are books to be flicked through by firelight. Unlike Victorian readers, dutifully conning pages to improve themselves, I indulge myself like a late-night TV watcher, zapper in hand, skipping from piece to picture, fiction to fact. Instead of a cup of improving tea I take a whisky. The flames from the fire glow in my glass and I'm transported from this rough, tough, go-get-'em hard boiled land I pretend to live in, back to an equally invented land of Victorian middle class duty, self-sacrifice and respect. The hard boiled "Godfather of British noir" relaxes within the dusty pages of old books.

Russell James' latest book is Oh No, Not My Baby *(Do-Not-Press).*

ROBERT WILSON

My only guilty literary pleasure is when I go to the dentist and read Hello magazine for the gossip and I'm not sure that counts. Occasionally I get hold of the Spanish version and that's even stranger as it features Hispanic minor royalty and aristos that I've never heard of but is still oddly satisfying.

Robert Wilson's latest book is A Small Death in Lisbon *(HarperCollins).*

JANET LAURENCE

I have always been a sucker for the soft underbelly of literature, the stories that hook you in with charm and romance. Georgette Heyer's historicals are favourite bedtime reading that I turn to again and again. But I can't quite feel guilty about enjoying Heyer; her light style, her research, her deft plotting, her delightful characterisation and her gift for irony, can all be admired.

The author I squirm to admit that I still read, albeit standing up by the bookshelves while hunting for something else, is Dornford Yates. To steal a look at the Berry stories is to be taken back to a world where men were gallant, ladies lovely and the countryside beautiful. I find the background of landed estates and privilege seductive, and the beautifully behaved characters charming, though Berry's witticisms and persiflage can be tedious. Technically, the stories are deftly told. What is totally shaming is to realise that their snobbism and anti-semitism completely passed me by when I first read Yates as a teenager. Now I see them warts and all - but still occasionally slip back into that sunlit world where crime was straightforward and honour of great value.

Janet Laurence's latest book is Canaletto and the Case of the Privy Garden *(Macmillan)*

SPARKLE HAYTER

I love books by the Jackies, Susann and Collins, and bad tell-all autobiographies by celebs, like Eddie Fisher. I also like naughty nurse porno novels from the late-1970s and early-1980s and *Richie Rich* comics. Should I feel guilty about that?

Sparkle Hayter's latest book is The Last Manly Man *from No Exit Press. She is quite proud of it, but nevertheless wishes she had written* Captain Underpants and the Invasion of the Incredibly Naughty Cafeteria Ladies From Outer Space (and the Subsequent Assault of Equally Evil Lunchroom Zombie Nerds) *by Dav Pilkey.*

KIM NEWMAN

These days, it's almost impossible to think of books as guilty pleasures. A true guilty pleasure would be something you read despite its lack of any qualities that would make an enthusiasm for it explicable to other people - books (or, perhaps, comics) that meant something to you as a child but which adult sensibilities tell you aren't actually any good even on their own terms (anyone who, like me, has tracked down, bought and read a particular Batman issue remembered from 1967 knows what I mean), or books that are so extreme in one way or another that you wouldn't recommend them to anyone else. However, as my life stands, I find all the reading that I undertake simply because I want to, as opposed to the sometimes chore-like reading I have to do as a critic (or, as this year, as a judge for a literary award), can't possibly be guilt-making. There is no pulp science fiction, crime or horror writer whom I admire who does not have his or her legion of like-minded fans. The same goes for the sometimes abstruse academic or reference books about popular culture that I am mildly addicted to. In order to feel guilty, you have to be the only person in the world - or, at least, that you know - who would even consider reading the damned thing. I suppose all that leaves in the guilt column are those few books I own that I have only the vaguest intention of ever actually reading - books picked up because of their strange cover art, lurid title or bizarre jacket copy. To whit, on the shelf I have of paperbacks (mostly picked up cheap off stalls) yet to be read, I find these items, which might well not live up to their covers: *When the Clock Strikes 13* by David Hanna ("They call themselves The Committee - neo-Nazis whose mad leader feeds on sex, mass murder, absolute power"); Ann Fettamen's *Trashing* ("Gentle Ann in the clutches of a stone-freak revolutionary mad-mob") which has blurb quotes from Jerry Rubin ("for freaking out - Ann Fettamen sure can DO IT!") and Abbie Hoffman ("the Nancy Drew of the revolution - makes Harold Robbins read like Homer"); Anthony Dekker's *Temptations in a Private Zoo* ("The Bear Garden begins where the Playboy Club leaves off") of which the Observer noted "a posh organised expense account orgy with slap up tarts and every kind of kink catered for". Eventually I will read these books; but for the moment, the most guiltily pleasurable aspect of them is that I can imagine just what they're like.

Kim Newman's latest book is Seven Stars *(Simon & Schuster)*

MARK TIMLIN

When Barry Forshaw asked me to do this, I scratched my head. I mean - what is a literary guilty pleasure? I read books about bad rock 'n' roll records and lousy movies, but I don't feel guilty about it. Then the perfect thing struck me - and I promise I've never told anyone else about this before. So keep it under your wig. It all started in the Sixties when (for a little bit of extra cash) my first wife decided to become an agent for Littlewoods.

One morning, bright and early, the carrier brought the catalogue, all five pounds of the bloody thing. I took a squint - and what did I find? Why, the lingerie section, of course. Blimey, I thought, this'll do. So when I was saying: "Nice shoes", or "I do like that shirt", you can guess were my fingers were really doing the walking. And now every time I see a GUS catalogue or Kays, or any of those brightly coloured six-inch thick volumes, I know where I look first. The models are so pure looking, so girl-next-door. But is that a hint of nipple? A shadow of pubic hair? You bet your sweet life it is. Then I got an American girlfriend, went to visit - and discovered *Victoria's Secrets* catalogue. And if you don't know what that is, I'm not going to explain. Use your imagination. Fucking hell, I thought. I'd died and gone to heaven. And even though she wore the kit, I still think I preferred the pictures. That's not all. I've also got *Caddy's Daddy* 1999/2000 catalogue of Cadillac spares from their inception to the present day. Let me tell you, the air filter for a '59 Bonneville or the hood ornament from an '83 Fleetwood really gets my juices flowing.

Mark Timlin's latest books are Quick, Before They Catch Us *(No Exit Press) and* I Spied A Pale Horse *(Toxic).*

CAROL ANNE DAVIS

I nominate second-rate erotica by writers who've been spurned by Mills 'n' Boon. You know, the type where a heroine with an exotic name is described as "going on a sexual odyssey". At the end she uses a carrot as a dildo and consequently finds herself. These books imply that having anal sex is like sliding a knife into chocolate mousse. I told one erotica writer that most of us who'd opened the back door had been biting the pillow. "Oh, I've never tried it," she said, looking mortified, "I've got irritable bowel syndrome so couldn't put anything up there." Other erotica characters are heavily bondaged then left alone for half an hour "to take their torrid anticipation to a crescendo". Deserting a lover who is bound and gagged is seriously dense. If they regurgitate last night's madras and duly asphyxiate you'll be the one wearing the handcuffs - whilst answering a manslaughter charge. There's some very good erotica out there, but the bad stuff is much more diverting. A single page can make you both cry with laughter and feel comparatively like a carnal connoisseur.

Carol Anne Davis' latest book is Safe as Houses *(The Do-Not Press).*

MARTIN EDWARDS

I admit it. I'm a sucker for those "how to write a bestseller" books. In fact, any book about the craft of writing exerts an irresistible fascination on me. Hard to explain, really, since I never take any of the advice they offer. Perhaps that explains why I don't outsell Patricia Cornwell and Ruth Rendell, but I doubt it. I don't want to be told to "write about what I know" for the thousandth time. It's incomplete advice at best: after all, I write about murder and I have yet to commit one. But I do find it intriguing to find out what works for other writers - just as I might enjoy discussing the same things in the bar at Bouchercon or Dead on Deansgate.

There's no doubt which of the "how to" books are the most appealing. The ones that have passed their sell-by date. My all-time favourite is Marie F Rodell's *Mystery Fiction: Theory and Technique*. It was published in 1954, which simply shows how much times have changed. The most hilarious chapter, written in solemn tone, is entitled "Taboos and Musts", which contains priceless tips about the handling of sex. I've never read any of Ms Rodell's own novels, but somehow I doubt whether they can match her crime writing manual for sheer entertainment value. A classic.

Martin Edwards' latest book is First Cut is the Deepest *(NEL)*

PETER LOVESEY

A difficult one. I've given this quite some thought, but all I could come up with was something by Isaac Asimov. No, not one of his detective outings, or even his science fiction. How about his *Lecherous Limericks*? Not many people know about that - and I imagine it doesn't figure in too many of his bibliographies.

Peter Lovesey's latest book is The Reaper *(Little, Brown)*

MIKE RIPLEY

I don't suppose that this counts as a guilty pleasure: in fact, I think Richard Matheson's *I Am Legend* is now considered something of a classic, so probably I have to discount that. I'm tempted to include the complete works of Nigel Molesworth, but I think I've come up with something that none of the other contributors will have picked. Most people have heard of *The Story of O*, but how many people are familiar with *Story of O, Part Two*? I bought that in Toronto, and consumed it at a sitting. Guilty enough?

Mike Ripley's latest book is Bootlegged Angel *(Constable Robinson)*

ROBERT HARRIS

Hmmm...well, I don't imagine that Richmal Crompton's *Just William* books are much of a guilty pleasure these days, but I wonder how many adults pick them up? I certainly do, and I'm not ashamed to say it - well, not too ashamed. Yes, the grubby William it is: I'm prepared to stand up and be counted.

Robert Harris' latest book is Archangel *(Arrow), with the film tie-in of* Enigma *imminent.*

PETER JAMES

I'm an aeroplane freak – and the Biggles books still have tremendous appeal for me. WE Johns has to be unacceptable enough, surely? Actually, the books are not as un-PC as people think...

Peter James' latest book is Faith *(Orion)*

GWENDOLINE BUTLER

I certainly feel guilty about reading *Harpers* and *Vogue* – but I continue to do so. Why? All those anorexic prepubescent models...

Gwendoline Butler's latest novel is The King Cried Murder *(CT Publishing)*

MAXIM JAKUBOWSKI

Gee, a difficult one! Somehow over the years I've quietly engineered my career and writing so that my guilty pleasures become socially acceptable: obsessive noir fiction, literate erotica, even drinking cola, rock and country music of the non-charts variety, so what is left that might be termed gently shameful? (scratches his brow) If push comes to shove then, let's confess to a non-literary guiltless indulgence for black silk shirts! Yes, I know it's a profound disappointment to my mini-legion of fans who expected something more perverse, but I learned years ago not to ever feel guilty!

Maxim Jakubowski's latest book is On Tenderness Express*(Do-Not-Press)*

VAL MCDERMID

Barry Forshaw tells the I'm not the only one to pick a Chalet School book as my guilty pleasure, but what can I do? Whenever I'm tucked up in bed with flu, *Chalet School in Exile* is just the thing. It may be a world away from my usual universe, but that's probably why it does the trick for me.

Val McDermid's latest book is Killing the Shadows *(HarperCollins)*

WOODY HAUT

Reading remains, whatever the material, a "guilty pleasure". Meanwhile crime fiction has become so pervasive that guilt hardly enters into its consumption. My guilty list would begin with the WW2 spy novels of Alan Furst, which I devour as soon as they appear. My entire knowledge of Eastern Europe during WWII comes from those books. I'd also cite the boys' baseball novels of John R Tunis. Written in the late 1940s, and influenced by Popular Front politics, the likes of *Highpockets*, *Keystone Kids*, *Good Field No Hit* and *The Kid from Tomkinsville* remain fascinating. Well-written, they concern a mythical Brooklyn Dodgers. Each focuses on a particular player and issue, from anti-semitism and racism to false pride and mob violence. Having first read them as a 1950s pre-adolescent in LA, I can still reel off the names and positions of the players. I bought Philip Roth's excellent *American Pastoral* simply because he mentions Tunis' novels. Thirdly, I'd pick the hardboiled poetry of Kenneth Fearing. Forget his fiction, however excellent some of it might be. Poems such as *The Face in the Barroom Mirror*, *Sherlock Spends a Day in the Country*, and *As the Fuse Burns Down* are a series of novels that would never be written. A final guilty pleasure: accessing internet book searches, an activity that has made collectibles widely available, inflated their price beyond measure, and turned every second-hand dealer into a rare book authority.

Woody Haut's latest book is Neon Noir: Contemporary American Crime Fiction *(Serpent's Tail)*.

FRANCES FYFIELD

When I was a serious student of heavy duty literature and the law, the not-so-secret pleasure was anything in the Mills & Boon library. Don't knock it; a lot of good writers start here and a lot of the books are as good as any romances in print , but it isn't the best ones which appealed. It was the worst. You know the kind, with lines like: *"as she came downstairs, she heard Bruno murdering Chopin on the piano…"*, or, *"his eyes rolled around the room"*. As an antidote to real life and peerless prose, this is sheer heaven.

Frances Fyfield's latest book is Staring at the Light *(Corgi)*.

MARGARET MURPHY

"What are your guilty literary pleasures?" Barry Forshaw asked. Guilty pleasures? Me? All my reading material is worthy, grown-up, intellectually

demanding - you should see the weighty tomes on my bedside table...

All right. Okay, you may find the odd graphic novel in the pile - so I'm a sucker for the superhero. To be specific Superman. What is it about those guys with bulging muscles and aching hearts? For me, the aching heart was the attraction. The need for comfort, for tender human contact, counter-balanced by the awful-wonderful secret he must keep. He's the nice guy from Smallville, honest and honourable, and no one demonstrates better that you don't have to be macho to be strong.

Perhaps the concept of good battling against the forces of evil fills a secret void in my atheistic psyche; whatever the cause, the harmless flirtation that began with borrowing my brothers' comics as a kid became a full-blown obsession. What else could it be, when a grown woman sits through the Saturday cacophony of brainless link-persons, just so that she can catch up with the Man of Steel? Though what Clark saw in the strident Lois Lane, I'll never know - for me, Lana Lang was the woman he should have fallen for. But isn't that just like a man? They always fall for the wrong women...

Margaret Murphy's latest book is Past Reason *(Macmillan).*

TOBY LITT

I have a confession to make... I *cheat*. [Angry shouts from female audience members.] God, man, it's really hard for me to admit this stuff. The shame it brings my friends, my family. The terrible hurt it causes my beautiful girlfriend. But you've gotta believe me... it's like an *addiction*. Something I just can't... really, I can't control it. I get so *involved* in the whole atmosphere of the thing. Those snatched phone conversations that, in a moment or two, seem to move my life on to a whole 'nother level. Those covert meetings in darkened rooms. (Just the two of us together. Losing all memory of the real, moral, out-there world. Gently touching those sweet curves with thumbs and fingers. Pushing all the right buttons.) [Gleeful whoops from male audience members.] But, man,... it gets to a point where I'm stuck, y'know? It feels like I've fallen into a room with a secret exit, and I just can't find that mother-BEEP! Or like I'm shooting BEEP chunks out of a crowd of BEEP zombies that never BEEP die! OK,. I'm cool... And it's like it's no use. I feel all maggoty with guilt. Man, I feel *rancid*. But still some mysterious, like, "force" draws me back. Once again, I'm entering the agents. I'm selecting my obscene assistant, approaching the counter, paying my sad way. And then I'm out on the street with my guilt all in my hands: *PlayStation Solutions*. The World's Best Selling PlayStation Tips Magazine... you've gotta help me. Please! I want out! I really want out of this sordid life I've been living. O BEEP BEEP! [Prolonged applause from audience.]

Toby Litt's Latest book is Corpsing *(Hamish Hamilton).*

NATASHA COOPER

"You can't go in there, miss; the master's eaten Hull's Cheese." Having dropped my copy of Georgette Heyer's *Venetia* in the bath once too often, I can't check the quotation for precise accuracy, but it's an example of the

magpie collection of wonderful slang that makes her novels such fun.

When I first read them as a child, I wallowed in the romance provided by her four distinct classes of hero: Mr Rochester types with evil tempers hiding secret vulnerability; suave sarcastic brutes with great estates and many mistresses; fragile wounded souls in need of TLC and money to save the family inheritance; and big blond bruisers with huge muscles and gentle instincts. Any of them could make my girlish heart flutter.

These days it's the jokes that tickle me, and the slang, and the way Heyer subverts the classic romantic plot to give the alpha male to the heroine who refuses to behave as a modest creature should. Not for Georgette Heyer (pace Joan Smith in *Misogynies*) the sweet gentle heroine taming the savage brute with her innocence; it's almost always the wicked, the extra clever, or the particularly strong woman who gets the goodies in the end. Great stuff!

Natasha Cooper's latest book is Prey to All *(Simon & Schuster) with her new outing as Clare Layton,* A Clutch of Phantoms *from HarperCollins*

CHAZ BRENCHLEY

Okay, I confess. Here I am – tall, dark and scary (I'm told), with a mind that runs to the extremes of human cruelty - and what do I read in times of crisis, where's my comfort-zone? The *Chalet School* books of Elinor M Brent-Dyer, that's where. For those not familiar, we are talking a series of sixty-odd novels here, boarding-school stories for girls, set largely in the Austrian Tyrol or else in Switzerland; the first was published in 1926, the last in 1970. And they're magic. Wherein the magic lies is hard to pinpoint. The plots are, let's say repetitive (stubborn / rebellious / spoilt girl joins the school, causes trouble, is redeemed and grows up to marry a doctor some volumes later), and the writing is rarely good and often excruciating; and yet, they are magic. I've been an addict since I was a small boy, when my sisters used to read them. Best news, though, is that I am not alone. I go to stay with a friend of mine, she tries to distract me with her own latest book, but it doesn't work. For bedtime reading, I trawl her *Chalet School* shelf for anything I haven't got. Ever been outed, Val...?

Chaz Brenchley's latest novel is Shelter *(New English Library).*

GARY LOVISI

I think the stuff that has to be the most fun for me is the 1950s British hardboiled gangster digests, Griff, Ace Capelli, dare I say it, Hank Janson, some of the Danny Spades, Darcy Glinto, Al Bocca and Ben Sarto's ain't bad either. Most of it written in the American idiom. Gray Usher (his actual name) was an excellent British hardboiler relegated to these gangster digests. I sift through it all to find the better stuff, and sometimes actually find it. It's raw, hardboiled crime pulp that pulls no punches, and it's fun to read, even if the closest most of these writers got to America was meeting some GI stationed in the UK during WWII.

Gary Lovisi's latest novel is Blood in Brooklyn *(Do-Not- Press).*

CHRIS PETIT

I find it hard to name a book as we now live in an age of confession and apology which makes almost everything permissible, so long as you say sorry afterwards. Mickey Spillane is accepted canon now (though I always like his sheer hysteria), and I have tried hard to think of fascist writers beyond the pale (Dennis Wheatley) but post-modernism allows you to cut up and reposition anything. Perhaps the only one that makes me feel guilty is P D James.

Chis Petit's latest book is Back From the Dead *(Macmillan).*

JAY RUSSELL

In a time when even the most lowbrow cultural artefact is ripe picking for academic vivisection, the very concept of guilty pleasure may be past its sell-by date. If soap operas and video games and theme park rides can be the stuff of high theory, what in the world is there to feel guilty about? Comic books, of course!

Now, believe me, I am aware of the plethora of learned treatises devoted to comics. I wrote one myself, once upon a time. (Well, I don't know how learned it was, but it was certainly machete-thick enough to qualify as a treatise.) But the question I had to ask myself here was: what would I be embarrassed to be *seen* reading by strangers on an aeroplane or tube train. Romance novels might fit the bill, but I don't like them and would never be reading one, so the "pleasure" half of the equation doesn't work. The cover art of some of the genre novels I read is almost enough to make me want to hide them, but I have no real guilt about the contents.

Comic books still embarrass the hell out of me. Because I do think the form is wonderful, I'm embarrassed to have to admit to being embarrassed by them, but then maybe I'm just too easy to embarrass. And I'm not just talking about superhero comics here - because they're almost all so bloody awful, I hardly ever read them. (Honest. I'm not just lying to cover my embarrassment.) But even the best comics, such as Acme Novelty Library, which I would defend with every sinew of writerly elegance at my disposal, tend to stay hidden in the Forbidden Planet bag as I'm riding the train back home. (And don't get me started on the embarrassment of those Forbidden Planet bags...) I want to be brave about this textual pleasure that dare not speak its name, but what's an overgrown boy to do? At least when I get them home, I don't read the comics under my covers.

Not anymore, I mean.

Jay Russell's latest book is Waltzes and Whispers *(Pumpkin Books).*

JUDITH CUTLER

Laugh? I could die every time I chortle over *The Black Countryman* magazine with a half of mild and a packet of pork scratchings. But you, dear reader, may not even realise there's a joke there. Try this for size:

Enoch (pronounced Aynuck), goes down the boozer and buys a dog, real cheap. He takes it down the cut (canal) and throws a stick along the tow-path. The dog wags its little tail and retrieves it. Now, Enoch's had a skinful, remember, and next time he throws, the stick goes across the water. The dog looks at him a bit old, but shrugs his shoulders, walks across the water and retrieves the stick. Enoch can't quite fathom this: he repeats the procedure. So, shrugging his shoulders, does the dog.

Only one thing for it. Enoch finds his friend Eli (pronounced Ayli) and drags him down to the cut. A throw along the towpath - the dog wags his little tail. A throw across the cut - the dog shrugs his shoulders and sets off across the water, walking back with the stick which he drops at Enoch's feet.

Eli looks at his friend aghast: *"Eh, Enoch: you been done. You been and paid five bob for a dog as cor (can't) swim!"*

Gerrit?

Judith Cutler's latest book is Dying by Degrees *(Headline).*

PHILIP FRIEDMAN

Not long ago my girlfriend and I took to reading to each other on long trips by car, switching off between driving and reading. One of the books we read was the first Harry Potter, which we'd picked up on a trip to London. This made me think about children's literature as a source of reading pleasure. That, and the fact that some friends had recently completed a quite wonderful stage musical based on R L Stevenson's *A Child's Garden of Verses*, turned me to *Treasure Island*. What a splendid book I found it to be, much richer and more interesting by far than my pallid recollection. I literally couldn't put it down. I don't where this is going to lead me...presumably to *Kidnapped* next, if I want to stay with Stevenson. But I'm now fascinated by the wider possibilities of books nominally intended for kids. I've had some Karl May (*Ardistan and Djinistan*, etc) on a shelf forever - bought them because I'd once read they were Einstein's favourites as a kid - but I have never attempted them. I suppose I'd better start with what I have at home, since a grown-up lurking in the stacks of the kiddie library is apt to draw the wrong kind of attention here in New York.

Philip Friedman's latest book is No Higher Law *(Headline Feature).*

HILARY BONNER

I am not sure that I really feel guilty about anything I read, but if I am ever found covering up a book with my hands while trying to look as if I'm studying Tolstoy, it will probably be because I am immersed in something aimed for rather younger readers than the average tome of Russian literature. I have a love of children's books, the sillier the better. A great favourite is a beautifully illustrated book called *The Butterfly Ball*.

*"Tantara, teroo!
I'm Harold the Herald,
Gadfly and trumpeter too,
Well equipped for my job, as you see.
My trumpet's a gentian,
My sword's in its scabbard,
My wife, let me mention.
Embroidered my tabard."*

OK, I know it's sad, but that always makes me chuckle. I bought the book as a gift for a child many years ago and it so enchanted me that I kept it (which is actually something of a habit). This last Christmas I bought *The Complete Borrowers' Stories* for a young cousin, started rereading them - I loved them when I was a kid, what an imagination Mary Norton had - and ended up buying a second set because the first one was going nowhere.

And that, I suppose, is my real guilty secret. I use young children as an excuse to acquire, or at least reread, books and poems aimed at them rather than give in and admit to myself that I'm really buying them for myself because I'm obviously still just a big daft kid. Shameful, really!

Hilary Bonner's latest book is A Deep Deceipt *(Heinemann)*

JON COURTENAY GRIMWOOD

"If you have never robbed a man - or a woman - of honour. If you have never ruined boy or girl..."

A bottle of blood-red Cahors, a couple of free hours and those words - short of sex there's nothing to beat it. At school, kept safe in the library behind locked glass-lined doors, was a collection of pre-war hardbacks. Red covers and rough-cut edges, spines heavy with blocking. The fact they were locked away meant I just had to read them... And all it took to force the ancient brass lock was a knife slipped between the doors and twisted. I didn't even crack the wood.

It wasn't pornography that the school kept safely hidden, it was historical fiction. Rows and rows of the stuff. A E W Mason's *Fire Over England*, G A Henty's *In the Reign of Terror*, Stanley J Weyman's *House of the Wolf*.

Some, including most of the Henty, were trite and unreadable. But Raphael Sabatini's *Scaramouche* and Weyman's *Under the Red Robe* were stunning: trash novels made great by accident. Books not about how society makes people but about what people make of themselves. About the cost of living up to your own lies. Just pass me the bottle of wine.

Jon Courtenay Grimwood latest book is redRobe *(Earthlight).*

PAULA GOSLING

My guilty literary pleasure began in childhood. They are the Oz books by Ruth Plumley Thomson, who continued the series after the death of Frank Baum. Her use of language is delightful, and made me realise that language can be fun, that you can play games with it, twist it and turn it to have more than one meaning, and in general squish it as raw clay for the sheer pleasure of it. I mean English, of course, having no sense of other languages myself. It is surely the most marvellous language for writers, a mongrel language, adaptable, accepting of new words (unlike French), capable of being either roughshod or as delicate as a ballerina as it steps across the page. Now, when I am ill, or even just feeling a little inept as a writer (which comes all too often) I turn to Ms. Thomson's Oz books to re-ignite that sense of joy in words. Not Austen, not Dostoyevsky, neither Chaucer nor Shakespeare, but just a juggler of language for the entertainment of children. And are we not all children still, within, when feeling small?

Paula Gosling's latest book is Underneath Every Stone *(Little, Brown & Co.).* Death and Shadows *has been released in paperback (Warner).*

PHIL RICKMAN

Rivals by Jilly Cooper. It was a late night encounter. I seemed to have read most of the paperbacks on the tiny stand in the motorway motel, except for the Tom Clancy, and this two-inch thick number with a red stiletto heel piercing a man's hand on the front and the face of Jilly Cooper simpering from the spine. Naturally, I asked my wife to buy it.

But isn't this how it always happens - the passing attraction that becomes a wild craving?

Rivals is about a bunch of flawed people - and one saint - chasing the franchise for a TV station in the Cotswolds. It has wild sex, tame puns and lines like: *"I want him"*, she thought helplessly, *"I want to be the woman who brings him fulfilment"*.

God, I loved this book. For me, it was never like this before. For a while, I just kind of hoped they'd win the TV franchise, then it became an urgent need. Finally, I knew that if they lost it I couldn't face the dawn. Suddenly, in comparison, *The Bonfire of the Vanities* seemed emotionally thin, and I learned what could be the most important lesson in novel-writing: true suspense is only possible (sob) when you really, really, *really* care.

Phil Rickman's latest novel is Midwinter of the Spirit *(Pan).*

PAUL JOHNSTON

Homer's *Odyssey*. Yes, I know - choosing an ancient Greek text is a touch pretentious, but it's the truth. Whenever I need to kickstart my spirits, I head for my tattered copy of *The Odyssey*. Maybe it's because I first came across it when I was about six (precocious, moi?); maybe it's because I'm deeply in love with the isles of Greece; or maybe, just maybe, it's because the old epic is actually the Western world's first crime story.

Think of it this way: you've got a hero, Odysseus, who's trying to get home after ten years' fighting. During the additional ten years the voyage takes him, he's persecuted by an unseen power (the sea-god Poseidon); he's attacked by a cannibalistic psycho (the Cyclops), who he blinds; he's serially unfaithful to his wife; and he's betrayed by his crew. Then, when he finally makes it back to Ithaca, he slaughters his wife's suitors and hangs the maids who slept with them from the rafters. Plenty of criminal material there.

Of course, there's much more to *The Odyssey*, and I don't go back to it simply to remind myself of crime writing's epic pedigree. I reread Odysseus's travails because they're psychologically convincing - the poem presents a world that's infinitely different from ours, but that world is peopled by characters we can instantly recognise.

And the scene in the underworld where the hero encounters his mother, whose death he didn't know about, would move even a pulp writer to tears...

Paul Johnston's latest book is The Blood Tree *(Hodder and Stoughton).*

DAVID DOCHERTY

I know I shouldn't but I always do. I feel that familiar itching in the palms, the clammy guilt, the glance over the shoulder to see if anyone is looking, the nagging knowledge that such reading should be confined to the privacy of the loo. Yes, you've guessed it, I'm addicted to Rupert's mighty organ, the deal old Current Bun. In common with all right thinking people I body-swerved Murdoch's *Sun* after the Wapping move and the disgraceful treatment of the Liverpool fans at Hillsborough; but I was drawn back after Saint Tony joined the paper as a columnist and accepted the wages of spin. I realised I could not understand New Britain and New Labour unless I gained insight into the mind of White Van Man (the *Sun*'s name for the everyman). I'm afraid *The Guardian*, my trusty companion to all things PC, was no longer enough of a guide to the world around me. It only slowly dawned on me that past page three and the right-wing bilge of some of its columnists, it's actually a bloody good read: a particular pleasure is the picture problem pages, in which pudgy "real-life" blokes and their leggy Essex girl wives / lovers / adulteresses agonise over the issue of three-in-a-bed sex (and one of those is a sheep). I tried to copy their style in my new book, but I'm afraid it takes decades of training. There, I've got that off my chest. I feel much better. Now let me tell you about my addiction to... No, that's for the privacy of the bedroom.

David Docherty's latest book is The Spirit Death *(Simon and Schuster).*

ROB RYAN

In retrospect he was a terrifying construct built from equal parts Jeffrey Archer (there was some scandal about a murder covered up in his youth), Dick Francis (*"Prince of thriller writers"*, the *TLS* proclaimed) and Stephen King (those astral plane thrillers such as *Devil Rides Out*), but even so, the yellow-spined Hutchinson paperbacks of Dennis Wheatley's work are my literary madeleine cake. I had, of course, ditched my own copies years ago, probably when I moved onto something loftier - Sven Hassel perhaps - but around two years ago I saw a dog-eared copy of *Traitor's Gate* in a charity shop window and bought it for 25p. I sat down to read the dated and artless prose and found myself fifteen again, rooting for Gregory Sallust (*"My God you must be made of solid gall"*, as his boss puts it) while secretly relishing the dastardly Gruppenfuhrer Grauber. Since then no charity shop is safe from my rummaging, even though, having bought several of them, I can never see myself finishing one of the 18th century Roger Brook tales, with their accurate, if dull, slabs of history crudely inserted (imagine Flashman without the finesse) and others are downright offensive - witness *Dangerous Inheritance* where the heroes *"still believe in all the British Empire stood for and that marriages between people with different coloured skins rarely brings lasting happiness."* However, there is always a compensation - it does feature a Rex van Ryn, a name I always fancied purloining. I also think my growing library of Dennis up there acts as a grim warning not to take all this publishing malarkey too seriously - as every jacket proclaims, Wheatley sold a million books per annum, penned more than fifty novels, and not a single title is left in print today.

Rob Ryan's latest book is Nine Mil *(Headline).*

STEVE HOLLAND

It started with a boyhood fascination for Page 3 girls and teenage years spent reading *Confessions* books and the occasional Sullivan magazine (Playbirds, Whitehouse) starring Mary Millington. Thus focused, my collector, gotta-make-a-list nature has doomed me to an obsession with saucy British sex magazines. That's saucy, not pornographic. Until 1971, you didn't even get a flash of pubic hair, and even after that breakthrough, British magazines were always softcore; adult books always accompanied sex with a snigger, and Valerie Leon's Hi-Karate adverts was the closest TV got to sex. And my guilty pleasure is? Pin-up magazines and "candid" story papers from the 1950s and 1960s. The (fictional) confession style of storytelling in these thin magazines (sometimes priced at 75 cents – did anyone believe they were genuine Yank mags?) usually stopped at a stolen kiss or a snapping suspender; the pin-ups were smooth-skinned statues in black and white, beautifully photographed by Roye, Harrison Marks or Russell Gay. Part of the pleasure is their naiveté. All of the guilt is that I actually spend money on this rubbish. (And I do. If you find some, call me.)

Steve Holland's latest book is The Mushroom Jungle *(Zardoz Books).*

JOHN CONNOLLY

The year: 1978. The place: Synge Street Christian Brothers' School, Dublin. The book: Ian Fleming's *Thunderball*, the cool Pan edition with two bullet holes in a front cover otherwise dominated by an expanse of naked flesh. The memory: a bemused Brother O'Grady examining the cover before handing it wordlessly back to the small boy who was reading it at the time.

I'm not sure if Brother O'Grady had ever read an Ian Fleming novel but, if he hadn't, that cover told him pretty much all he needed to know: we were talking sex and violence, but kind of expensive sex and violence (even now, you'd be hard pressed to convince a publisher to go to the trouble of making little bullet holes in the cover of your book). If he'd been interested, I could also have told him about the snobbery; the peculiar card games with rules I couldn't understand but which seemed to make the player irresistible to women; the fact that a disturbing number of those women seemed to have some physical defect (limps, dodgy eyes, pig ugliness); the sadism; and Pussy Galore, who really just needed a good man to sort her out. I guess that, even at age 10, I wanted to have women falling for me, preferably women without limps. I wanted to play *chemin de fer*, even if I didn't know the rules and my mum only gave me enough money for bus fare. I wanted to be able to tell the vintage of a wine by taste alone and have barmen all over the world know me by name because I was a classy guy, and not simply because I was a well-travelled alcoholic. But, most of all, I wanted a watch that doubled as a radio, and a car fitted with spikes and machine guns. I think I still do, which is why I still have a shelf of musty paperbacks and The Best of Bond on my car stereo. And my name...?

My name's Bastard, Sad Bastard.

John Connolly's latest book is Dark Hollow *(Hodder)*

MICHELLE SPRING

Diet books, especially the type that promise you will lose a stone in less than a fortnight. Unfortunately, reading them always makes me very, very hungry.

Michelle Spring's latest book is Nights in White Satin *(Orion).*

MICHAEL JECKS

There are few pleasures which can equal mine. Not literary. Every few weeks I take a day off. Yes, a whole day. I spend it without reading or typing, although I may well walk the dog, because on these days I produce BEER. Yes, I home brew. My God, you don't know how hard it is to confess! I'm just glad the truth is in the open at last. I simmer grains for an hour and a half, rinse them in hot water, then boil hops for another ninety minutes, before shoving the liquor away to cool. Throw in the yeast and within a fortnight I've got a delicious beer.

"Oh yeah?" you sneer? You reckon all home brew tastes of chemicals, do you? Well, I know what goes into my beers and they're all chemical free, which maybe explains why friends and I can each drink seven pints without a following headache - only in a spirit of scientific enquiry, you understand.

The only trouble is, although I make five gallons at a time, as soon as my neighbours hear it's ready, they all tend to drop in, so I have to make more quite regularly.

Michael Jecks latest books are The Traitor of St Giles *(Headline) and the paperback of* Belladonna at Belstone.

ANDREW TAYLOR

My literary guilty pleasures are too numerous to mention - Heyer, Blyton, Du Maurier (D and G) just for a start. But the one I really can't do without is Richmal Crompton's *William* books, with the Thomas Henry illustrations. Crompton wrote with wit, elegance and enormous intelligence. (You hardly notice that while she's making you laugh, she unobtrusively chronicles nearly half a century of provincial life.) And William Brown is a hero to die for. William remains my role model. I gave his name to both my first fictional hero, William Dougal, and my son.

Andrew Taylor's latest book is The Office of the Dead *(HarperCollins).*

PETER GUTTRIDGE

Literary guilty pleasure: The *Sherlock Holmes* Radio Show. Cue loud, cheesy organ music. A cheerful American voice: *"Petri Wine brings you ..."* More organ riffs. *"Basil Rathbone and Nigel Bruce"* - more organ - *"in the New Adventures of Sherlock Holmes"* - the organist goes nuts. Every Monday night for thirty-nine weeks each year between 1939 and 1946, the two stars played Holmes and Watson live on US radio.

On audiotape you can now get some sixty of those transmissions from 1945 and 1946. And - despite the high price, scrappy introductions and a disgraceful minimum of information - I've got 'em all. Including the lousy ones when the sponsor changed to Kreml hair tonic and the announcer was a dolorous guy who sounds like Marvin in *Hitchiker's Guide*. (Lousy because Rathbone's place had been ineffectually taken by Tom Conway, though they don't tell you that on the packaging.)

I love them - not least for their corniness and the delight of hearing Bruce flub his lines and Rathbone make eloquent the most banal remark. One or two of the episodes are faithful to Conan Doyle (*A Scandal In Bohemia*; *The Problem of Thor Bridge*), a few are either "inspired" by a Conan Doyle story or enact one of those stories Conan Doyle only referred to. (It's a rare thrill - sad life or what? - to come upon Wilson, the Notorious Canary Trainer brought to life in one episode.) Over the years many writers scripted the series - including Leslie Charteris - but most of the episodes on tape are by Dennis Green and Anthony Boucher. Thanks chaps.

Peter Guttridge's latest book is The Once and Future Con *(Headline).*

MIKE ASHLEY

My guilty pleasure is compiling lists. I can't stop myself. Anything that lends itself to a list and I just have to start. I can't bear incompleteness. It isn't just literary lists — anything from kings and queens to rivers, planets, stars — but it's bibliographies that can send me crazy. Oh what a sad, sad sight to see me slavering over a complete bibliography to Raymond Chandler or an index to Dime Detective. But woe-betide if there's a gap in it. I tell you — it's the road to madness.

Mike Ashley's latest book is The Mammoth Book of Sword and Honour *(Constable Robinson)*

BASIL COPPER

Guilty pleasures? Well, I suppose that this must include the forbidden subject of sex. But to people of my generation, brought up in the golden age of the Twenties and Thirties, sex did not exist. Things went on behind the scenes, of course, but it was a world of innocence to young people of my sort. We were absorbed by classical music and literature, Meccano, model railways and such like, plus the glamour of the cinema. In my teenage years, I came across the Marquis de Sade. He has been unfairly vilified over the centuries, but he was a much maligned man, spending most of his life imprisoned due to the schemings of an evil relative. Nearly all of his amorous adventures were in his own head, unlike the squalid world in which we now live. About fifteen years ago, I was in a London bookshop when I spotted a row of paperbacks of his *120 Days of Sodom*. A few days later, I was again in the same shop when I noticed that all the books had gone. Not, as one might suppose, due to a rush of eager customers, but they had been withdrawn on the orders of the authorities. Books can, it seems, still be subversive.

Basil Copper's latest book is Whispers in the Night *(Fedogan & Bremer).*

born in a vintage year:
peter lovesey

Photo: Phil Monk

This Spring Peter Lovesey becomes the first author of the new millennium to be awarded the CWA Cartier Diamond Dagger Award for a lifetime achievement in the genre of crime writing. Past recipients include such illustrious names as John le Carré, Dick Francis, Reginald Hill, PD James, Ed McBain, Ruth Rendell, and last year's winner Margaret Yorke. Lovesey began writing historical crime fiction long before such writers as Edward Marston, Ellis Peters (also a Diamond Dagger winner), and Anne Perry came on the scene. He made his debut with a number of novels featuring Victorian policemen Sergeant Cribb and Constable Thackeray. The books are currently being republished by Allison & Busby. However, these days the author is probably better known for his contemporary(and award winning¾Peter Diamond series set in Bath. A new non-series novel, The Reaper, recently published by Little, Brown suggested that this was, a good time for Adrian Muller to look at Peter Lovesey's long and varied writing career.

PETER LOVESEY was born in Middlesex, England, in 1936. "The same year as Robert Barnard and Reginald Hill," he says, adding with a smile, "A vintage year for mystery writers". Brought up in suburban London during World War II, he was evacuated to the West country in 1944 after the family home was destroyed by a flying bomb. These war

adrian muller

abracadaver
A Sergeant Cribb Mystery

'Sinister fun in a splendidly atmospheric setting'
The Sunday Telegraph

experiences, and those following in early peace time, were to influence two of Lovesey's later novels, *Rough Cider* and *On the Edge*. After completing his education at Hampton Grammar School, Lovesey went to Reading University in 1955. Failing his Latin exams meant that he was not eligible to study English because a qualification in the ancient language was a necessary requirement for the modern one. Being a reasonable artist he decided to study Fine Art instead. Part of the latter course included History and English as secondary subjects and due to submitting *"some quite interesting essays,"* as the author puts it, two of Lovesey's tutors, novelist John Wain and literary critic Frank Kermode, helped him get into English studies after all.

By now he had met Jacqueline (Jax) Lewis, his future wife, and he was eager to change courses for more reasons than one. *"The big incentive,"* he recalls, *"was that Art was a four year course and English three. I wanted to get married to Jax who was doing a three year course, so I swapped to English."* Lovesey, who recalls his time at Reading with much affection, says that, *"Whilst I didn't do anything remarkable, I managed to get a degree."* The statement is a good example of the author's modesty, because his entry in *The St. James Guide to Crime and Mystery Writers* shows that he graduated with Honours.

When Lovesey left university in 1958, a two year stint in the National Service was still obligatory in Britain, so he joined the Royal Air Force. With an eye on the future, he signed up for three years and completed a training course to become an Education Officer. The rank offered better wages, allowing him to marry Jax in 1959, and also gave him a head-start on a teaching career.

In 1961 he left the Armed Forces for a fourteen-year career in education. Starting out as a Lecturer in English at Thurrock Technical College in Essex, he became Head of the General Education Department at London's Hammersmith College for Further Education (now West London College) until he left to become a full-time writer. Lovesey enjoyed teaching and interacting with students, but disliked the inroads made on both of these areas by his administrative duties. *"There's so much paperwork, so many committee meetings, to the extent that it distracts from the real business of teaching,"* he says. By the time Lovesey ended his educational career in 1975, he had already established himself as an author, with two non-fiction books on sport, and six of the eight Detective Sergeant Cribb books.

The Cribb novels came about through the author's self-confessed lack in athletic ability. *"The first two books I wrote were about sport and their origin goes right back to my school days,"* Lovesey remembers. *"If you wanted to have any status with people in the school, you had to excel at sport. I was useless,"* he says laughing. *"I was really, really bad."* In an attempt to improve his standing, he may have been one of the world's first joggers. Shuffling around the back streets of the London suburb of Twickenham, he tried to improve his times but frequently, the author claims, ran into lampposts and was savaged by dogs. As a consequence, he sought a safer alternative to gamesmanship. *"I became one of those kids who didn't participate, but who knew and could talk about sport a great deal."* He would read all the papers and listen to all the commentaries on boxing, football, and so on. Gradually he began to dream about a career as a sports journalist. Later, when he was a teacher, he started to submit articles to magazines, initially without much success. It took a little while before he realised there was a little covered topic he could exploit: track and field history. Explains Lovesey, *"I thought that if I dug into the past I could find information for interesting character-pieces about great runners."* The research brought him into contact with many names in the world of athletics, some of whom became good friends.

People like Norris McWhirter, the founder of *The Guinness Book of Records*, and Harold Abrahams, one of the athletes portrayed in the Oscar winning film *Chariots of Fire*. After Lovesey had spent some ten years writing about sport, it was suggested that he might have enough material for a book. *"I thought about it and realised it would require more work,"* he says. *"So I began to expand some of the articles I had written and put them together into a book called The Kings of Distance."* Peter Lovesey's first book, focusing on the lives of five long distance runners, was published in 1968. It started off in the early nineteenth century with the story of Deerfoot, an American Indian, and closed some hundred years later with Emil Zatopek, the Czech athlete who dominated the Olympic Games in 1952. The book received good reviews and was chosen as Sports Book of the Year. In 1969 *The Kings of Distance* was followed by *The Guide to British Track and Field Literature 1275-1968*, a bibliography on sports writing, written in collaboration with Tom McNab. A definitive reference work on the subject, the guide is still used by collectors.

It was also in 1969 that Jax Lovesey spotted an advert in *The Times* which would have a major impact on her husband's life. It was for a competition to write a crime novel and, because the cash prize was about as much as her husband was earning in a year as a teacher, Jax suggested he should enter. After all, he had had two books published already. Lovesey was less confident. *"I pointed out that those had been non-fiction books about sport, and I had hardly read any crime fiction."* Jax was

CROOKS, CRIMES, RIDDLES & RHYMES
RECENT AND FORTHCOMING CRIME FICTION FROM

ALLISON & BUSBY

The A & B Crime Collection
CANDLELAND - *Martyn Waites (March)*
MURDER ON WHEELS - *Mary Scott (April)*
THE LONE TRAVELLER - *Susan Kelly (May)*
SKELETON AT THE FEAST - *Patricia Hall (June)*
THE THIRD MESSIAH - *Christopher West (Aug)*
All hardback - £16.99

MEET	**CONGRATULATIONS**	**WIN!**
Martyn Waites & Mary Scott at Crime in Store, London on 9th May at 6.30 p.m.	to Peter Lovesey on the award of the CWA Cartier Diamond Dagger Award	Peter Lovesey 'Cribb' novels in the competition in this issue

Crime Paperbacks
WHOEVER HAS THE HEART - Jennie Melville
NIGHT VISIT - Priscilla Masters A PRIVATE INQUIRY - Jessica Mann
KILLER'S PAYOFF - Ed McBain ABRACADAVER - Peter Lovesey
SEA FEVER - Ann Cleeves EVAN HELP US - Rhys Bowen
THE JOHN DICKSON CARR OMNIBUS - £10.99
THE DEATH OF AN IRISH SEA WOLF - Bartholomew Gill (May)
MONSIEUR PAMPLEMOUSSE ON PROBATION - Michael Bond (June)
SHERLOCK HOLMES AND THE DEVIL'S GRAIL - Barrie Roberts (June)
SNAPPED IN CORNWALL - Janie Bolitho (July)
STONE DEAD - Frank Smith (Aug)
RED MANDARIN - Christopher West (Aug)
All £6.99 except where stated

****

Watch for new Crime fiction every month from
ALLISON & BUSBY
114 New Cavendish Street, London W1M 7FD
send for our catalogue. Visit our website at www.allisonandbusby.ltd.uk
Telephone: 020 7636 2942 Fax: 020 7323 2023

persistent, however, and he finally agreed to have a go. For this budding novelist, the obvious idea was to use a background in athletics. He entered his manuscript, called Wobble to Death and, looking back, he is convinced that it was the novelty value of the story that won him the first prize.

Lovesey first came across wobbles—Victorian long-distance races lasting six days—when he was researching an article in the newspaper library in Colindale. *"They seemed very bizarre and extraordinary, involving all kinds of tricks that trainers and runners would use to try to hamper their opponents,"* he recalls. *"They would put laxatives in the refreshments, crush walnut shells into competitors shoes..."* However, it was a performance-enhancing drug that fired Lovesey's imagination. To improve their results, runners would take tiny amounts of strychnine. *"It is a stimulant if used in a tiny amount, but take a little more and you're writhing in agony!"* notes Lovesey. He immediately realised that the 'wobble' setting was a natural for a traditional whodunit: poison, murder, and suspects in a closed environment. All that remained was to find a detective to solve the crime. The author decided an ordinary policeman would be more interesting than a Sherlock Holmes-type character, and learned about police methods of the day. Enter Sergeant Cribb and his assistant, Constable Thackeray. It wasn't until Lord Hardinge, the publisher of *Wobble to Death*, handed Peter Lovesey his cheque and asked him what he would be writing next, that the first-time novelist thought about a sequel. *"I remember thinking that I could probably write another crime novel,"* he says, *"but for the life of me I couldn't imagine what it would be about. I didn't think I could go on mining the Victorian world of athletics for very long."* For the sequel, Lovesey stuck with the same detectives, and again turned to Victorian newspapers for inspiration. In the 1880s clandestine fist fights took place in the south of England. To get to the secret location, trains would be organised and people would end up in the middle of nowhere having to walk a short distance to the place where the fight would be held. This background was used in the author's second novel, *The Detective Wore Silk Drawers*. The books developed into a series, mostly exploring various forms of Victorian entertainment. *Abracadaver* dealt with music-hall acts, and *Mad*

Hatter's Holiday is set in Brighton, a popular seaside holiday resort. The fifth in the Cribb series, *Invitation to a Dynamite Party*, focused on Britain's early problems with Irish nationalists. *"In that book I used real events more than I had in any other up to that time,"* says Lovesey. *"I found out about Irishmen who, for many of the same reasons as the Irish Republican Army, were blowing up buildings in London in the early 1880's. Terrifying everybody, they were much more successful than the IRA, and actually damaged London Bridge and several of London's main railway stations. They even managed to get a bomb into Scotland Yard and blew up part of the building!"* *Invitation to a Dynamite Party* ended with an attempt to kill the Prince of Wales by means of one of the earliest submarines, a vessel built by the Irish. *Swing, Swing Together* was inspired by the craze set off by Jerome K. Jerome's *Three Men in a Boat*. The latter is a humorous tale of three friends boating up the river Thames. Jerome's book was a huge best-seller in its time, and as a result trips on the Thames became enormously popular. Reading of all this activity started Lovesey thinking, 'Let's have a situation where people join in the craze.... In *Three Men in a Boat* a corpse floats past the boat... Let's weave a story around that.' Also popular in Victorian times were spiritualists who 'contacted' the dead, and this subject was the inspiration for *A Case of Spirits*. The last Cribb novel, *Waxwork*, provided a major boost to Lovesey's writing career. Telling a gripping tale of a Victorian woman awaiting execution for murder, *Waxwork* was well received, won the author his first Crime Writers' Association Dagger, and caught the eye of June Wyndham-Davies, an English television producer who thought the subject might make an interesting television film. The dramatisation of *Waxwork* was broadcast in 1979, and starred Alan Dobie as Sergeant Cribb, and William Simons as Constable Thackeray. It proved so popular that Granada, the production company, decided to turn the other seven Cribb novels into a television series. Peter Lovesey was shown the scripts, and when he mentioned that one of them didn't feel quite right, the producers asked him if he would do the adaptation himself. The experience proved useful when Granada approached him with the request for a second series. Did he have any ideas for further stories? *"You don't turn down an offer like that,"* says Lovesey. *"I came home triumphantly and told Jax about it. She asked me when the company wanted the stories, reminding me that writing a book took me about a year. They wanted six plots in eight months!"* The opportunity and financial rewards were too good to pass up, and it was Jax who provided a solution to the problematic time factor. Lovesey explains, *"Jax always had some influence on the books. We used to discuss the structure of the story, and I would read the chapters to her as I was going along. So, to help me out with the television series, she said she would write three of the stories, if I would write the other three. That's how we did it,"* he says, concluding, *"We had our names jointly on the credits."* The television series, shown in some fifty countries, was highly successful, and also helped to further popularise the novels. Yet Lovesey decided against writing more Cribb books. One reason was the definitive portrayal of the detective. *"I don't in any way want to give the impression that I wasn't satisfied with Alan Dobie's performance of Cribb,"* he stresses. *"I thought he was brilliant in the part, but television is a very powerful medium. After I saw him play my character it was very difficult to get his portrayal out of my mind. The result was that I couldn't get back to the original concept that I had for Cribb."* Moreover, he had exhausted all his ideas for further stories when writing the television series.

Before concluding the Cribb novels, Lovesey wrote three books of contemporary fiction under the pseudonym of Peter Lear. The first, *Goldengirl*, focused on a super female athlete. Everyone from the girl's own father to big business men seek to exploit her, even when the distinct possibility arises that she will break down from all the pressure. *Goldengirl* was filmed starring Susan Anton and James Coburn, and problems hampered the film's release. *"In the book the athlete was an American competing in the Moscow Olympics,"* says the author. *"It was written about two or three years before the actual event was scheduled to take place. By the time the film was ready for distribution the Russian invasion of Afghanistan led the Americans to boycott the 1980 Olympics. That made it difficult for the studio to promote the film, and it did not do well at the box-office."* Two more novels appeared under he Lear pseudonym. *Spider Girl* is about a woman trying to overcome her fear of spiders. So much so that she becomes obsessed, turning almost spider-like herself. *The Secret of Spandau*, is a fictitious account of an attempt to spring Rudolf Hess from his cell in Berlin's Spandau Prison. There has always been speculation as to the motives of Hitler's deputy parachuting into Scotland in 1941. After the war Hess was sentenced to lifelong imprisonment in Spandau. More recently questions have been asked about the identity of the now deceased prisoner, with some people suggesting that the jailed man may not really have been Hess. Lovesey's theory is that the German prisoner-of-war knew too much sensitive information about the people who wanted make peace with the Germany. 'For me,' says Lovesey, *"the most intriguing thing was not Hess' 'true' identity, but the question of his sanity. It is a fact that there were attempts to brainwash Hess in his first few months in Britain. When obliterating his memory proved unsuccessful, he was imprisoned. The Russians were always blamed for keeping Hess in Spandau but,"* concludes Lovesey, *"I think the British had far more interest in keeping him there."*

In 1982, *The False Inspector Dew* was published, winning Peter Lovesey a Gold Dagger. The introduction to the novel suggests it is based on true events, and then teasingly leaves the reader to try and define which facts are real and which fiction. Lovesey had been reading E.L. Doctorow's *Ragtime* and was much influenced by the latter novel. *"Doctorow had used real people in his book and I found that very exciting,"* he says. *"I began to think I might do something similar in a detective novel."* Lovesey's plot was inspired by Doctor Crippen, the English doctor who murdered his wife, burying her in their cellar.

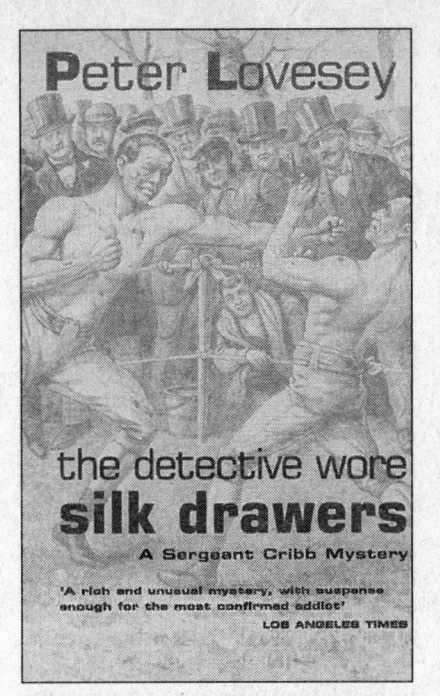

Crippen then attempted to escape to Canada with his mistress on an ocean liner. Unfortunately for the murderer, he was recognised by the Captain, who cabled that Crippen was on board. It was Inspector Dew who was sent ahead in a faster vessel to waylay Crippen in Canada and bring him back to face trial. Lovesey read Inspector Dew's memoirs and became more and more intrigued by the policeman's reaction to the murderer. *"Dew seemed to like Crippen, even though his name is now almost synonymous with someone like Jack the Ripper,"* says Lovesey. *"In his autobiography the Inspector called Crippen 'the little fellow' and 'my friend Crippen', portraying him as a Chaplinesque character. That, to some extent, is why Charlie Chaplin makes a brief appearance in my book."* A further area of interest for Lovesey was to see how much Dew identified with Crippen, wondering what motivated the murderer, and suggesting ways in which Crippen might have escaped. In the book Crippen becomes Walter Baranov, and the reader is left guessing to the closing pages whether the very likeable villain manages to elude the police. The clever plot-twists, and surprising ending earned the author his second dagger.

For his next novel, Lovesey stuck to the winning formula of mixing fact and fiction, setting *Keystone* in 1915 at Hollywood legend Mack Sennett's Keystone Film Studios. The plot has an aspiring English actor joining the Keystone Cops to solve a succession of crimes involving bribery, kidnap, and murder. Naturally the slapstick comedy of the silent-film era forms an integral part of the book. Up until *Keystone*, the author had not yet written a novel set in a period of time of which he had some personal experience. All this would change with his following two non-series books.

In *Rough Cider*, the Second World War forces a young city boy out of his everyday environment. He is evacuated to a 'safe', but alien location in the countryside, only to become a crucial witness in a murder case. Though Lovesey's evacuee experiences in Cornwall did not include murder, he still remembers them as unsettling due to the unfamiliar surroundings and strange local accent. Years later, after coming across a West-country recipe for mutton-fed cider, which involves a joint of meat added to barrelled cider for extra potency, an idea for a novel sprang to mind, and *Rough Cider* was born. *On the Edge* is about *"two women who become bored after the war and decide to murder their husbands,"* says Lovesey. The novel looks at the dissatisfaction of people who in peacetime were forced back into their old, often less exciting existence. For Rose and Antonia, the two women in *On the Edge*, the situation causes personal conflicts, leading them to kill their husbands. *"As with Walter Baranov in The False Inspector Dew I can identify quite a bit with Rose,"* says the author, describing her mitigating circumstances. *"Books that just paint the murderer as a complete blackguard aren't really that interesting. I try to get away from black and white characterisations in an attempt to understand a little of the motives of people. I think it's always fascinating for a reader to be able to understand what drives a person to murder. It's one of those universal questions you can only answer if you have been confronted by it yourself."* Jax Lovesey was especially helpful with *On the Edge*. *"Since it was a book about two women,"* says Lovesey, *"I checked with Jax quite a bit. I had an idea of how women talked, but it was the way women talk to men, not how they talked amongst themselves. So Jax put me right on quite a bit of that."*

Having set three subsequent books in the twentieth century, Peter Lovesey decided to return to Victorian times for his next novel. The author explains, *"I read about Fred Archer, the top jockey of his day, who at the age of twenty-nine committed suicide. His sister came in as he was holding a gun to his head and she heard him say 'Are they coming?' before he shot himself. I thought the incident would lend itself to a conspiracy theory: who were 'they', and what was it all about? It never became clear at the inquest or in the biographies of Archer."* In his search for information on the jockey, Lovesey found that Fred Archer, also known as the Tinman, frequently rode for the Prince of Wales—the latter being called Bertie by his family and close friends. *"I thought 'why shouldn't Bertie himself take an interest in the case?' I discovered that he had sent the biggest wreath at the funeral, and the more I thought about it, the more I realised that he was perfect to be the detective. As the Prince of Wales he had lots of time on his hands—his mother, Queen Victoria, gave him no responsibilities—so he spent his time playing cards, charming the ladies, and looking for things to do. Also, he was in a unique position: he could order the police to help him if he wanted or, when necessary, he could keep them at arm's length."* Having found his sleuth, the author went on to consider what form the book might take. During research for *The Secret of Spandau*, he learned that a substantial amount of documents regarding Rudolf Hess had been classified as 'secret', and their release controlled by a time embargo. What if something similar had occurred to Edward VII's personal papers? 'Declassification' is how Lovesey would explain the sudden appearance of *Bertie and the Tinman: The Detective Memoirs of King Edward VII*. The author recalls enjoying writing the novel in the first person, allowing his sleuth to solve the Tinman mystery, almost in spite of his bungling attempts. When *Bertie and the Tinman* was published one of the favourable reviews referred to the book as 'Dick Francis by gaslight'. With the year of Dame Agatha Christie's centenary nearing, Lovesey wondered whether it might not be interesting for him to write the next Bertie novel with a nod to the Queen of Crime Fiction. Taking some of the typical ingredients from a Christie plot—a country house setting, a murder occurring for every day of the week, and rhymes being sent as clues—*Bertie and the Seven Bodies* was written. A third book, *Bertie and the Crime of Passion*, took the Prince to Paris where he investigates a murder with the assistance of the great actress Sarah Bernhardt.

In 1991, over twenty years since *Wobble to Death*, after fourteen historical mysteries and numerous short stories, Peter Lovesey decided the time had come to write a contemporary crime novel. Ironically the title of the first book in this (unplanned) series featuring Detective Superintendent Peter Diamond was *The Last Detective*. When writing his first 'modern' crime novel, Lovesey had to consider how he would deal with unfamiliar subjects such as up-to-date police procedures and current forensic methods. Previously these matters had been relatively easy to write about because they were less complicated and fixed in time. A solution was soon found. *"The procedures and forensics are acknowledged but,"* says Lovesey, *"I've deliberately made my detective a dinosaur as far as those issues are concerned."* Having explained Diamond's contempt for the latest methods, the author also made the detective a loner, 'Which, for me,' he says, *"was more important. A police procedural should involve a great number of people, it's team work. It can be very difficult to engage a reader's interest when the credit for solving a crime is diffused through a number of people, and I prefer to write the kind of story where one person gets the credit and faces the problems himself."* The *Last Detective* won the 1991 Anthony Award for best novel. It also left Peter Lovesey with an unforeseen dilemma: *"Diamond has this great row towards the end of the book and storms out of the police force,"* says Lovesey, adding, *"Initially I had him continue with the case after being reprimanded. Then I realised that this character had such integrity, and that he was so volatile, that he would not stay in the force but would resign. So that's what happened. However, that left me with a problem when I started thinking about a sequel."* The dilemma was solved by turning the next Peter Diamond novel, *Diamond Solitaire*, into an international thriller. *"Peter Diamond has a job as a security guard in Harrods"*, explains Lovesey, *"but is fired when a Japanese girl sets off the alarms in his department. Intrigued by the little girl Diamond becomes involved with her lot when she is kidnapped, taking him first to New York and ultimately to Tokyo where the whole case is resolved."* In *The Summons* the author found an ingenious way to return Peter Diamond to the police force: one of the former-Detective Superintendent's old cases is drastically reopened, forcing the police to ask for his help. By the close of the novel Diamond can return to his old job stating his own terms. *The Summons* was nominated for an Edgar and won the CWA Silver Dagger for 1995. Diamond's next case, *Bloodhounds*, was published in the year following a brief controversy in the Crime Writers' Association regarding the value of traditional versus hardboiled crime fiction. *Bloodhounds* focuses on a group of crime fiction readers

Peter LOVESEY
The Reaper

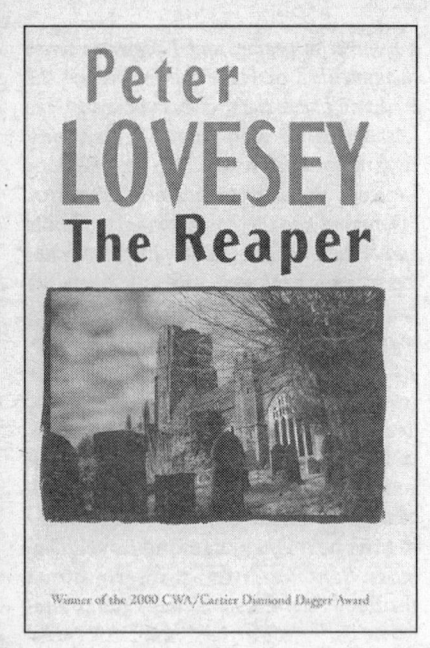

Winner of the 2000 CWA/Cartier Diamond Dagger Award

who gather once a week to discuss the merits of their preferred genre. When members of the reading group start being murdered, Diamond is called in to solve a variety of crimes. With the fictional skirmish following on so soon after the less drastic CWA discord, it might seem that Lovesey had found inspiration right on his doorstep. 'Well,' he says with a smile, *"it might be unwise to admit it, but there are real people in Bloodhounds."* He then swiftly points out why it would be pointless trying to identify any of his fellow writers, *"My characters are often based on real people. I start by thinking so-and-so is ideal for that particular character. Visualising my protagonists makes them more real for me. Then, as the story develops, they take on a life of their own and become involved with things their real-life counterparts would never consider doing. Therefore it would be unfair for me to say that a character is based on a certain individual because they have completely changed."* In 1996, for the second year running, the Silver Dagger was awarded to a Diamond novel.

As mentioned earlier, Peter Lovesey has also written many short stories, and they too have won numerous awards. Interested readers can find some of them in *Butchers and the Other Stories of Crime*, *The Crime of Miss Oyster Brown and Other Stories*, and *Do Not Exceed the Stated Dose*. Calling the short story form 'a delight,' Lovesey says, *"If I could make a living writing them I would be very happy to do so. They can be done in a short time and you can experiment with original, exciting ideas. You can take risks with short stories that you can't with a novel."* The ideas for the tales bubble up in Lovesey's mind when he is deeply involved in a novel, and he thinks of writing them as a reward to himself for finishing a book.

When writing a novel, he will have worked out a synopsis beforehand. This can run up to eight or nine pages, describing what will happen from chapter to chapter. *"It may alter a little as I go along,"* he says, *"but I have to be satisfied in my own mind that the structure is there before I begin."* It takes Lovesey eight or nine months to complete a manuscript and, whilst some of the research is done before he starts, much is also done during the writing of the book itself. Comparing notes with other authors on their writing methods Lovesey was amazed to realise that he is one of a small group of writers who know how their novels will end before they start writing them. 'In my experience,' he says, *"the majority of crime writers appear to prefer not be too clear about where the book is going. They say they can't see the pleasure in writing if they know what's happening. For me the pleasure comes from putting down the words, and finding the appropriate ways of saying things."* The author calls himself a very slow writer, writing approximately two hundred words a day at the start of a novel, but steadily increasing to six or eight hundred words towards the book's completion. One thing Lovesey rarely does is revision, remarking, *"What I write is what will go in the book."*

Presumably this writing process is exactly how the author's new novel *The Reaper* came about. Described on the dust jacket as being 'rich as the devil's food cake at a church fete', the mystery is set off when a bishop's body is found at the bottom of a quarry with a bible and a copy of a girlie magazine. As the police investigate whether someone helped the dead man move closer to his maker, further sudden deaths follow the bishop's demise.

Peter Lovesey's most recent Peter Diamond titles were *Upon a Dark Night* and *The Vault*. Looking back to his very first detective, Lovesey can draw certain parallels with his more recent contemporary creation. *"I suppose we have all been in jobs where we've had some contempt for our superiors, thinking we could do the job a whole lot better without them interfering! That certainly is true of Diamond and Cribb. Also, to some extent they're both protective about the information that they have gathered, not wanting to share it too much. That trait of being careful of revealing too much is also a convention of mystery writers: you want to* surprise *the reader, so perhaps you keep back a little."* He concludes with what could be a summary of his literary style, *"I try and write a fair book, a 'mystery' in the old fashioned sense of the word."*

(This is an updated version of an interview that appeared in the book *Speaking of Murder: Interviews with Masters of Mystery and Suspense.* Editors Ed Gorman and Martin H. Greenberg.)

BIBLIOGRAPHY:

NON-FICTION:

The Kings of Distance: A Study of Five Great Runners. London, Eyre and Spottiswoode, 1968; as *Five Kings of Distance.* New York, St. Martin's Press, 1981. *The Guide to British Track and Field Literature 1275-1968,* with Tom McNab. London, Athletics Arena, 1969. *The Official Centenary History of the Amateur Athletic Association.* London, Guinness Superlatives, 1979.

FICTION:

Wobble to Death. London, Macmillan, and New York, Dodd Mead, 1970. (Macmillan/Panther First Crime Novel Prize). *The Detective Wore Silk Drawers.* London, Macmillan, and New York, Dodd Mead, 1971. *Abracadaver.* London, Macmillan, and New York, Dodd Mead, 1972. *Mad Hatter's Holiday: A Novel of Murder in Victorian Brighton.* London, Macmillan, and New York, Dodd Mead, 1973. *Invitation to a Dynamite Party.* London, Macmillan, 1974; as *The Tick of Death,* New York, Dodd Mead, 1974. *A Case of Spirits.* London, Macmillan, and New York, Dodd Mead, 1975. (Prix du Roman D'Aventures) *Swing, Swing Together.* London, Macmillan, and New

York, Dodd Mead, 1976. (Grand Prix de Littérature Policière) *Waxwork*. London, Macmillan, and New York, Pantheon, 1978. (CWA Silver Dagger) *The False Inspector Dew: A Murder Mystery Aboard the S.S. Mauretania, 1921*. London, Macmillan, and New York, Pantheon, 1982. (CWA Gold Dagger) *Keystone*. London, Macmillan, and New York, Pantheon, 1983. *Butchers and Other Stories of Crime*. London, Macmillan, 1985; New York, Mysterious Press, 1987. *Rough Cider*. London, Bodley Head, 1986; New York, Mysterious Press, 1987. *Bertie and the Tinman: From the Detective Memoirs of King Edward VII*. London, Bodley Head, 1987; New York, Mysterious Press, 1988. *On the Edge*. London, Century Hutchinson, and New York, Mysterious Press, 1989. *Bertie and the Seven Bodies*. London, Century Hutchinson, and New York and London Mysterious Press, 1990. *The Last Detective*. London, Scribner, and New York, Doubleday, 1991. (Anthony Award) *Diamond Solitaire*. London, Little Brown, and New York, Mysterious Press, 1992. *Bertie and the Crime of Passion*. London, Little Brown, and New York, Mysterious Press, 1993. *The Crime of Miss Oyster Brown and Other Stories*. London, Little Brown, 1994. *The Summons*. London, Little Brown, and New York, Mysterious Press, 1995. (CWA Silver Dagger) *Bloodhounds*. London, Little Brown, and New York, Mysterious Press, 1996. (CWA Silver Dagger) *Upon a Dark Night*. London, Little Brown, and New York, Mysterious Press, 1997. *Do Not Exceed the Stated Dose*. London, Little Brown, and USA, Crippen & Landru, 1998. *The Vault*. London, Little Brown, 1999, New York, Mysterious Press, USA, 2000. *The Reaper*. London, Little Brown, 2000.

AS PETER LEAR:
Goldengirl. London, Cassell, 1977; New York, Doubleday, 1978. *Spider Girl*. London, Cassell, and New York, Viking Press, 1980. *The Secret of Spandau*. London, Joseph, 1986.

Win Lovesey Stuff!! Really!!

Just send your name and address, and the name of Peter Lovesey's *other* Victorian sleuth to the editorial address and receive a parcel of Cribb novels, donated out of the goodness of their heart by Alison & Busby!

writing the patient
michael palmer

ALTHOUGH I have always been an avid escapist fiction reader, I was perfectly happy with my life as an emergency room doc and never gave a thought to writing – that is, until I read Robin Cook's masterful thriller, *Coma*. Robin and I were classmates at Wesleyan University in Connecticut and trained together at Massachusetts General Hospital in Boston.

'If Robin and I have the same education', I asked my younger sister Donna one day, 'and he can write a book, why can't I write a book?'

'Because' she replied without a blink of hesitation, 'you're dull!'

There was the challenge. I started with an idea based in a true incident in the ER at my hospital, and wrote a book called *The Corey Prescription*, which I finished (at a page or so a night) in the spring of 1979. A friend working as an editor in one of the prestigious publishing houses in New York was kind enough to agree to read the manuscript with the two provisos:

1. If my book was ghastly, I had to be ready for him to tell me so and
2. I had to know in advance that it was going to be.

He called. Basically, his message was, 'Just as I thought, this book is God-awful and you don't know the first thing about writing a novel. However,' he added as I was melting onto the carpet, 'I promise you we can teach people how to write. What we can't teach anyone, and what you seem to have in some abundance, is a sense of what is dramatic.'

My friend then referred me to an agent who worked with new writers. She convinced me that there were so many problems with *The Corey Prescription*, that I had best start over with a new idea. My first attempt, a book about nurses and mercy killing called *The Sisterhood*, was published in 1982 after five drafts. During its creation, my wonderful editor at Bantam Books began teaching me the craft of writing. *The Sisterhood*, is now in it's 31st reprint and has been translator into more than 30 languages. It certainly gave my writing career a running start.

I continued working fulltime as a doc until my son was born 8 years ago. After that I left the ER and tool a part-time position working with the doctors who are ill – mental illness, physical illness, drugs and alcohol. I still hold that job and lobe the balance it gives my life. My 8 subsequent novels were published every threes years at first, then every 2 as my medical load deceased.

The Patient, is my 9th novel –10th is you count the fact that *The Corey Prescription* has now actually been published in 7 countries outside the US (though never here or in the UK). Unlike my other novels, there is no primal 'Oh my God, this frightful medical disaster could happen to me!' element in *The Patient*. Instead, it relies on the dynamics of the characters and the pace of the writing to create what I think is grinding, relentless tension.

AS with all my novels, *The Patient*, began with a 'what if?' In this case, it was 'What if he most mysterious, malevolent, remorseless terrorist in the world developed a brain tumour that needed delicate surgery?' He couldn't very well kidnap a neurosurgeon and have his procedure done in a motel room. In some disguise or other he was going to have to come out into the open. But he would be a man with back-up contingencies upon back up. Thorough and brilliant, he would be ready for anything.

Now all I needed was a protagonist, and I had myself a book. I chose Jessie Copeland because she is unassuming and as 'average' a person as a female neurosurgeon could possible be. It is the classic twisted genius vs. every person conflict that drives so may wonderful thrillers like *Marathon Man, Six Days of the Condor,* and *Silence of the Lambs,* three of my favourites, The story came together thanks to my dear friend at Harvard, world-renown neurosurgeon Dr. Eban Alexander. Eban brought me into the OR with him many times, and on rounds as well. I spoke with his patients and learned a bit about what it was like to confront the news they had a brain tumour, and subsequently, what it was like to have the surgery.

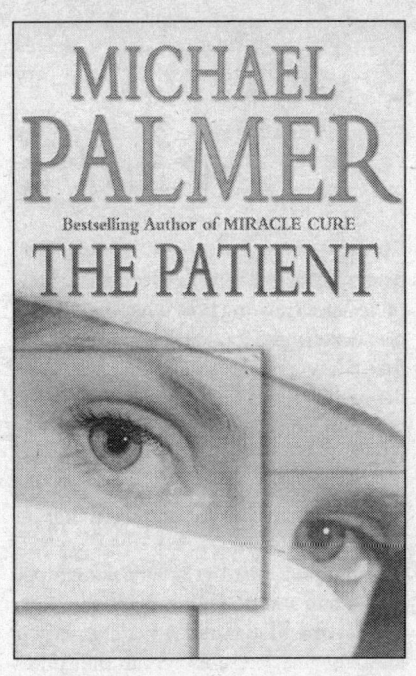

In addition to my deep sense of story, what I bring to the writing table are my feelings as a practising physician, and my knowledge of medicine and medical procedures. My aforementioned sister, Donna (a marketing consultant) is my first-line reader. It is her job to explain them to me in such a way that I am sure the lay reader won't be confused or put off. If she can't do it, it's back to the drawing board for me. I never want anything to pull readers out of my stories.

I am pleased with the effort I have made on each of my books to have them be the best work I can do. But *The Patient* is special. The pacing, the action, the medical scenes and the character interactions have all come out just as I had hoped they would – maybe even better. The novel has been chosen as the main selection of the Book of the Month Club here, and as a triple main of the BCA Book Club in the UK. Perhaps even more exciting, it was recently optioned for a feature film by Wylie/Katz Productions, a company owned by Noah Wylie-Carter on ER. My fingers are crossed. I think it would male a great film.

So there you have it. I am hard at work on the proposal for my next book. It keeps me right-sized to have written a bit here about my sister, Donna. After my first book made the bestseller lists she had a box of business cards printed up for me. They read:

Michael Palmer
Minor literary figure

Michael Palmer is published by Random House

honourable lying:
d w buffa

The author of The Prosecution *(No Exit Press) talks to CT.*

THE PROSECUTION is a sequel to my first novel, *The Defense*. Joseph Antonelli, who had left the practice of law, is asked by his friend, Judge Horace Woolner to prosecute a case against the chief deputy district attorney who is suspected of having his wife murdered. Just as the case against the chief deputy is coming to an end, another murder takes place. When Horace Woolner's wife is arrested and charged with that murder, Antonelli once again finds himself the attorney for the defense. The book is an attempt to deal with the question of lying; more importantly, the issue of when, if ever, it is a permissible, and perhaps even an honorable thing to do. It is a subject which, of course, in this country, the United States, we heard quite a lot about during the impeachment trial of the President. That was, in part, the reason I wanted to write the book. I would have to say that among the writers I most admire, there is none I admire more than Joseph Conrad...his influence may be in there at some point.

How do I regard my early unpublished work?' With indulgence, in the same sense that some people love their children, no matter how stupid and ugly they might be. It took me some time to learn the difference between writing the sort of non-fiction things which I had had published and fiction. In part, it's the difference between telling someone that something happened and showing how it happened. In a non-fiction piece, for example, you can write that a lawyer who lost at trial was very depressed about the outcome. In a work of fiction, you need to describe the way in which it changed the way he looked, the way he felt, the way he talked, to say nothing of the things he did and the things he thought.

I'm afraid I read very little contemporary fiction and prefer instead things written by writers long since dead. This, as you may imagine, presents certain difficulties when it comes to reading things I have written myself.

Violence can often be handled off-stage, as it were. In writing about a murder trial, for example, the murder has already taken place. Both violence and sexuality have largely lost their power to shock, which was never a very good reason for writing about them in any event. It seems to me that you ought to leave something to the reader's imagination, because if you don't, you're not likely to engage the reader in the first place.

The nuts and bolts of how I write: Every morning, for several hours, I write long hand with a fountain pen on long lined legal pads. I have never been able to write anything, except an occasional letter, on either a typewriter or, now, a word processor. As distinguished from a word processor, where everything you write stares back at you from the screen, the movement of the pen from left to right helps the mind to concentrate on the next thing you need to say. Because my handwriting is illegible, I then transcribe it onto the word processor, and make changes as I do it. I think you have to write every day, or nearly every day. Inspiration, if it comes at all, comes only at the point of a pen. In my case at least, nothing is ever quite the same as I think it is going to be once I start to put it down on paper. That does not mean that everything you put down on paper is worth keeping. The two most important possessions for a writer are a pen and a good book of matches.

I don't know if it's important for a writer to keep abreast of the other arts. I tend to doubt it, but that may be because I have serious reservations about the current state of the arts altogether.

There are two teachers who had a great influence on me. When I was a graduate student of political philosophy at the University of Chicago I had the great good fortune to study under both Leo Strauss and Joseph Cropsey. I could not have created the character of Leopold Rifkin in *The Defense* if I had not studied under Strauss.

Character is more important than plot, simply because if you don't care about the characters you're not going to care very much about what happens to them.

The Defense, *The Prosecution*, and my third novel, *The Judgment*, which will be out next year, are all set in Portland, Oregon. The fourth novel, which I have now started, is set in San Francisco.

I suppose I've had just about every experience with publishers, editors and agents it is possible to have. I could not find an agent who was willing to represent me. The only reason Henry Holt was willing to look at my first novel was because they had published a non-fiction book which I had helped write. I had an extremely good relationship with the CEO, Michael Naumann, but when he left to become Minister of Culture in the German government, I decided it was time for me to go as well. Fortunately, Wendy Sherman, who had been an executive at Holt and knew my work, decided to become a literary agent and I became one of her first clients. She auctioned my third novel, *The Judgment*, to Warner Books, as well as the next one after that. No Exit Press are my UK publishers.

I learned a long time ago not to write what I thought someone else might want to read. In that sense, I suppose I write for myself. But what I'm really trying to do is write as if I were explaining something to someone who was very serious about wanting to know it.

The importance of reading.

Precisely because there are so many other things thrown at us from so many different directions, reading is, if not more important, than certainly as important as it ever was. Reading requires, and teaches, a discipline that the more passive mediums of television and movies do not.

A writer should be someone of whom it could be said that he was never less alone than when he was alone. Someone else – someone famous – said that, but I can't right now remember who it was.

The next book, *The Judgment*, which will be published by Warner Books in the US, tells the story of someone sent to an insane asylum supposedly so he can avoid going to prison for a crime he may not have committed, and what happens when he realizes that he may never get out. As you probably have already guessed, it is entirely autobiographical.

michael cordy on michael cordy

I'M SURE you already know this, but records show that men commit over ninety percent of all violent crime. They are also responsible for virtually every war in history.

Now, just suppose you believed the reason for this was that mankind had evolved too quickly, becoming too successful too fast. What if you thought that the human male's natural aggression, which once protected our species and gave us mastery of the planet, had now become obsolete and counter productive—posing an actual threat to our survival? Now imagine that the technology existed to identify and modify the genes that code for aggressive behaviour in men? How far do you think society should go to curb man's aggression and eradicate violent crime?

How far would *you* go?

These are the questions I pose and explore in my new book, *Crime Zero*, published by Bantam. Ever since I was small I have asked myself bizarre questions like these, wondering what would happen if this or that occurred. I've never had a serious ambition to furrow my brow in earnest contemplation and become a Great Writer but I have always wanted to tell stories and use them to probe questions like these.

Most of my life I've spun yarns to any unsuspecting soul who would listen but I never believed you could actually earn a living from it. It was too much fun and too bizarre to be a real job. Then a few years ago, after a decade pursuing a perfectly respectable, well paid career in marketing I was struck by a question so weird and so wonderful that I couldn't shake it off. So with my wife, Jenny's encouragement I gave up everything to write my first novel.

The question was a simple one: If you found a sample of Jesus Christ's DNA what would you discover there? Would you find the genes of God—whatever they might be? I resigned from my job, marketing Martini and Bacardi Rum, and gave myself one year to write *The Miracle Strain*. It took two. After my first year I had written rubbish. Don't get me wrong, I had filled countless pages with type. For sheer volume of ink on paper I was your man, and many of the thousands of words I wrote were the correct ones. But sadly they weren't yet in the right order. Researching the whole area of genetics and developing credible characters was the least of my problems. I had to learn the basics of how to construct a full-length book. I hadn't appreciated that the hardest thing about writing a novel is just that: writing a novel. I had to unlearn most of what I'd studied for my English degree ten years before and learn point of view, structure, characterisation, pacing—all that stuff. Two years later in late 1996, bruised, battered and broke I finished my story of a geneticist who although an atheist must seek out the DNA of Christ to find his healing genes and so save his daughter's life. But although I now had a novel I had no agent or publisher.

The first two agents I approached rejected me. Then I got lucky. So lucky I now realise what a good title *The Miracle Strain* was, because after two years of strain a minor miracle occurred.

An agent who knew someone whose mother knew my mother agreed to read it. He liked it and within two weeks we had a British deal for a significant amount of money, then he took it to the Frankfurt Book Fair and sold it to Germany and Holland. Then, on the Friday evening after the Book Fair, sitting in my little house in Ealing watching some band called The Spice Girls on Top of the Pops, the phone rang. A caller with an American accent said he wanted to buy my book. I remember being annoyed that this stranger had called me at home while I was relaxing in front of the telly. "I'm afraid the book won't be out until next September. You can buy it then," I told him as politely as I could, still staring at the screen wondering which one of the group was called Scary Spice, and why.

I heard a throat being cleared followed by a patient sigh. "I don't think you understand. I am from Walt Disney and we want to buy the rights to *The Miracle Strain* to turn it into movie."

Suffice it to say that once all the agents came into play a deal was done and that night became one of the most surreal of my life. Only a few months earlier Jenny and I had cheered ourselves up by going out to dinner—to a very cheap place I hasten to add—and playing fantasy casting. Weeks later I was having lunch at The Ivy restaurant in Los Angeles, discussing with a real life Hollywood film producer whether Tom Cruise was old enough, or Mel Gibson cerebral enough to play the Nobel prize winning geneticist in the book. Meanwhile, at the next table Winona Ryder ate Caesar salad and Brad Pitt squeezed his way past me to get to the men's room. It was incredible. Even I would never dream of putting something so far-fetched in a novel.

The American publishing rights were sold the week after the film deal and *The Miracle Strain* has now been translated into almost thirty languages. The film is in development but I've learned very quickly that in Hollywood you should hope for the best and expect nothing. So although the film will be made, I'm not laying down any bets on when. I was asked to write the screenplay but quickly decided against that. Aside from the fact that I'd probably mess it up, I prefer writing novels. They may not be as glamorous as films but they are far more personal, offering a real one-to-one between the reader and writer. The reader can plug straight into the writer's vision, using his or her imagination to add their own colour and texture without some director or cast of thousands getting in the way. Plus when I get inspired by one of my daft questions I would hate to involve a committee exploring it.

For my new book, *Crime Zero*, the question was a logical flip on the one that inspired *The Miracle Strain*. If you could find 'good' genes with divine miraculous healing properties could you also find 'evil' genes that code for violent behaviour? At first I thought this was just too bizarre, then in the States I read of a real life case in Atlanta where a man called Stephen Mobley murdered a clerk in a Domino's pizza parlour. In cold blood Mobley shot the man in the back of the head and when he was sentenced to death he showed no remorse, gloating over his crime, even decorating his jail cell with domino pizza cartons. But what really got my attention was that his lawyers argued he should be spared the electric chair because of his genes. They claimed that because four generations of Mobley's had exhibited violent antisocial behaviour he shouldn't be held fully responsible for what was in his blood. Apparently he was your genuine natural born killer. I don't know the outcome and for all I know Mobley is still on death row.

The case spurred me on to research how genes could be responsible for violent behaviour and how the male brain differs from the female. I learned how certain neurotransmitters such as serotonin link the civilised cortex with the animal area of the brain, acting as a brake on impulsive behaviour, effectively contributing towards guilt and conscience. I also explored how other neurotransmitters are responsible for more aggressive responses, such as the fight or flight reflex, and how these combined with male hormones like testosterone can trigger violence and reduce empathy for others. I knew that like any physiological process in the body, genes had to instruct these brakes and boosters. So the impression I gained was that the main reasons the notions in *Crime Zero* won't become a reality in the near future will be due to ethics, not technology.

I also spent time developing my characters to try and personalise the story and bring the issues to life. The hero is a male criminal psychologist who doesn't believe in genetics; he believes that we are products of our past not our genes. But then a whispered revelation from a killer on death row changes his entire view of the world. He is thrust into a conspiracy so vast and so ruthless that the evolution of humankind is at stake.

What I love about novels is that you can look at all the politically incorrect stuff about men and women, free will and predetermination, without having some film executive breathing over your shoulder saying: "But you can't do that, because you'll offend this or that person." I enjoyed just seeking out the facts, the more bizarre the better. One scientist, a woman as it happened, even argued that men could be viewed as cancer cells in the 'body human'. Originally men were healthy and positively helped the species, but now they had become unnecessary and positively dangerous. They had to be 'treated' or removed. She helped me formulate the radical solution for making men evolve that I explore in *Crime Zero*, effectively altering what men are and changing the future of humankind.

I'm already working on my third book now, trying to resolve yet another bizarre question bouncing around in my head—and this time it's a *real* mind-stretcher. But although I finished *Crime Zero* almost a year ago I still think about the questions behind that book—and as a man the story can still make me feel on edge. But then I take a deep breath and tell myself, isn't that what thrillers are supposed to do?

joyce holmes:
skating on thin ice

Admirers of the redoubtable Ms. Holms (crime writer and ex-detective herself) have been beating on CT's doors asking for a piece for some time now, so we're using the occasion of her recent Headline title Thin Ice *as a springboard for the following. We asked Joyce: was this a tough book to write?*

WORKING ON *Thin Ice* was quite a challenge. The mystery concerns the kidnapping of a three-year old boy, the child of a single parent who is the nursing sister in the geriatric award of a cottage hospital. When it emerges that the young mother's boss died recently in a slightly iffy road accident, it begins to appear that there may be some connection between the two incidents The love/hate relationship between Fizz (now in her second year at Law school) and her unwilling employer Buchanan (a young

Edinburgh solicitor) is still changing and developing. When in *Payment Deferred*, Fizz galloped into Buchanan's well-ordered life like a fifth Horseman of the Apocalypse, she'd just returned to Edinburgh after working her way around the world. She was frighteningly independent, selfish, manipulative, and had her own highly individual morals. She was also diminutive, baby-faced and wore an expression of unassailable innocence. Buchanan thought she was the anti-Christ. But over the last three books, they have grown to understand each other a little, and by the middle of *Thin Ice*, Buchanan is beginning to admit to himself that he wouldn't necessarily kick Fizz out of bed. This, however has probably less to do with her charms than with the fact that, for the past 18 months (ever since he met Fizz, in fact), Buchanan's love life has been that of a priest with a small parish. Precisely why Fizz keep putting the skids under his girlfriends is still not something she cares to think about to deeply, but we can make a reasonably good guess.

Readers sometimes ask how I myself became a detective. This was a piece of pure opportunism on my part. I noticed the offices of the agency in Edinburgh, and decided on the spot to brass-neck my way in and pick a few brains. Luckily, there was a sign in the window offering fax services, and that gave me my way in. However, before I could ask to have a fax sent, the guy I spoke to admitted that they were in total chaos because their receptionist/typist had just run off to America with his boyfriend. With the speed of light, I said "This is your lucky day!" And got behind the desk by the time they discovered that I couldn't type, and was crap on the telephone, I had ingratiated did myself with the two ex-CID guys were running the place and they kept me on. At first I was given the job of taking depositions from eyewitness for the defence lawyers. This was enormous help in my writing because I was hearing first-hand accounts of violent crimes, accounts which frequently differed quite markedly from how one would imagine such things. Subsequently, I did surveillance work: mostly marital, but a few insurance frauds. This was more exciting because I never knew when some guy would realise that I was spying on him and decide to take a swing at me. This was a great incentive to be good my job.

I read very little detective fiction these days. This is because if it's good I hate it, and if it's crap I don't want to read it. So it goes without saying that I avoid Val McDermid and Ian Rankin like the plague—if they are that good I don't want to know about it. As for the other current exponents of the genre—I wouldn't run down another writer for a hundred pounds—but if any of your readers care to make the offer they can see my agent.

My books are pure escapism. I don't expect them to change anybody's life. But, having said that, I do hope I'm saying something relevant about how people choose to live their lives and what is right for one person is not necessarily what everyone should aim for. I'd like to think that when my readers finish one of my books, they'll feel like they've been on holiday with amusing and entertaining friends, and maybe feel a little sorry that it's all over.

I'm now on my third editor (in three years) at Headline—almost as many as the driving instructors I went through in my ten-lesson driving course. I'm not aware of stressing them out particularly, but then I wasn't aware of stressing out my driving instructors either.

I'm frequently asked if Buchanan and Fizz will ever become an item. I'd like to see them get-together, but it's obvious that, if they do it will knock the series on the head, so it will have to be the last Fizz and Buchanan mystery. I already have the title: *Buchs' Fizz*.

everything worked:
stuart pawson on sex, crime and dagger winners

MY LATEST BOOK is called *Some by Fire* (published by Headline) and is number six in the Charlie Priest series. It starts back in the Sixties, when he was a rookie sergeant, and explains the bond between Charlie and his sidekick, Sparky. We then leap to the present, and they solve a crime that was committed when they first met. The story involves a crooked tycoon who manipulates share prices by criminal means. It's the best so far, but I would say that, wouldn't I?

My strongest influences come from average books that make the best sellers list, invoking the 'I can do that' response in me. Truly great books—and there are some wonderful ones around, but rarely on the Crime shelves—leave me wondering if I ought to find another outlet for whatever talent I may possess. I started by reading and analysing a few of Dick Francis's, from when he was at his best. He seemed to be doing OK.

And I'm a great admirer of Len Deighton. He invents these devastatingly accurate metaphors, and when I read him I'm constantly wishing I'd said that. One day I probably will.

I was lucky in that my first book, *The Picasso Scam*, was taken by Headline, but that means I don't have a great canon of unpublished work to fall back on in an emergency. Once, on holiday, I wrote a science fiction story about alien creatures which, it transpired, were not from another galaxy but from the bottom of the deepest ocean, where they lived off the chemicals coming up through the Earth's crust. This was long before those tube worm things were discovered. It's still in a drawer, somewhere. That was my very short sci-fi stage, and is about the sum total of my early efforts. I've always been an avid letter writer, which is good training.

I keep a weather eye on the crime scene, but not much more than that: recommended books; the dagger winners; and ones by writers I've befriended. For choice I read about scientific subjects, by people like Richard Dawkins. Proper science, not UFO nonsense. I don't have favourite writers, just favourite books. Everybody is capable of producing a lemon, somewhere along the line. I have a definite leaning towards America, and enjoy Ed McBain, Joseph Wambaugh and Martin Cruz Smith. I've just finished reading *The Floating Egg*, by Roger Osborne (Jonathan Cape), about the geology of the Yorkshire coast, and before that it was *Fugitive Pieces* by Anne Michaels, which made me seriously think about swapping my word processor for a fishing rod.

It's my proud boast that I wrote the shortest description of the sex act in modern fiction: *"everything worked."* What more does the reader need to know? OK, so it's not great erotic literature, but it didn't slow-down the plot. Sally Beaumont takes four pages to say the same thing, and she sells a lot more books than I do, so readers must want that sort of stuff. Personally, I find reading about it to that extent nearly as interesting as studying the menu in the window of a restaurant that's closed. Just for the record, I've extended my repertoire a little since then.

It's possible for a writer to be anything he or she wants: that's the beauty of the medium, but if you write about the real world then your political stance will usually emerge. To be overtly party-political would be to alienate 50% of your potential readership—there are no dog-haters in fiction for the same reason—but politics in the wider sense can provide a background or a springboard for a story. The big-stage issues are galloping consumerism and over-population, and I'd add one about little fish in big ponds wanting to be big fish in little ponds. There's enough potential material there for a lifetime of writing. Most of us pussyfoot around, slipping in the odd unobtrusive comment about inner city deprivation or such, because we have been told that we shouldn't preach and we shouldn't be self-indulgent. We give our characters a few opinions, then put the alternative point of view in someone else's mouth because we believe in fair play. Ben Elton jumped in feet first and kicked his readers in the teeth over issues he felt strongly about. He was a revelation, just what the crime-writing scene needed.

The fashion industry is something I take great delight in knocking, particularly clothes with the label on the outside, and I voice my derision through Charlie. I had one character wearing a *Calvin Bollocks* T-shirt, which hopefully amused a few readers but I doubt if it caused a single fashion victim to bin his silly underpants.

My background is in engineering, which is unusual for a writer of fiction, but it gives me certain useful techniques. I plan a lot, and make copious notes and diagrams, so I never have writer's block. When I sit down at the word processor I always have a destination in mind, but then the characters take over, and I often find myself elsewhere. I started writing after being made redundant from the mining industry, so I have the luxury of calling myself a full-time writer, but it's an exaggeration. I type in the mornings—my target is 850 words—and do my thinking/planning/research during the rest of the day. The word processor is a wonderful tool. There is now no excuse for sloppy writing, although it does encourage verbosity.

I write in the first person, because it suited the first book, but it was a big mistake. It consumes material like a council incinerator. If you write in the third person you can describe an event—the murder, say—from the victim's point of view, the murderer's point of view, the police officer's point of view, the Archbishop of Canterbury's point of view, and so on. When you write in the first person, the telephone rings in the police station and off you go. New writers take heed.

I don't particularly try to hide who the villain is. If Charlie makes a discovery I usually share it with the reader. I hate books where the detective smiles knowingly and keeps it to himself. I might do it once per story, but that's all. I've heard some writers say that they don't know themselves who the culprit is until near the end, but if that's the case, who cares?

I aim for plausibility. I could say realism, but that word has taken on a context of its own. I populate the books with believable but interesting characters, some of whom commit brutal crimes. The stories are often bleak, but I leaven them with humour. The police force is chiefly a male-oriented industry, like coal mining was, with a great leg-pulling culture, and that's what I endeavour to portray. People tell me the books are funny, but that's not my intention. I say that some of the characters in the books are humorous. Originality is high on my list, and I like to push at the boundaries of human behaviour. There are, of course, no boundaries. The secret is to make the reader believe that *that character* could have behaved like that. Then there has to be a story, with lots of hooks linking one part with another, and I try to put it across in an interesting manner. After all that, I just hope that there's something there to appeal to the reader.

Talking about realism, my two real-life police inspector friends, who help me a lot, recently retired from the force after serving their thirty years. They celebrated by bicycling from Lands End to John o' Groats, consuming vast quantities of Guinness on the way. Can you imagine any of the TV cops doing that? No, but Charlie Priest might.

A novel without a plot is like a pina colada without a sparkler. I always feel cheated if a book I've invested several hours of reading time in just fizzles out, leaving the reader to provide his or her own ending. What's even worse is when the writer hangs the characters on an historical event, let's say the sinking of the Titanic or Captain Scott's last expedition, and gives everyone completely fictitious personalities. It's a cop-out, writing by numbers, no matter how brilliant that writing is. Plot requires effort and imagination; characters are observation and reporting. Every novel should come with a free plot.

At a superficial level I wish I was working in America and could base my stories in New York or Los Angeles. The availability of guns there and the different laws regarding private detectives and bail bond agents give a lot more scope for certain types of stories. And the language is different. *"Getcha ass outa here"* loses something with a Barnsley accent.

the washington heights (and depths) of
george p. pelecanos

eddie duggan

SOME WRITERS are known for the characters they create, others for the places in which their stories are set: Los Angeles will always be associated with the novels of Raymond Chandler and, more recently, James Ellroy, while San Francisco will always be Dashiell Hammett's burg. The settings are so integral to the work of these writers that the cities are like characters. As any mystery-reader worth his or her salt will tell you, George P. Pelecanos's novels are set in Washington DC, and the streets, clubs and bars of the North American capital are vividly portrayed in Pelecanos's fiction.

George Pelecanos, who has seven novels under his belt (seven novels have been published in the US, five in the UK), is at that interesting—if not critical—stage in his career in which his books are well received by critics—you'll look long and hard to find a bad review of a Pelecanos novel—but are not yet clocking up sufficient sales to make Pelecanos 'a big name' like, say Grisham or Ellroy.

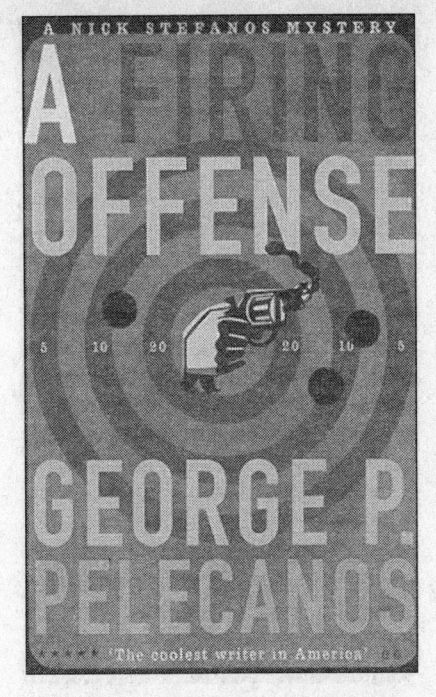

Perhaps the forthcoming film of *King Suckerman* will have an effect on Pelecanos's book sales. Serpent's Tail seem to be working hard at keeping Pelecanos in print in the UK, having just re-issued the three Nick Stefanos novels, namely *A Firing Offense*, *Nick's Trip* and *Down by the River Where the Dead Men Go*. Also, 1999 saw Pelecanos's first trip to the UK, which included two reading and book-signing sessions in London, as well as an appearance at the Edinburgh festival in August.

For those who've had their heads in the sand for the past few years, here's the low-down on Pelecanos to date.

Pelecanos, a third-generation Greek, was born in Washington DC in 1957. He grew up in the 1960s and 70s against a backdrop of the civil rights movement and the riots that followed the killing of Martin Luther King, with an accompanying soundtrack of disco, funk and punk music while doing his best to stay drunk, stoned and chase girls. Pelecanos worked in a variety of jobs, from a delivery boy for his father and grandfather, each of whom ran a snack stand in Washington, to a salesman and later manager of the Washington DC branch of a chain selling domestic electrical goods. The similarities between Pelecanos's life and that of the fictional Nick Stefanos stand out, as Chandler might say, like a tarantula on a fairy cake.

There is also a harrowing incident with a hand-gun in Pelecanos's past that has a deep resonance in his fiction. As a teenager Pelecanos accidentally shot a friend in the face while messing about with his father's handgun and, although the friend survived, Pelecanos was deeply traumatised by the event. In an interview with Eric Brace in Washington's *UNo MAS* magazine, Pelecanos describes the incident which took off the side of his friend's jaw, the bullet leaving an exit hole 'the size of a dime' in his friends neck [1]. In *Down By The River Where the Dead Men Go*, perhaps the most violent and traumatic of the Stefanos books, Nick Stefanos sees his friend LaDuke shot in the face in a scene which is strikingly similar to the accident described by Pelecanos, the fictional scene focusing on the shot-away jaw and the dime-sized exit wound in the neck. Without wishing to offer a Freudian 'explanation' for the Pelecanos formula, once the reader is aware of this harrowing incident in Pelecanos's life, one may be able to see in this event, which took place when Pelecanos's own father was out of the house, the germ of the theme of the absent father, a recurring feature in Pelecanos's fiction.

Pelecanos decided in an existential moment that he no longer wanted the stifling life of a manger of an electrical goods store, and that he would rather write. So, while still working as a store manager in the late 1980s, Pelecanos began writing *A Firing Offense* in longhand in exercise books. After revising it, he typed it up and hawked it around agents, all of whom rejected it. Pelecanos then sent it direct to St Martin's Press who, after sitting on it for a year, bought it (the St Martin's Press edition is now quite collectible with Internet book dealers asking over $100 a copy).

The result of this moonlight scribbling was a debut novel in which the settings and main character closely resemble Pelecanos's own personal background. As well as sharing the DC setting, the novel's main character, Nick Stefanos (the names Stefanos and Pelecanos are not dissimilar) works in a chain selling domestic electrical goods in the late 1980s. Something of a dope-head with wide musical tastes, Stefanos becomes embroiled in a search for a missing employee of Nutty Nathan's. By the end of the novel Stefanos, like Pelecanos, has left the electrical goods store. But while Pelecanos left retailing to take up the pen, Stefanos applies for a PI license and the series is underway.

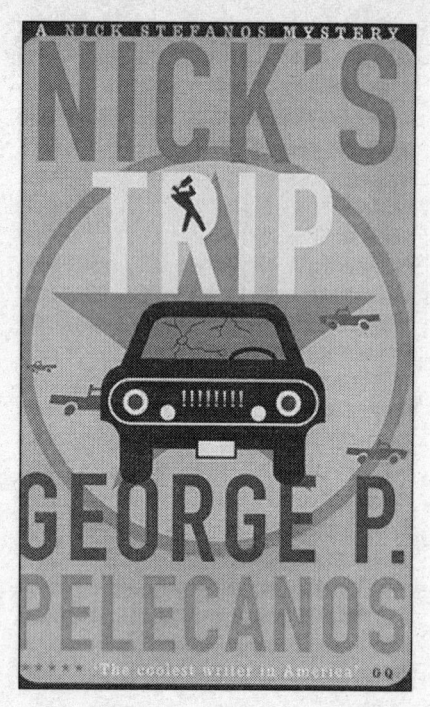

The second book in the Stefanos series is *Nick's Trip*. Set in 1989, the novel opens with Nick Stefanos taking a job as a bartender at a bar called The Spot as there is little PI business coming his way. Stefanos is then asked to find April Goodrich, the wife of an old school friend. The case involves a journey out of DC and into neighbouring Maryland as well as a journey into the past as Stefanos interrogates his own memories; the quaint trait of drinking and driving becomes firmly established as Stefanos's preferred modus operandi.

Pelecanos's third novel is a departure from the Stefanos saga. *Shoedog* is something of a homage to the 1950s paperback original of the type penned by Jim Thompson and David Goodis. Set again in DC, it tells the story of Constantine, a drifter who becomes entangled in a quest for lost loot from a robbery. The title, by the way, is a reference to a shoe-store salesman (and of course Pelecanos also has a stint as a shoe salesman on his CV). *Shoedog* is now out of print in the US, and there are no plans to publish it in the UK. Pelecanos returns to the Stefanos series with *Down By The River Where the Dead Men Go*. Set in 1990-91, the character of Stefanos continues to develop, not least in terms of his appetite for booze and recreational chemicals. The emotional relationship that Stefanos struck up during the previous case with Lyla McCubbin, managing editor of *DC This Week*, is brought to an unsatisfactory conclusion and, chronologically speaking, Pelecanos leaves Stefanos stranded at the end of this third case as subsequent books have been set in a time before Stefanos is granted his PI license. In the later books Stefanos is relegated to walk-on parts as Pelecanos develops the other characters in his version of Washington DC: a young Stefanos meets Dimitri Karras in *King Suckerman* and Stefanos also appears in a cameo role as a shadowman in *The Sweet Forever*.

In the two novels written after *Down By The River*, namely *The Big Blowdown* (US 1996) and *King Suckerman* (US 1997, UK 1998) Pelecanos continues to develop as a writer. Although *The Big Blowdown* has been well received by critics in North America, and Pelecanos has described this novel as his personal favourite, it has not yet been published in the UK. Set in the 1930s, 40s and 50s, it tells of the protection rackets of organised crime that operate in DC and how a group of immigrants—including Nick Stefanos Snr and Peter Karras, the grandfathers of Pelecanos's contemporary protagonists, Nick Stefanos and Dimitri Karras—become embroiled in violence when they decide to stand up to the shakedown merchants. While *The Big Blowdown* is not quite The Great American Novel, it is hailed by many as Pelecanos's best to date.

King Suckerman, short-listed for the 1998 Golden Dagger Award, is usually described as Pelecanos's 'blaxploitation novel'. Here Pelecanos introduces more of the set of characters who will continue to develop in what will be Pelecanos's 'DC Quartet'. Set in 1976, the novel introduces Marcus Clay, a black Washingtonian, who owns the record store, Real Right Records. Clay's friend, Dimitri Karras, is also an employee. Clay and Karras go to score but, in an unanticipated turn of events, end up ripping off the dealers, and a violent chase around DC ensues. The novel explores the familiar themes of masculinity, friendship and fatherhood.

The DC Quartet continues with *The Sweet Forever* in which Karras and Clay find themselves caught up in another drugs-related ripoff. Set in 1986, drug-gangs now have a high profile and the atmosphere is taut with the threat of violence underscored by racism and corruption. Many of the characters appear to be dissatisfied with their shallow consumer-driven lives. There's a potential contradiction here for Marcus Clay who, as a member of the entrepreneurial class, has a vested interest in promoting consumerism, but Pelecanos doesn't develop this beyond Clay showing some concern about investing in more or less CD or vinyl stock in his record stores. While Dimitri Karras enjoys booze and coke and casual heterosexual couplings, Pelecanos suggests that he is spiritually empty and, while we can see Pelecanos appear to be taking something of a spiritual turn, it's worth looking out for the way in which the crucifix is symbolically deployed on a couple of occasions.

Generally speaking, while Pelecanos's plotting is generally very tight and the action is well paced the 'good' characters—such as the 'innocents abroad' and Marcus Clay—tend to be coated with a bit too much sugar in places.

There are also a few unlikely conversations that take place between characters, such as Nick Stefanos's telephone conversation with April Goodrich's doctor in *Nick's Trip*, and a couple of conversations between bad guys Tyrell Cleveland and Anthony Ray in *The Sweet Forever* which come off like clumsy plot patches which, if publishers employed editors to actually edit, ought to have been weeded out.

One of the more enjoyable aspects of Pelecanos's yarns is the way in which the characters' lives intertwine. Like some great drugs 'n' violence infused soap opera, Pelecanos's DC expands in all directions, chronologically backwards and forwards and outwards to embrace more characters. A young Nick Stefanos, for example, pops up in *King Suckerman* and *The Sweet Forever* while Dimitri Karras has a habit of recollecting events in Stefanos's past, as well as his own, and he has an awareness of events which took place in *The Big Blowdown*.

More problematic is the way in which deviance is inscribed: for Pelecanos, homosexuality seems to be a way of coding characters as deviant. For example, in *King Suckerman*, anal rape—or sexual deviancy—is used as a way of underscoring bad guy Wilton Cooper's social deviancy. Similarly, in *Down By The River Where the Dead Men Go*, the head of a drugs and porno-flick operation is marked as doubly deviant by his homosexuality while, in the same book, Karras's friend LaDuke faces up to his own terrible past by his admission that his father had a predilection for young boys. In *The Sweet Forever* the cruel Anthony Ray (whose great uncle was 'a big man down on 7th Street back in the 40s') forces Eddie Golden to perform fellatio It would be refreshing if the version of masculinity Pelecanos constructs were broad enough to accept male homosexual behaviour as something other than deviant.

Shame the Devil is the final episode in the so-called DC Quartet. This will be published in the UK by Orion. Set in 1995, it has Nick Stefanos and Dimitri Karras meet up again. While rumour has it that a major character will be killed off in *Shame the Devil*, Pelecanos, understandably is giving nothing away. We can only hope that Marcus Clay will blot his copy book with Clarence Tate's daughter or, better still, with Clarence Tate. However, with the shadow of Catholicism beginning to fall across Pelecanos's DC, and with the evocative title *Shame the Devil* lined up as the next installment, it's a safe bet that the more spiritually stable characters (i.e. Marcus Clay) are already home free while the future—and salvation—is not so certain for the morally ambiguous characters like Nick Stefanos and Dimitri Karras, and it's a pretty safe bet that the non-heterosexual characters are always already damned.

Stefanos has fathered a son, Kent (in *Nick's Trip*) but in the warped father-son world that Pelecanos has built, the child is a product of artificial insemination as Stefanos donated his sperm in an act of selflessness to his lesbian friend Jackie Kahn, who left DC for San Francisco immediately after this less-than-immaculate conception. Perhaps the 'fatherless' Kent Kahn will return to present Stefanos with a set of father-son problems that the old stand-bys of sex and drugs and rock 'n' roll just can't resolve. We'll just have to wait and see. Meanwhile, Pelecanos has already written the book that will follow the so-called DC Quartet. *Right as Rain* is slated for US publication in 2001 and, while there is as yet no UK date set, it is likely that UK publication will follow soon after.

NOTES

(1) Eric Brace, 'The Hard and Heart of It: George Pelecanos shines a new light on the mystery novel', UNoMAS Magazine <http://www.unomas.com/featuresgeorgepelecanos.html>

the simple truth: david baldacci

mark campbell

David Baldacci was born in Richmond, Virginia in 1960. Before he started writing thrillers, he spent ten years as an attorney in Washington DC. His first novel, Absolute Power, *was bought by Warner Books in the US, and since then three more books have followed, all published in this country by Simon & Schuster.*

Baldacci's rags-to-riches life story (he reportedly earned £4.5m for Absolute Power, *if you include the film rights) has been described as 'corny' in some quarters. In fact, in true John Boy Walton style, instead of splashing out on a fast car with his first millions, he invested it in trust funds for his two children. But let's not begrudge the man his dues—his novels are tautly paced filmic adventures that richly deserve their place in the bestseller charts.*

I met up with him at the Savoy Hotel, London, during a publicity tour for The Simple Truth.

You left your job as a lawyer to start writing, but what interests me is that if you had a completely different job, do you think you'd still end up as a writer?

I think I would—I have been writing fiction since I was a kid. I really wanted to be a writer all my life, but I didn't have the ability to make a living of it back then. It's something I just needed to work at. Actually I was a writer before I became a lawyer, but I became a lawyer because I was interested in the law, and I could make a good living at it—I *was* good as a lawyer. But writing is what I wanted to do, and if I'd gone and been a carpenter or an electrician or an engineer I still would've done the writing.

Were you encouraged at school?

Oh, very much. When I was at Grade School, storytelling was the sort of thing I liked to do best. Sometimes I would tell stories to get out of trouble with parents or school officials.

You mean lying.

Well...fiction! [Laughs] As I went to High School and explored more fiction writers, I realised that I wanted to be able to do what those writers did. The fact that a writer could capture my attention completely was a power that I really wanted to have. I spent many years learning the craft, and I had teachers who encouraged me as a writer. I didn't let anybody know I was writing—that was my own personal thing—and while I was practising law for almost ten years, nobody knew except my wife and my parents. But without all those years of practising, there's no way I could tell a story well enough that anybody would want to read it.

Presumably as a lawyer you had to have a very logical mind – no room for any padding?

When I wrote legal briefs, I had to persuade people using the same set of facts the other side was using, which I think was really good training for the writing that I do now. It taught me patience, because I would work on cases for years at a time, and do a little piece each day. So many aspiring writers try to do too much too fast, and then they get frustrated and quit—it happens all the time.

I understand you had to deal with a lot of rejection letters to begin with.

Lots of rejections. I think of being rejected as a badge of honour! Lots of very cruel rejections, but that just goes with the territory. If you can learn from the rejection, if there are comments about the work, then learn from it. If it's just a personal attack, and basically they're saying "Go to Hell", my advice would be to forget it and move along.

If you received a constructive rejection, would you then revise your story and send it back?

No, I would take those comments and then focus them on new stories. I wrote a lot of different things over the years, and I think it's important to hop around and see what sort of thing you're comfortable with. I wrote short stories, screenplays and novels, and I think it's good to dabble in all of those.

Do films play an important part

in your childhood?

Well, I enjoy movies a lot, but I don't pretend to understand how Hollywood works, or doesn't work. I mean I've certainly got a taste of it with the various film projects I've got involved in, and it's a miracle that anything gets done in Hollywood. But I tend to write visually because I wrote screenplays before I wrote novels, and I like to be able to paint word pictures—if the reader can see it in their head, it's much more entertaining to read, because they can really participate. I try to paint very vivid pictures about locations and characters to make the story more compelling. And oftentimes that may make my books more interesting to filmmakers, but not all the time—some of the subject matter I write about, they're not interested in.

Tell me about your first book, *Absolute Power*. The movie was changed to keep the central character Luther Whitney alive, wasn't it?

Yes, very much so.

I've read in various press releases how you just looked at the $1m cheque they paid you, and that kept you going...

[Laughs] Well, it's funny, I have a couple of different reactions to that. When I first saw the movie at the Hollywood premiere I was very upset, because even though I'd read the screenplay and knew it was going to be different, seeing it different was far worse than reading it. It was so different, I wondered what the people in the theatre were thinking—did *they* think I wrote all this stuff? The secret service agent being killed by Clint Eastwood with a lethal injection to the neck—that's not in the book at all. It was almost like somebody was holding up a baby in front of the audience and saying I was the father—I knew I wasn't, but no-one would believe me. But then after that I got more realistic, and said, "Jesus Christ, it's just a movie. And they made it from your book—it'll always be your book. People went to the movie, they either enjoyed it or they didn't, and you got paid a lot of money—move on. Life's too short."

Do you think it's a good movie, despite the changes?

I thought it was incredibly suspenseful in parts, particularly in the mansion when he's trying to escape. I knew Clint was going to get out alive, but I was still saying, "Run, run!" when I was watching it. It did very well in the States.

Your second book was *Total Control*. Who was the central character in that?

There were two. Sidney Archer, the wife of Jason Archer, and Lee Sawyer, who's an FBI agent. Sidney was a lawyer, a young mother, who was told that her husband died in a plane crash, and she comes to find out that he was never on that plane, and he's been accused of all these horrible crimes. She sets off to try to find the truth, and at the same time the FBI is trying to find her husband. It's a very complicated plot, and it has a lot to do with computers, plane crashes and financial issues.

Did you make a conscious decision to make your second book as different to the first as possible?

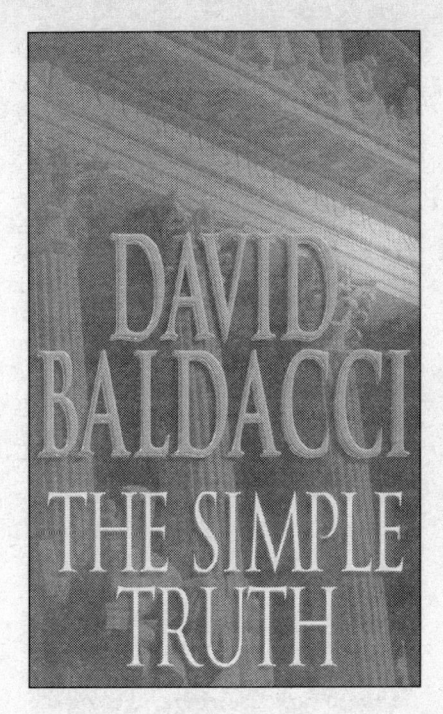

Even though the second book had a lawyer in it as well, it really had very little to do with the practice of law. In a way, I made it difficult, because the main character was a woman and so I had to write from a woman's point of view, which was a great challenge for me as a man. But I got some good advice from my wife.

So you got someone to look at it and see that it rang true.

Yes, my wife, definitely. If you don't write it realistically, woman know how other women talk and react in all sorts of situations, and if you don't have that right, then people will just close the book.

What was the main difference when writing as a woman?

In certain emotional situations, women and men react very differently. Men withdraw—they want to brood on it themselves—or if they have any kind of reaction, typically it's physical. Whereas women communicate in times of stress—they're consensus builders, and they create a desire to communicate, to convey information to people to try and work through it. I did a presentation once, and someone asked me, "When you write about men and women, do you ask men for their advice, and women for theirs?" and I said, "Yeah, I have a standard rule. If I need to know something about a man, I'll ask one and get his opinion on it, and then I'll ask a woman to make sure the man's right!" [Laughs]

Did you then go straight on to write your third book?

Yes. Now *The Winner* is completely different from the other two. It's about fixing the United States National Lottery, and it's got the best villain I've ever come up with—Jackson. There's this very young, poor woman—LuAnn Tyler, the heroin—and she has nothing. This man Jackson comes to her small town and says to her, "I can make you rich. I can get you out of this miserable life. I can make you a winner—all you have to do is play the lottery. Any numbers you want to play, I'll guarantee you win $100m." It's a Faustian tale, a deal with the Devil. She accepts, and then comes to learn there's a heavy price to be paid for that. Jackson represents the evil that comes with being the winner of a huge amount of money. I don't know how it is here, but in the States, it's been absolute misery for lots of people who've won the lottery.

So is her life ruined?

Jackson has a special reason to make her the winner, but something happens which he doesn't expect, the police go after her, and she has to leave the country. But when she returns ten years later, Jackson finds out. He's like Hannibal Lector without the blood and gore—you never know where he's going to turn up. He's truly a master of disguise. I spent a long time researching with make-up people, because I wanted to show people how he changes his appearance. So Jackson goes after Tyler, trying to stay one step ahead, and she has one friend, a man with a mysterious past who befriends her, and she's really not sure if he can be trusted. The story ends in this violent confrontation between good and evil, and at the end you find out who's really the winner, and who's not.

Sounds like you're a fan of The X Files.

Yeah, absolutely. In this day and age, I'm not sure that we know who anybody is. The world is becoming so impersonal. You can communicate on a little mobile phone to people 5,000 miles away, and with computers you've got your whole life history on a little microchip—it's very easy to destroy people and create new ones.

Does that worry you?

I think the world is changing faster than we can adapt to. Forty years ago, if you'd read *Brave New World* or *Nineteen Eighty-Four*, where all these changes were lumped together, you'd think, "Oh my God, I hope it never comes to that." But change happened so gradually over the years that we're at the same spot, collectively, as where those books told us we'd be.

Tell me about your newest book, *The Simple Truth*.

It starts with Rufus Harms, a black man who's been in prison for twenty-five years for murdering a white girl when he was in the army. Rufus remembers killing her, but he doesn't know why. And twenty-five years later, sitting in prison, he gets a letter from the US Army and something is revealed to him—even though he murdered the little girl, he's not guilty of the crime, and he wants out of prison. He turns to the Supreme Court, only to find that in his case it is not designed to deliver justice at all. So he has to turn elsewhere, to bring the simple truth out. There's a lot of family confrontation, and it's a very classic dilemma that you find in fiction—good trying to overcome bad, and truth coming out over people not wanting it to, because it will destroy them. I've always liked to deal with characters facing extinction, and there's no greater human instinct than survival. People who are normally law-abiding will do really dangerous things.

Is this Good vs. Evil power struggle a theme that runs through all your books?

Very much so, because it happens every day. Lots of us do stupid things in our lives, and most of the time the repercussions are not terrible, but sometimes when you do something really stupid, it haunts you the rest of your life.

Are you working on a new novel now?

I just completed it. It's entitled *Saving Faith*, and it'll be out in the UK next year. I also wrote an original screenplay that's out in Hollywood now. It's a family drama set in the 1950s, and it's been optioned for a film. I'm hopeful it'll get made, but you have to understand that 99% of what Hollywood buys, it never makes. I was approached some months ago by Paramount to create a television mystery series of stand-alone dramas, like *Columbo*, which was part of the NBC Mysteries in the 1970s. They want to do a new version of that for the '90s, and they asked me, Ken Follett and Robert Parker to each create a series. We did, and now they're trying to put the whole package together. Other than that, I travel around, and do talks and speeches.

And get more sleep? I understand when you began writing, you used to work through the night...

Yes, though it doesn't seem like I get any more sleep than I used to. Because of my kids, I adapt my writing schedule around them, so even though I work long hours during the day, sometimes I still have to write at night. Plus I do a lot of charitable work, and it's hard for me to say no. They're all great causes, but they're all very time consuming. I find myself far busier than I ever was, even as a lawyer writing in the middle of the night. Twenty-four hours in the day aren't enough any more!

Are you happy?

Very happy. I spent ten years as a lawyer and I can't say I loved it—I was always working for someone else. I remember a few months before *Absolute Power* sold, I had a screenplay out in Hollywood and the producer of *Speed* read it and loved it, and took it out to all the studios; but it didn't sell. And the very next day I had to fly to New York and spend *three days* reviewing property leases. I went from this high of thinking I was going to sell this screenplay to spending three days away from my family in this hotel room with these obnoxious bankers. That was probably one of the lowest points in my life, because what I really wanted to do was earn my living as a writer. So when I think what I can do nowadays, like spending time with my kids, I know I'm truly blessed.

sarah cauldwell

an appreciation, by hrf keating

SARAH CAULDWELL, who died of cancer at the age of 60 on January 28, was the daughter of Claud Cockburn, the radical journalist (who flew the coop shortly before her birth). She published only three books, with a fourth, *The Sybil in her Grave*, due out in America shortly. They were, however of such high quality, of such wit and such ingenuity of plot, that she rose at once to the topmost branches of the criminous tree. Before turning to crime fiction, however, she had a highly distinguished career in other fields. With a degree in classics from Aberdeen, two in law from Oxford (with one in French law from Nancy), she became a member of the Chancery Bar and later had a career in banking, that enabled her eventually to devote her time to the often perilous reaches of fiction. At Oxford she made her mark in other fields than the academic. She became known as a pipe-smoker – anyone who knew her after this will carry an ineradicable picture of her lighting and re-lighting, puffing and pausing—and more importantly, she was a pioneer in securing women their place on the debating floor of the Union.

In 1981 she burst on the crime-writing fully armed with *Thus Was Adonis Murdered*.

For all the rest of her output, *The Shortest Way to Hades* (1984) and *The Sirens Sang of Murder* (1989) as well as *The Sybil in her Grave*, she retained the same characters, her sleuth Professor Hilary Tamar (whose actual sex is never made clear: an ingenious ploy. which delighted readers), with most of the investigation in the hands of a group of young barristers, the delightfully named Cantrip and Ragwort, and the formidably intelligent Julia Larwood and Selena Jardine, neither averse to the pleasures of the flesh, both well able to leave the grosser details to the imagination. Her handling the often tricky subject of the sexual imperative is a sign of a writer with a deep, if prettily veiled, knowledge of human beings at their lowest and the highest. It gives to what might have been merely frivolous books, however laugh-aloud funny, a backbone of integrity likely to ensure them readers for many years to come.

serial writer: max allen collins

MAX ALLAN COLLINS is perhaps best known for the 16 years he spent scripting the Dick Tracy comic strip, and perhaps best unknown as one of America's top producers of movie tie-in novels (*Dick Tracy, Maverick, Waterworld, Air Force One, Saving Private Ryan*). Crime fans are aware that he has won two Shamus Awards (and gathered five more nominations) for his series of Nate Heller thrillers, now numbering ten and going strong involve his softboiled hero in some of the most famous hard-boiled crimes of the century. Sadly, no Heller novel has appeared in the UK since Sphere brought out a beautifully illustrated edition of his debut, *True Detective* in 1984. It's a collector's item now. His series thrillers include seven novels about a Nolan, a professional thief, five starring an assassin named Quarry, and four featuring Elliott Ness. Collins is also a film-maker, having scripted *The Expert* for HBO, and written and directed *Mommy* and *Mommy's Day* for Lifetime Cable. His documentary, *Mike Hammer's Mickey Spillane*, received its UK premiere at the National Film Theatre as part of the NFT's Mickey Spillane season (see

michael carlson

Crime Time 2.6 for a review), and it was then I spoke with Max, and I began by asking him if his prolific output might be working against an appreciation of his work. And it doesn't take much of a question to start Max flowing...

Well, it flows from my being a working writer—this is what I do—and publishers don't want a new Nate Heller novel more than about every 18 months, and they don't want much else...but *Private Ryan* (Max wrote the movie tie-in novelisation) is selling millions, which is great. Still, I'd like to have all the Heller novels back in print! Tie-ins don't really count. The movie people look at them the same way they do lunch boxes, so you're free to do what you want as long as you stick to the basics of the film, but even so, no one respects that sort of writing. But respect is a moot point, because I came out of comics, so I was way in the back of the bus to begin with. I don't worry about that. If I'm going to have millions of copies out there why not have my name on them—I always insist on an author biography on those books, and hope it will work to sell my other books.

Are they hard work?

I don't work from the finished film, but from the shooting script...so when I see the film it's like it was based on my script. You have to be able to visualise the story, which is why I think my comics background helps, as I think it's helped my own film-making. If I stay tight to the plot, I have a lot of freedom. I can throw out the dialogue 100%, because it usually won't play in novel format. It's a nice supplement to writing real books, and my goal it to make it seem like this was the novel the film was based on. A lot of people now believe I wrote *Saving Private Ryan*, the movie (laughs). It also lets me genre jump, to westerns and war stories, and I love that freedom.

You seem to be a serial writer...

Well, all those series are accidental. I didn't set out to create them, and it caused problems sometimes, like my Mallory series, which was really low concept, was a one-shot but the publisher then asked for four more. My first book was *Bait Money* (1973), which I wrote in college, and it featured a tough guy, sort of *High Sierra* type outlaw, and obviously influenced by the Richard Stark Parker books, but in the original version Nolan died. Donald Westlake (Richard Stark) was a hands-on mentor for me, as much as Mickey, whom I didn't actually meet until 1981. I knew I was doing pastiche; well, once was homage but twice is ripoff! Anyway, the seventh publisher to reject the book had also spilled coffee on the only manuscript copy, so my agent asked me to try changing the ending as I retyped it. So I changed it, and the kid comes back and saves Nolan, and by God it sold and they asked for more. Eventually I did seven Nolan books, and there was a prequel which was published in a fanzine when I was 19. Now when they approached me to do more, I asked Don Westlake, and said, look I'm doing Parker, and he said, oh no, go ahead, they're different enough. I think the character of John, the kid, humanises Nolan. There's the scene I love where he says, in the way *"you shouldn't've killed my partner"*, *"you shouldn't have killed my dog"*.

After the Nolan books, you began another series, starring Quarry, a hit man.

I'm very proud of those books, I think they were innovative and they'd get more credit if readers today were more familiar with them. I was doing hit men 20 years before Tarantino, and my friend Lawrence Block. I still get more fan mail about Quarry than anything else, I think because they were dark before anyone really knew about dark. On the other hand, if Quarry had hit like I think it should've I'd probably be doing my 30th one now, and I'd be lapsing into self-parody! The Heller series is richer, and has more potential to delve into changing emotions. Heller is a different character depending on what age he is—people picked up on that when I started jumping around in time with him, but the major line of demarcation is World War II—post-war he's much tougher, more inclined to violence, somewhat more like Mike Hammer. Pre-war he's a wise-guy, post-war he skips saying it. The Nate Heller series came out of two impulses. First was my childhood love of historical fiction: *The Captain from Castile*, *The Prince of Foxes*, the work of Samuel Shellabarger, which is forgotten today, but no one has noticed that in the Heller books. Those books had characters who all were real, except for the protagonist, who's young and thrust into classic situations. The other impulse was my love of private eye books in the 1970s, when the literary devices of the great private eye writers were reborn. I come out of Mickey Spillane, Hammett, Chandler, Cain, McCoy, Burnett. In the 70s this was an anachronism, but people found ways to make it work. So I was re-reading *The Maltese Falcon* and I noticed it was 1929 and Sam Spade and Al Capone were contemporaries. It occurred to me that Spade could encounter a Philip Marlowe-type private eye. I thought why not look for a famous unsolved crime, and the murder of Chicago's Mayor Cermak was my first thought, and I originally wanted the Dillinger story too. I did the novel on spec, without a contract, which was an outlandish gamble at the time, everyone, including my agent, said don't do it. And they were almost right! I was on page 590 and I was almost in tears. Of course being a tough guy I wasn't in tears!

My wife Barbara and I sat up and decided we had to take Dillinger out of it to make it manageable, and thus we had a series in waiting. There's a difference between period writing and historical fiction. I have to make these as accurate as possible, so I use a researcher, George Hagenauer, who was in comics with me, and whose uncle lived next door to Elliott Ness. Originally I was going to have Heller quit the Chicago police because they were corrupt, but George said, *"first off, you've got to be corrupt to get ON the Chicago force!"*, so that mind set helps keep Heller from being the traditional knight in tarnished armour, though he will usually do the right thing in the end. In the first book I made sure Heller despoiled a virgin. Loren Estleman told me he didn't like *True Crime* because Heller broke most of the 'mean streets' rules of Raymond Chandler, but that was intentional. By the way, Heller's office in Chicago is a real building, it's the same flop house the Blues Brothers blow up at the end of their movie. I don't know how much longer they'll want Nate Heller. I'm contracted through number 13. I'd like to do 20, because I've done ten and I really feel like I'm about halfway. The new one (*Majic Man*, 1999 Dutton USA) is set in part in Roswell New Mexico, and deals with the death of James Forrestal. The next one will be quirky, dealing with the Leopold and Loeb murders. Heller was 19 years old, and at the University of Chicago, and Elliott Ness was there at the same time.

Ness pops up a lot, and of course you've done four novels with Ness as the hero.

I think *Butcher's Dozen* (1988) the second of the four Ness novels, is one of my best books. I'd like to being Ness back to investigate the Coconut Grove fire in Boston, but publishers want series novels. I did a novel, *The Titanic Murders* (1999 Berkeley Prime, USA) which obviously was sold off the back of the success of the film. I discovered that the crime writer Jacques Futrelle was one of the people who went down on the ship, and that was the idea. The publisher loved it, but said *"we only give three book contracts, it must be a series"*. *"But the detective DIES on the Titanic,"* I said. I'm going to do one on the Hindenburg tragedy, with Leslie Charteris, the creator of the Saint, as the detective. He did fly on the Hindenburg, though not on that voyage. So Ness would have to be a series. He did work fighting VD in America during the war! But I see his series converging with Heller. I'd like to bring them together on the Black Dahlia murder, with other walk-ons.

Of course, James Ellroy has staked out the Dahlia as his own.

And it's a great book, but it doesn't intimidate me at all. I'd still relish taking on the material, but out of respect for his success I'll probably leave it about ten years. My goal has been to do the JFK assassination, basically as the last Heller novel, but do it out of order. When I showed my solution to my publisher he was afraid of it. Jimmy Hoffa, Joe McCarthy: *Majic Man* is the first of a wave of 1950s Heller, and the deeper you get the more interwoven the history is. And then there's Jack Ruby, who goes back to Chicago and Barney Ross.

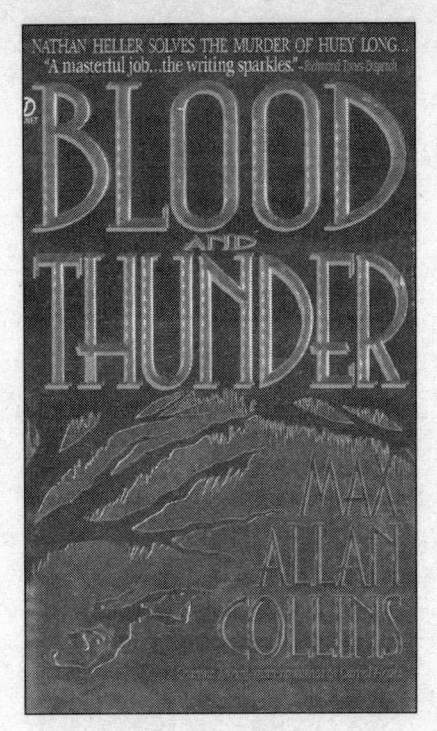

Heller's also an interesting character because you've already established him in contented retirement, which makes some of his encounters bittersweet....

Yes, in *Stolen Away* (1991) Heller disappoints Evelyn Walsh McLain, as he does a lot of women (laughs). It ends *"...and I never saw her again."* Now she actually turns up, historically, on the fringes of three other stories, but I was committed to writing her out. This happens a lot. The three guys who got Capone with Ness were assigned by the government to the Lindbergh kidnapping, because they thought it might be part of the same case. They also show up in the Huey Long assassination. That's real.

Just down the street from his hotel, Max had found remaindered copies of his novelisation of the TV series, NYPD. The first, Blue Beginning (1995 Signet USA) is interesting, because it is, in effect, a prequel to the TV show.

Yes, I got to do two continuity implants with those novels. The first sets the scene with Sipowicz and the gangster, their feud, and the second plugged the gap between the first two series. But they didn't do well in sales.

You're still active in comics...

You know, I learned more about writing comics than anything else. But 15 years was long enough with Dick Tracy; I basically got fired for insubordination by a new editor at the Tribune Synidcate. I did a graphic novel, *Road To Perdition* (1998 Paradox), which was optioned by the Zanuck Company as a possible script, but I got a little tired doing it, I'm such an old man for comics, I'm too mainstream, which makes me an aberration there. (laughs). There's only two things you can do in comics now, avant garde arty stuff or adolescent garbage. You can't do a solid mystery story or a western. If 'The Searchers' were a graphic novel, you could not sell it. There has to be some middle ground between art and junk, well, there is, but it's good TV like *NYPD Blue*!

So you dropped comics and took up movies?

The most expensive hobby I've ever had! But it's even worse, I'm getting too old to tilt at all those windmills! I'd had scripts optioned three times, twice in Hollywood and once in Italy, but no films made, so I thought I'd try myself. We shot the exteriors of *Mommy* in Beta SP, the rest in 16mm, and cast Patty McCormick, who as a child actress starred in *The Bad Seed*, as an adult version of the character she played then. *Mommy* is *The Bad Seed* backwards. We had Jason Miller, who played in *The Exorcist*, and Mickey did a cameo role, and those names got it onto cable. You know, Mickey's been in four movies and I've directed two of them!

Can you write while you're directing?

I have to work hard to open a 3-6 month window to blow on shooting and editing. Movie projects just never seem to end. But I love it. It's like a giant toy of my second adolescence. It does try to suck all the time and energy out of a person, though. I've got a Mike Hammer script for filming with Jay Bernstein, who produces the Mike Hammer TV shows. I've also got two properties under option, the other with Disney, and I want to do the screenplay. But it's funny, they obviously respond to my writing, but when it's suggested I try the screenplay they back away in horror! But I understand the difference between novels and movie writing; I can turn one into the other. Novels are interior, movies are exterior.

Tell me about the Mickey Spillane documentary...

You know, Mickey is a pop culture juggernaut. He's also a master of answering in non-sequiturs, which makes him a tough interview.

Tell me about it! *[see Mike's interview with Mickey in Crime Time 2.6!]*

When Mike Hammer burst on the scene, he could do no wrong, like the Beatles. It's incredible that someone so popular could be so savaged. Everyone loved Hammett and Chandler, but everyone now wants to hate Mickey. One of my goals is to make sure he is not forgotten. I want him to regain his position as the third of the crime writing triumvirate, with Hammett and Chandler. It isn't Ross MacDonald and it sure as hell isn't Robert B Parker. I was so pleased to show the film here, with Mickey, but you know, it was even more wonderful that Adrian Wootton had programmed the original 3D version of *I.The Jury*. I'd never seen it before, I thought I'd die before I ever saw John Alton's 3D photography. It's a fitting tribute to Mickey, and I'm glad I had a part in it.

living with crowner john: bernard knight

WRITERS OFTEN claim that their characters take them over and after living with Crowner John for some four hundred thousand words, I sometimes wake in the morning wondering at which end of the millennium I am! I'm beginning to believe that Sir John de Wolfe, appointed the king's coroner for the county of Devon in 1194, actually existed. His brother-in-law, Richard de Revelle, really was the sheriff at the time, as many of my characters are firmly planted in fact—but of course, I don't know if Richard had a brother-in-law, do I? These tortuous thoughts plague historical novelists, but fascinate us at the same time.

The latest offering in the Crowner John series is *The Awful Secret*, and concerns John's entanglement with two renegade Knights Templar, who are threatening to divulge a secret that will "rock Christendom to its very roots", as the blurb says. Interlaced with the main story is a sub-plot about murder and piracy centred on Lundy and the north Devon coast, which again has a basis in fact. I've deliberately been a bit cagey about the nature of the 'awful secret', not wanting a hit-squad from the Vatican to call upon me—but at the end of the book, I've offered a list of sources for those readers who want to delve more deeply.

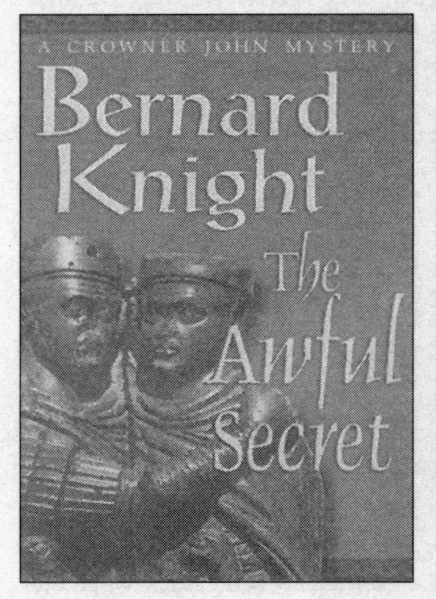

The twelfth century fascinates me and I have written several previous novels about it, though they were based in Wales. One was about Princess Nest, a mistress of Henry I, whose nephew was Giraldus Cambrensis—the other about Prince Madoc, a pre-Columbian voyager to North America. I would have liked to have placed the coroner yarns in Wales, but we didn't have them until well after the English conquest in 1282.

The idea for this series came from my professional interest in the origins of the coroner—I've even lectured in China about the origins of the Chinese 'coroner' judges, well over two thousand years ago. Though they probably existed in Saxon times, it was the Normans who revived coroners in 1194, mainly as a fiscal enterprise to help raise the huge ransom for Richard the Lionheart, who was kidnapped in Austria on the way home from the Crusades. It seemed a pity to let the idea rusticate in academic articles, so I floated the idea of turning them into crime novels and Simon & Schuster commissioned three and later asked for more.

I've been writing for donkeys years, ever since I edited the medical students' magazine in university. Whilst an army medical officer during the Malayan Emergency, I soaked up all the whodunnits in the Naafi library, then tried my hand at one when I returned to my first forensic job in London. A Daily Mirror court reporter gave me a one column-inch plug and the next day a publisher wrote asking to see the manuscript, which I'd only half finished!

In the next few years, I wrote half a dozen contemporary detective novels under the pen name of Bernard Picton, as in those days doctors were supposed to keep a very low public profile. Then I drifted into radio and television drama and documentary scripts, together with the two twelfth century Welsh novels and very successful biography of the Chief Forensic Pathologist of New York City. After this, medicine reclaimed me for well over a decade, as I turned out ten textbooks, before escaping to Crowner John a couple of years ago. I've been very lucky, in that I've almost never written 'on spec', but always to a commissioned idea, so my bottom drawer has only two old manuscripts that have failed to find a home.

People ask me who influenced my writing—and the answer is no-one, as far as I'm consciously aware. I've no particular favourite authors, though being in the death business, I suppose the police procedural style appeals to me most. I think I enjoy Ed McBain most of all, but these days I prefer to read history than fiction.

Folk often want to know how I work, but I think they would be disillusioned if they knew the truth. Though theoretically retired, I seem to have less time than ever, so writing is squeezed into odd hours, usually late at night—at least until the deadline is breathing down my neck, when panic speeds up my two typing fingers! I love doing the research, especially for Crowner John, but I find the actual business of getting words on paper to be hard labour on a par with digging an allotment with a blunt spade. I plan out the plot sequence before starting, though usually the story tries to wander off the rails, having a mind of its own. The days have long gone when

I hopefully started a book on page one with "It was a dark and stormy night, with clouds scudding across the face of the moon", as one tends to seize up by page forty, unless one has a clear idea of where the yarn is going—especially the ending. A one-page flow diagram is my starting point, with X,Y and Z as the main characters. Then I choose names from my bank of actual twelfth century Devon people, and add them to my 'bible', in which all the characters have their bio-data recorded, from the date of birth almost down to the number of their teeth! This is to avoid the not-so-infrequent errors that readers spot, such as the blonde on page seventeen who becomes a brunette by page eighty-two! This is followed by a chapter synopsis, where I make a provisional story-line for the contents of each chapter.

For me, writing seems a constant battle against distractions—I sit at the keyboard confidently determined to knock out four thousand words that night, but first I need a drink of water or to go to the bathroom, then the chair is the wrong height or the cat needs putting out—anything rather than get on with it! The word processor is a mixed blessing, as although it would be impossible to go back to typewriter again, the thing offers endless opportunities for fiddling with the margins or the type-face—great excuses to delay the actual writing.

Once I've started, what seems to happen is that I see a silent film playing in my mind and my fingers write a description of what I'm viewing, almost a voyeuristic process. I've read somewhere that there are two types of writer, the visual and the auditory. I'm certainly the first, as I can't easily hear my characters speaking. I have to make a conscious effort to put words in their mouths, whereas I can see the action as if I'm a hovering spirit. On that point, perhaps I *am* a hovering spirit, as my wife thinks my previous incarnation was in the twelfth century and that if I underwent retro-hypnosis, I'd claim to be Crowner John's kitchen boy—though I think I was Giraldus Cambrensis! Disturbingly enough, when writing the third book, *Crowner's Quest*, I quite arbitrarily used Berry Pomeroy Castle as one locale, then made the de Pomeroy's, whom I'd never heard of before, prime villains in my plot, associated with the treacherous revolt of Prince John. Later, I was astounded to discover that my fiction was all true! I'm sure I had no pre-knowledge of this, even on a subliminal level.

Since Ellis Peters—rather than Umberto Eco, as so often claimed—there has been a huge upsurge in historical mysteries, with new writers appearing all the time. I feel this springs from the reading public's eternal interest in a puzzle, coupled with escapism and nostalgia for the imagined past, be it Roman, Norman or Victorian. This has its disadvantages for authors, as the chances of television or film rights are slim, due to the huge cost of historical productions. Even the Cadfael television series was a bit of flop—the streets were far too clean for the twelfth century!

The author has constantly to be on guard for anachronisms—and not only in the physical *milieu* of the period, though that's hard enough to achieve. There are psychological and mind-set anachronisms to avoid, putting words or sentiments into characters who would never have thought that way at that time. For instance, one of my editors was dubious about me letting Crowner John wonder whether there was a better way of dealing with a thirteen-year old petty thief than hanging him, as she maintained that this would never have occurred to any law officer in 1194.

I try to get things right, as readers are quick to pick up any mistakes—I recently had a letter from France correcting my spelling of a single word! I have a stock lecture about forensic howlers in modern detective fiction, the worst offenders being some of the famous names of the 'golden age', so I strenuously try to avoid historical clangers. In this mental video I view when writing, I see all the muck in the streets of Exeter, the raucous and ragged crowds and the smoky hovels of most of the population. Without wishing to be snide about my rivals, I have read a few historical novels where a good plot would have been better placed in the present. I remember one sited in a famous English city where, in spite of the stated antiquity, the whole ambience was so modern that you could almost hear the buses passing in the background!

The language is another problem—I have a foreword in all my books explaining that as the characters in Devon would then have spoken either Early Middle English, western Welsh or Norman-French, there was no point in trying to write dialogue in 'olde-worlde' style, with 'gadzooks' and 'prithy' in every sentence. It's similar to the incongruity of so many films and television dramas, where the Nazis speak amongst themselves in English with a German accent!

Though I write partly to please myself, I always have the readership in mind and feel that if a book won't sell, it wasn't worth writing. Literature is communication, and if the recipients don't want it, then the exercise is futile. I was once briefly on the Literature Committee of the Arts Council, but I didn't last long, because of my philistine attitude that it was a waste of public money to support authors and poets who couldn't get published, as no-one wanted to read their stuff. Publishers are a hard-headed bunch, but they have to be, as those that aren't, don't survive. I've always got on well with the dozen I've dealt with—though I must admit that sometimes their editing of my breathless prose, which took me hours to perfect and then gets junked, can wreak havoc with one's blood-pressure.

Well, I've had enough of the new millennium for now, I'm off to the twelfth-century, to plod through the garbage of the Exeter streets down to the eye-watering smoke of the Bush Inn, for a jar of foul ale while I spy on Crowner John fondling the landlady!

crime from canongate

Brian Ritterspak looks at a new imprint, and talks to one of its stars, Douglas Winter.

IT'S ALWAYS REFRESHING to hear that a publisher has increased their commitment to crime fiction—but this can be a double-edged sword, when the resulting list is ill thought out and uninspired. No such problems with a redoubtable candidate: and the notification of the Canongate Crime list engendered anticipation, which receipt of the first batch of books more than fulfils. The big hitters include Andrew Vachss and Douglas Winter, and there are considerable contributions by Anthony Bourdain and Jon Jackson. Jackson's *Hit on the House* introduces the dry and idiosyncratic Detroit Detective Sergeant Fang Mulheisen and his nemesis, hit man Joe Service to a UK audience. The writing is pithy and electric, with the kind of off kilter characterisation rarely found in British crime fiction.

Chad Taylor's *Shirker* is a terrifying examination of savage murder and sexual compulsion across time; uncertain moments, but this is a narrative voice that shows real promise.

With Tony Bourdain's *Bone in the Throat*, we've got the kind of funny and caustic examination of drugs, murder (and even haute cuisine) that makes for a truly satisfying read.

No doubt Canongate are trusting that Andrew Vachss' new novel, *Safe House* will give their list the gravitas it needs, but with hardly a bum note sounded in this initial overture Vachss simply takes his place among the rest. This isn't vintage Vachss, but quite compulsive enough to be doing with.

Douglas Winter's *Run* comes with Peter Straub's encomium, and it's hard to disagree with him, even though his recommendations adorn almost as many books as Stephen King. This is a crime thriller of real energy.

And speaking of Douglas Winter…

You are an attorney. What made you decide to write a novel?

I've been fortunate to find some success as a writer while pursuing a career in the law; but until RUN, I wrote only nonfiction, criticism, and the occasional short story. I didn't have time to devote myself to a novel. Then came the crash of Northwest Airlines Flight 255 at Detroit, Michigan—a horrifying air disaster that produced an epic lawsuit when Northwest and its insurer refused to accept responsibility. I lived on the road for years, and moved to Detroit to try the case: a jury trial in federal court that lasted nineteenth months, then spawned a series of appeals that went on for years. We won the case convincingly. And although it was a triumph professionally, it was a terrible loss personally—years of my life spent without family and friends, without writing, without joy. In the aftermath, I knew I had no choice; if

I was going to find some kind of meaning for myself—and in this kind of tragedy—and if I was really going to think of myself as a writer, then it was time to write a novel. And the novel was *Run*.

How would you describe *Run*?

It's is a thriller. I use that description in its best sense, meaning that I wanted this book to stir the emotions of readers, to excite them with its words and ideas, to keep them turning the pages—and, most of all, to make them feel for its characters and its story and, hopefully, in turn, to make them feel about the story beyond the story. Because *Run* isn't meant simply to entertain, but also to encourage readers to think about certain timely and controversial issues.

What is a "run"?

My title is intentionally duplicative—and, I suppose, duplicitous—as the reader soon learns. In its first sense, "run" refers to the transportation of illegal weapons: gunrunning. The story's opening afocuses on a doomed alliance between white suburban criminals and an inner city gang in an intricate plan to move a cache of weapons from Washington, DC, to Manhattan. But we soon learn that there is another "run"—a run inside the run, one that transcends common crime.

You said that the background is based on facts gathered from actual events. How did you do research for the book?

I knew enough about guns—and about domestic gunrunning, and the complex cultural (and constitutional) problem of guns—to know that my story would work not merely as fiction but also for its factuality. Once I was writing, I spent a lot of time interviewing, talking, reading, and just living the book. Some of my law enforcement sources are credited in the acknowledgements; they included everyone from police in several cities—street cops and brass—to FBI and ATF and Secret Service agents. I talked with people on both sides of gun control issues—from Sarah Brady's Handgun Control, Inc., to the NRA—and to gun manufacturers, military types, and a few people who shouldn't be mentioned. I lurked in gun shops, armouries, ranges. When I was finished, I consulted a few weapons experts, notably Andy Stanford of Options for Personal Security, to confirm that I had done things right. But I also spent a lot of time imagining, which is probably the best kind of research.

Who was the model for Burdon Lane?

Burdon is never described in *Run*. That was intentional: he's meant to have a bleak everymanish quality; but in a painful sense, I suppose he's based on me—and particularly on some of the bad places inside me, the places in all of us where we accept, very passively, the violence and the cruelty and the bigotry of our world. In that sense, Burdon is meant to represent our burden: that, however many platitudes we offer about what we "believe," only those who finally take some kind of action may avert damnation—and, perhaps, find redemption.

You display a great ear for the "cop talk" and "street talk." How were you able to perfethis?

I like to listen. As a lawyer, I prided myself on the ability to know when *not* to talk. As a writer, it's a challenge to give readers a sense that they can actually hear the characters speaking. The late George V. Higgins was a master of this kind of writing: he wrote dialogue better than most people can speak it.

I also love the poetry of everyday conversation, the ways in which voices shift with context. The courtroom, for example, has a language that's unique, oddly forced, often stilted, replete with ritual. Street talk is the opposite, it's utterly freestyle and, like rap—which certainly inspired me in writing *Run*—it's unafraid. And there's something honest there, amid the posturing and the profanity, that you just don't find that often in more "civilised" contexts.

Why is there so much violence depicted in *Run*? (Is this an accurate depiction of the violence attached to this livelihood?)

Violence is integral to *Run* because, let's face it, the book is meant to confront our culture of violence—and, of course, guns. And the reality of the book had to extend to its violence, so there are some unflinching glimpses—the kind that films and television rarely offer—into the aftermath of gunplay. I wanted to assure that Run did not glamorise its events, and that readers understood the terrible toll of violence.

As for the connection between violence and illegal guns: The ATF recently announced that, between 1996 and 1999, almost 500 guns sold by one dealer in Maryland had been linked to crimes. There is a certain inevitability here, since the only purpose of a gun is to kill.

How much is organised crime involved in gunrunning operations?

As *Run* tries to underscore, the problem with gun trafficking—and arms dealing—is that bad guns can reach the hands of bad people in a myriad of ways, from a street corner exchange to an organised run to an international operation involving our government. Certainly weapons are moved freely throughout the United States by organised (and unorganised) crime—often as an adjunof the drug trade.

Do you think we have lost the war on the distribution of illegal firearms in this country?

No. But to be honest, it hasn't been much of a war; it's been more like a skirmish. We desperately need a national solution to what, as the sad events of this past year show, is a public health problem: the problem of guns. And the states suffer in the absence of federal regulation. Washington, DC, for example, may have the strictest gun laws in the country, but it also has six times the number of crime guns per capita as New York or Boston. In part, that's because it is surrounded by two states that freely allow gun sales.

As *Run* hopefully suggests, the problem of guns is complex, and deeply rooted in our culture; but the solution, really, is a very simple one. It takes courage, however; great courage.

What is next on the horizon for you?

I've written a biography and critical study of novelist, artist and filmmaker Clive Barker, which should be published within the year. But I'm working now on a new novel. As in *Run* I want to explore the collision of American perspectives and cultures, to take these seemingly unequivocal positions—pro-this, anti-that—and to force them into something other than a traditional confrontation. My motto, I like to think, is to "unexpect the expected." We've had more than our fair share of traditional thrillers—it's time for something different.

the right sort of ferment: philip friedman

I'VE READ RAVENOUSLY since I was a kid, all kinds of things from all eras, but I never intended to be a writer, so I wasn't sitting there going *"Oh, I'd love to write the way that writer does."* I don't know that I can single out any particular influence. It all goes into the hopper, and whatever comes out, comes out. My earlier work was probably most influenced by the top-level thriller writers of the time, and I particularly admired British spy thriller writers, who managed to tell a good story and still be literate and even smart.

I read everything that Lawrence Block writes, no small feat, but otherwise I'm fairly spotty about following people. I prefer variety, when I have the time to read outside my own research, which keeps me pretty busy. Every time I wrote a new novel, I typically buy twenty or thirty books on related subjects, almost all history or politics or other nonfiction.

I just attended a fascinating seminar on violence in the media at the New York University Law School. Having heard a person of great intelligence make the argument that entertainment-media violence is dangerous, I remain unconvinced, at least by the 'social-science' argument. I do believe that some real-life crimes are influenced by, say, violent movies, but I don't see a case (for instance) that the kids who are said to have imitated *Natural Born Killers* would have been model citizens without that movie. And *NBK* was a sort of extension of *Badlands* which was itself patterned on a real crime, so it's hard to know where the influence begins. I think writers and producers have some moral obligation to think hard about material that's purely pandering to a taste for the violent, but I haven't noticed that anybody's seriously worried that teenage slasher movies put cheerleaders across the nation at risk. And frankly I'm more concerned about showing young people looking cool smoking cigarettes, killing activity that's a lot more likely to be imitated.

I do a lot of research, most of which involves talking to people who do the real work that I write about. I try to formulate as much about the characters and storyline as I can before I start writing, but everything always changes as I get into the book itself. My writing hours per day vary between zero and sixteen. When I'm deep into it I can put in twelve or more hours a day of writing, revising and thinking about the book, for as long as a couple of months, with only a few half-day breaks.

The battle in a courtroom is inherently dramatic, and crime — especially serious crime — can potentially illuminate the deepest aspects of human desire and emotion. Still, there are many ways to approach he subject, some more surfacey, and some that attempt a fuller examination of the motivations and interactions of the characters, and how all that fits into the broader society. I'm fond of saying that there are two principal kinds of recreational reading pleasure, one like waterskiing and one like scuba diving. I think of my books as being like scuba diving, but with one of those motorized sleds to pull you along.

I was fortunate enough to have a wonderful teacher in high school. Bob Geller taught a course that was entirely reading plays, in historical sequence from ancient Greece through the mid 20th century. We must have read 80 plays, and discussed them, along with the politics, art and culture of each period we studied, and Bob Geller was an absolute inspiration. Then he changed professions and became an acclaimed producer of high-quality TV drama, notably a series called *The American Short Story*, which won all kinds of prizes and was the first American dramatic series bought in its enirety by the BBC. Though Bob and I had been out of touch for a few years, while I, too, was changing careers — from maths to law to writing for the movies (and novels) — we reconnected, and we've been closest friends for the many years since. He has continued to be a mentor and advisor… and as the years have passed I've become an advisor of his, as well. He's even made me a director of his production company.

For the first three of my legal novels I had a very yeasty relationship with my publisher, who was also my editor. Donald I Fine was legend in New York publishing, famous for his skill and his temper. We sometimes clashed but it was always productive. Unfortunately, after a very long and notable career, he succumbed to cancer while I was writing *No Higher Law*. On your side of the pond, I've been happy in my relationship with Headline, in London. They're all terrifically responsive people, and full of energy and imagination. As for grisly experiences early in my career, I've certainly had them. And not only early. My books are very much about the world as it really is, offering my readers a chance to get inside the skin of people who lives are very different from their own. But in doing the writing I definitely need to get away and isolate myself. I've been very successful in doing this at a place called the Virginia Centre for the Creative Arts, a retreat for writers and visual artists and composers, where I spend many weeks at a stretch.

Philip's latest book is No Higher Law *(Headline).*

dark detectives
(oooh - spooky!)

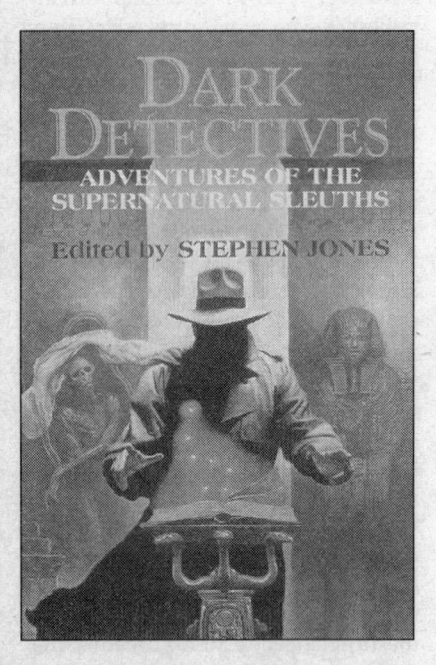

Like our own Mike Ashley, Stephen Jones is one of the very best editors of anthologies this country can boast, and his work in the horror field is non-pareil. However, we can welcome him to these pages for a wonderful new collection called Dark Detectives: Adventures of the Supernatural Sleuths *(Fedogan & Bremer, £20.95) a selection that includes both classic writers such as William Hope Hodgson along with the multitalented Jay Russell and Kim Newman (whose* Seven Stars *sequence is studded throughout the book). We asked Jones, Russell and Newman to tell us how a book—and their contributions to it—came about.*

A SLEW OF SUPERNATURAL SLEUTHS
STEPHEN JONES
PSYCHIC DETECTIVES. Phantom Fighters. Ghostbusters. Call them what you will, for more than thirty years I have enjoyed reading about fictional sleuths investigating the strange, the bizarre and the horrific.

Although it is generally accepted that the modern detective story began with Edgar Allan Poe's *The Murders in the Rue Morgue* (1841), in which the author introduced French detective C Auguste Dupin, who solved a grotesque murder through logical deduction, it was Sir Arthur Conan Doyle who created the celebrated formula from which most subsequent "psychic sleuths" (and of course their faithful assistants) would be moulded.

From Doyle's Sherlock Holmes solving the mystery of *The Hound of the Baskervilles* (1901-02), through the case files of Algernon Blackwood's extraordinary physician *John Silence* (1908), to Seabury Quinn's ninety-three stories about dapper French detective Jules de Grandin in the pages of the pulp magazine *Weird Tales*, some of fiction's most memorable detectives have confronted the supernatural while protecting the world from the forces of darkness and evil.

After writing and editing more than sixty books in the horror and fantasy genres, I decided it was about time that I tried my hand at putting together an anthology which combined my love of the macabre with detective and crime fiction. The result is *Dark Detectives: Adventures of the Supernatural Sleuths* ($29.00), the first of a proposed three-book hardcover series from Minneapolis publisher Fedogan & Bremer's Mystery imprint.

In many ways, this present volume can be viewed as a follow-up to both my earlier anthologies, *Shadows Over Innsmouth* (1994) and *The Mammoth Book of Dracula* (1997), which were based around H P Lovecraft's ichthyoid Deep Ones and Bram Stoker's undead Count, respectively. As with those previous books, *Dark Detectives* contains a combination of new and reprint fiction and is assembled along a loosely-constructed chronology (stretching from Ancient Egyptian times through to the Twenty-first Century).

The reprints are William Hope Hodgson's classic ghost story *The Horse of the Invisible* featuring Thomas Carnacki, who uses a combination of contemporary science and occult wisdom in his battle with the supernatural; Basil Copper's *The Adventure of the Crawling Horror* involves London's second most famous consulting detective, Solar Pons (actually created by young Wisconsin writer August Derleth in 1929), who relies upon his deductive reasoning to solve another strange case, aided by his chronicler Dr Lyndon Parker; Manly Wade Wellman's *Rouse Him Not* features Manhattan playboy and dilettante John Thunstone, who is armed with potent charms and a silver swordcane as he seeks out deadly sorcery wherever he discovers it; *De Marigny's Clock* is investigated by Brian Lumley's Titus Crow, who is a world-acknowledged master in such subjects as magic, archaeology, palaeontology, cryptography and the dimly forgotten or neglected mythologies of Earth's prime; R Chetwynd-Hayes' *Someone is Dead* is the first adventure of "the world's only practising psychic detective", Francis St Clare, and his attractive assistant and gifted materialistic medium Frederica Masters; and Clive Barker's *Lost Souls*, in which private investigator Harry D'Amour is drawn to the dark side against his will and forced to walk the line between Heaven and Hell.

Comprising the new fiction written especially for this volume is *Our Lady of Death* by Peter Tremayne, in which the writer's popular Seventh Century religieuse and advocate Sister Fidelma has her first encounter with the supernatural; *Vultures Gather* by Brian Mooney features occult researcher Reuben Calloway and his friend Father Roderick Shea involved in a tale of African magic and supernatural revenge; *Bay Wolf* by Neil Gaiman is a prose poem in which lycanthropic private investigator Lawrence Talbot once again confronts a modern mythological monster; and the always clever Jay Russell's *The Man Who Shot the Man Who Shot the Man Who Shot Liberty Valence* drops Hollywood child actor turned lowrent private investigator Marty Burns into another movie-mystery. Having been closely involved with Marty's creation for Russell's underrated debut novel, *Celestial Dogs* (1996), it is always a pleasure to include one of the character's offbeat cases in a new anthology.

However, the undisputed jewel in this volume (pun intended), is Kim Newman's multi-part short novel, *Seven Stars*, in which such characters as Charles Beauregard, Edwin Winthrop, Richard Jeperson, Sally Rhodes, Dr Shade, the vampiric Geneviève Dieudonné and many others over the decades challenge the influence of an alien weirdstone that has the power to annihilate mankind. Inspired by Bram Stoker's 1903 novel *The Jewel of the Seven Stars*, Kim and I discussed in detail how his eight-part story cycle would form a unifying nucleus for the book. Kim imaginatively borrows bits from Stoker's volume, much as he co-opted the author's vampire for his successful *Anno Dracula* series, but he soon mixes in the Egyptian plagues, the machinations of the Diogenes Club, stolen mummies, stage and screen actor John Barrymore, the Swinging Sixties, demonic multimedia magnate Derek Leech, cyberspace science fiction and an apocalyptic climax featuring the author's very own legion of superheroes. It's an audacious and creative entertainment that attempts to pull together the threads of the alternate worlds and characters found in the author's other books and stories.

Of course, there have been previous anthologies of psychic detective stories: Michel Parry's *The Supernatural Solution* (1976) and *Ghostbreakers* (1985), Peter Haining's *Supernatural Sleuths* (1986) and Charles G Waugh and Martin H Greenberg's identically titled 1996 volume all immediately come to mind.

However, I don't believe there has quite been a volume like *Dark Detectives* before. Along with some of the greatest fictional detectives (and their faithful amanuenses) who have ever confronted the bizarre and the unusual, you'll also find a detailed overview of the genre, numerous pen-and-ink illustrations by Chicago-based artist Randy Broecker, and a stunning wraparound cover by the inimitable Les Edwards.

So once again the forces of darkness are abroad and occult powers are gathering. In the everlasting battle between Good and Evil, these investigators of the unusual set out to solve ancient mysteries and unravel modern hauntings with the aid of their unique powers of deduction and the occasional silver bullet.

For the supernatural sleuths, the game is afoot...

Stephen Jones lives in London. He is the winner of two World Fantasy Awards, three Horror Writers Association Bram Stoker Awards and two International Horror Guild Awards, as well as being a twelve-time recipient of the British Fantasy Award and a Hugo Award nominee. One of Britain's most acclaimed anthologists of horror and dark fantasy, he has edited and written more than sixty books.

For more information check out his web site at:

http://www.herebedragons.co.uk/jones

HARD TIMES AND ELDRITCH HAPPENINGS
JAY RUSSELL

Marty Burns is undeniably a Dark Detective, albeit one who is showing signs of lightening up. Marty wasn't originally intended to be an explorer of the great Oogy-Boogy, it just kind of happened. The novel in which he debuted, *Celestial Dogs*, began life as a mainstream crime novel about a former child-star-cum-detective fallen on hard times. The story was going to be about dirty doings in Hollywood—are there any other kind?—but somehow a flock of Japanese demons appeared. And the rest is history. Having established his credentials as a very strange attractor indeed, it only seemed (super)natural that Marty continue to encounter the inexplicable. In his second adventure, *Burning Bright*, Marty came to England to face down Nazi nasties, grey golems and all new manners of weirdness. And we ain't talking Marmite.

I'm a great fan of fiction which mixes and plays with genre categories, and as *Dark Detectives* so entertainingly proves, there is a long and rich tradition of melding the conventions of horror and detective fiction. The problem is that publishers hate books which don't fall into neat categories, and I believe that Marty Burns has developed visibility issues because he is neither fish nor fowl. The books get great reviews and I'm delighted with the feedback from readers, but booksellers seem puzzled as to where to place the books. Because there are supernatural elements, they generally go in the horror section, where few readers dare to tread. Horror has been a severely depressed genre for six or seven years now—though not nearly as depressed as the writers who produce it. As a result, and much as I enjoy mixing things up, the third Marty novel—tentatively titled *Greed & Stuff* and due to be published late this year or early next year—is a more traditional crime novel, with just a hint of the otherworldy for old time's sake.

Which is not to say that Marty is

entirely through with things that go bump, shriek and splat! in the night. The Man Who Shot the Man Who Shot the Man Who Shot Liberty Valence is part of a series of loosely linked short stories featuring Marty, all of which play off film titles and which are "about" the movies in one way or another. Some of these stories will be supernatural tales, though not all. Sullivan's Travails, featured in my collection *Waltzes and Whispers*, contains considerable comic spookiness; What Ever Happened to Baby June, in Steve Jones' *White of the Moon*, is a straight psychological thriller. I plan to send Marty to Hell—literally—in his next short story, along with Abbott and Costello. Really. What happens, you see, is...

Oh, you'll just have to read it to find out.

One of the delights of the anthology is Kim Newman's Victorian *Seven Stars* sequence, with the redoubtable Charles Beaureagerd; here's a glossary of characters:

SEVEN STARS WHO'S WHO

CHARLES BEAUREGARD. Beauregard appears in the first three novels in the Anno Dracula cycle, *Anno Dracula*, *The Bloody Red Baron: Anno Dracula 1918* and *Dracula Cha Cha Cha* (aka *Judgment of Tears: Anno Dracula 1959*). In the timeline of those novels, as in the stories here, Beauregard is a stalwart adventurer, something between a spy and a detective, who serves the interests of the Diogenes Club (q.v.) and the British Empire in the late Victorian era and rises to a high position in British Intelligence during World War One. Like Richard Jeperson, Beauregard is one of the first characters I created. I wrote stories about him, or featuring him, when I was a teenager, and even began a novel—*Beauregard in the Fog*—that would have prefigured some of the game-playing of Anno Dracula by pitting him against Fu Manchu, with other Victorian heroes and villains (Alan Moore, please note) in the background.

THE DIOGENES CLUB. Sir Arthur Conan Doyle created the Diogenes Club, and introduced it in *The Greek Interpreter*, the story which also brings on stage Sherlock Holmes's brother, Mycroft. Later, in *The Bruce-Partington Plans*, we learn that not only does brother Mycroft work for the British government but, under certain circumstances, he is the British government. The extrapolation that the Diogenes Club, where Mycroft is to be found, is the ancestor of Ian Fleming's Universal Export as a covert front for British Intelligence is not original to me, since I copped it from Billy Wilder and I A L Diamond's script for *The Private Life of Sherlock Holmes*. My version of the Diogenes Club, central to the stories collected in *Seven Stars*, also appears, albeit on that alternate timeline, in the Anno Dracula cycle.

GENEVIEVE DIEUDONNE. The Geneviève of this collection is the third alternate I've presented for this French-born vampire. The first—with no accent in her forename—appears in the books I wrote as Jack Yeovil for Games Workshop: *Drachenfels*, *Beasts in Velvet* (a cameo), *Geneviève Undead* and the novella *Red Reign*. The second, probably primary, Geneviève is the heroine of *Anno Dracula*, a background presence in *The Bloody Red Baron: Anno Dracula 1918* and returns in *Dracula Cha Cha Cha*. She'll probably show up in the next volume, *Johnny Alucard*. The Geneviève of *Seven Stars* has only previously been glimpsed in the novella *The Big Fish* (cf: *The Gumshoe*). The three can be told apart because their middle names vary, but they are at heart the same girl.

MORAG DUFF. Scots politician and future Prime Minister, Morag Duff appears in my story *SQPR* (see: *The Original Dr Shade & Other Stories*), and also turns up as a satellite of Derek Leech (q.v.) in my novel *The Quorum*. In my notes on 'SQPR' in the Dr Shade collection, I confessed my shortcomings as a prophet since the premise was that John Major lost the election he won the week the story was published. However, I spoke too soon since every policy and attitude I ascribed to Morag Duff seems now to be a plank of Tony Blair's New Labour government.

ROGER DUROC. Religious fanatic, mercenary of the future and general trouble-maker Duroc is a major villain in the Dark Future cycle I wrote as Jack Yeovil for Games Workshop: *Route 666*, *Demon Download*, *Krokodil Tears* and *Comeback Tour*. He was co-created by Eugene Byrne—there was going to be a Eugene solo novel (*The Violent Tendency*) in the sequence, and we would have collaborated on the big finish *United States Calvary*—and we took the name from the little boy in the Longman's Audio-Visual French course we were both taught in the early 70s.

THE GUMSHOE. My story 'The Big Fish', available in *Shadows Over Innsmouth* (edited by Stephen Jones), *Cthulhu 2000* (edited by Jim Turner) and my collection *Famous Monsters*, is a conflation of the styles and characters of H P Lovecraft and Raymond Chandler. The first-person PI narrator of 'The Big Fish' isn't quite Chandler's Philip Marlowe, since his mean streets have even darker corners, but he tries hard; 'The Trouble With Barrymore' is a direct sequel to 'The Big Fish'.

ROB HACKWILL. Rob Hackwill, the monster hero of the Where the Bodies Are Buried films, debuts in my story 'Where the Bodies Are Buried' (see: *Famous Monsters*, or the collection *Where the Bodies Are Buried*) to haunt Robert Hackwill, the small-town politician whose bullying inspired writer Allan Keyes to name the character after him, and reappeared in 'Where the Bodies Are Buried II: Sequel Hook' (in the same places) to haunt Keyes himself. The two stories here complete the cycle. Hackwill, the bully-turned-councillor, appears also in my novel *Life's Lottery*, while the monster (and Keyes) rate a few mentions in *The Quorum* and the novella 'Out of the Night When the Full Moon is Bright' (in *The Mammoth Book of Werewolves*, or *Famous Monsters*). The real Robert Hackwill, whose name I stole, is an announcer for Euronews, one of those cable channels.

RICHARD JEPERSON. My first efforts at fiction, which date back to the early 70s when I was learning to type, featured this character (I even completed a Jeperson novel when I was 16, a vampire story). It was appropriate to resurrect him when I decided to do a series set in that period and paying homage to the likes of The Avengers and the Jon Pertwee vintage Dr Who and the 120 page paperbacks I used to buy (Peter Saxon's The Guardians series, Frank G. Lauria's Dr Orient books). I also brought back his sidekicks Vanessa and Fred. I see Richard as a cross between Dr Strange and Jason King, and hope he'll be back.

CHANTAL JUILLERAT. Like Roger Duroc, Chantal—ninja nun, computer exorcist—was created for the Dark Future series; she is the heroine of *Demon Download*, and I have a terrific picture of her by Martin McKenna (the face of Audrey Hepburn, the body of Diana Rigg) framed above my desk. The Chantal of 'Where the Bodies Are Buried 2020' lives in a different timeline and decade, and isn't used up yet.

CATRIONA KAYE. Like Edwin Winthrop, Catriona was created for my play *My One Little Murder Can't Do Any Harm* (1981). She pops up all over my work, in the novels *Jago* and *The Bloody Red Baron: Anno Dracula 1918* and the story 'The Pierce-Arrow Stalled, and ...' (*Famous Monsters*).

ALLAN KEYES. Brit-born, Los Angeles-based horror writer-director Keyes (think Clive, think Wes, think John) is the creator of Rob Hackwill, the monster. Besides the 'Where the Bodies Are Buried' stories, he shows up briefly in *The Quorum*.

DEREK LEECH. My collection *The Original Dr Shade & Other Stories* features three stories revolving about possibly demonic, certainly malign, yet refreshingly honest multi-media tycoon Derek Leech: 'The Original Dr Shade', 'SQPR' and 'Organ Donors'. The last is a curtain-raiser for *The Quorum*, and establishes the adversarial relationship between Leech and single mother/private detective Sally Rhodes. Leech is often a background presence in my stories (cf: the 'Where the Bodies Are Buried' series, 'Out of the Night, When the Full Moon is Bright'). At his most diabolical, he is the narrator of *Life's Lottery*.

KATE REED. Katharine Reed was originally going to be a character in *Dracula*, but Bram Stoker never managed to include her. To make up for that, she has increasingly become central to my Anno Dracula cycle, showing up in all the novels and the novella 'Coppola's Dracula' (first part of the forthcoming Johnny Alucard). Since Mina Harker in Dracula has one friend (Lucy) who is beautiful and flighty, it struck me that her other friend should be gawky and sensible, which is how we arrive at Kate. I also gave her some of Stoker's own Dublin Protestant background.

JEROME RHODES. The son of Sally Rhodes (q.v.), Jerome is conceived in 'Organ Donors', a toddler in *The Quorum* and a grown-up investigator in 'Where the Bodies Are Buried 2020'. I named him after my nephew, who is about the same age.

SALLY RHODES. Private eye Sally Rhodes appears in a clutch of stories collected in *The Original Dr Shade & Other Stories*: 'Mother Hen', 'The Man Who Collected Barker' 'Twitch Technicolor', 'Gargantuabots vs the Nice Mice' and 'Organ Donors', but gets her largest canvas in *The Quorum*, which explains how she picks up the boyfriend she has in 'Mimsy' and further explores her relationship with Derek Leech (q.v.). She also turns up in *Life's Lottery*, to set a good example.

IAIN SCOBIE. Besides his appearance here, he gets a mention in *Life's Lottery* for the benefit of those who are paying attention.

DR SHADE. A scientific vigilante from British pulp magazines, who makes a sinister venture into the real world, Dr Shade was created for 'The Original Dr Shade', which was first published in *Interzone* and has been often reprinted. As an aspect of Derek Leech, he also lurks about in *The Quorum*. A movie script, *The Original Dr Shade*, co-developed with Adam Simon, is sitting on a shelf somewhere.

EDWIN WINTHROP. WWI veteran-cum-manipulative-psychic investigator Edwin Winthrop first appeared, with his girlfriend Catriona Kaye (q.v.), in the play *My One Little Murder Can't Do Any Harm* (1981), in which he was played by me and exposed a villain by feigning his own death during a seance. He is a leading character in *The Bloody Red Baron: Anno Dracula 1918*, and shows up also in *Jago*, *Demon Download* and 'The Big Fish'.

ELIZABETH YATMAN. She was in the crowd in *Jago*, and her sister Mary is a major character in *Life's Lottery*. I've never quite figured out just what made Elizabeth such an extreme character, but she strikes me as the most appalling of the many monsters I've made.

corpsing with toby litt

You may be tired of hearing about the newest crime-writing sensation: but we've got the man himself...

I HAVE NEVER BEEN SHOT. But for a number of years I was obsessed with trying to imagine how it would feel. *[Unpleasant and painful—Ed]* (Sigmund Freud, come on down!) I think this obsession (and I don't use that word about myself more than once or twice a decade) began when I read George Orwell's *1984* (at school, in 1984, for 'O' Level). At the end of the novel, as you probably know, our hero Winston Smith loves Big Brother. He is so happy that he doesn't want to risk ever being unhappy again. He was walking down the white-tiled corridor, with the feeling of walking in sunlight, and an armed guard at his back. The long-hoped-for bullet was entering his brain.

At one point in my life, the idea of being about-to-be shot used to come into my mind every night just before I fell asleep. (strange boy.)

It was this image, the image of a bullet entering a body, that began *Corpsing*. The sentence I worked over and over, as the opening of the novel, read: The first bullet (there are to be six: evenly distributed—three for her, three for me—though not equally destructive) enters Lily's body approximately two inches beneath her left breast.

(This, of course, ended up not as the first sentence, but lodged within the body of the book.)

For a while, that image was all I had.

Eventually, I came up with the next sentence. Slowly, or if not slowly then gradually, or if not gradually then at least moment by moment, leaving no gap in actual proceeding time, jumping no millimetre completely, the bullet begins its inevitable passage into Lily's thorax.

After this, it soon became clear that the remainder of the novel was a simple matter of tracing that single bullet in two directions: back up the gun-barrel, hunting the source of its motivation; onwards through the body, chasing its full consequences—physical and otherwise.

The bullet was now going into a fictional character, Lily. And I had to find out who she was, too. As I won't be able to talk about the motivation part without giving too much of the plot away, I'll concentrate on the full consequences part. I decided I needed to find out as much as possible about what it's like to be shot, and what happens inside of you when you are.

I was sick of seeing people in movies getting shot flippantly. Gatted Tarantino-style. There's a scene from an action movie, can't remember which, that particularly narked me. Arnie or Brucie or whoever is fighting his way up an escalator, all the time coming under heavy machine-gun fire from baddies. As he goes, he uses a couple of innocent commuters as human shields. Their death, paralysis, pain, is irrelevant. It isn't the point. (Some of you may also recall the "No-one thinks about the henchman's wife and children" gag from Austin Powers, International Man of Mystery.) Being shot isn't as simple as bang-bang-you're-dead.

Yet there is a problem. Most accounts that ordinary people give of being shot, like most accounts that ordinary people give of any extremely traumatic event, are couched in cliché. They almost always refer to a feeling of unreality. As if they themselves had been in a film, a work of fiction. Asking people to describe being shot is a bit like asking Ole Gunnar Solskjaer to describe what scoring his extra-time European Cup winning goal felt like. If I could find anyone who actually had been shot, I wasn't likely to get much out of them I hadn't already got from seeing a hundred such people interviewed on TV.

Plus, why assume that everyone who is shot experiences it in the same way? When my characters were clearer, then I'd know how they would react to the actual physical event.

So instead I concentrated on what I could find out for sure: what goes on inside the body. This is where it gets a bit gory.

I needed to do some book research. First stop: the British Library. This was when it was in the British Museum. I looked up Gunshot Wounds on the computer, and got two immediate hits. When I ordered the books, however, I was made to sit in what I once heard Will Self call The Seats of Shame. This was a large table and twelve chairs right beneath the eye of the Issue Desk librarians. If you wanted to read de Sade, this is where they put you. Imagine my discomfort.

I decided to take down the publisher's details, and order the book so that I could read it at home. This was my main source: Vincent J.M. Di Maio's *Gunshot Wounds: Practical Aspects of Firearms, Ballistics, and Forensic Techniques*.

I also boned up on anatomy with the *Colour Atlas of Human Anatomy*, a book I found in Blackwells on Charing Cross Road. (This, incidentally, though no-one ever asked, was my Book of the Year 1998.) An extraordinary publication, it uses photographs of real dissected bodies. Not the crappy, primary coloured illustrations of your Biology Textbook at school.

I also needed to learn about the different types of guns that might do the shooting. This led me to American gun-enthusiast magazines. The scariness of these is a by-word.

Hitting the Internet, I came across plenty of gun manufacturer websites, and found the non-sequitors of their sales pitches horribly delightful. The constant emphasis placed upon how safe their weapons are was particularly excruciating.

Rather than choose a real gun, in the end I decided to make up my own: a Gruber & Litvak. It is a .40 which operates with a modified Browning-type action. It is available in three finishes (matte black, blue or stainless).

I did also, surprisingly, talk to some real people. Whilst writing, I had a useful conversation with Steve Collins, an ex-policeman who used to work for SO19, the armed division of the Met. He was promoting his memoirs, *Good Guys Wear Black*. When I asked him how someone might get hold of a gun, he said, Walk in to the right pub in South London, get talking to the right person, and you can be tooled up within half an hour.

Publicity following the Jill Dando shooting subsequently confirmed this ease of access.

Eventually, I gained enough expertise to write this kind of stuff.

As the bullet passes through the cohesive but elastic tissue of the muscles, a cavity of greater diameter than the bullets own is temporarily created—around and behind it. For all of five to ten milliseconds after the bullet passes, this ripping-rippling emptiness pulsates—in and out, in and out—spreading damage laterally, through to tissues the bullet itself hasn't even touched. This phenomenon is technically known as cavitation.

A gunshot is a paradoxical thing for a writer. In one sense, as soon as the trigger is pulled and the bullet leaves the barrel, its consequences are inevitable; in another, there is always the chance—while the bullet moves onwards in slow-motion—that it will miss, or at least miss the vital organs. Until the worst has happened, it's still not certain.

In this, it's a bit like reading a crime novel. Your reading of it won't in any way change the terrible things that happen to the characters. But you can hope against hope that, this time, things won't turn out quite so bad. And even if they do there, is always the fascination of watching disaster as it strikes.

And did all this help with the obsession? Well, I no longer think about being shot every night just before I fall asleep. Some nights, but not every night.

cuban crime

jose latour interviewed peter walker

With the publication of Cuban crime writer José Latour's Outcast, *a previously closed world has opened up to us—if only slightly. This is the first Cuban crime book written in English to be published in the United States and readily available here in the UK. Havana based Latour is "one of Cuba's most popular crime writers" and, under the pseudonym Javier Moran, he is the author of six previous books—including* Preludio a la Noche (Prelude to the Night) *and* Medianoche Enemiga (Midnight Enemy). *These facts alone should make us sit up and take notice, but* Outcast *is full of surprises, and for all sorts of reasons makes for an intriguing, surprising and sometimes uncomfortable read in the way it makes us look at ourselves afresh.*

I contacted the publishers—New York based Akashic Books—and requested an interview with Latour which, for obvious reasons, took place via email. Latour limited me to six questions for various reasons but mainly because he was redecorating. I asked him to tell me about himself, the background to his writing and his popularity in Cuba.

I was born in what Christopher Columbus—probably overjoyed that he had proven his theory—described as *"the most beautiful land human eyes have ever seen."* Well, as we now know, the Great Admiral had not proven his theory, and with regard to Cuba maybe he lay it on thick, but not too thick. As centuries went by, the Pearl of the Antilles came to be a country privileged in having what many foreigners describe as one of the kindest people on earth. Today it is a place of enchantment where natural beauty and human decency blend.

That is the background to my writing. A lovely corner of this planet with many soft-hearted humans and lousy luck. Ruthless colonialists ransacked it for a little over four centuries; it's located much too close for its own good to the most powerful nation in history; then for sixty years it endured crooked politicians, greedy businessmen, and gangsters; lives presently in a social experiment of utopian visions and goals lacking vital natural resources, suffering from mismanagement, an unjust embargo, and totalitarianism. It also has, like other places, models of virtue and criminals, whores and nuns, selfish and selfless people, hypocrites and idealists.

Is there a richer background for a writer? If you were born and raised here, you can't escape it. Not even if you live abroad for the better part of your life. Unfortunately, I lost many years in bureaucratic jobs. I regret that. By now I would have produced twice as many books. But it was impossible to earn a livelihood from writing only.

As to popularity... Here, crime fiction is extremely well-received, so almost any Cuban crime writer becomes popular, whether he is good, average or bad. I guess I'm not one of the worst.

I asked Latour about his crime and literary influences.

I became a voracious reader at a very tender age, maybe at eight or nine. I read Don Quixote for the first time when I was twelve or thirteen. I read it again in my twenties, thirties, forties, and fifties. Same thing with the works of Shakespeare, Balzac, Dostoyevsky. I admire the literature produced by Alejo Carpentier, Jorge Luis Borges, Mika Waltari, John Steinbeck, Winston Churchill.

In the 50's I read hundreds of crime books in English. Among the Britons: Conan Doyle, Christie, Michael Innes, Margery Allingham (ah, her *Tiger in the Smoke*). Chandler, Queen, Gardner, Prather and Spillane were the Americans who made a lasting impression.

Then I got disconnected from Western crime literature until the International Association of Crime Writers was founded in 1986. Immediately books flowed and I came to know authors like Manuel Vazquez, Rolo Diez, Ricardo Piglia, and Paco Taibo, all of whom write in Spanish. In America I discovered, among others, Don Westlake, Joe Gores, Elmore Leonard, Larry Block, Martin Cruz Smith, John D MacDonald, Joseph Wambaugh, John Grisham and Carl Hiassen. I've also read some British colleagues: Susan Moody, Janet Laurence and June Thompson. Also Chris Niles, from New Zealand, who sets her novels in London and Sydney.

The main part of the book is set in a realistically portrayed Florida—especially the Cuban community. I asked Latour about the Cuban-American community, his relationship to it and how he researched this part of the book.

I travelled extensively through twenty-eight states of the Union as a teenager, but the only American city I can say I know a little is Miami. I was fourteen years old the first time I spent a month there. I went back in 1956 and 1958. Then for thirty-four years I was unable to visit. When I finally returned in 1992, I found a completely different place. But to write acceptably about a town, city or country that you don't know well, research is the name of the game.

For a Cuban living here, it's not difficult to study the Cuban community in Miami. I have many relatives and close friends living there, none of whom are criminals. The criminals in Outcast are figments of my imagination.

I asked Latour how he felt Outcast had been received in Cuba and his perception of the way it has been received in 'the West'.

As far as I know, *Outcast* is not for

sale in Cuba. If someone has read it here, I haven't learned about it. If by 'the West' you mean America and Europe, my perception is that in the US it has received more attention than I hoped for. There have been nice reviews in several publications. My publisher has a distributor in the UK but I haven't heard anything about sales and reviews.

Latour is the Vice President for Latin America of the International Association of Crime Writers. I ask him to give me an outline of Cuban and Latin American crime writing. Are there, for example, any other Latin American/Cuban crime writers he admires?

To my knowledge, there was only one attempt at fictional crime writing in Cuba before the late 40s. A few young writers, half-jokingly, decided that each would write one chapter of a novel. The result was not spectacular.

In the late 40s and early 50s some good short stories were published in Cuban magazines. The first Cuban crime novel was written by Ignacio Cardenas in 1971. The 80s was a golden era in which more than seventy titles were published, many of them of average quality, some frankly bad, a few very good. From 1991 to 1995, due to financial reasons, only two crime fiction novels were released. From 1996 to date the publishing industry has recovered somewhat and several rather good books have reached readers.

Latin American crime fiction is alive and well. Very well, I would say, if the right authors and books are chosen. As Vice President of IACW, I should refrain from mentioning my favourite writers and titles, but it is a shame that some of the best are unknown outside Spanish-speaking countries. Maybe the high cost of translations is a reason for this, but I assure you that English-speaking readers are missing some exceedingly good Latin American crime literature.

Outcast is a very good hard-boiled thriller in which the central character, Elliot Steil, escapes from the failing and restrictive socialist state only to land in a corrupt Miami where, literally, everything has a price. The transformation of mild mannered Steil as he searches for answers to why someone would want him killed is the core of the book. This alone makes for a compelling read but Latour isn't content to leave it there. Given his background how could he? One of the things that makes Outcast *so interesting—and important—is the way Latour is able to blend political issues effortlessly throughout the book. Elliot, musing on the world around him says:*

"America confuses liberty with libertinism…my homeland and this country face the same fundamental issue: the limits of control. In Cuba laws etc. rule almost everything a person can do and you end up feeling enslaved. In the US respect for individual rights seems to have turned freedom into a form of anarchy in certain social strata."

Difficult choices which face all of us. Whilst the Cuban revolution is failing—the illegal American blockade, rationing, shortages, bureaucracy and a one Party state have all taken their toll—the education and health system are at least available to all as a right and not at a price.

Cuban kids are so bright they are usually placed a grade or two ahead of their American contemporaries in American schools whilst, at the same time, having to cope with shootings and drugs.

Latour is a fierce critic of American capitalism. Elliot has to find a way to survive and ends up working for a businessman who is making millions selling illegal CFC's and destroying the environment into the bargain—thus turning Hiassen et al on their heads. There are no easy answers. The experience of Cuban immigrants has often been harsh. As he explains in Outcast (with a slight touch of Marxist analysis and one that could apply to the world situation as well);

"The centres of real power in Federal and State Governments and higher education appeared to remain firmly in Anglo hands. Once in a while a few crumbs were dropped to the best and brightest of first and second generation immigrants. Letting them in was one thing, relinquishing power was another."

Given Latour's literary influences it's fair to say he's written a modern version of Dickens A Tale of Two Cities. It's one of the big questions; do we try to change an imperfect world or can we only change ourselves? Latour isn't 'pro-socialism' or 'pro-capitalism' but he seems to be, of all things, pro-humanity. In Steil's developing relationship with his girlfriend, for example, he draws strength from her feminism: "Through her he was recovering a little faith in humanity". But this is a view built on a foundation of fatalism. Freedom is indeed "man's most pressing need" but governments are as imperfect as human nature. There is simply no such thing as paradise. "The world," Steil remarks, "is sick... some diseases are common to all societies, others need specific environments to survive."

Finally I asked Latour about his future plans. His next novel will also be in English, there's an interview with CBS in January, a trip in February to the US, and he is rewriting The Fool, an earlier work, to be released by Akashic this year.

Your question includes my answer. He who lives by the crystal ball ends up eating glass. Let us wait and see.

I'm not sure what to make of this answer—other than perhaps it is a touch of Cuban fatalism. Johnny Temple at Akashic Books tells me that The Fool is "...a story about a Cuban sugar-trader who is tricked into playing a role in an international drug-money laundering operation. Much of the action takes place in southern Mexico—both in a city and in the jungle. It is written very well, extremely suspenseful, and the character development is incredible." Definitely one to look out for.

Where does all this take us? I don't know. There may not be any answers—only very good questions—but I'm always impressed at crime writings ability to be at the cutting edge. And maybe Latour is better placed than most to make us stop and take stock of the ways we choose to live in this world—and, of course, to tell a great story along the way.

OUTCAST BY JOSE LATOUR
AKASHIC BOOKS £7.99

Cuban crime writer José Latour makes an impressive English-language debut with *Outcast*, a noirish guided tour through both Havana and Miami's Cuban community that will push buttons. Guaranteed.

Burnt-out Havana school teacher Eliot Steil's dreary existence is disrupted by a mysterious American who comes a-calling, offering a shot at freedom and riches. But it turns out the American dream isn't quite so easily achieved. The mild-mannered Eliot becomes a sort of criminal Superman once he's on the other side of the Straits of Florida—living outside the law, stealing cars and running hot goods, and prowling for those who would have him dead. Eliot handles it all with a gloomy fatalism that asks no quarter and salutes no flag. He concludes that the same end awaits us all: *"Funerals, I guess. Grieving, silent people saying goodbye to a loved one."* Latour may not take sides in the prolonged, pointless pissing contest between communism and capitalism—but he doesn't pull any punches either. The worker's paradise and land of the free are both held up to Eliot's fierce vision, and both are found sadly lacking.

A great book? No, merely a good one. It peters out at the end, and at times seems curiously removed. Still, even if it offers no easy answers, it certainly asks some very hard questions. And in light of the recent Elian Gonzalez case, that's enough to make it an important book. Read it and weep.

KEVIN BURTON SMITH

Kevin Burton Smith is the creator and editor of The Thrilling Detective Web Site, which is devoted to the appreciation of fictional private eyes—hard-boiled and otherwise—in literature, film, television, and other media. He lives in Montreal, where it's legal to Cuban cigars and American cigarettes. But it's not paradise, either. The Thrilling Detective Web site is at: www.colba.net/kvnsmith/thrillingdetective/

Outcast is readily available in the UK. Akashic books are at:
  www.akashicbooks.com
  email: akashic7@aol.com

hammet, chandler and cain: new approaches

ray and dash...

Raymond Chandler

The author of the much-acclaimed Seven Stars *and* Life's Lottery *(Simon & Schuster) adds his tuppence-worth to a long-standing debate among crime-writing aficionados.*

I am prepared finally to concede against my instincts that the Beatles are a better pop group than the Rolling Stones (even if you lump together the horrible individual post-split work of the Beatles and include it in the canon to set against every terrible album the Stones have done since 1970), and I prefer the Bonzo Dog Doo-Dah Band to either because I feel closer to their engagement with the popular culture I've also chosen to play with. However, I've never come down on either side of the Chandler/Hammett debate Both writers strike me as enormously seductive (their prose is about the best antidote you can have as a teenager after reading too much, say, Lovecraft): Hammett is stripped-to-the-bone, not-a-word-wasted reportage, always giving a you-are-there feel; Chandler began as a poet, and his voice is whimsical, pleased with the strange meta-

kim newman

phors, laced with a sense of the exotic that has matured as his world has faded into historical fantasy. Their visions of America are dark, but only superficially concerned with the real sense of despair that haunts, say, Cornell Woolrich.

The Op and Marlowe are both romantic loners, and thus beyond real hurt—the antithesis, I suspect, is Jim Rockford, a Los Angeles private eye who is inextricably tied to the world by family and friends, constantly dragged into cases through personal obligations and eternally disappointed by people he genuinely likes. I think we shouldn't make too much of Hammett's real experience as a detective; Chandler certainly saw more violence, human beastliness and horror in any day on the Western Front than Hammett did coughing through years of sick days on the job in San Francisco. Hammett does have a real political sense that the merely cynical Chandler lacks and was, unlike Chandler, able to conceive of sympathetic, attractive and believable *rich* characters in *The Thin Man* (notably, Chandler couldn't finish *The Poodle Springs Mystery*, which has the *The Thin Man* premise of the poor detective married to the wealthy heiress).

In their careers, both great men strike me as tiresomely self-dramatising, simultaneously whining that no one took them seriously because they wrote detective stories but never able to finish any of their supposedly serious projects (which all sound a whole lot less interesting than another thriller as good as *Red Harvest* or *Farewell, My Lovely*), and complaining bitterly about the treatment of the writer in Hollywood while neglecting their own work to rake in big bucks for screenwriting assignments. All the biographical stuff I've read about them makes me sympathise with anyone who had to deal with them as an editor, publisher, agent, producer or life partner (why has the whining, paranoid drunk been such a model of American literary behaviour since Edgar Allan Poe?). Hammett's writing career was over twenty years before he died, though he never quite admitted it; and Chandler slowed down drastically as soon as he was comfortably rich from Hollywood.

Each barely managed in their entire careers a half dozen slim novels and enough stories to fill a couple of collections—someone like Stephen King probably puts out more words in a single year than Ray and Dash did in their whole working lives. Then again, maybe Ross MacDonald and Ed McBain wrote too many books, lessening the impact of each individual effort with uniform excellence. As a set, MacDonald's Lewd Archer books are as essential to the development of the private eye field as the oeuvres of Hammett and Chandler, but he was just too professional and personally decent to make the same noise. Archer is a step away from the Op and Marlowe, towards Rockford—he hasn't got the superhuman dissociation from the world that makes his predecessors great detectives and tends to solve the case by understanding the people involved rather than sneering at them.

There's a strange disjunction between the *Black Mask* school and the science fiction magazines: the best thriller writers came to the pulps in early middle age after drinking their way through several careers and managed quite small outputs, while the science fiction writers were kids who had never really done anything and went on to be enormously prolific. The founders of science fiction also hung around a lot longer, and in some cases are still cranking out sequels to their early hits (even if they're dead, like Isaac Asimov and L Ron Hubbard), giving the impression that the field is still a grazing area for dinosaurs. There are a great many unreadable continuations of books from the 40s and 50s on the shelves, next to work from writers not born when *Foundation* (or even *2001*) came out. How would the detective/thriller/noir field look if James Ellroy or Joe Lansdale had to compete with bloated seventieth sequels to *The Maltese Falcon* or *The Big Sleep*, cranked out either by the plugged-into-the-mains original authors or by amanuenses hired to flesh out sketchy outlines dropped from the pens of the great men?

In all honesty, neither Hammett or Chandler was a great *mystery* writer: Hammett always had the pulpish one-damn-thing-after-another plot method, and *The Dain Curse* is every bit as contrived, unlikely and in its perversity guessable as anything by Agatha Christie, while *The Thin Man* just pulls out a nonentity as the arbitrarily-unmasked killer; Chandler cobbled together two or more novelette plots in his great novels, sometimes with brilliance (one of the great clues in literature is the liquor-glass ring on Marlowe's business card in *Farewell, My*

Dashiell Hammett

Lovely, which tells the PI that the two cases he is working are actually the same case) and, perhaps influenced by *The Maltese Falcon* and his own misogyny, he always has the strongest woman in the book turn out to be the killer, a quirk he might never have recognised in himself and which renders all his whodunits (except the marginal *Playback*) transparent. These books are so much a part of the canon now that anyone who sits down to read *The Maltese Falcon* will almost certainly from the film know who killed Miles Archer (though perhaps the killer of Rusty Regan, different in the book, is more of a surprise). How did these books go down with readers interested in the whodunits rather than the cool writing and the filmland associations? There must have been many who saw through *The Big Sleep* in the first chapter and reached in relief for the next impenetrable John Dickson Carr.

Together, Chandler and Hammett are responsible for that strange, sadomasochist mix of homoeroticism and homophobia that remains an oddly recurrent aspect of hard-boiled writing, consciously in James Ellroy and riotously unconsciously in Mickey Spillane. Think of the lovingly-described brutal beating Ned Beaumont takes in *The Glass Key* and the treatment of the gunsel in *The Maltese Falcon*, and Marlowe's mix of snide put-downs of effeminate characters (the lavender-scented Marriott in *Farewell, My Lovely*) with odd little crushes on other men (most heartbreakingly, Terry Lennox in *The Long Goodbye*). Both write great female monsters, but are less happy with good girls: Nora Charles of *The Thin Man* is a good try but nothing like as convincing as Bridgid O'Shaughnessy-Wonderly-Thursby-Whatever in *The Maltese Falcon*; you'd be hard put to remember Anne Riordan from *Farewell, My Lovely* even though she turns up again in a late short story as Marlowe's squeeze, and the jury is still! out on Linda Loring, supporting character in *The Long Goodbye*, who marries Marlowe in the *Poodle Springs* fragment.

It may be that the flaws of this pair of major writers are as important as their inarguable virtues. Certainly, many of their successors have chosen to imitate and elaborate their failings as often as they have built upon the foundations they lay down. Now they belong to the historical past, I shouldn't be surprised if their fictional worlds are as often revisited as the London of Sherlock Holmes: there was a collection of 'authorised' marlowe pastiches a few years ago (and I wrote an unauthorised one, *The Big Fish*) and Robert Parker finished *Poodle Springs* before turning out a blah sequel to *The Big Sleep* (*Perchance to Dream*) and once the estate gets sorted out the temptation to provide more Sam Spade cases must be irresistible. Both voices are deceptively easy to imitate, but their personalities are more elusive. In creating a genre, they began a process that continues in many media: in 70s cinema, Roman Polanski and Robert Towne's *Chinatown*, Robert Altman and Leigh Brackett's *The Long Goodbye* and Arthur Penn and Alan Sharp's criminally underrated *Night Moves* hommaged, critiqued and extended the Chandler/Hammett legacy, and their most important modern interpreters may not be the horde of PI scribblers but Joel and Ethan Coen, who have taken their material (Hammett in *Blood Simple* and *Miller's Crossing*; Chandler in *The Big Lebowski*) as core texts and spun off in all manner of direction.

And Eddie Duggan looks at some interesting Chandleriana...

RAYMOND CHANDLER'S PHILIP MARLOWE: A CENTENNIAL CELEBRATION EDITED BY BYRON PRIES, I-BOOKS £9.99

Although the blurb on the back describes this volume as offering "*twenty five new stories featuring America's favourite detective*", it is in fact, a repackaged edition of a collection published in 1988 to mark the centenary of Raymond Chandler's birth. While the stories are not as fresh as the publisher might have us believe, the undertaking is still interesting: editor Byron Preiss commissioned a group of Philip Marlowe stories from contemporary crime writers, each offering a pastiche in the style of Raymond Chandler. The contributors include a raft of familiar names: Max Allan Collins, Sara Paretsky, Simon Brett, Stuart Kaminsky, Robert Crais, Edward Hoch and Ed Gorman. The original collection offered 23 stories. In this repackaged edition, two extra stories are added (owners of the original tome may be interested to know that the two additional stories are available on the publisher's website <http://www.ibooksinc.com/mar_info.htm>). The original introduction, penned by Chandler's biographer, Frank MacShane, is now shunted to the back as an *afterword*, and Robert B. Parker's introduction to the 1988 edition of *Playback* is recycled as the introduction here. The book design has been improved for this reissue. The original collection offered illustrations between each of the stories; these stylised graphics are more attractive in this larger trade paperback format. A map of LA locations, labelled *Philip Marlowes Los Angeles*' has been added, which brings a nice touch, though the monotone reproduction fails to capture the vivacity and style of the old Dell *map back* series of paperbacks, published in the 1940s. In his foreword, Byron Preiss remarks that this collection is intended to *"honour Chandler rather than steal from him"*. The danger in such an enterprise is not so much that it might 'steal' from Chandler as lurch into a poor-taste parody. Despite the risk, the collection actually works rather well, and the authors do manage to capture something of the essence of Chandler's style—in almost every story there is a descriptive phrase or a piece of dialogue jumps off the page, somehow more convincing—more Chandler, rather than Chandleresque—than its neighbours. The collection is arranged to offer one Marlowe story for each of the years from 1935 to 1959, spanning the years between the first Marlowe story and the year of Chandler's death (the inclusion of two additional stories in this edition gives 1959 three stories). The chronological arrangement causes the cultural background to shift as time progresses: from the depression of the 1930s, through the war years of the 40s, and on through the 1950s; the chronology also means that these ersatz Marlowes age as the stories progress so, by 1958, Marlowe has Poodle Springs and a failed marriage behind him. It is slightly ironic that this tribute offers twenty-five Marlowe stories, which is more than the number of Marlowe stories that Chandler wrote himself (even allowing for the fact that Chandler's Marlowe was sometimes called Dalmas or Carmady). One original Chandler story is included, *The Pencil*, the last Marlowe story Chandler wrote (in 1958), published posthumously in *Manhunt* magazine in 1960 (and in the same magazine, the following year, as *The Wrong Pigeon*). The value of this collection is not that it offers an introduction to Chandler or Marlowe, but that it offers an enjoyable diversion for the Chandlerphile, and Chandler fans will undoubtedly find a place for it on their bookshelves.

dashiell hammett:
detective, writer

EVERYONE READING this will almost certainly have heard of Dashiell Hammett, that most original writer of detective fiction who drew on his experience as an operative for the Pinkerton detective agency when he started writing crime stories. Look at the blurbs on the crime novels at your local bookshop—Hammett's name will appear again and again, the benchmark against which so many writers of 'tough' or hard-boiled fiction are still measured, the magical name which is used to invoke the highest achievement—so many writers are hailed as 'the new Hammett' or are promoted by blurb-writers to take a place 'alongside Hammett and Chandler.'

It is remarkable that a man with so short a writing career as Hammett could transform detective fiction and, at the same time, cut so deep a benchmark as to set the standard by which others will be measured and judged for the next seventy-five years, but that is precisely what Hammett achieved. Hammett's career as a writer was short

Cover from the rather lovely Folio Society Maltese Falcon.

eddie duggan

one. He started by selling short filler-pieces of dry wit, then longer pieces and then short stories during 1922, becoming established as a contributor to the legendary pulp magazine *The Black Mask* in 1923. Knopf published his first novel, *Red Harvest*, in 1929 after serialization that year in *Black Mask*. In 1933, Hammett's fifth and final novel, *The Thin Man* was published in the magazine *Redbook* before book publication by Knopf the following year and, with that, Hammett's writing career was effectively over.

So who was Dashiell Hammett, detective, drinker, invalid, writer, and radical?

Dashiell Hammett was born Samuel Dashiell Hammett in St Mary's County, Maryland, May 27th, 1894, the second of three children born to Richard and Mary Hammett. The Hammett family had been comfortable, but Richard Hammett, a drinker and womanizer, was unable to maintain the prosperity of previous generations. He was also involved in local politics but, after switching his political allegiance, became so unpopular that the family had to leave St Mary's County. The Hammetts moved to Philadelphia in 1900, and then to Baltimore the following year. During this period the young Samuel Hammett enjoyed a reasonably unremarkable childhood, although he was an avaricious reader.

Richard Hammett became too ill to work in 1908 and, so the story goes, Samuel had to leave college to take a job as a messenger in order to help the family finances, but Samuel Hammett was glad of the chance to give up school. Young Hammett had trouble keeping jobs however, because of his poor timekeeping. The reading habit that kept Hammett up half the night caused him to be frequently fired for lateness.

In 1915 Sam Hammett answered a newspaper advertisement which led to him being taking on as an 'operative' or a detective at the Baltimore office of the Pinkerton Detective Agency. Here his varied employment history was seen as something of an advantage and his Pinkerton role provided him with the variety his previous, mundane jobs had lacked.

The Baltimore branch of the Pinkerton agency was headed by Jimmy Wright, who trained Hammett in the art of 'shadowing' or following suspects. Hammett would later use the short, stocky Wright as the physical model for his plump, middle-aged, nameless detective character, the Continental Op. Hammett extended his homage to the Baltimore branch of the Pinkerton Agency by naming his fictional detective firm The Continental Detective Agency: in Hammett's day the Pinkerton office in Baltimore was located in the Continental building.

In June 1918 Hammett enlisted in the ambulance corps, and was posted to a camp some twenty miles outside Baltimore. Within a few months Hammett became one of the many victims of the world-wide epidemic of Spanish flu which was spread around the world by various armies leaving the European theatre at the end of the First World War. By May 1919 Hammett's condition had developed into tuberculosis and, in July, he was discharged from the army as an invalid.

Hammett returned to Baltimore for a further stint of detective work. However, his poor health caused him to be hospitalised again and, in December 1919, Hammett was declared 50% disabled. Meanwhile, the decade about to open is one of optimism and prosperity: after the war in Europe, a lighter mood is encouraged by the boom in advertising (in which Hammett will soon play a part as a copywriter), and promises of happiness and freedom flicker against a backdrop, in America at least, of scandal and corruption, as the Volstead Act becomes law and 'the noble experiment', the prohibition of the production and sale of alcohol, allows for corruption and organised crime to take a firm hold on America. Overnight, the huge profits to be made from supplying bootleg liquor means that everybody from the bellboy to the mayor is on the take. Illegal drinking joints—speakeasies—operate in every town. The cultural soundtrack is jazz and the mood is decidedly upbeat as women bob their hair and hemlines and the dancefloors resonate with racy dances like the Black Bottom and the Charleston. This is also the decade of the motor car: the great American symbol of freedom, opportunity and mobility (as well as the getaway) sweeps across the country almost overnight—seven million cars are on the road in America in 1920, by 1929 the number will be 23 million. Following his release from hospital, Sam Hammett moves across the country to Washington, in the colder northwest. Here, in May 1920, he joins the Spokane branch of the Pinkerton Detective Agency. In the same year, two entrepreneurs, H. L. Mencken and George Jean Nathan found a pulp magazine, *The Black Mask*, in the hope that sales of this title will support their ailing slick magazine, *The Smart Set*. The strap line of *The Black Mask's* first issue, dated April 1920, declares it 'An Illustrated Magazine of Detective, Mystery, Adventure, Romance and Spiritualism'. It will be a few years yet, however, before the new-style, tough, detective-hero, emerges from the cradle of its pages.

By November 1920 Hammett's health has failed again, causing him to be admitted to a lungers' hospital near Tacoma, Washington. During periods of respite from this bout of illness, Hammett courts and seduces Jose Dolan, one of the hospital nurses, whom he will later marry. In February 1921 Hammett and several other patients are moved south to a hospital near San Diego, California, in order to benefit from the milder climate. At the same time, Jose Dolan, who had been transferred to a hospital in Montana, finds she is pregnant and is discharged from her nursing job. Meanwhile, Warren Harding takes office as 29th US President: by 1923, however, Harding will face prosecution for his corrupt or, at best, inept presidency, which includes selling his cronies the Teapot Dome military base, containing vast oil fields. While corruption appears to run to the very core of American society, Harding avoids impeachment by dying in mysterious circumstances, possibly poisoned by his wife for his infidelity.

In May 1921 Hammett is considered well enough to be discharged from hospital and, in June, he moves to San Francisco where, in July, he marries

Jose; they move into an apartment at 620 Eddy Street and Hammett works off-and-on as a part-time Pink in San Francisco. Pinkerton's San Francisco Branch was run by Phil Geaque, Hammett's model for The Old Man, the head of the fictional Continental Detective Agency. In October 1921 Jose produces a daughter, Mary Jane, and Hammett has to sleep in the hall of the apartment to minimise the risk of infecting the baby with TB. His poor health also causes him to give up Pinkerton work and, by December 1921, Hammett quits the Pinkerton Detective Agency for good. Hammett would later claim to have been involved with the Fatty Arbuckle case, and also to have discovered a cache of stolen gold on a ship just before it was due to sail: some critics and biographers are uncritically accepting of Hammett's claims, but Richard Layman is more skeptical, suggesting Hammett, as a successful author, was knowingly exploiting his past.

After taking a writing course in 1922, Hammett began to write and sell advertising copy on a freelance basis. He also tried his hand at other forms of writing and, by October 1922, has sold a short, droll anecdote, 'The Parthian Shot', to Mencken and Nathan's *The Smart Set*. In December 1922 Hammett published his first piece in *The Black Mask*, under the pseudonym Peter Collinson, a name he had used for several earlier short pieces. 'The Road Home' is the tale of detective doggedly pursuing his human quarry into the jungle. Although he is wracked by thoughts of home the detective presses on with the pursuit when anyone else would have given up. This trait will be a feature in Hammett's later Continental Op stories.

Another of Hammett's early *Smart Set* pieces stood out from the short sardonic sketches. This was 'From the Memoirs of a Private Detective', which appeared in *The Smart Set* in March 1923. The piece consisted of 29 short paragraphs in which Hammett recalled incidents or made wry comments about various aspects of detective work, such as 'Three times I have been mistaken for a prohibition agent, but never had any trouble clearing myself' and 'That the lawbreaker is invariably ... apprehended is probably the least challenged of extant myths ... [T]he files of every detective bureau bulge with the records of unsolved mysteries and uncaught criminals.'

Writing and drinking through the night, ex-detective Hammett managed to publish fourteen stories in six magazines in 1923, half of them in *The Black Mask*. After 'The Vicious Circle', a recursive blackmail story published as Collinson in June 1923, Hammett's next appearance in *The Black Mask*, also as Collinson, is in October 1923 with 'Arson Plus', the first Continental Op story. This debut tale of a character that will prove to be popular with *The Black Mask*'s readers tells the story of a complex insurance fraud and a fabricated death, which the Op uncovers through observation and perseverance.

The Op is an interesting character in the history of detective fiction: he does not have a name, he is referred to simply as 'the Op'. Although the stories are told in the first person, the Op reveals few personal details. As well as withholding his name, no details of his background or his family are given: we know that he is middle-aged, plump, unmarried, and does his job because he likes it and is good at it. His dedication to the job forms the basis of the detective's code. As the Op remarks to Princess Zhukovski at the end of the 1925 story, 'The Gutting of Couffignal', 'I like being a detective, like the work, and liking the work makes you want to do it as well as you can ... I don't know anything else, don't enjoy anything else, don't want to know or enjoy anything else.'

The Op is also significant because of the way in which he works. Hammett's Pinkerton experience shows through in detailed descriptions of the painstaking investigative procedures that characterise the Op stories. Unlike the cosy world of the country house detective, in which there is a place for everything and everything slips back into place at the story's end with the villain in custody and (social) order restored, the world of the Continental Op is one in which apprehension of the criminal is, as Hammett intimated in 'From the Memoirs of a Private Detective', by no means a certainty. The process of investigation involves careful searches, tedious stake-outs, and ongoing team work—a far cry from the twist of Abyssinian tobacco found on the carpet of the study that leads the cerebral detective to infer that the brigadier was dispatched by the housekeeper's demented half-brother.

In the world of the Continental Op, murder and other crimes are committed by people with base motives like jealousy, lust or avarice. Characters with habits to support, like Porky Grout, the cowardly stool-pigeon in 'The Girl With Silver Eyes' (1924), are likely to give away what information they might have for the price of a hit of nose-candy. If the detective can't prove a criminal committed one crime, he may well be able to fit him up for another, as in 'The Golden Horseshoe' (1924), in which the Op frames a murderer for a crime he didn't commit in order to send him to the gallows to pay for another murder. These are the qualities which led Raymond Chandler to comment in his essay 'The Simple Art of Murder' that 'Hammett took murder out of the Venetian vase and dropped it in the alley ... [He] gave murder back to the kind of people that commit it for reasons, not just to provide a corpse; and with the means at hand, not with hand-wrought dueling pistols, curare, and tropical fish. He put these people down on paper as they are, and he made them talk and think in the language they customarily used for these purposes'.

The language Hammett used to tell his stories, and the language he put in the mouths of characters, also contributed to what made his work stand out. While Ernest Hemingway is credited with a particular form of realist writing, Hammett was developing a similar style, which captured the speech patterns of ordinary people, and of the professional detective. Hammett also kept the words needed to tell a story trimmed to the minimum. This gave his stories an economy of style and a particular feel. One of Hammett's best opening lines must be 'It was a wandering daughter job', which immediately draws the reader into the milieu of the 1929 story, 'Fly Paper'. *Black Mask* editor Joe 'Cap' Shaw was so taken with Hammett's style that he would encourage other writers to emulate it, hence it was said Shaw strove to 'Hammetize' *Black Mask*.

The settings of The Op stories, generally but not always San Francisco, were portrayed with an accuracy that would allow a reader familiar with the city to follow the characters around, or a reader unfamiliar with the city to develop a sense of its geography and atmosphere. The effect of the accuracy of setting, the attention to detail in detective work, the language used, the characters' motivations, and the backdrop of social and moral corruption was such that Hammett's Continental Op stories became a cornerstone in the genre; Hammett developed a style and, in so doing, set a standard by which 'tough' or realist crime writing is still judged.

Hammett continued to write stories for *The Black Mask* through to the mid-1920s, and for other publications, including *Brief Stories, Sunset Magazine* and *Argosy All Story Weekly*, using various pseudonyms—Peter Collinson, Daghull Hammett, even Mary Jane Hammett—as well as Dashiell Hammett, the name he settled on by 1924.

Of the twenty-eight Hammett stories published in *The Black Mask* between 1922 and 1926, twenty were Op stories (one Op story, 'Who Killed Bob Teal?', appeared in *True Detective Stories* in November 1924). When Jose delivered a second daughter, Hammett asked *The Black Mask* editor Phil Cody for a rise. Cody couldn't increase Hammett's rate, even though Hammett's Op stories (along with Carrol John Daly's Race Williams yarns) were among the most popular in the magazine. This caused Hammett to give up 'blackmasking', as he called it, to take a job as an advertising copywriter for San Francisco jeweller Albert Samuels.

While with Samuels Hammett wrote advertising copy and articles about advertising, and conducted an office affair; however, ill health caused Hammett to give up his job with Samuels after six months. Hammett also moved out of the family home. The explanation usually offered by biographers is that TB caused him to live apart from Jose and the girls: whether or not that was the case—perhaps his drinking or philandering, or the fact that Hammett was not the father of Jose's first daughter, precipitated the separation; whatever the cause, the marriage soon broke down.

When Hammett stopped writing Op stories sales of *The Black Mask* noticeably dipped, with the result that editor Phil Cody was replaced by Joe Shaw in 1926. Shaw read back issues of the magazine and was particularly struck by Hammett's work. Realising there were no more Hammett stories on file, Shaw contacted Hammett and persuaded him back to the fold by asking for longer stories. As Hammett was paid by the word, this had the effect of increasing his earnings from 'blackmasking'; with this and his disability allowance, he was able to support himself and Jose and the girls. Although Shaw was the third *Black Mask* editor to publish Hammett's stories (the first was George Sutton, who preceded

Cody) Shaw is usually credited with developing a particular style in the magazine inasmuch as he encouraged other writers to think about their prose, to strive for the economy of style which characterized Hammett's writing. While the tight writing and liberal use of underworld argot gave *Black Mask* its distinctive quality; the clipped, aggressive style and vernacular expression was not unique to *Black Mask* but should be seen, along with Hemingway's writing, as part of a developing trend in American realism in the 1920s. After shortening the magazine's title to *Black Mask* in 1926, Shaw published twenty-four Hammett stories between 1927-1930, including four novel serialisations; thus, under Shaw's editorship, Hammett produced all his major works.

Hammett's first story for Shaw was 'The Big Knockover'; the first installment of a two-part saga that pitches the Op and the Continental Detective Agency against organised crime. The story bristles with underworld slang and evocative nicknames, such as Paddy the Mex and The Dis and Dat Kid. The opening line is typically blunt and atmospheric: 'I found Paddy the Mex in Jean Larrouy's dive.' 'The Big Knockover' tells of the gathering of at least a hundred and fifty crooks, drawn from all over country, in order to simultaneously rob two San Francisco banks. The scenario provides more shootings and a higher body-count than a clutch of Tarantino movies, and The Op displays his own capacity for violence as he follows the gang's trail. At the end of the story the criminal mastermind escapes, and the Op resumes pursuit in the sequel, '$106,000 Blood Money'. In the second episode, corruption is seen to extend as far as the Continental Detective Agency, and to a fellow operative. The Op employs natural justice to achieve his desired ends, which is to apprehend his quarry and protect the reputation of the Agency.

Encouraged by Shaw, Hammett worked up to even longer stories. He undertook his most ambitious writing project to date, four linked stories, which ran in *Black Mask* from November 1927 to February 1928. This would be Hammett's first full-length novel, originally entitled *Poisonville,* but finally published by Knopf in 1929 under the title *Red Harvest*. Engaged by the editor of the town's newspaper, the Op travels to Personville, which the locals refer to as Poisonville, a more accurate name for a small town riven with corruption. On his arrival the Op finds the reforming newspaper editor has been murdered. The Op persuades the murdered man's father, Elihu Willsson—who owns the mine and the newspaper and once ran the town—to allow him to carry on with the case. Willsson brought in gangsters to help him beat the union during a miner's strike. However, the gangsters and their thugs refused to leave, and Willsson lost control of the town. The mercenary Dinah Brand, who appears to be about to burst out her clothing, is one of Hammett's more memorable female characters. She provides the Op with female company as she shares gin, laudanum and repartee with him until her untimely exit. The Op infiltrates the gangs and, typically, plays both ends against the middle, bringing the book to a violent conclusion.

The body-count is typically high (hence the title, 'red harvest') and the Op finds the violence getting to him as he declares 'getting a rear out of planning deaths is not natural. It's what this place has done to me ... If I don't get away soon I'll be going blood-simple like the natives.' Get away he does, but cynically remarks that the town is all set to go to the dogs again. Some find in *Red Harvest* a marxist critique of capitalism. Others find in it a realistic tale of violence and corruption, with plenty of action. It caught the attention of the critics and André Gide recorded in his journal that this was 'far superior' to Hammett's other novels, although Peter Wolfe has it about right with his observation that, exciting as the story is, there is too much action for the plot to sustain.

In 1928 Hammett wrote another series of linked stories which Knopf would also publish as a novel. The stories ran in *Black Mask* from November 1928 to February 1929, before appearing as a novel later that year. Hammett later referred to *The Dain Curse* as 'a silly story'. It tells the story of a woman with a troubled background, Gabrielle Leggett, who gets caught up with a San Francisco cult. Gabrielle apparently carries the Dain family curse, which gives the novel its title. As well as investigating the cult, the Op investigates Danielle's past. There are, however, rather too many peripheral characters, too many mysterious elements and too many shifts in location for a coherent plot, with the result that the book is goofy-gothic. There are interesting elements, however, as Hammett includes some ironic touches: the Op is pitted against a writer, suggesting Hammett knowingly incorporated two aspects of himself in the plot, the detective getting the better of the writer (physically, the tall, white-haired writer resembles Hammett); a character named Collinson also puts in an appearance. This would the last full-length tale to feature the Op.

By 1930 *Black Mask's* circulation had risen to over 100,000 per issue, but the end of the pulp era is already in sight: writers were beginning to move to more lucrative Hollywood and radio markets and, by 1935 in the depths of the depression, sales would slump to 60,000. Hammett had yet to reach his peak however. This would come after his next series of linked stories, *The Maltese Falcon*.

Here Hammett introduced a new detective, quite different from the Op: he worked not for an agency, but with a single partner. He was taller, younger and slimmer than the Op, and he had a name: Sam Spade. The subjective first-person narrative of the Op stories is abandoned too as Hammett adopts an objective, third-person, narration for his latest yarn. *The Maltese Falcon* ran in *Black Mask* over five issues, from September 1929 to January 1930. Although his marriage was effectively over—Hammett moved to New York with Nell Martin in the autumn of 1929—the book would carry a dedication: *To Jose*.

In *The Maltese Falcon* Hammett combines suspense with characterisation and a well-paced plot to produce his most successful novel, which will be acclaimed a classic—'the best detective story America has ever produced', according to critic Alexander Woollcott—and will feature at or near the top of any list of 'best detective novels'. Set in San Francisco, the action begins when a woman engages Spade to find her missing sister; later a Middle Eastern character shows up in Spade's office with a gun, and soon after Spade's partner, Miles Archer, is shot dead from close range. Spade is suspected of carrying out a second fatal shooting to avenge Archer's death. The woman, Bridgid O'Shaugnessy, and the Levantine, Joel Cairo, are searching for a bejewelled statuette of a bird, as is Caspar Gutman. Spade agrees to help recover the falcon. Spade is ambiguous enough to be a convincing anti-hero, representing, as he tells Gutman, not only his clients' interests, but also his own. While the quest for the fabulous object turns up a wild goose rather than a black bird, by the end of the tale Spade's clients and their associates are dead or in jail: perhaps Hammett is suggesting that the search for honesty or integrity in a private eye is also something of a wild goose chase.

The action takes place over a five-day period, and the chronology is carefully worked out. A manageable range of characters moves the plot along through a series of crisp, lively dialogues. Subtle clues pointing to the identity of Archer's killer—powder burns on a dead man's coat, the dates on rent receipts—are deftly placed, and the denouement between Spade and Bridgid O'Shaugnessy brings the tale to a powerful climax.

While there are clear differences between the Op and Sam Spade, there are some similarities too, Spade echoes the Op's words to Princess Zhukovski as he remarks to Bridgid O'Shaugnessy 'I'm a detective and expecting me to run criminals down and then let them go free is like asking a dog to catch a rabbit and let it go.' Both Spade and the Op go beyond acceptable legal or moral limits in order to get the job done.

It was in New York that Hammett finished his fourth novel, *The Glass Key*. The work was serialized in four parts in *Black Mask* between March and June, 1930, before book publication the following year. More experimental in form than *The Maltese Falcon*, this work split the critics. Some found the style of this elusively-titled novel too off-putting, its coldly objective third-person narration preventing identification with any of the characters. James M. Cain remarked in an interview that he found it unreadable, commenting, 'forget this goddamn book' while Robert Edenbaum declared it 'Hammett's least satisfactory novel'. Others, such as Will Cuppy writing in the *New York Herald Tribune* in April 1931, thought it 'about twice as good as his *Maltese Falcon*', and later critics also argue that *The Glass Key* is Hammett's *meisterwerk:* Julian Symonds, for example, called it 'the peak of Hammett's achievement'.

The Glass Key is a story of political corruption. Politicians and gangsters happily co-exist. Ned Beaumont, a gambler, sets out to clear his friend and his boss, local politico Paul Madvig, when he is suspected of the murder of Senator Ralph Henry's son. Complications arise because both Beaumont and Madvig are in love with Janet Henry,

Senator Henry's daughter. While *The Glass Key* demonstrates Hammett's economy of style—the tightly written first chapter lays out the complex Madvig-Beaumont relationship in just 20 pages—it depicts brutality in the savage beatings Beaumont endures to defend Madvig and, through its complex plot, shows a society rife with corruption. Hammett also places clues for the reader as carefully as those found in any country-house mystery.

After the critical and commercial success of *The Maltese Falcon*, Hammett was engaged as writer by Paramount, and then Warner Brothers, giving him his first taste of Hollywood. Here he will meet Lillian Hellman and the pair will enjoy a stormy relationship that will last for the rest of Hammett's life. He stayed in Hollywood only a short time before returning to New York where he met William Faulkner who became a drinking friend. It was here in 1931 a drunken Hammett and Faulkner turned up in tweeds at Alfred Knopf's black-tie dinner party and Hammett passed out on the carpet.

Despite his celebrity status and literary success, Hammett was broke during the early thirties. Having left the penny-a-word pulps behind, he published several short stories in higher paying magazines, including three Sam Spade tales, and in 1933, the lengthy 'A Woman in the Dark' is serialised in *Liberty* magazine. Despite this flurry of creative activity, Hammett is still unable to pay his bills and, in 1932, slips out of an expensive New York hotel without paying, and moves into Nathaniel West's NY boarding house. Here he starts work in earnest on his last novel, *The Thin Man*, which he had already begun but abandoned (the first attempt at *The Thin Man* and the Sam Spade stories are included in the *Nightmare Town* collection). After initial publication in *Redbook* magazine in 1933, *The Thin Man* was published by Knopf in 1934. It will prove to be Hammett's most commercially successful project due to a series of spin-off films with Dick Powell and Myrna Loy playing the husband-and-wife detective-team, Nick and Nora Charles. However, *The Thin Man* lacked the hard-boiled edge that characterised Hammett's earlier writing. Nick and Nora Charles spend much of their time in comfortable surroundings, drinking and exchanging witty comments, an amusing echo of the Hammett-Hellman relationship.

The book aroused some controversy because Nora asked Nick 'didn't you have an erection?' when he wrestled with one of the female characters. The question was excised from both the *Redbook* publication and the British edition, but Knopf reinstated it, drawing attention to it in publicity material: 'Twenty thousand people don't buy a book within three weeks to read a five word question.'

Hammett's last original short stories were published in *Colliers Magazine* between January and March 1934 (two of the three are included in *Nightmare Town*). MGM bought the rights to *The Thin Man* and a film was released the same year. When MGM engaged Hammett to write a sequel, he moved into a six-room suite in the Beverly-Wilshire Hotel to work on the story and, after two months of drinking and partying, managed to produce a 34-page typescript. This though was enough for MGM, and Hammett's contract was renewed for another three years, although he would miss meetings and deadlines through drunkenness.

After Hammett's turn to urbane whimsy with Nick and Nora Charles, six Hollywood films were made from his stories between 1934 and 1936, which provided a good income. Hammett spent money easily, however, living in expensive hotels and he rented Harold Lloyd's 44-room mansion; he threw lavish parties, hired limousines and servants, and, according to biographer Joan Mellen, kept himself entertained with prostitutes. Hammett was drinking to legendary excess during this period, and all the biographies recount an incident in 1937 or 1938 when, after an extended binge, friends (the Hacketts or the Bracketts, depending upon the biography) paid Hammett's hotel bill and put him on a plane bound for New York, c/o Lillian Hellman, in order to dry out.

Hammett's last original work of fiction to be published in his lifetime was the *Secret Agent X-9* comic strip, syndicated in Hearst's newspapers from 1934 as a rival to the popular *Dick Tracy* strip. Hammett was engaged by Hearst to write the comic strip because of his reputation as a writer. Alex Raymond, creator of *Flash Gordon*, provided the illustrations for Hammett's prose. Hammett only wrote three adventures for the strip before his contract was revoked. The strip continued long after Hammett left however, employing a succession of writers.

Although Hammett's writing career was effectively over—he had repeatedly failed to deliver a new novel to Knopf and the publisher ended Hammett's contract—he had an income from Hollywood as a screen-writer and from films based on his earlier work. He would also earn money throughout the 1940s from radio series based on his characters, and from radio adaptations of his novels.

Hammett becomes bored with Nick and Nora Charles, describing them as 'insufferably smug', and he began to miss meetings and deadlines. He got involved with the Screen Writers' Guild, a group concerned with the rights of screen-writers. American paranoia-politics at this time is such that involvement in groups concerned with workers' rights can lead to blacklisting as 'a communist' or trouble-maker. Hammett's contract with MGM is terminated. Hammett moves to NY where he signs petitions and lends his name to anti-fascist causes, and speaks against fascism at a communist-sponsored rally in NY. He also writes the screenplay for *Watch on the Rhine,* based on Lillian Hellman's play.

The FBI suspect Hammett is a communist organiser and begins to monitor him. However, after America enters the war following the Japanese attack on Pearl Harbour, Hammett re-enlists—despite his advanced years (he is 48)—and the FBI lose track of him for two years.

As a soldier in the Army Signal Corps, Hammett is posted to the cold and inhospitable island of Adak, in the Aleutians, an island chain stretching from Alaska's Pacific coast toward Japan. Here, with a small team of men he edits an army newspaper called *The*

Adakian. In the Aleutians, Hammett is known as Sam or 'Pop'. Although he is writing no new material other than for the newspaper, his novels are reprinted by Dell in 25 cent paperback and Spivak begins publishing his old short stories in digest form. Films of his novels are being made (*The Maltese Falcon* with Humphrey Bogart as Sam Spade in 1941 and *The Glass Key* with Alan Ladd as Ned Beaumont in 1942) and several radio versions of his novels are broadcast. In 1943 Warner Brothers release *Watch on the Rhine*, which earns Hammett an Academy Award Nomination for Best Screenplay. In 1944 Chandler publishes his famous essay, 'The Simple Art of Murder' which celebrates Hammett's contribution to hardboiled fiction—in the past tense.

Discharged from the army in 1945, Hammett returns to New York where he teaches a mystery-writing class. He abandons another novel, 'The Valley Sheep Are Fatter'. While Hammett is still unable to finish a writing project, two radio series based on his characters, *The Adventures of Sam Spade* and *The Fat Man* (based on the Continental Op) begin in 1946. Although Hammett is credited with some involvement in these series, he has no creative input. In the same year he becomes President of a left-wing group called the Civil Rights Congress.

Drinking heavily, Hammett is hospitalised briefly in 1948. On his release from hospital he briefly gives up drinking. Warner Brothers, who own the film rights to *The Maltese Falcon*, initiate a claim for breach of copyright regarding the character Sam Spade in the radio series *The Adventures of Sam Spade*.

Hammett goes to Hollywood to write a film treatment for William Wyler, but cannot do it. He also claims to be working on a novel, but is unable to produce more than a few pages. He has, and will continue, however, to contribute to structure and dialogue in Lillian Hellman's plays.

The Civil Rights Congress had put up bail for eleven members of the American Communist Party, charged with conspiracy. After four of the 11 absconded, Hammett, as President of the CRC, was called to testify. It was thought that contributors to the bail fund might be harbouring the four. Hammett, however, refused to answer questions, and was jailed for contempt. Overnight, Hammett became *persona non gratia*: radio series based on Hammett's characters were dropped from the schedules (*The Adventures of Sam Spade*; *The Adventures of the Thin Man*; *The Fat Man*); Universal took Hammett's name off the credits of *The Fat Man*; a re-run of *The Maltese Falcon* was cancelled, and Spivak ceased publishing the Hammett digests.

Nineteen fifty-one was a bad year for Hammett. Ironically, he won the copyright case against Warner Brothers, and retained rights to the character Sam Spade, but the radio series had been already been dropped. On his release from prison, Hammett is broke financially and in health terms: the spell in prison didn't make the sickly Hammett any better, and the IRS demanded $111,000 in back-taxes, making an attachment to Hammett's earnings. To cap it all, *Black Mask* finally folded.

Unable to maintain his NY apartment, Hammett moved in with Hellman at Hardscrabble Farm. However, Hellman is forced to sell the farm in 1952 to meet a tax demand from the IRS, according to William F. Nolan, or to pay legal costs after being called before the HUAC, as Richard Layman has it. Hammett moves into a cottage on a friend's estate where, living as a recluse, he will fail in his attempt to write a novel ('Tulip') about a man who cannot finish writing a novel.

In 1953, at the height of the cold war, Hammett is called to testify again, this time before the Senate Internal Security Sub-committee, another of Senator Joseph McCarthy's anti-communist interrogation committees. When Hammett is asked what he thinks about keeping the books of communist sympathisers on the shelves during the fight against communism, he replies 'Well I think—of course, I don't know—if I were fighting communism, I don't think I would do it by giving people any books at all'. As a result, Hammett's books were taken off the shelves of state-department libraries.

Unable to live alone due to his rapidly declining health, Hammett moves in with Hellman in 1957, living with her on Martha's Vineyard in the summer, and in her New York house in the winter. After suffering a collapse in 1960, Hammett is admitted to New York's Lenox Hill Hospital where, on January 10th 1961, he dies, aged 66. The cause of death is a cancerous lung tumour, complicated by emphysema, pneumonia, and heart, liver, kidney, spleen and prostate disease. The man who was once described by his drinking pal, screenwriter Nunally Johnson, as living as if he 'had no expectation of being alive much beyond Thursday' finally succumbed to the ravages of a life of excess.

In a final twist of irony, Hammett, who had enraged the US State by refusing to kowtow before the state interrogators, is buried—to the chagrin of the FBI—in Arlington National Cemetery, Washington, alongside US heroes and past presidents. He had, after all served his country twice, took a stand against fascism, and contributed to the national literature.

After Hammett's death, his will was nullified because of the debt to the IRS. Hellman managed to secure his copyrights for herself for $5,000, making a payment to the government to clear Hammett's debt. Hellman also managed to gyp Hammett's wife and daughters from a share in the royalties which, by Joan Mellen's calculation, amounted to 'hundreds of thousands of dollars'. Until Hellman's death in 1984, she obstructed researchers, and sought to control Hammett beyond the grave. Joan Mellen's joint biography of Hellman and Hammett exposes much that Hellman had managed to suppress in earlier Hammett biographies. Mellen reveals Hammett's daughter Josephine managed to secure the copyrights of the novels during the 1990s.

Currently, all of Hammett's novels are in print in the US, and most are available in a single volume, entitled *The Four Great Novels*, in the UK, where *The Thin Man* remains in print. The novella *The Woman in the Dark* was published in hardback in UK and US editions in 1988. Three volumes of stories complete the essential collection: *The Big Knockover and Other Stories*, with an introduction by

Hellman (first published in 1966) is readily available; this collection contains the fragment 'Tulip' and nine other stories. While *The Continental Op*, edited by Steven Marcus (first published in 1974) has gone out of print, second-hand copies of this seven-story compilation are easily found. Knopf published twenty stories in *Nightmare Town* in the US in 1999 (reviewed in *Crime Time* 2.6); Amazon.co.uk can deliver a copy of this to a UK address within 48 hours.

Further reading: the Hammett biographies Richard Layman, *Shadow Man, The Life of Dashiell Hammett* (London: Junction Books, 1981).

William F. Nolan, *Dashiell Hammett: A Life at the Edge* (London: Arthur Barker, 1983).

Diane Johnson, *Dashiell Hammett: A Life* (NY: Random House, 1983).

Joan Mellen, *Hellman and Hammett* (NY: HarperCollins, 1996).

And…

NIGHTMARE TOWN BY DASHIELL HAMMETT, KNOPF, UK£15.72/ US$25.00 HARDBACK.

William F. Nolan's introduction to this collection offers a useful summary of Hammett's writing career, sketching in what might be called the 'authorised version' of Hammett's life. Nolan perpetuates, however, some stories about Hammett which ought, by now, to be treated with more caution or simply put right. For example, Joan Mellen's 1996 dual biography, *Hellman and Hammett* (reviewed by me in *Crime Time* 6), the first biography of Hammett to be written without the cloying threat of litigation from Lillian Hellman's estate, revealed what had been concealed by others—that Jose Dolan's first daughter, Mary Jane, was not in fact Hammett's child at all (Mary Jane Hammett died in 1992 without knowing this). There is no hint in the introduction that Nolan has read Mellen's work, or has revised his views on Hammett's domestic arrangements since his own Hammett biography, *A Life at the Edge* (1983).

While Nolan has probably published more words on Hammett than any other critic, there is scope for a little more scepticism in this introduction. Richard Layman realised as long ago as 1986 that, by the time Hammett was the leading light of the so-called 'hard-boiled school' of detective fiction, any statement Hammett made about his past as a detective should be treated with care, if only because Hammett might be inclined to enhance his own past as a form of self promotion. One example that Layman discusses in *Shadow Man: The Life of Dashiell Hammett* is an episode concerning the recovery of lost jewellery which Hammett had recounted on more than one occasion. The way Hammett told it, he had been responsible for locating a stash of stolen jewellery in the funnel of a ship the day it was due to set sail for Australia, the point being that his detective skill had cost him a trip to Australia. As Layman reads it, however, by the time anyone was interested enough in Hammett to be bothered about his detective past, Hammett-the-author was in a position to benefit by talking-up his exploits as a detective. Moreover, through research, Layman had established that Hammett was not actually employed as a Pinkerton operative at the time he claimed to have been salvaging stolen jewellery. Here then scepticism is backed up with research. Meanwhile, Nolan appears to be happy to cite Hammett's longtime lover Lillian Hellman as a reliable source: it has been shown on any number of occasions that, as a pathological liar whose 'memoirs' are highly elaborate fictions, Hellman should be treated as anything but a reliable source.

Niggles about the introduction aside, this is a wonderful albeit long-overdue collection of Hammett material. The opening story is 'Nightmare Town', which provides the title for the collection as a whole. In this 1924 story Hammett departs from the usual setting of the twentieth-century city for the desert-town of Izzard, where things are not as they seem and organised corruption is the order of the day. The marvellous opening scene, Steve Threefall's arrival in Izzard, displays Hammett's eye for detail, fondness of drink and his witty style.

The collection makes some material available that has long been unavailable or hard to locate. Seven of the twenty stories feature the Continental Op, Hammett's nameless detective. Some of the early Op stories, along with *The Maltese Falcon*, can be counted as Hammett's most accomplished writing. Here we find 'House Dick' (aka 'Bodies Piled Up') from 1923; a slew of stories from 1924: 'Night Shots', 'One Hour', 'Zigzags of Treachery', 'Death on Pine Street' (aka 'Women, Politics and Murder') and 'Who Killed Bob Teal', and one tale from 1925, 'Tom, Dick or Harry' (aka 'Mike, Alec or Rufus'). 'Zigzags of Treachery', a complex tale of blackmail, is one of Hammett's better Op yarns, not only for its pacing and plot, but also for the way Hammett manages to work in to the story some advice for the reader on the art of shadowing.

Although the collection reprints the three Sam Spade stories, these are not particularly notable ('A Man Called Spade', 'Too Many Have Lived' and 'They Can Only Hang You Once'). Hammett knocked these out in the 1930s while he was living fast and spending his Hollywood income as fast as it came in, so they are not written under the same conditions as his earlier shorts. While Nolan's introduction describes these as 'crisp, efficient and swift-moving', the first two are dismissed by Richard Layman in *Shadowman*, his biography of Hammett, as 'simple rewrites of earlier stories' while the third is 'so simplistic no model is necessary'. That said, 'They Can Only Hang You Once' has a great opening line: 'My name is Ronald Ames said Sam Spade'. The stories did provide Hammet with a means of establishing ownership of the character Sam Spade, a character Warner Brothers wanted to claim ownership of at a time when CBS were broadcasting *The Adventures of Sam Spade* on the radio. Although the radio stories were not written by Hammett, CBS played up Hammett's reputation as the creator of Sam Spade.

The collection ends with a pair of Thin Man tales: 'A Man Named Thin', a San Francisco based tale featuring the detective-poet, Robin Thin. Although Hammett wrote this story in the mid-to-late 1920s, that is, at about the time he worked for jeweller Albert Samuels, it was not published until 1961. Here, Hammett amusingly implicates his real wife Jose Dolan in a jewel robbery, placing 'Mrs Dolan' in the story, complete with a bag of groceries. The final story is the so-called 'The First Thin Man', featuring San Francisco detective John Guild. Hammett began this story in 1930, but abandoned it, unfinished. It was the later 'New York' version, with Nick and Nora Charles, which was published as Hammett's last novel in 1933. 'The First Thin Man' takes a theme Hammett had used several times before, pitting a writer against a detective. This is of course the theme that bedevilled Hammett, the detective who became a writer and wrote himself out in a decade.

This collection is an essential companion to the two earlier volumes of Hammett short stories, *The Big Knockover and other stories* (1966) and *The Continental Op* (1974). Although you probably won't find it on the shelf in your local bookshop in the UK, Amazon.co.uk will deliver it to UK addresses in about 24 hours, for £16.60 which includes postage. What are you waiting for? Buy it now.

twisted hopes and crooked dreams: james m. cain's double indemnity

> *"To me, a claims man is a surgeon. That desk is an operating table. And those pencils are scalpels and bone chisels. And those papers are not just forms and statistics and claims for compensation, they're alive, they're packed with drama, with twisted hopes and crooked dreams..."*—Barton Keyes, Double Indemnity (1944)

IF EVER A BOOK was filled with twisted hopes and crooked dreams, it is *Double Indemnity*. To James M Cain, its author, it was a 'piece of tripe', written to cash in on the startling success of his first novel, *The Postman Always Rings Twice*. Cain, nervously approaching his second full-length novel which he had in outline, was not finding his new career as a novelist easy. His agent, Edith Haggard, was flooded with requests for a new murder story by the best-selling author; Cain responded with articles about food, stories about failed actors who made their comeback on the back of a hippo and children's birthday parties. He needed money: both RKO and Columbia had sniffed around the film rights to Postman when it was in galley form and still under Cain's original title, *Bar-B-Que*, but Joe Breen, director of the Production Code Administration, had persuaded them it was a picture that was not going to be made. The finished book was sold to MGM for $25,000, but Breen wrote to Louis B Meyer in March 1934 rejecting it as in-

Barbara Stanwyck and Fred McMurray in the screen version of Double Indemnity

steve holland

crime time 3.2

117

decent, and citing then current objections from lawyers about their depiction on screen—Cain's twisted lawyer Katz would have incensed them[1]. MGM stalled on the project, which wouldn't see the light of day for twelve years.

The editor of Redwood magazine was one of Haggard's most insistent clients when it came to Cain, and Cain finally submitted a short, 29,000-word novella. Redwood rejected it. With *Serenade*, his next full-length novel, still unfinished—Cain wanted to travel to Mexico to research the ending—he considered rewriting the novella, *Double Indemnity*, up to novel length, but before he could get started, Haggard sold it to Liberty magazine, who serialised it in early 1936, with sensational reader response. Not surprisingly, Hollywood snapped at this hot property, with five studios bidding for the rights. The price had reached $25,000 again when, once again, Joe Breen decided that the story would not fit the Production Code as it dealt *"improperly with an illicit and adulterous sex relationship"*; it violated the Code in having the two killers escape from justice and in offering too much detail of the murder they had committed, which would lead to *"the hardening of audiences, especially those who are young and impressionable, to the thoughts and facts of crime."*[2]

Any thought of putting the film on screen was put on hold for eight years. Cain himself thought *Double Indemnity* not worthy of putting into hardcover, although he softened, and it appeared with two other short novels in the collection *Three of a Kind* (Knopf, 1943), a bestseller following in the tracks of *Serenade* (1937) and *Mildred Pierce* (1941), the play based on Postman (first performed in 1936) and even a spell of screenwriting, albeit only briefly and not very notably.

If Cain's contribution to Hollywood as a scriptwriter was poor, he was a fine source of material; three moderately successful films had already been made from Cain's stories: *Wife, Husband and Friend*, 1939, from the story *Two Can Sing*; *When Tomorrow Comes*, 1939, from *The Modern Cinderella*; and *Money and the Woman*, 1940, from the eponymous story; Postman had even been filmed, but in—and with the action transferred to—Italy by newcomer Luchino Visconti as *Ossessione* [Obsession] (1942)[3]. In America, it was 1944 before one of Cain's smouldering, sleazy crime noirs finally made the big screen, and its twinning of sex and murder made it, not surprisingly, a smash hit.

The key phrase in *Double Indemnity* is *"straight down the line"*. It's a carefully chosen phrase used at carefully chosen moments, first to cement the pact between the killers, Walter Huff and Phyllis Nirdlinger, like a handshake on a deal. Later, it appears again when the first element of the plot falls into place, Mr Nirdlinger's signature on the blank personal accident policy form, *"with double indemnity straight down the line for any disability or death incurred on a railroad train"* (p260). The phrase is reflected in the other key element of plot: for Nirdlinger's dead body to be found on the railway track.

In the movie the phrase is used like a mantra, on four occasions, usually repeated by both killers. In the movie you become aware of many straight lines: the diagonal blocks of light behind Walter Neff in the corridor, the darkness that encloses him in the frame of the door as he enters the office; doorways and diffused light sources behind the main characters help create the foreground darkness through which the characters move. More straight lines—the bars of the stairway—separate Phyllis Dietrichson and Neff when they meet for the first time, a scene replayed when they meet again. It can become something of a game looking and reading meaning into everything: at that first meeting, Neff mentions her ankle bracelet and Phyllis uncrosses her legs and sits up in her chair, legs pressed together. You can see straight lines everywhere if you try hard enough. Watch the film, pick out your own favourites.

While the interplay of angles and light is an important aspect of film noir, the phrase is put to different use in the book, not just in the way it is used to signal important plot elements; it is significant that as soon as the characters stop playing straight with each other, doubts and uncertainties begin to pick at their confidence and unravel their carefully woven plot. The film had certain alterations forced on it in order to conform with the Hays Code of Practice. The book is a nastier piece of work, but more subtle in its inferences.

The style of writing was slashed down to the bone. The East Coast journalist used to writing satirical pieces in rube dialect had made the transfer to West Coast straight talking, stripping out anything that did not move the story along. This is most noticeable in the dialogue between characters, which does away with the conventional 'he (or she) said,' and its variations ('he growled', 'she sighed'), and pared down descriptive passages. Cain hated the comparisons made by critics between his work and Hemingway's, and admitted in his introduction to *The Butterfly*, that *"this skinning out of literary blubber"* was a conscious decision, one he had practised before reading Hemingway[4]. He had, he said, read less than twenty pages of Dashiell Hammett, and did not consider himself a member of the hard-boiled or any other school of writing. His fiction is, if it must be categorised, impeccable crime noir and moves with the hiss and crack of a whip.

The plot is an archetype, not invented by Cain but skilfully adopted by him for a good proportion of his novels. In its simplest form the crux is: man and woman meet and wish death upon one's partner; the story turns on what happens when their wishes come true.

Cain wastes little time in *Double Indemnity* introducing his protagonists: they meet on page two and half-way through chapter two are plotting the husband's death. It is to Cain's credit that he makes this credible.

Walter Huff is an insurance salesman for General Fidelity of California who arrives at the home of Mr Nirdlinger to pitch him a renewal policy on his car. Here he meets Phyllis Nirdlinger for the first time, *"maybe thirty-one or -two, with a sweet face, light blue eyes, and dusty blonde hair. She was small, and had on a suit of blue house pyjamas. She had a washed out look"* (p242). Hardly the entrance of a femme fatale, but as they talk inconsequentially about her husband maybe insuring through the Automobile Club, Huff begins to take notice of her shape beneath the suit, *"a shape to set a man nuts"* (p243). She wonders if his company handles accident insurance. A chill creeps up the back of Huff's neck: experience tells him that nobody asks for accident insurance—they have to be sold it. She asks him to come back the next day, and Huff leaves, bawling himself out *"for being a fool just because a woman had given me one sidelong look"* (p244).

Back in the office we are introduced to the head of the Claim Department, Keyes, a fat, peevish man, always in some kind of argument with other departments, but a wolf when it comes to a phoney claim. At their meeting he praises Huff for his appraisal of a suspicious customer who has tried to gyp the company by setting fire to his own truck.

Delaying their meeting, Mrs Nirdlinger contacts Huff again three days later. Now she wears a white sailor suit and a blouse tight over her hips; she knows she is in good shape and no longer looks washed out. She brings up the subject of accident insurance again, perhaps something she can take out on her husband's behalf...? Huff's fifteen years of experience tells him to drop the renewal and everything else about this woman like a red-hot poker. But he doesn't. Instead, he puts his arm around her and kisses her, and, after a second or so, she closes her eyes and kisses him back.

At their next meeting, Huff confronts her directly. *"You're going to drop a crown block on him... it's all you've thought of since you met me, and it's what you came down here for tonight"* (p250). Having peered over and seen monsters, Huff seems to be backing away from the edge of the abyss, but knows that she will be back after sweating blood for fear that Huff will confess their conversations to someone. When she returns the next evening, he offers to become her accomplice—*"You are going to do it, and I'm going to help you"* (p251).

Why would he do this? *"You for one thing,"* says Huff, then adds 'Money' (p252), which is corny enough for plot purposes; Phyllis Nirdlinger, however, sees through this tissue, commenting *"You mean you would—betray your company, and help me do this, for me, and the money we could get out of it?"* An interesting response: not *"you would commit murder"* but *"you would betray your company"*. She considers the betrayal the key here, and she is spot on, as Huff later reveals when he compares insurance to laying down bets: *"It's the biggest gambling wheel in the world... You bet that your house will burn down, they bet it won't, that's all"* (p256). And: *"I'm a croupier in that game. I know all their tricks, I lie awake nights thinking up tricks, so I'll be ready for them when they come at me. And then one night I think up a trick, and get to thinking I could crook the wheel myself if I could only put a plant out there to put down my bet. That's all. When I met Phyllis I met my plant"* (p256).

Both killers disassociate themselves from the murder: for Huff it is a wager, playing the odds that he can fool even a wolf like head of claims Keyes; Phyllis is rather more schizophrenic, inventing reasons for this seemingly motiveless crime (*"He's not happy. He'll be better off—*dead*") and then admitting "*There's something in me that loves Death. I think of myself as Death, sometimes. In a scarlet shroud, floating through the night. I'm so beautiful then. And sad. And hungry to make the whole world happy, by taking them out where I am, into the night, away from all trouble, all unhappiness…*" (p252). The idea and discussion of death excites her to sexual passion.

The mechanics of the murder are simple: to collect the double indemnity on the insurance, Nirdlinger needs to die in a railway accident, and for Walter Huff there is no other option if he is to test himself to the limit. He realises that it would be impossible to kill Nirdlinger on the train, and plans to kill him beforehand and impersonate the dead man on that final leg of the journey to where his corpse has to be found. It's neat and nasty and fulfils Huff's three-point programme for the successful murder: Help, Opportunity and Audacity.

In Cain's hands, the murder is spread over three chapters which cover the killing, the impersonation, and finally the escape. It has all the elements of plotting and preparation you can find in Mission: Impossible—only here the planning involves the death of an innocent man, the setting up of alibis and the rooking of an insurance company. Although we rarely see inside the minds of the killers (something Cain shies away from), there is definitely an element of voyeurism in watching this murder being so coldly set up (one of the reasons a film version was originally denied); the defining moment is Nirdlinger's death. This has been carefully planned in the mind of the killer, and although Huff tells his readers "*I won't tell you what I did then*" (p272), they are left to fill in the gaps, to think like a killer and decide why he cannot strangle Nirdlinger or kill him any other way. Huff breaks the man's neck.

It is immediately after the murder that things begin to go awry. In the car on their way home, Phyllis runs a red light, unable to concentrate (she says) because of the radio, which Huff needs to listen to as part of his alibi. He notices that her shoes have been scuffed by the gravel on the tracks. Before long they are snarling at each other—"*She raved like a lunatic*"—and Huff threatens to sock her. Back at home, once he has completed his alibi, Huff throws up with the realisation that he has killed a man and put himself completely in Phyllis' power: "*There was one person in the world that could point a finger at me, and I would have to die. I had done all that for her, and I never wanted to see her again as long as I lived*" (p279). Fear curdles love into hate.

Complicating this dislocation of the two lovers is Nirdlinger's nineteen-year-old daughter, Phyllis' step-daughter, the beautiful Lola. Huff has seen her on a number of occasions, usually in the company of her boyfriend, Bernanino ('Nino') Sachetti. After the murder, Phyllis phones to say that Lola has been acting funny, hysterical, and, soon after, Lola visits and shares her suspicions that Phyllis was responsible for her father's death, as she suspects Phyllis was for her mother's: an ex-nurse specialising in pulmonary diseases, Phyllis had allowed her mother to die of pneumonia. Huff begins to fall for Lola, suspecting that he has been used as a cat's paw: for all his planning, the scheme has come to nothing. *"I didn't have the money and I didn't have the woman"* (p298).

His other problem is Keyes, who rules out suicide as a possibility, giving a glorious speech wonderfully transferred to the screen by Edward G Robinson in the movie. His method is primarily analytical, using tables of probability to spark his instincts, but the rest of down to experience and hunches, and in a moment of intuition realises that if death by falling from a slow-moving train is statistically unlikely, Nirdlinger had to be dead already when he hit the tracks; that means a partner on the train to commit murder, or that Nirdlinger was never on the train. The solution to both Keyes' and Huff's problems seems to lie in Nino Sachetti. Nino is seen visiting Phyllis and provides Keyes with a suspect for the role of partner; to Huff the new affair is a two-fold boon as it brings Lola to him on the rebound and as a patsy to take the fall for Phyllis' death.

Huff makes that decision when Norris, the boss of General Fidelity, chooses to bluff Phyllis out by refusing to pay on the policy and make her take the company to court. His love for Lola is built on a slightly more solid foundation of seeing her three or four nights a week; Phyllis, he reasons was just *"some kind of unhealthy excitement"*, but his love for Lola is *"a sweet peace that came over me as soon as I was with her"* (p302).

The plotting and alibi-making elements of the book fill another chapter as Huff sets about killing Phyllis after arranging to meet her in Griffith Park. Stealing Nino's car he waits for Phyllis to arrive.

He waits.

He hears a twig crack and winds down his window, and she shoots him in the chest. *"I wasn't the only one that figured the world wasn't big enough for two people, when they knew that about each other"* (p309). He staggers to his own car before passing out—to awaken in hospital where Keyes believes he has found his killers: Nino Sachetti and Lola Nirdlinger, both of whom were found at the scene. Keyes still needs to know the answer to many questions—why try to kill Huff? what did they gain? his silence? about what?—which he'll know soon enough, he says, once the police start giving them the rubber hose treatment. And Huff confesses, to save Lola, and over the next few days he's allowed to write down his confession (which we have been reading). He learns more about Phyllis, how—before she befriended the first Mrs Nirdlinger—she had been the head nurse at a sanitarium run by Nino Sachetti's father. He had died soon after a number of children had also died, one of them a relation of Lola's mother, who now inherited a package of property that would have gone to the child. Phyllis Nirdlinger is a colder-hearted killer than any of us had previously suspected, her motive simple greed, spiced with psychosis.

In confessing, Huff wants Keyes to release Lola, only to be told that she already has been and is waiting to talk to him. When Lola leans forward to kiss him, he turns his head. *"I knew I couldn't have her and never could have had her. I couldn't kiss the girl whose fa-*

ther I killed" (p321).

The confession is mailed to Keyes, and Huff escapes onto a ship bound for Mexico. Watching the Mexican coast, he discovers himself next to Phyllis, and with nothing to look forward to, with the Captain knowing who they are and likely to have the police waiting, and with Huff's lung bleeding, they make a pact. She dresses herself in the red silk of her Death outfit and they wait before going over the side of the ship so they can see the fins of the sharks cutting the water in the moonlight.

In translation for the big screen, a number of cosmetic changes were made. Walter Huff became Walter Neff (Fred MacMurray), Phyllis Nirdlinger became Phyllis Dietrichson (Barbara Stanwyck), and Keyes (Edward G Robinson) was given a first name—Barton—and his role expanded. The cast was superb, and the results a classic of film noir, but its achievement in even reaching the screen was even greater for the obstacles its producers had to overcome. Rejected by the Hays Office in 1935, it was 1943 before anyone seriously tried to revive it as a movie project. Producer Joseph Sistrom at Paramount brought it to the attention of director Billy Wilder, who was enthusiastic, but could not persuade his then writing partner Charles Brackett to have anything to do with adapting the novel. Instead, Wilder was introduced to another writer of hard-boiled stories whose abilities with dialogue were evident in his novels; for his part, Raymond Chandler was attracted by the money on offer—$750 a week—but hadn't a clue about how to construct a screenplay.

The relationship between Wilder and Chandler as they co-wrote was rocky: Chandler was a rookie, older, and an ex-alcoholic. Wilder found him a sour writing partner. For his part, Chandler thought Wilder was drinking too much, womanising too much and rude; at one point he even wrote a letter of complaint to Sistrom.

But once Chandler had learned that his job was not to write the camera directions, only to concentrate on the characters, atmosphere and dialogue, the two turned in a remarkable screenplay which was unexpectedly passed with only minor changes by the Production Code Administration.

There were changes from the novel: although much of the dialogue was retained verbatim, or almost verbatim, the screenwriters tightened up a few plot snags and simplified some of the other action, made the first meeting of Walter Neff and Phyllis Dietrichson a more flirtatious and memorable encounter, and extended their affair beyond the murder where Cain had them bickering almost from the moment they dropped the body on the tracks. The Griffith Park scene was moved to the (studio-set) Dietrichson house and Huff's affair with Lola became Neff's attempt to distract her from investigating her suspicions of Phyllis and her affair with Nino, whom Neff cannot bring himself to frame.

The oddest moments are reserved for Barton Keyes: a company man, although preferring the way business was carried out under the father of the present owner, he allows one fraudster to walk out of his office after signing a waiver on his claim, and forgives Neff once he has confessed his crime, allowing him to walk out of the building, and, when he collapses (he has been shot), lighting a cigarette for him. The film is allowed to end on this moment of redemption, although a further scene of Neff in the gas chamber was shot.

Cain thought it was the best adaptation of any of his books and stories, and the film is a classic in its own right. But the story was Cain's, innovative in its scrutiny of the act of murder, remarkable in its depiction and concentration on two killers as lead characters, stylishly and coldly told, and without any measure of doubt one of the best crime noir stories ever published that delves into the twisted hopes and crooked dreams that underpin human nature.

NOTES

Background material on Cain is derived from James M Cain by Paul Skenazy (Continuum Publishing Co., New York, 1989), the introductory material to *The Baby in the Icebox*, and other short fiction edited by Ray Hoopes (Holt, Rinehart & Winston, New York, 1981), and Cain's entry in *20th Century Authors* edited by Stanley J Kunitz & Howard Haycroft, (New York, H W Wilson Co., 1942) and its supplements. Quotes from the novel are taken from *The Five Great Novels of James M Cain* (Picador, 1985) which is still in print.

1. When the film was finally made in 1946, the Katz of the movie was not the Katz of the book.

2. Quotes from Joe Breen's reaction to *Double Indemnity* are derived from *Censored Hollywood: Sex, Sin and Violence on Screen* by Frank Miller, Atlanta, Turner Publishing, 1994, p134.

3. Because of wartime restrictions, the film had to be approved by the wartime Fascist government who okayed the script, but were shocked by the way Visconti had shot the finished film. It was temporarily shelved, but released after Mussolini saw and enjoyed it. Now considered an early example of neorealist school of European cinema.

4. It is more clearly a development from his writing of satirical dialogues and a reaction against his constant use of 'I says' and 'he says' in his early short stories. In his West Coast writing, he owed more of a debt to Ring Lardner, the writer of sports stories.

"BUTLER IS THE LAST TRADITIONAL ENGLISH CRIME WRITER WE HAVE — AND ONE OF THE VERY BEST" - *CRIME TIME*

THE KING CRIED MURDER!
by GWENDOLINE BUTLER

WELCOME to Georgian-era Windsor Castle for the first in a series of historical crime novels by Britain's finest practitioner of the traditional mystery.

Set in the same period of the film The Madness of King George, a young Fanny Burney, not yet the famous actress she is to become, is a lady-in-waiting to the Queen. The life of the entire castle is affected by the wanderings and ravings of the deranged monarch, and Fanny does the best she can to soothe her mistress in the midst of her troubles.

And then the murders begin…

Major Mearns and Sergeant Denny, ex-secret service men in India and Canada are employed by Prime Minister Pitt to keep an eye on the King—and foremost in their minds is whether he is in some way involved in the killings. Fanny, who loves the theatre, will leave the relative safety of the castle to visit the town's theatre. Mearns and Denny find they must watch over her as well as the King.

Because in some strange way she has a connection to the murders…

Available from all good bookshops or by post from CT Publishing, Dept CT32) PO Box 5880, Edgbaston, Birmingham, B16 9BJ (Postage and Packing free) - or buy on the web from www.crimetime.co.uk

ISBN: 1 902002 15 6   Price: £16.99 Hardback

CT PUBLISHING, PO BOX 5880, BIRMINGHAM B16 8JF.

flying the flag
(the stars and stripes, that is)

mike ripley

Author of the award-winning 'Angel' series of comedy crime novels, Mike Ripley is celebrating ten years as crime critic for the Sunday/Daily Telegraph, in which time he has reviewed over 500 books. Here he reflects on how the last decade of the century came to be dominated by American crime writers.

Eleven years ago, way back in the 20th century, a well-known and very well-respected crime editor told me in no uncertain terms: "Americans don't sell in this country".

The context was an argument, started by me, about why the crime writers I liked—Elmore Leonard, James Ellroy, James Lee Burke, Charles Willeford and Carl Hiaasen—were not better known here, or even compulsory reading for a GCSE course in being a rounded human being.

At the time, Leonard was getting critical acclaim but not impinging on the UK bestseller lists. Ellroy and Burke had cult status but little exposure in High Street bookshops and virtually none in libraries. Charles Willeford had had a brief flurry of critical success just before his death with the Hoke Mosely books (subsequently championed by No Exit Press), and Carl Hiaasen's first two novels had been published and remaindered with stunning speed and cynicism, although later he was to be rescued by Pan/Macmillan.

For the crime fan who realised that some of the best and most innovative writing was coming from America it was a depressing scene, but the 1990s changed all that. At the end of a century which had begun with *The Hound of the Baskervilles* and *The Riddle of the Sands*, three of the top selling crime hardbacks in 1999 were by Americans (Thomas Harris, John Grisham and Patricia Cornwell) and two out of the top five paperbacks (Grisham and Cornwell again).

Overall, about a third of the crime fiction published in the UK has been American since around 1996 and 32% of the catalogued titles coming in the first six months of 2000 are also. The larger publishing houses all have a Yank among their big guns. Little, Brown have Cornwell; Century have Grisham and Hutchinson have Richard North Patterson; Hodder have Elizabeth George (writing British cosy crime of all things) and Jeffery Deaver; Harper-Collins have the much-overlooked James Hall; Viking have Leonard; Macmillan have Hiaasen and Sue Grafton; Orion have a nap hand with James Lee

Burke, Michael Connelly and Robert Crais.

In the *"should be better known"* category, Bantam have picked up John Ridley, Hutchinson have Robert Ferrigno and Headline have a gem (though perhaps they don't know it) in Sam Reaves.

Just as British breweries felt they had to have a foreign-sounding lager in the early Seventies, so publishers have to have American crime on their lists these days and I for one am certainly not complaining. There is nothing wrong with the mainstream moving westwards, just as long as it doesn't become McDonaldised.

The smaller publishing houses should make sure it isn't, for they have been in the vanguard of promoting (and preserving) good American mystery writing and are still on the cutting edge. It is imprints such as No Exit who have brought James Sallis, Eddie Bunker and Daniel Woodrell (surely one the most original voices of the last decade) to this country. Serpent's Tail are likewise to be lauded for introducing Walter Mosley and George P Pelecanos, and Canongate for new names such as Jon A Jackson and Anthony Bourdain and for reintroducing Andrew Vachss to the UK after far too long away.

So the Americans are here and in force. In sheer economic terms, three of them—Thomas Harris, Cornwell and Grisham—sold 1,567,166 copies of their *latest* hardbacks and paperbacks (not their backlist) in 1999. By my crude calculation, at cover price without discounts, that is £14,223,507.20 of retail sales in this country alone. Three authors, five titles, fourteen million quid. That's the logic.

But back in the late 1980s, such a scenario seemed anything but logical.

Between 1976 and 1989, only three Americans (four if you count ex-pat Paula Gosling who lives here) featured in the Crime Writers' Association's Dagger awards: Martin Cruz Smith for *Gorky Park*, Scott Turow for *Presumed Innocent* and Sara Paretsky for *Toxic Shock*.

The subsequent decade to 1999 has seen the CWA honour: Patricia Cornwell (twice), Walter Mosley, Carl Hiaasen, Doug Swanson, Janet Evanovitch, Laurence Shames, James Lee Burke and Dan Fesperman, not to mention a belated Diamond Dagger for Ed McBain.

In the early 1980s, the prospect looked totally remote. The (otherwise) excellent *Whodunit? A Guide To Crime, Suspense and Spy Fiction* edited by Harry Keating and published in 1982 (and surely worth a second edition for the 21st century), featured 118 *living* American crime writers. But of these, less than a fifth were listed as having written new novels since 1979. Among those were some famous names—Mary Higgins Clark, Joseph Hansen, George V Higgins, Robert Ludlum and Tony Hillerman—and some perhaps less famous ones: Louise Kallen, Mary McMullen and William X Kienzle.

Surprisingly, the young James Ellroy, who must have had two books under his belt in America by then, was not mentioned. Amazingly, neither was Elmore Leonard, who had turned from westerns to crime and had already published six or seven crackers, including *Mr Majestyk, 52 Pick Up,*

The Switch, Cat Chaser, Gold Coast and *Split Images*.

So, no indication there either of the American invasion to come.

But the critics, the more adventurous reader and a handful of aspiring British writers, had noticed the coming sea-change.

Within the space of a few months spanning 1988-89, Elmore Leonard's *Freaky Deaky*, James Ellroy's *The Black Dahlia* and George V Higgins' *Outlaws* all appeared in the UK to immense critical acclaim.

Hollywood was beginning to take a renewed interest in the work of shamefully forgotten noir writers such as Jim Thompson and Charles Williams and in Britain itself, a new crop of crime writers—Mark Timlin, Denise Danks, Phillip Kerr et al—were bursting into print, all cheerfully acknowledging their debt to the American school of the hardboiled rather than the British tradition of detective fiction.

Exactly ten years ago in my January and February 1990 crime round-up columns then in *The Sunday Telegraph*, eight out of the fourteen novels I reviewed were American, and two Canadian, which seemed quite daring in those days.

Not that the Americans in question were exactly revolutionary or dangerous in their approach to crime fiction, with the possible exception of the posthumous publication of Charles Willeford's *Kiss Your Ass Goodbye*, a title which raised surprisingly few eyebrows among Telegraph readers, I'm delighted to say. The others in the frame were: Robert B Parker, in the days when he only wrote one book a year, John Camp (now better known for serial killer thrillers as John Sandford), Deborah Valentine, Jeremiah Healy, Charlotte Macleod, Robert Goldborough and Elizabeth George.

[Of the Elizabeth George—*Payment In Blood*—I wrote: "Miss George does have intelligent things to say, particularly on the nature of jealousy, but her version of Britain inspires xenophobia, not sympathy." I think that still stands.]

Interestingly enough, it was only a matter of months, in the summer and autumn of 1990, before the more hardboiled American style came to dominate the round-up column. New names began to appear as lead reviews: the previously-ignored Carl Hiaasen, Robert Campbell, Gerald Petievitch (still one of the best but unheard of for several years now), Sue Grafton (then on 'G' in the alphabet), Lawrence Sanders, Loren Estelman, James Ellroy, James Lee Burke and, in September 1990, a first novel by 'Patrica Daniels Cornwell': *Postmortem*.

Cornwell's novel was the breakthrough.

Without the aid of big movie or television tie-ins, Cornwell's often gruesome medical/forensic mysteries have carved out a British readership which all but a handful of domestic crime writers can only dream of. Regularly selling over 800,000 paperbacks a year in Britain, Cornwell undoubtedly appeals to women, the majority of the book-buying and reading population.

As too do the novels of that other lynch-pin of the American invasion, John Grisham. Since the appearance of *The Firm* in 1991, just about every one of his legal thrillers has sold over

600,000 paperbacks here, again with a firm following among female readers taking an unexpected interest in the American legal system.

Both Cornwell and Grisham have been much copied here and in the US and now suffer the embarrassing and dubious marketing ploy of having their rivals promoted with *"As good as... Or your money back"* offers.

Their success opened the floodgates for American crime. The 1998 Paperback Fastseller list compiled by *The Bookseller* showed that 44 out of the top 100 selling paperbacks of all genres, fiction and non-fiction, were crime or thrillers. Twenty-five of those forty-four were by Americans. The new Paperback Fastseller 100 list for 1999 shows a disappointing drop to only 30 crime/thriller titles, but again the majority (17) are by Americans (four by Tom Clancy alone!)

Even that recalcitrant crime editor, who said *"Americans don't sell"* back in the late 1980s, must surely have seen the light by now.

Admittedly, not many of those Americans in the Paperback Fastseller list, accounting for well over 3.5 million paperbacks last year, were household names a decade ago. Tom Clancy may well have been around, but Cornwell, Grisham, James Patterson, Richard N Patterson, Michael Connelly, Tami Hoag and Jeffery Deaver were not.

Not that all American crime finds its way across the Atlantic, far from it. There are some exceptionally talented American writers who find great difficulty in getting a British publisher, probably because they are not easily pigeonholed—'serial killer', 'legal thriller' and 'hardboiled' being the standard categorisations. Among such softer boiled writers are Margaret Maron, Walter Satterthwait, Justin Scott, Joan Hess and K K Beck (now Mrs Michael Dibdin). All are fine writers, well worth a look.

It was Cornwell and Grisham who opened the doors for American mysteries in this country and it is no exaggeration to claim they are now a dominant force in British reading habits, at least when it comes to crime. [Harry Potter, Catherine Cookson, Terry Pratchett and others reign supreme in other genres.]

Of the British contingent in the 1999 paperback Top 100, Gerald Seymour, P D James, Jack Higgins and Ruth Rendell/Barbara Vine were established pre-1990, but to match the 90's decade of new American talent, we have only Ian Rankin (and he's technically late-80s), Minette Walters and Robert Harris.

The implications of all this are probably widespread and significant but will not be clearly seen for many years.

One of the immediate effects, though, is the often unseemly 'me too' marketing scrabble on the part of certain publishers to find 'the next Grisham' or 'the next Cornwell'. There is also the rather odious technique of lumbering a first author with the 'As good as' special offer. In 1998, Kathy Reichs' *Deja Dead* got the *"As good as Patricia Cornwell or your money back"* promotion, which always draws the instant *"It isn't, keep your receipt"* come-back. This year, Mo Hayder's *Birdman* gets the *"As good as Thomas Harris or your money back"* treatment, which is a terrible millstone to hang round a new author's neck.

Whatever the pros and cons of this sort of marketing (and, to be fair, the very slick campaign for Kathy Reichs did result in big sales), the point is that here are two new authors to this country, instantly *compared to Americans*. Would that have happened ten years ago? A critic might have made references to Chandler or possibly Ross MacDonald when reviewing, but in a mass market promotion direct to the book-buyer on the cover? Unlikely.

The point is that Harris, Cornwell and Grisham are not just successful writers, *but household names* which can be recognised in the 4.7 seconds (or whatever it is) that a bookshop browser takes to spot a cover he or she fancies.

Whether they remain household names is another matter, as fashions change and, increasingly, change at a faster pace. If I was asked who 'invented' the legal thriller, the old buffer in me would probably say Cyril Hare, but the realist would recognise that the question referred to the American legal thriller and the answer would be Scott Turow. But the name on top of the public mind is now John Grisham, although Turow is still around and writing, it is said, better than ever. It wouldn't surprise me to find some publishing marketing whizz kid in the year 2005 promoting the new Scott Turow with an *"As good as John Grisham or your money back"* sticker.

[As an aside, I once asked an eminent clinical psychologist, giving a lecture on criminal profiling, who 'invented' criminal profiling. Without batting an eyelid, he said: 'Thomas Harris'.]

Another effect of the American invasion has been, perhaps ironically, the temptation for British crime writers to try their hand at setting their novels in America. It has been said that this could be because they have one eye on the American market, but equally these days it might be because they have two eyes on the British market.

Phillip Kerr, with one eye firmly on Hollywood, and Tim Willocks were among the first. Michael Dibdin, who now lives there, produced the excellent *Dark Spectre* and Denise Danks, more recently, has taken on California in *Torso*.

A younger generation have gone straight in to the American scene: Adam Lloyd Baker, with his much underrated *New York Graphic*; Rob Ryan with *Underdogs* last year and *Nine Mil* this; Lee Child, soon to publish *The Visitor*, the fourth in his Jack Reacher series; and, the most successful of all, John Connolly (OK, so he's Irish) with *Every Dead Thing* and *Dark Hollow*, bestsellers both.

Is this the way the future lies?

For the domestic British reader (and writer) that future might look grim, especially with Inspector Morse dead and buried and Adam Dalgliesh rumoured to be facing marriage (and retirement?) later this year.

The paranoia stakes were also raised back in August by my old mate Mark Timlin, who has done more stirring than Delia Smith, in his crime column in the *Independent On Sunday*, when he suggested that the only crime worth reading was American or set in America. This was broad-brush stuff, albeit with a point, and home-grown crime writing is far from dead and buried as long as the likes of Ian Rankin, Minette Walters, Frances Fyfield and Val McDermid are still around, and I've not heard that Ruth Rendell is planning to retire either.

There is also new, young talent coming through, although no Brits made it on to the short list of the Crime Writers' John Creasey Award for first novels in 1999. Watch out for Andrea Badenoch, Denise Mina, Emer Gillespie, Max Kinnings and Stephen Booth in the longer term, and remember you heard of them first here. In the shorter term, I would expect to see Julia Wallis Martin making her mark on the Fastseller charts for 2000 or 2001.

So don't run up the white flag, or the Stars and Stripes, just yet. In fact, look on the bright side.

Ten years ago, we had a proud track record in this country (thanks almost exclusively to small publishers) for keeping in print or reprinting American noir classics. Authors such as Jim Thompson, David Goodis and Charles Williams were available here but not in their native land. Today, that tradition is maintained—again mostly through the smaller houses—and books by Lawrence Block, John D MacDonald, Andrew Vachss and the early 87th Precinct mysteries of Ed McBain are, thankfully, in print.

The success of the Cornwells and the Grishams must surely have smoothed the path for other Americans into the mainstream book trade. It needed the sales of a Cornwell or a Grisham to persuade publishers and booksellers that Americans could sell and today's more discerning fans no longer have to scour the land for James Ellroy, Carl Hiaasen or James Lee Burke. They have also had the added pleasure of discovering Mosley, Pelecanos, Woodrell, Shames, Ferrigno and a host of others.

So don't worry about this American mystery imperialism (as Gore Vidal would call it), enjoy it.

There was, however, one notable downward swoop on this learning curve of American crime fiction, which really has to be put on the record.

In July 1990 I was asked (at gunpoint) to review *The World Cup Murder* by Pele, no less, in partnership with one Herbert Resnicow and published by— oh, the shame—the No Exit Press. The book was a vain attempt to explain soccer to an American audience and was set at a World Cup Final, in New York, where the USA have to play East Germany for the Jules Remy. And guess which 42-year-old Brazilian coach has to come out of retirement and score a hat-trick in the last fifteen minutes for the USA?

Without doubt, this was one of the greatest crime writing turkeys of the Nineties, possibly ever.

"Politically as subtle as a Rambo movie and as gripping as a Scottish goalkeeper" I wrote at the time. After ten years of careful reflection, I would amend that sweeping judgement.

Scottish goalkeepers have got better.

collecting crime
mike ashley

Mike Ashley has written and/or compiled nearly 60 books covering a wide range of subjects from science fiction and fantasy to mystery and horror and to ancient history. He has a keen interest in the history and development of genre fiction, particularly in magazines, and has a collection of over 15,000 books and magazines. Amongst his mystery anthologies are *The Mammoth Book of Historical Whodunnits*, *The Mammoth Book of Historical Detectives*, *Shakespearean Whodunnits*, *Shakespearean Detectives*, *Classical Whodunnits*, *The Mammoth Book of New Sherlock Holmes Adventures* and *Royal Whodunnits*—and he is currently compiling *The Mammoth Book of Impossible Crimes*. He is also working on a biography of Algernon Blackwood.

AVON CALLING

The last twenty years have seen a rapid increase in interest in early paperbacks, both American and British, and there is now a healthy collector's market, with conventions, magazines and websites dedicated to the subject.

I love paperbacks almost as much as I love magazines—and after all, paperbacks emerged from the magazines, to a large degree. There's something about the feel of a paperback, the look of the cover, even the smell of a book, that makes it all so alluring. And that's <u>before</u> you read it. Add to this the work of Raymond Chandler, Cornell Woolrich, Agatha Christie, Leslie Charteris, James M Cain—and the fact that their values, in very good or mint condition, can be in the hundreds of pounds, then it makes them all the more desirable.

I'm going to concentrate on my favourite American publisher from the first decade of the paperback, the 1940s—Avon Books. I can always come back to other publishers—especially Dell Books and Popular Library—and other eras another day. But maybe a little scene setting first.

There have been paperbound books for decades, right back into the Victorian era, and I'm not about to go into the semantics of what is or isn't a paperback book here. I think we all know what they are. The first paperbacks, as we recognise them today, began in Britain in July 1935 with the launch of Penguin Books under the direction of Allen Lane and in the United States in June 1939 with Pocket Books under Robert DeGraff.

Penguin included just two crime books in its first ten: *The Unpleasantness at the Bellona Club* by Dorothy L Sayers (#5) and *The Mysterious Affair at Styles* by Agatha Christie (#6). Both these books are in the standard rather dry Penguin format of the early years and though these books are collectible, simply because they're early Penguins, and can fetch prices of £50 or more in very good condition, I don't find them especially desirable.

It's the early American paperbacks that draw me. Now, interestingly, in the first ten titles from Pocket Books—which began, incidentally, with a fantasy, *Lost Horizon* by James Hilton—there was only one crime novel, and it was English not American. It was *The Murder of Roger Ackroyd* by, who else?, Agatha Christie. The contrast with the staid Penguin covers is immediate. The cover, by Isador Steinman, shows the murder victim slumped down with a knife in his back. The style was reminiscent of the pulp magazines, a phenomenon that had never really blossomed in Britain. The price of the paperback was 25 cents, at a time when many pulps were still 15 or 20 cents. It was still considerably cheaper than hardcover editions which were around $2.50. Even the cheapest of the cheap hardcover reprints were about 75 cents, so the paperback was a bargain. Just about all of the first ten Pocket Books, each published in a print run of 10,000 copies, sold out within a few months. A mint or even near mint copy of the Christie volume will fetch around $250-$300 in the States, where the real collector's market is, and could be anything between £75 and £100 in Britain.

Lee Wright, who edited the Inner Sanctum series of mystery novels for Simon and Schuster, and who later edited several mystery-fiction anthologies for Pocket Books, asked DeGraff why he had only published one mystery novel, and queried how sales had gone. "The sales were terrific," DeGraff responded. "Then you should do two or three a month," Wright responded.

And so DeGraff began to increase the number of mystery novels amongst his otherwise fairly standard selection of books, which included classics and titles popular at the time—usually because of a current film. For some reason—probably contractual—DeGraff did not corner the market in Agatha Christie. After all these were still experimental days. But he did begin to publish other highly popular mystery novelists of the day. During the remaining six months of 1939 he issued *The Chinese Orange Mystery* by Ellery Queen (#17), *Murder Must Advertise* by Dorothy L Sayers (#21) and *The Corpse With the Floating Foot* by R A J Walling (#24). Walling—now there's a forgotten name. There's nothing by him in print these days, but back in the thirties he was rather popular, with a long running series featuring insurance investigator Philip Tolefree, several of which had the formulaic *The Corpse With ...* title. I've only read a couple of them, and they are very typical English mysteries of their day, rather dated now. But then if Gladys Mitchell's Mrs Bradley can resurface there may yet be hope for Tolefree. Certainly it's unlikely anyone would put much value on a paperback edition of any of his books, except for the fact that it was one of the early Pocket Books, and then suddenly the price rises to around $50, or probably £20 in Britain. It just shows.

Success invariably breeds imitation, and it wasn't long before Joseph Meyers jumped feet first into the paperback pool and launched Avon Books in November 1941. Back in the 1970s, when I corresponded with Donald A Wollheim, who was an editor at Avon Books in the late 1940s, he told me his memories of Meyers. He regarded him as uncultured and dictatorial, without an ounce of finesse in his body. Meyers didn't need it. He was streetwise and had a quick eye for the market—sometimes, too quick, changing his mind at a moment's whim and going off in several directions at once. It's worth remembering that the forties was a turbulent period in publishing. By the end of the forties, pulps were on their way out, digests seemed to be on their way in and paperbacks were still playing second (or third) fiddle. Meyers had his finger in every pie, including comics, and shuffled things around in whatever way he thought could make a quick buck.

But if that's what went on behind the scenes, out front it was glorious. Avon paperbacks have to be the most garish, over-the-top, sensationalised paperbacks of all, with delightfully lurid and sexy covers. That makes them collectible. In fact of all the early paperbacks, Avons are amongst the most collectible, with correspondingly high prices.

No sooner had Avon Books appeared that Pocket Books took them to court for stealing their format and appearance, and indeed masquerading as a 'Pocket Book' by using the phrase 'Avon *pocket-size* Books' on the cover. The case swung back and forth between the courts and the appeal courts. The end result was that provided Avon took the offending 'pocket-book' logo from the cover and stopped using the red page-end staining also used by Pocket Books, they were at liberty to use the pocket book format. In fact, any publisher was. Meyers, by his impetuous but keenly honed business nous, had opened up the way for the pocketbook industry.

Avon's book editor at the outset was Herbert Williams, Meyers's nephew. Williams was a very capable editor but in 1946 had a falling out with Meyers (not difficult) and that was how Wollheim became Avon's book editor. Also at Avon in the mid-late 1940s was Sol Cohen, who edited the comic books. When Williams served in the Armed Forces during the war years Louis Greenfield stepped in as editor. Greenfield was an avid mystery fan, and a friend of Rex Stout, so it is no surprise that the concentration of crime fiction books increased during 1943 and 1944.

Meyers was heavily into mystery fiction for Avon Books. The early Avon Books aren't numbered though they were properly identified in later catalogues. The very first Avon Book, just for the record, was *Elmer Gantry* by Sinclair Lewis, but otherwise seven out of the first ten titles are mysteries. These were *The Big Four* by Agatha Christie, *Dr Priestly Investigates* by John Rhode, *The Haunted Hotel* by Wilkie Collins, *The Plague Court Murders* by Carter Dickson, *The Corpse in the Green Pyjamas* by R A J Walling (ah-ha!), *Wilful and Premeditated* by Freeman Wills Crofts and *Dr Thorndyke's Discovery* by R Austin Freeman.

That's some list. The appearance of Walling shows that Meyers was keeping an eye on the Pocket Books list. In fact there was a more blatant example of follow-my-leader, because Avon also published a book by James Hilton, a story collection called *Ill Wind*. No wonder Pocket Books accused them of muscling in on their territory.

Let's look at those books in a bit more detail.

The Big Four (originally Collins, 1927) is perhaps the least typical of Christie's early books. It's a series of closely connected stories where Hercule Poirot is pitted against an international crime syndicate whose leaders, bent on world domination, seem more like renegades from a Sax Rohmer novel, and Poirot trying to operate like Simon Templar. When the *Daily Mail* reviewed it in 1927, they commented that it would not suit those who had "come to expect subtlety as well as sensation." Which explains why it was right up Avon Books' street.

John Rhode (1884-1965) was an immensely prolific writer, producing three or four books a year for fifty years. His real name was Cecil Street, an army officer, who also wrote mysteries as Miles Burton. His first book as John Rhode, *A S F* (Bles, 1924), was a thriller about cocaine smuggling. With *The Paddington Mystery* (Bles, 1925), he introduced his best known character, Dr Priestley (his first name was Lancelot, but as with Morse, it's hardly ever mentioned). Priestley was a former mathematics professor but fell out with the university (in a show of irascibility that I suspect was also typical of Street's army background). He now works privately, mostly as a pedantic commentator on the views of others. Like Sherlock Holmes, or more typically S F X Van Dusen, the Thinking Machine, mixed with a dash of Dr Thorndyke, Priestley applies logic to his investigations, and as the series continues (and it ran to over seventy books) he became increasingly an armchair detective letting others do the legwork. Avon's first choice was the ninth Priestley book, originally published as *Pinehurst* (Bles, 1930) in Britain. I'm surprised Rhode's books aren't more collected than they seem to be—he's gone in and out of favour, though I like him immensely. This early Avon paperback is worth around $60-$75 in the States or about £20-£25 over here.

The full title for the Wilkie Collins volume, which was #6 in their first ten, was *The Haunted Hotel and 25 Other Ghost Stories*, so it's really an anthology. No editor is credited but it was actually cobbled together by Herbert Williams from two out-of-copyright volumes, Collins' own *The Haunted Hotel* (Chatto & Windus, 1878) and an anthology *25 Ghost Stories* compiled anonymously by W B Holland back in 1904. This Avon title has been frequently reprinted, sometimes under variant titles and sometimes with changed contents. It's not that marvellous a volume, as the fictional ghost stories are mostly well known, though there are some purportedly true stories which are less well known. Collins' novel isn't always included in the later printings and is actually the best thing in it, though it's a better detective novel than it is a supernatural one. Again it would be less highly collected were it not one of the first Avons, and is around $30-$50 in the States and about £15-£20 in Britain. What makes the title intriguing are the number of variant printings, most of which also have variant covers, so for an Avon completist, this title is a real nightmare!

The Plague Court Murders by Carter Dickson (Morrow, 1934) is a little gem. Dickson was, of course, the thinly disguised alter ego of John Dickson Carr. This book was the first of his Henry Merrivale mystery novels, although Humphrey Masters so dominates the start of the book that the Avon edition proclaims it to be "A Chief Inspector Masters Mystery" in a shield on the cover, which makes it an intriguing item straight away. This novel is wonderfully eerie as Masters and Merrivale attempt to get behind an apparently haunted house and the tricks of a medium to solve a baffling murder and other mysteries. Because it's the first paperback edition of a much prized author this volume comes more expensive, around $60-$75 (or £25-£30 in Britain).

The Corpse in Green Pyjamas brings us back to Walling, and a chance to say a bit more about him. His full name was Robert Alfred John Walling (1869-1949), and he had been writing stories for the magazines since the 1890s, so his career stretched over fifty years, though he did not start his detective novels until 1927. Although most of the books feature the insurance investigator Philip Tolefree, as I've already mentioned, Tolefree works alongside two police inspectors, Pierce and Garstang, both of whom occasionally have novels all to themselves. Julian Symons classed Walling under the 'humdrum' writers of the twenties and thirties, and his work is certainly formulaic and very typical of the period. But they're good, harmless fun and the fact that both Pocket Books and Avon picked on him to launch their series show just how popular he was in his day. In fact Avon printed another Walling novel as their sixteenth title, *Murder at Midnight* (Morrow, 1932), which features Inspector Garstang, so he should not be dismissed too lightly. The Avon Wallings can usually be found for between $20 and $30 (or around £10-£15).

Wilful and Premeditated (Dodd, 1934) is the American title of the Inspector French novel *The 12.30 from Croydon* (Hodder, 1934). It might at first seem an odd choice to start with, but Williams was a perceptive editor. If you know the Inspector French series, then you'll know they are almost like 'inverted' detective stories. That is it's easy to work out who committed the crime—it's always the person with the strongest alibi. The fun is how that alibi is broken. And French, just like Columbo, years later, doggedly worked his way through dates and clues and timetables often interwoven into the most labyrinthine puzzles, until he got his man. They're tremendous fun. What's special about *Wilful and Premeditated*, is that for once Crofts gets deeper into the psyche of the murderer, with chilling results. It is, without a doubt, the most sensational of the Inspector French novels and therefore ideal for Avon. Crofts (1879-1957) was a civil engineer by training and worked on the railways for many years so you can bet that this is full of authentic detail which these days make these stories remarkable time capsules of a period long lost.

The tenth release was *Dr Thorndyke's Discovery* (Dodd Mead, 1932) by R Austin Freeman (1862-1943). This was the US title of *When Rogues Fall Out* (Hodder, 1932), one of the later Thorndyke novels, but the Great Fathomer was as sharp as ever, still up to date in all the latest scientific developments, and still ready to march on for another eight or nine years. Thorndyke was the first of the real scientific detectives. The first novel, *The Red Thumb Mark*, had appeared as far back as 1907, but although some of the science now seems quaint, the stories remain fascinating. Both this and the Crofts edition fetch around $30 (£15).

I've dwelt in detail on the first ten because they were Avon's showcase. What I find interesting is that, with the exception of Carr, all of these books were by English writers, and Carr's has an English setting (to some extent he's an adopted English author). It may be that rights to these volumes came cheap, but I think it's more because the English mystery was so popular in the thirties (and we're only at 1941 here), whereas the hardboiled mystery was still establishing itself. Those books were still in print and paperback rights less easy to acquire, but they would come.

In fact the next move was slightly unexpected. Starting in July 1942 Avon began to issue a digest-sized paperback under the heading 'Murder of the Month'. This soon metamorphosed to 'Murder Mystery Monthly' (hereafter MMM). Although these are sometimes called paperbacks, technically they are digest magazines, because Avon acquired the serial rights to the novels rather than the book rights. In fact Meyers was only imitating what Lawrence Spivak was already doing at Mercury Press. Spivak had launched American Mercury Books in 1937 starting with a reprint of James M Cain's 1934 classic *The Postman Always Rings Twice*. By March 1940 this series was divided into Mercury Mysteries and Bestseller Mysteries. In Fall 1941 Spivak also started *Ellery Queen's Mystery Magazine*. Meyers wasn't about to launch a new magazine, but a mystery series in digest format was a good idea. Remember that although with hindsight we know that the paperback now dominates the stalls, this was less obvious in the early 1940s. Meyers was hedging his bets. Moreover, if the book sold well in the digest series, he had an option to the paperback rights, which he could invoke if necessary. The covers of all of these monthly digests boasted "A $2.00 Mystery for 25c" and also declared "Complete and Unexpurgated." The identifying imprint was of the head of a skeleton which looks like it's wearing a wig, though I presume it was supposed to represent a remnant of hair. Nevertheless, you couldn't mistake this on the stalls.

His first choice for 'Murder of the Month' is a slightly odd one—*Seven Footprints to Satan* by Abraham Merritt. Merritt's work is mostly fantasy—and was extremely profitable for Avon during the 1940s, which boasted several million copies of Merritt's books in print—so most of the titles, like *The Moon Pool* and *Dwellers in the Mirage*, look out of place in this series. At least *Seven Footprints to Satan* was a thriller, with the supernatural fairly low key—in fact it was a disappointment to most Merritt fans when it was first published. It's about a super-criminal who masquerades as Satan. Anyone brought to him has to climb seven steps to his throne. Four of the steps are good and if you step only on those you win your heart's desire. But if you tread on the three bad steps you are ever after a slave of Satan. The House of Satan is a bizarre place full of corridors and mirrors and dark depths—a place almost impossible to escape from. The story is really great fun, and when I first read it, about thirty years ago, I thought it would make a good episode of *The Avengers*.

The second Murder Mystery was *The Mysterious Mickey Finn* by Elliot Paul, another name from the past. At this time Paul was hot stuff because of the success of his pre-war memoir, *The Last Time I Saw Paris* (1942) and this was an opportunity for Meyers to print the softcover edition of the first of Paul's Homer Evans mysteries. I'm pretty sure these books are all out of print now, though I know Dover Books had them in print in the mid-eighties, so they might still be available. The Evans mysteries are set in Paris and are full of bizarre characters who could just as easily have walked straight out of *The Fast Show*! The plots are almost surreal, and though the mysteries are serious and well thought through, each book has a sense of farce. Apparently Evans was supposed to be a parody of van Dine's Philo Vance, but he's more endearing that Vance. I'm sure these books would do well again if reprinted today. Maybe they didn't do too well for Meyers, though, because he didn't reprint *Mickey Finn* in pocketbook format until 1950.

What puzzles me about the Avon Murder Mystery series is that it never seems to be as highly collected as the more traditional Avon paperbacks. I can't think why. They are impressive productions, often with excellent covers (alas the artist is rarely credited) and they are, more often than not, the first true paperback edition of certain books. This becomes rather important as we proceed to the big guns.

I'll skip over the next few monthly digests and zoom in on volumes #6 and #7, because these are the real gems amongst the Avon Books, and allow me to widen the discussion. In 1943 Meyers achieved a very timely deal with A A Knopf, the publishers of the novels of James M Cain. Meyers had already secured serial rights to *The Postman Always Rings Twice*, James Cain's blockbuster, which as I've mentioned had already been put in digest form as the first of the American Mercury books. Meyers brought this out as MMM #6. But Meyers's real coup, was in obtaining serial and paperback rights to a trilogy of novellas that Cain had written, and which had proved too short to issue as separate hardcover books. Knopf planned to issue them as an omnibus volume, *Three of a Kind*, in early 1944.

Because he acquired serial rights, Meyers got them into print first. The first of them, *Double Indemnity* appeared as MMM #16 in late 1943, just ahead of the excellent 1944 Paramount film adaptation by Billy Wilder, starring Fred MacMurray and Barbara Stanwyck. Meyers brought out the paperback edition in early 1945 (Avon

#60) thus catching both ends of the market. The second of them, *The Embezzler*, Meyers released as MMM #20 in early 1944, bang in time to cash in on interest arising from the *Double Indemnity* film. The third volume was a novella and two short stories, *Career in C Major*, which he issued in early 1945 as #22 in another digest series, *Avon Modern Short Story Monthly*. Avon Books thus had all of Cain's major titles in print at the time that *The Postman Always Rings Twice* was released as a film by MGM in 1946, starring John Garfield and Lana Turner—still the classic version in my mind.

Apart from *Career in C Major*, which never seems to have been particularly collectible, and which you can find for under $20 (£10) in very good condition, the other volumes are much desired. Because *The Postman Always Rings Twice* had already seen an earlier paperback printing, the Avon edition is less valued, and you can get in very good condition for around $20-$30 (£10-£15 in Britain).

But the Avon edition of *Double Indemnity* is the true first edition and I've seen copies going for $200 or more (and certainly over £100 in Britain). By comparison the later Avon Books printing (#60 in early 1945), which many might think was the first paperback printing, only fetches around $20. Much the same applies to *The Embezzler*, where the MMM edition fetches up to $150 (£100), whereas the later paperback (#99 in 1946) is around $20.

A similar story applies to Raymond Chandler. In 1943, again by arrangement with Knopf, Avon Books brought out a paperback edition of *The Big Sleep*—not once, but twice! The standard paperback edition, Avon Books #38, came out in October, and I have frequently seen this referred to as the first paperback edition. But it wasn't. Six months earlier the novel had appeared as *MMM #7*. According to Frank MacShane's *The Life of Raymond Chandler*, that edition sold 300,000 copies, though Chandler would only have made $1,500 from that. Avon's usual deal was that they paid a royalty of just one cent per copy sold, and that was to the original hardcover publisher who shared it 50/50 with the author. Avon, on the other hand, once you deduct royalties and the 34% share that went to the distributor, netted $54,000.

Collectors always seem to favour the later paperback edition. That sells for at least $100, if you're lucky (or about £75 in Britain), but you can get the earlier digest edition for around $40-$50 (or about £40-£50 in Britain).

At this time Chandler was known to the book-buying public for his four big Philip Marlowe novels, *The Big Sleep*, *Farewell, My Lovely*, *The High Window* and *The Lady in the Lake*, two of which had also been blockbuster films. Not all Chandler fans may have known that he had been selling stories to the pulp magazines for the last ten years. Meyers scored another coup by bringing out not just one but three collections of Chandler's stories. *Five Murderers* came first. This contained five stories from *Black Mask*, including his earliest "Blackmailers Don't Shoot". This collection first appeared as MMM #19 in February 1944 and was reprinted as Avon Books #63 a year later. Prices vary considerably, though the later paperback edition usually goes for around $100 (£70). I've seen prices for the earlier digest ranging from $40 (£25) to $150 (£100).

The second collection was *Five Sinister Characters*. Again this was a digest MMM first (#28, February 1945) and a paperback second (#88, April 1946), and the prices are much the same as for the first volume.

The one that seems to get all the attention is the third, *Finger Man*, which was #43 in the MMM series (September 1946). The straight paperback edition was delayed until 1950 (Avon Books #219). This time the digest edition is much more desirable. Prices are now hovering around $200 (and certainly over £75 in Britain) whilst the paperback is usually around $60 (£35). The odd thing about *Finger Man* is that this includes one of Chandler's rare fantasy stories, "The Bronze Door", first published in *Unknown* in November 1939. But it's probably the fact that that story was not included in the omnibus of Chandler's short fiction, *The Simple Art of Murder* (Houghton Mifflin, 1950), that makes that collection so much in demand.

So, although Avon Books began traditionally with a bevy of English mysteries, by the mid forties it was heavily into the hard-boiled school, which was so well suited to the books brash covers and gutsy format. In addition to Chandler and Cain, Avon published Frank Gruber, W R Burnett (including *Little Caesar*), Dwight Babcock and Cornell Woolrich (both as himself and as William Irish).

With Woolrich, Meyers again struck lucky. He published *The Black Angel* as a MMM (#27) in November 1944 and then released it as a paperback (#96, August 1946) to coincide with the Universal film. He also published two collections of Woolrich's short stories, both as William Irish. *If I Should Die Before I Wake* (MMM #31, June 1945; book #106, October 1946) can easily fetch $100, even $150, in the digest format, and maybe $50 in the paperback, and proportionately less in Britain. The real teaser, though, is *Borrowed Crime and Other Stories* issued as MMM #42 in September 1946, but not subsequently reprinted as an Avon paperback. This is a very elusive title and certainly commands well over $200 (£130) when it surfaces.

One other development is worth mentioning here. Louis Greenfield's friendship with Rex Stout allowed Avon to develop a new magazine, *Rex Stout's Mystery Quarterly*, which first appeared in early 1945, dated Spring. It was a digest-sized magazine, clearly intended as a rival to *Ellery Queen's*. It was almost entirely reprint, so was more like a regular digest-size anthology—much the same as *Avon Fantasy Reader* two years later. It contained a good range of stories by authors already published by Avon plus a few other surprises. The first issue led with a Dashiell Hammett Continental Op story from *Black Mask*, rubbing shoulders with Agatha Christie, John Steinbeck, H F Heard, Dorothy L Sayers and even W W Jacobs. Later issues included stories by John Dickson Carr, H P Lovecraft, Cornell Woolrich, Vincent Starrett, John Collier, Eric Ambler—an interesting mix, and an enjoyable magazine. Although it was later retitled *Rex*

Stout's Mystery Monthly it never did sustain a monthly schedule—typical of Meyers's publishing whims—and was dropped in 1947 after Williams left. Wollheim helped assemble the final, ninth issue. Issues aren't that easy to find these days, not in good condition, and a full run would cost a good £100 or so.

When Herbert Williams returned from the War the concentration of mystery fiction slackened slightly. However, due to a family rift between Meyers and his sister (who was his business partner and Williams' mother) Williams left within only a few months. Williams was probably glad to go, because Meyers was placing increasing emphasis on salacious and violent covers and taking any opportunity to retitle books to give them more titillation. Donald A Wollheim, who had only just started working with Williams in developing the *Avon Fantasy Reader,* found himself the editor-in-chief. As the new kid on the block Wollheim had to go along with Meyers's ideas, but didn't like it. A notable example was the whipping cover put on *Europa* by Robert Briffault (Avon #272, 1950) or the totally irrelevant torture cover on the 1951 reprinting of Merritt's *The Ship of Ishtar* (Avon #324).

For a couple of years, until he acquired some assistants, Wollheim was in total editorial charge. He was seeing through so many books that some of the existing digest series had to go.

If the titles published in the late 1940s don't excite quite so much as the early 1940s, it's only because they are the quiet after the storm. Between 1941 and 1946 Avon introduced into paperback some of the best and most exciting mystery fiction available. And even afterwards they hadn't quite lost the touch. In 1948 they published the first paperback edition of Robert Bloch's *The Scarf* (Dial, 1947), though under the title of *The Scarf of Passion* (Avon #211). This was Bloch's major step forward in crime fiction, getting into the mind of a serial killer, and the book that started him down the road to *Psycho*. This edition goes for around $50-$75 (£35-£50).

I hope I've shown that there's a more to Avon Books than at first seems—and remember, I've concentrated on the crime fiction. They published plenty more besides, and a full run of Avon Books from the 1940s, even just the 300 paperbacks, let alone the various digest series, will be worth between £8,000 and £10,000.

"BUTLER IS THE LAST TRADITIONAL ENGLISH CRIME WRITER WE HAVE — AND ONE OF THE VERY BEST" - *CRIME TIME*

COFFIN FOLLOWING
by GWENDOLINE BUTLER

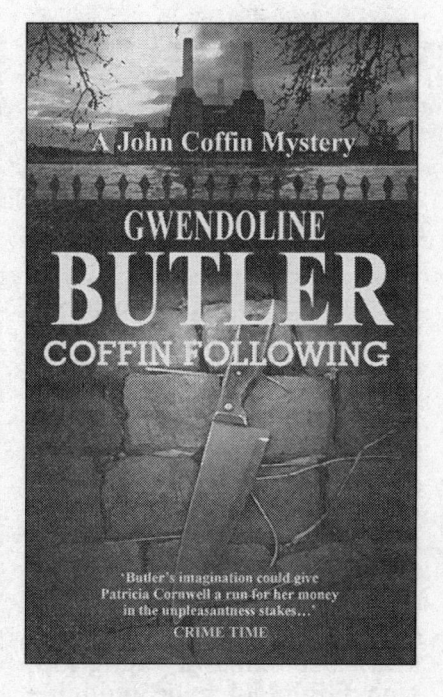

NO ACT OF VIOLENCE ever truly dies away; the effects of it go on for ever. The old princess, relic of an Eastern European royal house, could see plenty of it in her crystal ball: John Coffin on the run, three separate women and three separate acts of violence.

There was the ghostlike girl in the upper room, the girl from Wolverhampton and the princess herself, who studied the psychology of poisoning. John Coffin had left his wife and his job after he had been concussed while making an arrest. Moving from place to place within his own part of South London he finds himself in a nightmarish web of violence. Yet he can never be sure whether what he sees is really happening or whether it is something emanating from his own disturbed mind...

Available from all good bookshops or by post from CT Publishing, Dept CT32) PO Box 5880, Edgbaston, Birmingham, B16 9BJ (Postage and Packing free) - or buy on the web from www.crimetime.co.uk

ISBN: 1 902002-10-5   Price: £4.99 Paperback

CT PUBLISHING, PO BOX 5880, BIRMINGHAM B16 8JF.

candleland

martin waites

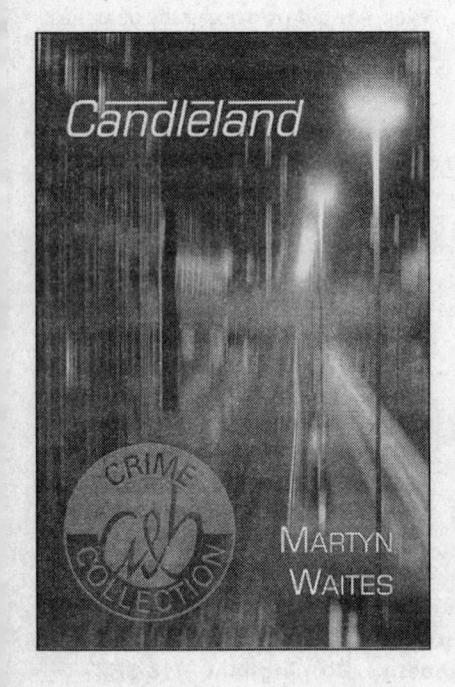

Extract from Candleland by Martyn Waites Published by Alllison &Busby in hardback at £16.99

HE HAD SEEN them come and go; sidling up to the door, doing a coded knock, slipping folded money in, getting a poly-wrapped bundle in return. Some were even allowed inside. Occasionally a big flash car would pull up, Beamer or Merc, stereo bleeping and thumping fit to crack the tarmac, and a couple of young black guys dressed like wannabe gangsta rappers would get out, go inside then back in the car and away. Sometimes a young kid, who didn't look to be in double figures, would ride up on a pedal bike, shove something through the slit in the door and zoom off again. Once, a young mixed-race guy, well-built with muscle, wearing a leather bomber, trainers, oversized jeans, with dirty blonde cropped hair, emerged from the flat. Despite the February cold, he wore nothing underneath the bomber, which was unzipped as far as his flaunted six-pack. His posture said he knew how to handle himself. Standing four-square and squat at his side on a leash and harness was a Staffordshire bull terrier, muscle-packed back-up. He looked up and down the street, his attitude expecting either armed police or paparazzi to come running, and when none did, strode off, leading with his dick.

Larkin had read his way through the papers twice, eaten a full English that was surprisingly good, and drunk three cups of coffee that, while not winning any awards, were comfortably the right side of poisonous. He wanted to keep watching, but out of the corner of his eye he could see the sole worker in the cafe, a small, aged West Indian, eyeing him suspiciously from his perch behind the counter. He seemed to be the only person working there, but Larkin kept catching glimpses of shadowy figures in the darkened kitchen area which was cordoned off from the front of the cafe by an old beaded curtain. Larkin didn't know what they were doing in there, but he doubted they were dishwashers. The last thing he wanted was to outstay his welcome in an area like this. The night was begining to cut in, so Larkin decided to pay his bill and leave. He'd plan his next move later.

Larkin moved to the counter, took out some cash from his pocket. The West Indian was dressed in a dirty shirt covered by an apron so multi-coloured with unidentifiable stains it resembled a mid-period Jackson Pollock. He never took his eyes from Larkin all the time he rang up the money in the cash register. Leaning across to give Larkin his change, he spoke.

"Haven't seen you in here before," he drawled in a rich Jamaican accent.

"No," said Larkin.

"You're not from round here." The man's left hand played under the counter. Larkin speculated what was there: a gun, baseball bat, machete, or even a panic button that would bring two dozen steroid-pumped friends running. He decided to choose his answers carefully.

"No, I'm not."

"You givin' a lot of attention to that place opposite. You police? Mr John Law himself?" The man's posture stiffened. He was bracing himself.

At least Larkin could answer honestly. "No, nothing like that. I'm just looking for somebody. Someone in there might know where she is."

Some of the man's hostility dropped away. A look of intelligence, of calculation, entered his features. "They won't tell you. Even if they know. They bad, bad boys." Bitterness crept into the man's voice.

"I know, but that place is the only lead I've got."

The man stared straight at Larkin, genuinely curious. "Who are you, then? What you do?"

"My name's Stephen Larkin. I'm a journalist."

The West Indian's eyes suddenly twinkled. A smile edged its way to the corners of his mouth. "A journalist? A newspaper reporter? You lookin' for a story, man?" He puffed his chest out. "Don't waste your time with those boys. Let me tell you the story of my life."

Larkin smiled. Why does everyone I meet want me to write their life story today? he thought. "I'm not working at the moment. I'm just doing a favour for a friend. Find his daughter for him."

"An' take her home?"

Larkin nodded. "Hopefully."

The man's face became serious, as if he was considering something, weighing up a painful decision. Suddenly, decision apparently reached, he broke into a wide grin. His hand dropped from whatever it was behind the counter. "Let me tell you my story. And who knows? If you listen good, and pay attention to an old man, and I take a liking to you, white boy, I might just be able to get you in there." He gestured towards the crack house.

"Really?" Larkin couldn't hide his surprise.

"Really." He looked round the cafe. "Now, my customers seem to have deserted me today, so what say I shut up early and find us something a bit stronger than coffee to drink. That sound good to you?"

Larkin smiled. It certainly did.

The man, whose name was Raymond, "but everyone be call me Rayman", closed the cafe, took off his apron, poured two huge shots of Jamaican rum and began to talk. The shadowy figures still moved about in the kitchen, but since they posed no immediate threat, Larkin tried to ignore them and listen to the story.

Rayman came to Britain from the Caribbean in the Fifties. "I was nine years old. Windrush. My parents thought there more jobs here, the land of opportunity." He sighed. "Ha. My father was trainin' to be a doctor. You not writin' this down?"

"I'm listening," Larkin replied.

The answer seemed good enough. Rayman continued. "Anyway, only work he could get here was shovlin' coal." He laughed bitterly. "Told him make no difference he wouldn't get dirty. His skin already too black. This wasn't the country we were promised, with fine buildings an' good manners an' all that. We were called wogs an' told to get back to the jungle. I saw all this, saw my parents stick in there, saw their dreams just disappear. I wouldn't go the same way. I's goin' make somethin' of my life."

He told Larkin of his drift into petty crime, "the only openin' for a black man in those days". Stealing, shoplifting to start with, then it escalated. "I was earnin' me good money, dressin' well, had fine-lookin' ladies on my arm. Good times. Then someone said he like to sleep with one of my ladies and pay well for it. So I got me a string of them, hired them out." He paused to take a mouthful of rum. "But it was all fun, you know? Nothin' heavy, you know what I'm sayin'? We all got somethin' out of it. I wasn't hurtin' no one, the ladies got fine clothes, money in their pocket, I din't beat them up or nothin' . . ." His eyes misted over as he travelled back over the years. "Yeah, we all enjoyed it." Larkin doubted that, but didn't interrupt his cosy criminal history.

Rayman had started to deal cannabis, "just weed, nothin' stronger," and run a shebeen. "Man, that was a success. High times for all. The black man loves to gamble, loves to drink, loves his women. An' I supplied all three. But then the big boys, the gangsters wanted to take over an' I knew it was time to get out."

"So what did you do?"

"Bought this place an' a couple others round here. Good times a-comin' Maggie said. So I listened. Became a businessman. Started some Caribbean restaurants, owned some property round here." He looked around. "All I got left now is this." He gestured towards the shadowy kitchen. "An' my weed dealin'." He shook his head. "Should have known better'n trust that white bitch."

Larkin agreed, and the conversation, fuelled by the rum, began to meander. Three glasses later, they had managed to sort out the majority of Britain's problems, and had an enjoyable time of it, but Larkin was still no further forward to gaining access to the crack house.

Rayman sat back, drained the last of his rum. "So, you like my story?"

"Yeah," said Larkin.

"But you're not goin' to write about me?"

"Not just yet."

Rayman laughed. "But you listened, an' we talked an' had us a fine time, an' that's good enough." He leaned forward, suddenly conspiratorial. "An' now you wanna know how to get in that crack house across the street?"

Larkin leaned in too. Partners in crime. "Yeah."

"Lemme think about it," Rayman said, sitting back. "Come here tomorrow for your breakfast an' we talk again."

"You've got a great way of getting repeat business," said Larkin.

Rayman laughed again, pointed. "You're not bad for a white man." He stood up. "You better leave now." He nodded towards the shadowy kitchen, his face suddenly serious. "I got me some business to attend to."

Larkin left, promising to return and made his way back through the estate. The darkness was full on now, and he attempted to stick to well-lighted areas, which wasn't easy. The further he got from the centre of the estate, the more relaxed he began to feel. He was even relieved to see the trendsetters of Hoxtonia sitting in their bars, oblivious to what lay around the corner. He wished he could have joined them.

He thought of Rayman and his promise. Could he trust him? Probably not. Should he be contemplating the course of action he was about to take? Probably not. Did he have a choice if he wanted to find Karen? Probably not.

With a sigh of relief at making his way out of the estate in one piece but for little else, he made his way back to Clapham.

The next morning found Larkin again in the cafe, coat collar up, tabloids spread in front of him, mug of coffee at his side. Upon entering he had been surprised to discover not Rayman behind the counter but a surly young black guy.

"You waitin' for Rayman?" the man asked.

Larkin answered that he was.

"Sit there." The man gestured to a table. "He be here soon."

Larkin had done as he was told, and sat there, waiting. He had thought of sitting at another table other than the one the man had specified, just to annoy him, but didn't think it was worth it. The man had just stared at him and stood in front of the doorway to the back of the kitchen, arms folded. He looked more like a sentry than a cafe worker, thought Larkin. His build showed he could handle himself, the faint scars on his face showed he had handled himself, and the bulge in his jacket pocket looked too heavy to be a mobile phone.

Larkin swallowed hard. The coffee seemed to be going down in lumps. He didn't quite know what he was getting into and he still had time to back out. He could just get up and walk away, and that would be that. Instead he stayed where he was and tried to read his paper. Waiting for Rayman to arrive.

About fifteen minutes later, the door opened and Rayman entered.

"Hey, my man Larkin! I knew you'd show."

Larkin turned. The man who had spoken bore only a passing resemblance to the cafe owner he'd met yesterday. This man looked like Rayman's flashy twin brother. He was dressed in a long leather coat, buttoned up, with only the top of a roll-neck sweater showing. All in black. He exuded confidence and focus, with a dangerous kind of swagger. Larkin's doubts had grown from chrysalis stage to full-blown butterflies.

"Hello Rayman," Larkin croaked.

"You didn't disappoint me. Good." He walked towards the back of the cafe and said over his shoulder, "Come on, white boy, we got work to do."

Larkin dumbly followed, the young guy following him. That was it, he was in now.

Once past the bead curtain, he found the back room had a kitchen area where food was prepared and stored, a table and chairs, and some weighing and measuring equipment shelved on one side. Larkin knew immediately what that was. He pointed towards it.

"You still dealing, Rayman?"

"Sure am, man. Can't make a livin' servin' up slop round these parts." His amiable Jamaican accent had been replaced by a much harder East London one. "You met Kwesi, my lieutenant?"

The young guy gave an imperceptible nod.

"We met," said Larkin.

Rayman smiled. "His mother named him Winston but he named himself Kwesi. Wanted something African, take him back to his roots even though he lived all his life round here. Isn't that right, Tottenham boy?"

Kwesi said nothing, just stood impassively. Rayman let out a harsh cackle.

What the fuck have I got myself into? thought Larkin.

"We not messin' about, this is what we do," said Rayman sitting at the table. Kwesi sat also. Larkin followed suit. "You go to the door of the crack house." He pointed at Larkin. "An' say Lonnie sent you. That's important. Lonnie."

"Who's Lonnie?" asked Larkin.

Rayman smiled. "Some junkie. OD'd over there. They'll know. Just sound like you're a junkie, moan a bit. Tell them you're desperate. Sound convincing, they let you in. When you're in there, ask them about the Scottish girl you're lookin' for." Rayman sat back looking pleased with himself.

"That's it?" said Larkin.

"You think it won't work?" asked Rayman with a twinkle in his eye. He sat back, turned to Kwesi. "White boy don't trust Rayman! Don't think he can cut it no more!" He leaned forward again. "Then you better take this." He snapped his fingers. Kwesi produced an automatic from his jacket pocket and laid it on the table in front of Larkin. "Take this." Rayman's eyes were as cold as the gun. "They won't argue with that."

Larkin sat back in disbelief. "Sorry guys," he said, "I think you're confusing me with Bruce Willis. I'm a journalist not a gunslinger." He tried to laugh but the sound died in his throat.

Rayman became deadly serious. "You want the girl? You do as I say."

Larkin looked from one to the other. Two stone faces stared back at him. It was too late to walk out now. He reached across and picked up the gun. It felt heavy in his hand, cold, powerful. He could see why some people thought it was an easy way to respect. He pocketed it. "Now what?"

Rayman gave a chilling smile. In the kitchen's half-light he looked like a devil who'd sweet-talked a soul into Hell.

"Now we do it," he said.

Larkin walked from the cafe to the crack house, watching the street all the time. He could feel Rayman's eyes on him without looking back. The weight of the gun was dragging at his side, and that's where he wanted it to stay. When he reached the steel door he banged on it. No reply. He banged harder, hurting his knuckles in the process. A speaker phone by the side of the door spoke to him.

"Yeah," said a suspicious, monosyllabic voice.

"Here we go," Larkin thought. "Oh, man . . ." he drawled in his best East London druggie drawl, "I need some gear, man . . ."

"Whosis," said the voice, too flat to be considered a question.

A bad Keith Richards impersonator, thought Larkin to himself. "It's Stevie, man . . ."

No reply.

"Lonnie sent me . . ."

"Lonnie," said the voice, almost betraying curiosity.

"Yeah, I think it was Lonnie . . . think that's what he said . . ." Larkin let his voice deliberately trail off. The speaker phone fell silent. What else could he say to persuade them? "Come on, man, I got cash . . ."

"Waitaminnit," the door said, and lapsed into silence.

Larkin stood there for what seemed like a small eternity until he eventually heard the sounds of bolts being withdrawn and locks released, then the door opened a crack.

"In," said the voice. Larkin entered.

The place was a tip. Old, ripped sofas on threadbare carpet, a scarred coffee table covered in junk food containers and gear. Coke can pipes, lighters, spoons. All illuminated by a bare, overhead bulb. The one incongruity was in the far corner, a brand new top-of-the-range TV and video with an expensive-looking CD system beside it.

The guy who'd let Larkin in was wearing oversized jeans, box white trainers and a T-shirt. He was white, or rather his race was Caucasian, since he looked and smelt like he was a stranger to soap and water. He was also, Larkin reckoned, not much older than eleven or twelve. The way he glanced suspiciously over Larkin's shoulder told him there was no one else in. He began to eye Larkin suspiciously.

"Who you?" he asked, slamming the door and nervously fingering the back of his jeans waistband.

Gun, thought Larkin, better move quickly.

"I want to talk to you about someone who used to live here," he said in as calm a voice as possible.

"You're not after gear!" the kid shouted. His hand went for his belt but Larkin was on him. He grabbed the kid and shoved him against the wall, keeping his right arm firmly across the kid's neck. With his left hand he grabbed the gun from the kid's waistband and pointed it at his face. The kid, cockiness now gone, suddenly resembled the scared child he was.

"Now look," Larkin began in his most reasonable voice, "I don't want to hurt you. I'm not the law, I just want some answers to a few questions, then I'm gone, OK?"

The kid nodded hurriedly.

"Good," said Larkin. "Now go and sit over there." He gestured to the sofa. The kid, once released from Larkin's grip, moved shakily towards it and sat down.

The gun felt unpleasant and alien in Larkin's left fist and he didn't like having to do it, but he continued to point it because that was the way the kid had made the play. It may be the only way to make him understand, thought Larkin sadly. Using the gun confirmed his earlier thoughts about it. It did give him a thrill, but also a feeling of disgust. He wanted this over with as quickly as possible.

"There used to be a girl who lived here. Karen. Scottish accent. Remember?"

The kid shook his head.

"Thought not," said Larkin. "You probably weren't born then. What's your name?"

"Karl."

"OK Karl," said Larkin. "Think harder. A girl called Karen. Scottish. Yes?"

"You'll have to ask Theo," muttered Karl, his head aimed at the floor.

"And who's Theo?" asked Larkin.

Suddenly he heard the sound of a key in a lock and turned towards the front door. It opened and there stood the huge, mixed race-guy with the pit bull that Larkin had seen the day before. He was still dressed for a summer's day, still exposing skin. It was hard to tell who looked the fiercest.

"Theo!" shouted Karl, relief all over his face.

That answers one question, thought Larkin.

Theo ignored Karl and stared straight at Larkin. "You'd better have a good reason for bustin' into my house, you motherfucker, or you're dog-meat."

Oh fuck, thought Larkin.

Larkin knew he had to think quickly and act even faster. Weighing up his options he swung the gun on to the dog.

"That bastard comes near me and *he's* dogmeat," he snarled, with a toughness he didn't feel.

Theo and the pit bull stopped in their tracks.

"Sit over there." Larkin gestured to where Karl was. Theo, eyes burning with anger and hatred, perched himself on the edge of the worn-out sofa, body erect, like a firework waiting to explode. The dog stood beside him, eyes never leaving Larkin.

"You're makin' a big mistake, man," said Theo.

"We'll see," Larkin replied. "Now that I've got your attention, though, I want to ask a couple of questions. Karl says you're the man with the answers, Theo."

Theo stared at Karl, mentally snapping the boy's bones. Karl looked from one to the other, not knowing who to be the most scared of.

"I'm sorry, man," Karl was almost in tears. "He said he was a friend of Lonnie's . . ."

Theo looked sharply at him, as if he'd been slapped. Then gradually, a look of slow understanding crept over his features. He sat back, relaxing slightly. A bitter smile curled the edges of his lips and he managed to dredge up a short phlegmy laugh.

"Fuckin' Rayman," he said.

Larkin was taken aback. "What?"

"You're from him, ain'tcha? He put you up to this, fuckin' foolish old cunt." Theo's confidence seemed to be rising with every word. He puffed his chest out, rippling his pecs in the process.

Larkin was thoroughly confused. This wasn't what he had expected. He tried not to let it show, though, since he was still the one with the gun, the one in control. But not for long if he didn't do something about it.

"I don't know what you're talking about," spat Larkin.

"Yeah you do," Theo replied. "Rayman. He's doin' it again. I bet he gave you some bullshit, got you riled up, stuck a shooter in your hand an' sent you here." He sneered at Larkin. "What he do? Give you his poor old Jamaican shit? You been 'ad, man."

Despite the gun, Larkin felt his grip on the situation slipping. He gave it one last go. "I don't give a fuck about that. Just tell me about the girl. She was Scottish. Name of Karen."

"I din't have no Scotch girl. You got the wrong man."

Theo sat, arms folded, thinking he was in charge now. Larkin decided something drastic was needed to refresh his memory. He pointed the gun at the floor between Theo's feet and fired.

His legs jerked up, trying to dodge the bullet and the splinters. The dog sprang back, barking as it went. Karl covered his eyes and screwed his eyes tight shut. The noise of the blast was deafening in the small space. Larkin's ears were ringing like he had been to a Metallica concert.

"Don't fuck me about!" Larkin shouted, probably too loud because of the ringing. He knew he would have to move quickly in case the noise alerted the police, although he doubted they would venture into this area. "Tell me!" he shouted.

"That Scottish bitch was sent by Rayman," Theo blurted out. "To fuckin' Trojan Horse the door open, just like you. Her an' that other whore, they tried to rip me off. It got nasty, the cops came, an' I had to fight to get my name back." He sounded sullen and sulky now.

"Why does Rayman want to get in here?" asked Larkin.

Theo looked at him like he had two heads. "Whassamatter with you, you thick or somethin'? I got all the trade in this area. I got the dealers, the suppliers. I'm the man. He's nothin', he's history. He wants my business!" Anger was welling up inside Theo.

"Listen," said Larkin, his own anger rising as he realised how he had been used. "I don't care about you and Rayman. I just want to know what happened to the girl. Tell me, then I'm gone."

Theo fidgeted in his seat. Either his attention span was wandering and he was getting bored, or some tiny living creatures from the sofa were trying to make their home in his clothes. Even the dog was looking restless. "How the fuck do I know? Whores like that, junkie whores, come and go all the time. After the police came I never saw them again."

Larkin stood for a moment, weighing his options. That looked like all he was going to get. "OK. I'm going to walk out of this door, then I'm gone. Out of your life forever, right?"

Theo just sat there. "Fuck you, man."

Larkin turned to the door and undid the locks, all the time keeping an eye on the two men and the dog. Especially the dog. It looked like a muscle-formed spring, coiled and ready to go at any second. He opened the door to leave, but got no further. For there stood Rayman and Kwesi, all razor smiles, both holding two of the meanest twelve gauge-pump-actions he had ever seen, both itching to use them.

"Well, Stephen, my man, how's it going?" said Rayman, crossing the threshold.

"You fucking used me!" snarled Larkin.

Rayman gave out a laugh. "Used you? You white liberals always ready to listen to a poor black man with a sob story."

"I'm not a liberal," growled Larkin, anger and fear fighting for prominence.

"So you say," he laughed again. "But you listened. An' you believed me." He turned to address Theo. "I'm in charge now, boy. You're history."

Hatred burned in Theo's eyes. "The bosses'll get you."

Rayman gave out another cold laugh. Mr Cheerful. "The bosses don't scare me. They'll do business with me. Like they used to with you."

The two men stared at each other. Theo and his pit bull against Rayman and his human pit bull. Larkin decided to leave them to it and quietly made for the door.

"Where you goin'?" asked Rayman without turning his gaze away from Theo. "Don't you wanna know about your girl?"

"Theo told me. You were her pimp, right? You got her stoned, made her come on to Theo, and when he was distracted tried to muscle in on his patch. But it didn't work. Is that what happened?"

Rayman shrugged. "Sounds about right."

"So where is she now?"

Rayman gestured with his left hand. "Vanished like the mornin' mist..."

Larkin looked at Theo and Rayman. They were standing in the middle of the room, eye to eye, toe to toe, squaring off to each other, lost in their own private grudge war. Karl sat on the sofa, eyes darting between the two, wishing he were somewhere else. Larkin reckoned they were no longer a threat to him so he made his way to the door, holding onto the gun just in case he was wrong. He moved past Rayman, who didn't remove his eyes from Theo. He laughed.

"A pleasure doin' business with you boy. Drop by anytime."

Larkin looked at him, wanting to say something – anything – just to have the last word. Nothing came. Karl looked up as Larkin reached the door. His expression was one of wonder that Larkin was able to walk out so easily, mixed with envy and fear because he couldn't do the same.

Too late, mate, thought Larkin. You're in it for life. However long that'll be.

He clashed the heavy steel door shut behind him as he left.

Larkin stood outside on the street, looking from right to left, shaking from rage, anger and adrenalin. The road was deserted. He swore under his breath and turned left. Glancing down at his quivering fist, he was amazed to see Karl's gun still in it. He looked round for a place to dump it and, seeing a litter bin that was still standing, headed towards it.

No, he thought, if I dump it there, some kid might find it. And then, on the heels of that thought, another one: some kid already had it. I took it off him.

In the gutter was a drain with a broken grille. Perfect, he thought, and dropped the gun down it. He heard the satisfying plop, then took the other gun, the one Rayman had palmed him, out of his pocket and sent that one down too. As he stood up to go, he caught a glimpse of movement from the corner of his eye, something that made his heart skip a beat. Theo's pit bull coming towards him at full pelt.

It was too late to retrieve either gun, so he turned and ran. But it was no good, the dog had his scent and was after him, a relentless missile of slavering muscle and bone, bounding along at breakneck speed.

Larkin ran as fast as he could. His legs raced, his heart pounded and his lungs had a sharp menthol ache as breath went in and out. He gave a quick glance over his shoulder, checked that it was still gaining. It was. His attention elsewhere, he didn't notice a chunk of gutted engine debris on the pavement in front of him. He hit it with his foot, stumbled, tried to right himself, but it was too late. His balance lost, he went over.

The dog was still bearing down on him and even if he made it to his feet, there was no way he could outrun it now. He lay on the pavement, his mind racing. He was done for. Suddenly he saw a whole rusted wheel hub, minus the tyre, lying to his right. Just as the dog was almost on him, he grabbed it.

The pit bull leapt, jaws open, primal blood lust in its eyes. Larkin quickly brought the wheel hub up, groaning at the weight, and caught the dog on its neck. He heaved with all his strength, putting his rage at Rayman and Theo into it, and propelled the dog high in the air, over his head.

Larkin dropped the hub and turned sharply. The dog landed on its back, looking more surprised than anything. It started growling, readying itself for another attack. Larkin was on it fast. He swung the wheel hub, catching the pit bull as it charged on the side of its jaw. It went down and he heard something crack, accompanied by a reluctant whimper. The injury didn't keep it down for long though, and it soon righted itself, ready for another charge.

Larkin was running out of options when suddenly from around the corner came the screech of tyres. He looked up to see a Saab, his own car, come hurtling towards him, Andy at the wheel, driving like the hordes of Hell were pursuing him.

Larkin got to his feet, the dog still running towards him. Andy sized up the situation immediately and drove the car straight for the pit bull. He mounted the pavement and with a dull thud, machine and canine connected. The dog was thrown up in the air, coming to land against the concrete wall of one of the tower blocks.

Larkin ran round to the passenger door and dived in. With another squeal of tyres, Andy spun the car around and they were off. He gave a cock-eyed smile to Larkin as he drove.

"Cavalry to the rescue!" he shouted, laughing.

Larkin just stared at him, panting, shaking. "Where the fuck have you been?" He was furious. "All you had to do was wait in the street and pick me up when I came out."

Andy knew that Larkin was in no mood to argue. "I couldn't get parked!" he said, indignantly. "If I'd stopped anywhere round there the fuckin' wheels would have gone, wouldn't they? I'd 'ave ended up on bricks. So I just circled round."

"You're so fucking unreliable! D'you know that?"

It was Andy's turn to be angry now. "Unreliable? Unreliable? Who just saved your fuckin' life back there? Ay? Ay?" He stared at Larkin, taking his eyes off the road, and narrowly missed an oncoming car. "If it wasn't for me you'd be half a fuckin' pound of badly wrapped mince by now."

Larkin fell silent. Andy had a point, but he wasn't prepared to admit it yet. They sat like that for a while, until Andy asked Larkin how it had gone. He told him.

"I was used, Andy, fucking used."

"And we're no further forward."

Larkin sighed heavily. He was coming down from the adrenalin, the post-rush blues were kicking in. The truth of the situation was begining to sink in. "Nope. A dead end." And then in a smaller voice, "We've lost her, mate."

They drove back towards Clapham in silence.

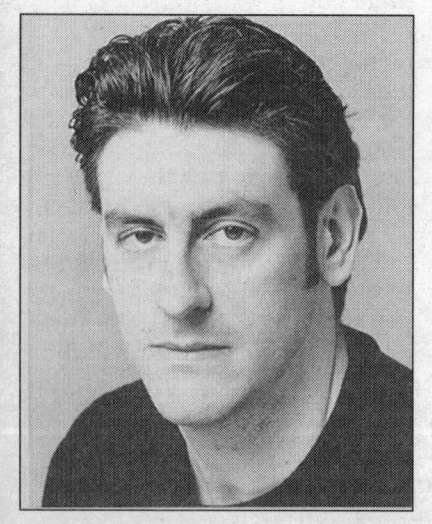

PRAISE FOR MARTYN WAITES

Candleland

'Martyn Waites's *Candleland* bears witness to the flowering of a major new talent…If Phillip Marlowe had been born later, British and Geordie, these are the mean streets he would be cleaning up."—Maxim Jakubowski, The Guardian

'Now working on his third novel, *Candleland*, Waites is shaping up as a compelling and confrontational challenger to the Brit Noir throne, his prose bearing all the hallmarks of a master in the making.'—Bizarre

Little Triggers

'The plot, involving corruption and child abuse, is as dark as a Northumberland winter midnight, and just as chilling. The writing keeps the tension taut and brittle, the characters as real as today's bills…Rough, bitter and cynical, *Little Triggers* is contemporary British noir at its best.'—Jim Driver, Shots

'Snappy dialogue and the plot crackles with tension.'—Mike Ripley, The Daily Telegraph

Mary's Prayer

'*Mary's Prayer* is an assured, powerful debut from a writer sure to find his place in modern crime fiction. Contemporary noir with a distinctly Chandleresque flavour, a significant contribution to the genre.'—Andrew Vachss

murder on wheels
mary scott

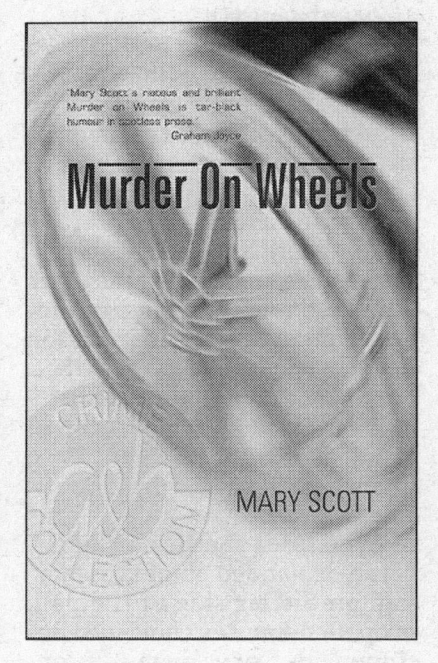

*Extract from Murder on Wheels by Mary Scott
Published by Alllison &Busby
in hardback at £16.99*

'HI SUPERMAN. Been riding any horses recently?'

'Hi cripple.' Bryan removed his large-brimmed black hat – his trademark – manoeuvred his wheelchair sideways in order to lay the hat on a table and grinned at John.

'Not surprised you're late.' John eyed Bryan's studded leather jacket which strained over one shoulder and drooped over the other, the distorted fabric of the waistcoat and black tee-shirt beneath it, the leather trousers clinging to his twisted legs, the boots neatly laced around his wasted ankles. 'Must take you all morning to get into that stuff.' John himself was arrayed in shapeless beige slacks and a yellow crew-necked sweater with a food stain on the front. John's carer was decidedly less meticulous than Bryan's.

'Had a whale of a time last night,' John went on. 'Went to a fancy dress party.' He was lying, of course, he never went anywhere much except to the Centre's Christmas social and for a week at Centreparcs in the summer. But Bryan played along as he always did.

'What d'you go as?'

'Took all my clothes off,' John edged his own chair a little closer as he prepared for the punchline, 'and went as a petrol pump.'

Bryan gave a bark of laughter. He knew full well that absolutely nothing below waist level functioned as far as John was concerned.

'Only thing I wore,' John raised a permanently clenched hand and gestured at his chest, 'was a notice. "Out of Order".'

'Meet anyone?' asked Bryan.

'Absolutely. A dead ringer for Miss Shaggable. Blue eyes, blonde hair, all the right equipment.'

'What did she think of your notice?'

'Only went and moved it, didn't she? Want to know where she put it?' He stopped abruptly. 'Hey, hang on. Here comes the original.' He paused. 'I give you,' he flung his hands wide and trumpeted, 'Miss Shaggable of the year. Our Marion.'

Marion swanned across the polished floorboards in immaculate white trainers. She was in her late twenties – a few years younger than both John and Bryan. But instead of sitting in a wheelchair she walked on her own two legs. And what legs! Long, smooth, tanned even at this time of the year. Above the legs a black linen mini dress grazed the surface of her bum. Around her neck was a thin gold chain. Golden hair fell to her shoulders, framing an oval face. Marion, the gorgeous volunteer, had come, as she always did, to brighten their days. And Bryan hated her for it.

How much had she heard of John's remarks? Everything, Bryan hoped, that would be bound to wind her up. But for the moment she said nothing, betraying her distaste for John's sexism by nothing more than a slight pursing of her pretty mouth. Instead she moved across the room, among the other wheelchairs, encouraging their inhabitants to form a circle for the Activity, bending to listen to their often garbled words, demonstrating by every movement of her perfect body the unconscious power the able-bodied wield over the disabled.

'Who does she think she is?' Bryan demanded of John, as Marion, on the far side of the hall, propelled Laura's chair into position with a sweet, compassionate smile. 'Bloody Florence Nightingale?'

'No lamp,' responded John. 'And better tits.'

The Activity Room was the largest in the Centre. Out of the corner of his eye Bryan could see things going on in the smaller, white-painted rooms which led off the central space. Art in one, pottery in another, gardening in a third. In the Activity Room itself the products of some of these sessions – crudely daubed paintings in primary colours and a collection of dog-eared photomontages – adorned the walls. Everything, everywhere, everyone was bright and busy and falsely, determinedly jolly.

It took a while for Marion to have all seven of the group arranged to her taste. She pushed golden-haired Karen into a prime position in the circle. Karen was sweet-natured as well as pretty – pretty from the neck up that is – and could always be relied on to respond with what Marion called 'a positive attitude' to whatever either staff or volunteers suggested. Then she propelled old Mr D, his head nodding like that of a toy dog in the back window in a car, into place.

The worst aspect of being disabled, Bryan reflected with his usual bitterness as he watched the manoeuvres, was not the constant pain, not the inability simply to get up and go where you chose, not the way people trundled you around as though you were a piece of bulky furniture: no, it was the fact that you had, quite literally, been cut down to size. When people – when women – approached, they bent down to you as though you were a child. Your entire life was lived at waist level – exactly as though you were a child. He had mentioned this to John once and John had nodded, heaved a deep sigh and pronounced, 'Yeah. Six inches up or down and you'd be at boob or crotch level. Scenery'd be greatly improved.' Bryan had given one of his sharp barks of laughter.

'But,' John had gone on seriously and sadly, 'they never seem to think of these things. No imagination, people with legs.'

Meanwhile, this afternoon, Marion now seemed satisfied with the disposition of her charges. She moved into the centre of the circle.

'Today,' she announced, 'we have a visit from the Mushy Pea Community Arts Group.'

'God, not drama again,' complained Bryan sotto voce to John.

'Don't knock it. If it's improvisation and you pick your subject right, you've every chance of copping a feel.'

Neither had spoken loudly enough for Marion to catch the words, but she directed a quelling look at them with her liquid blue eyes. She didn't like whispering in the ranks. What she liked – she now took pains to explain to them – was to offer them an opportunity to explore the implications of their disabilities. She went further than that: to celebrate their disabilities. Bryan looked over at Laura, her limbs twisted into their familiar, grotesque shape, her only communication with the outside world a screen on which, after you had asked her something and waited thirty seconds, her response would scroll, letter by letter, slowly across the silver surface. Not much to celebrate there. He didn't know what was wrong with Laura, in fact he didn't really know what was wrong with anyone here. Left to themselves the Centre's users talked about anything and everything – sex, politics, what they'd seen on TV last night – except their disabilities. It was only do-gooders like Marion who insisted they 'confront', at every possible opportunity, the way they were.

Now Marion was going on about the positive qualities inherent in being 'differently abled'. Bryan sneered silently. If being 'differently abled' was such a great deal, how come people with legs that worked didn't spend all their time 'confronting' the fact that they could run?

'Which is to say,' marion was now saying, 'that you all have special qualities which people like myself don't necessarily enjoy.'

'Tell that to my sex drive,' said John, far too loudly, while Bryan wondered why they all had to be lumped together in this way: as though being in a wheelchair, and not the many other complex emotions, desires and interests, was what defined you as a person.

Marion turned to John, an expression of disapproval on her face, tempered by an obvious effort at patient compassion for those less fortunate than herself.

'It's not as if,' she enunciated carefully, 'I haven't mentioned this before. The Activities are for the benefit of everyone at the Centre. Everyone should be free to enjoy them to the full in his or her own way. But if that enjoyment means spoiling someone else's enjoyment ...' Bryan shot a look at Karen who was now waiting, with an innocent, anxious expression, for the opportunity to show that, in spite of her limitations, she could shine, '... then the person who is doing the spoiling must learn to moderate his or her behaviour. And now,' marion turned to a gap in the circle of chairs, exposing the backs of long, shapely thighs to her audience, 'let's have a big welcome for our guests today.' And everyone made a more or less successful effort at bringing their twisted hands into contact with each other.

The Mushy Pea Company turned out to be a group of obscenely fit young people in skintight, tie-dyed costumes of various, bilious shades of green. They came hurtling, somersaulting and cartwheeling into the immobile circle, energy radiating from their lithe bodies, enthusiasm shining from their faces – as though they believed their efforts could magically imbue their silent watchers with the qualities they themselves so histrionically expressed. When they spoke, they did so in loud, ringing tones with, after every half a dozen words, a pause which would on the printed page have appeared as !!! or ???.

'For God's sake,' said Bryan to John, 'it's like being back in school.'

'You're just jealous because even your carer couldn't squeeze you into one of those get-ups. Look at the bum on that one,' and John pointed to the nearest Mushy Pea girl.

An hour later. An hour in which they had all strained and struggled. Not just to manoeuvre their chairs in accordance with the movements of the improvisation which they had been required to devise. But with the effort of, as the Mushy Pea people put it, finding something positive to improvise about being in a chair. John had ignored all of the Community Arts Group's suggestions and Marion's scarcely concealed frowns and dragooned the uncomprehending Karen into an improvisation breathtaking in its salaciousness. Bryan looked on with only half his mind on the sequence he was devising with Kenny. Kenny was one of the few of them who wasn't in a wheelchair. He had learning difficulties and recently – as part of his preparation for independent living – had been required to make his way on his own to the sessions at the Centre. Which meant he always got distracted by something en route: which meant he was always late.

'Doesn't it go quick?' he keened at Bryan, as he had, mid-Activity, each afternoon for the past three weeks. Then he carried on waving his arms in a vaguely jangling fashion over his head, occasionally swooping towards the wheelchair and flourishing his open palms in Bryan's face. For some reason (accepted by the green-clad mob as celebrating an alternative mode of movement) he was being the sea ebbing back and forth across a beach.

'I went to the seaside once,' he explained, 'for a whole day.'

Initially Bryan had said that his contribution to 'alternative modes of movement' would be to be a large, black rock, capable of withstanding whatever buffeting the waves threw at him. It would be years, he added, embroidering on his theme, before even minute signs of erosion were visible on his surface to the naked eye.

But both Marion and the Mushy Pea people were united in opposition. He couldn't just sit there! they chorused. He would have to be a pebble – several pebbles if he preferred – and go with the flow. With a sigh he did as they said. He wondered, wearily, for the umpteenth time, as he swivelled his chair right and left, why he came to the Centre. But he knew the answer. At first he had come because they had insisted it would help him come to terms with what had happened; and because there was nowhere else to go. Now he came for a dose – as bracing as a shot in the arm – of John's outrageous, acerbic, over-the-top heckling: for John's undiminished courage in refusing to act the part allotted him. And why did John come? He knew the answer to that too, he reflected as he swung in a parody of a dance around Kenny's agile, but unco-ordinated frame. John came because this was his only opportunity to rebel against his fate. He came because the Centre was a substitute for the family who had long ago abandoned him in a long-stay hospital. He came because here he could rebel to his heart's content; and no one would throw him out. After all – Bryan spared a moment for a fleeting glance at John and nearly collided with Kenny as the latter flung himself over-enthusiastically into an imitation of a bursting breaker – the house John shared with five other people – some with mental as well as physical disabilities – wasn't exactly a bed of roses. Not that John ever complained, in fact he was studious about avoiding any mention of the place. But Bryan could tell.

And now the Activity was over. John was at his elbow, nudging him.

'See that Karen? Reckon she really meant what she said to me in the improvisation? Improvised, yes, but it might have come from the heart. Okay, she's a cripple, but beggars can't be choosers. Be seeing you, mate.' He turned his chair in Karen's direction, then turned back. 'You'll be waiting for the library, won't you?' Bryan nodded. John turned his chair once more and moved away.

The library. For a year now books had been Bryan's major solace. At home, now he was at home, his kind, meticulous carer reminded him every moment of his disabilities. He would fetch this, adjust that, stoop with infinite patience to tie Bryan's feet into his black, laced boots. He would lift Bryan onto the toilet, ease him, with the help of the specially fitted hoist, into the bath. Bryan had been lucky with his carer. He had been lucky too to get a housing association flat. The association had fitted all the adaptations so he didn't, as John did, have to live in a shared house. He was lucky with the physical things. But just because you were in a wheelchair didn't mean you'd lost your mind. Nor your appetite for action. So, apart from the diversion of his repartee with John, books had become Bryan's sole source of excitement. Why, then, did he feel a dragging reluctance as he wheeled himself in the direction of the reception hall outside which, in a few moments, the mobile library would pull up?

He knew why. At first his passion had been for thrillers. Frederick Forsyth, Ken Follett, stories whose action took him, as his career once had, across the globe. Then, as he began to come to terms with his own newly limited world, his horizons narrowed to more domestic tales: to whodunnits. He'd read them all. A solid course of Agatha Christie, followed by Dorothy L. Sayers, P.D. James, Ruth Rendell, even an excursion (which he did not enjoy) into the lesbian sleuth novels published by The Women's Press. Once each of them had posed an impenetrable, absorbing puzzle. Now, by half-way through, he always had the villain taped.

Raji was pushing a trolley of books through the swing doors of the main entrance. He stopped when he saw Bryan.

'Got a Patricia Cornwell for you. Or if not, the new Nicci French. Or Reggie Nadelson? Or take all three. You're allowed that many.'

Bryan nodded and thanked him and stowed the books in his lap. Raji turned his attention to helping a couple of other Centre users select videos and CDs while Bryan trundled back into the Activity space where Marion had reassembled her charges after their refreshment break. She always helped with the refreshments; many of the Centre's users were unable to swallow a carton of orange juice without assistance and others of them dribbled. She turned to Bryan with a smile of bright enthusiasm.

'More books? The amount you read you ought to try your hand at creative writing. Especially as you say you can solve all those. Perhaps we should get a tutor.'

Bryan forbore to remind her that she had invited a perfectly good such tutor to the Centre only a month ago, that everyone had enjoyed the tutor's visit and that she was not asked to return because she failed to encourage them to focus, for even a minute of the session, on their disabilities. He also forbore to mention that Marion's idea of creative writing had one thing in common with the other Activities she arranged: they were all pointless. The Centre's users improvised Drama, but none of them had a hope in hell of becoming even amateur actors; they did Pottery and produced lopsided artefacts which no one would ever display, let alone buy; they practised Percussion and achieved the vilest cacophony Bryan had ever heard; and they raised plants from seeds and cuttings for the Centre's grubby garden, which were promptly trampled or uprooted by teenagers from the estate. He forbore to mention these things because he hadn't the least ambition to write about crime. Reading about it allowed him a vicarious involvement in dramatic action. To write about it would be to admit that he could never have a slice of that action in the real world ever again. No, if he were to pursue his passion for detection any further – he looked down with apathy at the books in his lap – he would far rather solve an actual crime. But of course no one would ever ask him, he would never have the opportunity to do such a thing. But there was always – the idea struck him suddenly – the other side of the coin. He could commit a crime – technically he was already doing so. He toyed idly with the idea. After all, he had the proven ability to plan, to keep things under wraps, to lay a false trail, to fox the opposition. Any crime he committed – he was sure of it – would be perfect, utterly undetectable by the likes of Miss Marple or Chief Inspector Wexford. It would be a crime, he thought, enjoying the sudden, now unfamiliar excitement at a new project, an excitement which had once been part of daily life, that would baffle the best brains which Scotland Yard could deploy in its solution.

But a crime, he reflected, excitement ebbing away, required a victim. Still, no harm in trying on the idea – the first real one he'd had for months – for size. He studied Laura, twisted in her chair, her mouth working soundlessly. Might be doing her a favour to put her out of her misery. Or there was John; after all, if you looked at him objectively, stripped of his bravado, what kind of a life did he have? The same question might be asked of any one of the group, himself included, now gathered, a captive audience, around Marion's perfect form.

It was Marion's voice that intruded on his reverie, brought him back to earth with a bump. Far from being the criminal brain of the century, he was a useless cripple. For Marion was insisting cheerily that he decide in which aspects of making decorations for the Christmas social he would like to be involved. She had a quantity of crepe paper and Sellotape and scissors and brightly coloured ribbons laid out on the table beside her. She was reiterating – he obviously hadn't heard her first time round – that the Mayor would be coming and they must all do their best to put on a good show if they wanted to be sure of next year's funding. And Bryan was back in kindergarten being told over and over – so often that it made a lasting impression on him for years to come – that he must join in, must learn to practise practical skills.

He shot Marion a look of pure, black venom. He'd never learned them. He'd learned to use his brain to earn money, his body to face danger. But he was hopeless with his hands, always had been, couldn't even put up a shelf, always paid someone else to do even the most simple domestic tasks. How many cripples, he thought, a bubble of hysterical laughter rising to his lips, does it take to change a light bulb? He must ask John sometime and see what he came up with.

Luckily for him John had filled the lengthening, expectant silence. 'Not the Mayor again!' he announced loudly. 'It's the feel-good factor. For her, not for us. Laying hands on a few cripples. Have you seen the hairs on her chin? I reckon she's a lesbian.'

Marion opened her mouth to speak, but again John got in first.

'If they really had our interests at heart, they'd hire a few strippers. Chippendales for the girls. And get a licence to sell booze. I can't even remember how a decent pint tastes. And as for getting out of my head, forget it. Tell me this...' he paused, tilting his face up towards Marion, his eyes as bright as a bird's, '... why is it only people with legs get a chance to get legless?'

He had drawn Marion's fire away from Bryan. She was fully occupied with reproving John. Was that what John had intended, had he read on Bryan's face what Bryan felt? If he had, he'd never say so. In the meantime, the moment had passed and Bryan was agreeing that yes, he thought he was quite up for cutting stars out of silver foil.

The afternoon was over. Disabled transport was at the door. Bryan's carer Edward was there with the car.

'See you down the pub later?' called John as he was wheeled away. That's what he always said when they parted, though Bryan and he never met in any pub and, as far as Bryan could tell, John never had the opportunity to drink any alcohol at all.

Bryan waited as Edward lifted the three hardback volumes from his lap. He settled his black hat on his head and turned to look at Marion shrugging her shoulders into a stylish, maxi-length, black overcoat. Where was she going now, what kind of active, satisfying life did she lead when she had finished with her slumming? He hated her, he thought, as Edward laid a gentle hand on his shoulder. He hated her for being so bright and so beautiful. For being so perfect and so patronising. But he didn't hate her enough to hurt her.

'No more than two children in the shop.' The words were roughly printed on a scrap of card ripped from a cash-and-carry carton, and the card was taped inside the Patels' shop window. Lee and Danny and Rick were all twelve years old, but only Lee could read the sign without pointing to each letter in turn and mouthing the words under his breath. And only Lee had worked out a scam so they could get what they wanted.

This is what they did. Under his instruction they waited until a woman with three small children went into the shop (children with parents didn't count as children), then Lee tagged along as though he was one of the family. Inside, Mr Patel stood to the left, by the till, and Mrs Patel sat to the right; that way they had a clear view along the shop's two aisles. But – Lee had sussed this – there was a blind spot at the further end of the shop where the two aisles met. All he had to do was to get Mrs Patel to follow him along the aisle – he picked several items from the shelves, furtively, as though he meant to pocket them – and entice her round the blind spot and into the left hand aisle. Then Rick and Danny – Lee made sure he never did the actual nicking himself – had a clear field among the alcopops in the right-hand aisle. Meanwhile Lee legged it out along the left-hand aisle, pushing past the toddlers, shouting and waving his hands as though he was running away from something, as though he had something to hide. Which he didn't. If Mr and Mrs Patel decided to call the Bill, they'd find him squeaky clean. But they never did. They just went sadly back into their shop and resigned themselves to a routine of watching the aisles and selling very little of anything.

Lee led Rick and Danny, racing and whooping, to the other end of the mall. They peeled the caps from the bottles with their teeth, drank, then competed at hitting pigeons with the caps. That soon got dull. Lee led them to the Community Centre where they peered through the window and made faces at the people in wheelchairs inside.

But that wasn't much of a buzz either.

'Let's go see if my mum's home,' suggested Danny.

'Let's go see if my sister's got anything to eat,' proposed Rick.

'Might as well go back to school.' Lee's voice was thick with scorn. And then – as always – he came up with the best idea. 'Let's go to the park and burn the shelter down.'

The shelter stood beneath barebranched trees, lapped by a thick carpet of the leaves the trees had shed. It was made of weatherproofed wood, its roof was painted red. In the spring old men sat there with their grey-muzzled dogs. In the summer couples had it off inside. This autumn someone had spray-canned graffiti all over it.

Lee and Danny and Rick had tried to burn it down several times before. But they'd always ended up with a smouldering, disappointing wisp of dying smoke. This time Lee had the other two kids bank piles of dry leaves around the walls: and this time it worked. The leaves caught, crackling, then ignited the wood of the shelter. Hot flames lapped towards the three of them, warming them. It was nice here. But it would be time, soon, for Lee to order them to go: someone was bound to see the blaze and then the Fire Service would be on the scene.

Rick hummed the theme tune from London's Burning.

Danny hummed the theme tune from Casualty.

And then they all saw it. A figure upright and incandescent in the midst of the flames.

DCI Dawson closed the file which lay in front of him on the unfamiliar desk, deposited it on the stack of files to his left and opened another. They all made depressing reading. Three officers up on assault charges. One set for a disciplinary for sexual harassment. A serious complaint from leaders of the ethnic minority communities of rampant racism in the force.

Community relations in general practically non-existent. Morale and clear-up rate low, bully-boy tactics rife. But then he knew he was on a sticky wicket when he applied for the transfer. That's why he was here, at what was, in his view, the sharp end of the Met's operations – as the new Guvnor of the CID force with the worst record of any in the whole of London.

He sighed grimly as he thought of the sullen response from his assembled team to his initial pep talk. Male almost to a man, they were among the most unprepossessing lot he had come across since he joined the force. Broad-shouldered, thickset, with necks like bulls and brains, he judged, to match. They'd clearly gone out of their way to make the most of the menace of their bulk: crew cuts were the order of the day and their clothes – heavy black leather jackets, boots and jeans – must make them a walking, terrifying nightmare to innocent people on the streets. But he saw behind the facade. They were pot-bellied, they were flabby, lax; soft from years of having it their own way. He doubted any one of them could run a hundred yards without wheezing and certainly they all stood to gain by losing a couple of stone in weight. They soon would. Mentally as well as physically he'd have them leaner, fitter, trimmer within months. As fit as he was. He smiled again as he recalled first the disbelief, then the brutish challenge in their eyes. He knew what a picture he himself presented. Six foot two, yes, but in all other respects as like to them as chalk to cheese. He'd watched them taking the measure of his wiry body, noting the neat, silver-grey suit, the perfectly knotted dark grey tie, the carefully pressed shirt (he, too, dressed for effect) and he knew they'd push him as far as they could. But he also knew – as they didn't – that beneath his facade was a core of pure steel.

He wouldn't just change the way they looked, he'd change their attitude. And fast – had to if he was to turn the reputation of the neighbourhood around. Because it wasn't only his team who presented the toughest challenge he'd ever faced. The manor they policed was one of the grubbiest, poorest, most crime-infested corners of the capital. Surrounded on all sides by the affluent suburbs of northwest London, Crandon had become synonymous with urban ills since the 1980s. Poll tax riots, race riots, just plain for-the-hell-of-it riots – Crandon had staged them all. Parts of it had been no-go areas for years and now it was peopled almost entirely by a seedy underclass. He closed another file, rose and looked out of the grime-streaked window of his new office at the grey wasteland below. Tower blocks on the horizon, in the middle-distance a litter-strewn apology for a park with graffiti defacing the walls and derelicts

crime time 3.2 167

on every bench; closer still a scrap yard, its tatty premises protected by anti-climb paint and razor wire. He shifted his gaze higher and to the left and there was the skyline of civilised London: the Telecom Tower, the dome of St. Paul's and beyond, the glittering apex of Canary Wharf. It might have been a million miles away.

So might New Scotland Yard. He recalled briefly the view from the window there as he had stared out over busy, affluent Victoria Street. His eyes followed a green No. 24 bus as he waited for the panel's decision. Surely they could not refuse his application. It wouldn't be promotion, only a sideways transfer, so it was no skin off the Met's nose financially speaking. And he'd been chained to a desk job for more than two years now.

They hadn't refused. And here he was. He returned to his desk and his reading. Crandon had, in the main, been developed in the sixties and seventies. The local council had poured money for social housing into the area, and had created a ghetto. Benefit fraudsters, drug addicts, sickos, winos, the unemployed, the unemployable, problem families, single parents, extended clans of refugees who spoke no English; all these had been decanted from the better-off suburbs to a place where they would cause no nuisance to their neighbours – because their neighbours were also a nuisance.

A sink neighbourhood comprised of sink estates, and the worst of them all, the scum in the wastepipe, was the Carleton Park Estate. Built as a model community with landscaped lawns and a shopping mall all its own it had swiftly degenerated into a violent slum. The picture was familiar, he thought, as he absorbed the details. Only here it had gone to extremes. Carleton Park Estate had been used in the late eighties as a dumping ground for homeless families. Which meant dysfunctional families. Which meant an intolerably high child density. Which meant – ten years on – an explosively high concentration of teenagers with nothing to do and nowhere to do it. One by one the major chains had deserted the purpose-built retail outlets in the mall. No Boots, no Safeways, not even a Nisa store. No one who lived on the estate had money to buy consumer goods, but plenty of them had the temerity to try to steal them – a perfect recipe for economic decay. All that now remained were a couple of beleaguered, steel-grilled shops run by – he turned the page and found his assumptions confirmed – a Mr and Mrs Patel and a Mr Singh. The seedy pub (which, he inferred from his reading, did more trade in drugs than it did in alcohol) was managed by a Jerry O'Flaherty. The minicab company was run by a Mr Ali. Only the fish and chip shop had a proprietor – one Joe Parker – with an indigenous, family-lived-here-since-the-year-dot sort of name.

So that was it. The Carleton Park Estate was his starting point, the proving ground for his radical, kill or cure tactics. First he'd begin the re-education of his force, then he'd put them all, man and boy, on the case. This time next year, he thought, his enthusiasm rising above the grey pallor of his surroundings, the Carleton Park Estate would be safe for decent people to walk at night. For there were decent people there. Pensioners terrified to step outside in case their lives and their savings were at risk. Families struggling to bring up law-abiding kids. Ethnic minority community leaders with the interests of the people they represented at heart. Local councillors who wanted to do the best for their constituents. He would get them all on his side, just as he would the men under his command. The drab room in which he sat – besieged by hostile staff, becalmed in a sea of petty crime – receded as he envisioned a future of ordered, orderly, neighbourly and above all normal people going about their normal business. Zero tolerance, he thought. Mop up the winos. Drive the drug users off the streets. Crack down on petty theft. Catch the TWOCers red-handed. Liaise with the council to create defensible space. He would clean this place up if it killed him. For DCI Dawson wasn't just a policeman. He was – that rare bird – a man with a mission. He felt the flush of excitement rise from his neck and stain his face at the thought of the rewards ahead.

A rap on his door.

'Come!' he barked.

The door opened a fraction. One of the most pug-faced, the most bullish of his subordinates inserted his head into the gap.

'Thought you'd want to know, Guv. Report's come in from the Carleton Park Estate.'

'A domestic? Ram raiders?' DCI Dawson was on his feet ready to meet the challenge.

'Actually, Guv,' the man's eyes were thin, black, spiteful pinpricks of malice. 'It's a bit more serious than that.'

MARY SCOTT

... is the author of an award-winning literary novel, *Not in Newbury*, and a collection of short stories, *Nudists May be Encountered*. her many stories have been published in magazines and anthologies including the *Penguin Book of Contemporary Women's Short Stories*.

PRAISE FOR MARY SCOTT

Not in Newbury
"Mary Scott is an adventurous and challenging writer whose portraits of London life are both precise and mordant – a raare combination!"—Jim Crace

Nudists May Be Encountered
"A confident new writer with a truly fresh way of writing."—Malcolm Bradbury

"Each story forms an exquisitely executed comment on male-female relationships, observed with a wit and observation that mark the debut of a fine talent."—Time Out

the puppet show
patrick redmond

The Puppet Show by Patrick Redmond Published by Hodder in Hardback at £16.99

Prologue
Bow, East London, 1984

'Where's Michael? Why isn't he here? I want to say goodbye.' Sean put down the bag he was carrying and stared at the ground. His face was flushed, his lip starting to tremble.

Susan Cooper, who had been following with his suitcase, took a deep breath. 'I told you, Sean, we can't find him.'

'But I want to say goodbye. I won't go without saying goodbye!'

The two of them stood on the pavement outside the Children's Home. It was a square slab of Victorian grey stone; the only detached house on its side of the street. Facing it was a council estate, a concrete maze that blocked out the sun and cast the narrow street into shadow.

Tom Reynolds, waiting in the car, now turned off the engine and made as if to get out. Susan shook her head. They were running late as it was. A few more minutes and there was no chance of avoiding the rush-hour traffic. A group of boys from the council estate played football in the road, trading insults with every shot, oblivious to the farewell scene that was being enacted before them.

She shivered. Though only early October, there was a sharpness in the wind that warned of approaching winter. An elderly couple walking by, laden with groceries, gave Sean a sympathetic look. Silently she cursed Michael. She really didn't need this now. 'I told you, Sean,' she said, more sharply than she intended, 'we can't find him. I'm sorry, but that's how it is.'

'Then I'm not going! I don't want to go! You can't make me!'

His gentle eyes were full of fear. Immediately she felt ashamed. Crouching down beside him, she brushed a lock of blond hair from his forehead. 'I'm sorry. I didn't mean to snap. We have tried to find him, really we have. You know what he's like. He's probably just got held up.'

'He doesn't want to be here.'

'Of course he does.' She kissed his cheek. 'He's your best friend. He wouldn't want to miss this.'

'He said he hated me and that he was glad I was going away. He said—' Sean's eyes were filling with tears '—he said that foster parents just act nice to trick you, and once I'm in their house they'll keep me in their cellar and pay the social worker not to say anything and …'

Susan made soothing noises. 'He's just teasing you. The Andersons are kind people, Sean. You don't think I'd let you stay with people who weren't kind, do you?'

He didn't answer. She took his chin in her hand and looked into his face. 'Do you?'

Slowly he shook his head.

'They've got that lovely big garden and two dogs. You'll be happy with them, Sean. I promise you will.'

A horn blasted, followed by a raised voice: a driver cursing because the road was blocked by Tom's car. She couldn't delay any longer. 'Let's get you settled. Tom said you can sit in the front and listen to one of your tapes.'

Tom opened the passenger door and grinned at Sean. 'Ready then, mate?' There was another blast from the horn. Tom leaned out of his window. 'Hang on!' He ruffled Sean's hair. 'Let's see if we can break the land speed record on the motorway, eh?' Sean managed a smile while Susan helped him fasten his seat belt. 'You will come and see me?' he asked her anxiously.

'Try and stop me.'

He still looked worried. 'You won't forget about my photograph? You will keep looking?'

'Of course. We'll find it. Don't worry.'

She watched the car move away down the road. The boys from the estate let the vehicle pass, then continued with their game. As she watched, an unspoken prayer echoed in her mind. Oh God, please let this be a happy ending. He's only nine, and he's suffered enough. He deserves a happy ending.

Sadly, she turned and walked back into the house.

Michael stood at the end of the

road, watching Susan hug Sean.

His school bag hung from his shoulder. He should have been back an hour ago. Instead he had wandered the streets, killing time. It should have been over by now.

He could tell that Sean was crying. Knew that he was frightened. Knew whose fault it was too.

Shame rose up in him, together with other, more complicated feelings he didn't want to acknowledge. Angrily he pushed them down. Sean was a baby and deserved to be scared.

He turned away, towards the tiny garage on the corner. The forecourt gate was unlocked, and he darted across it, jumped on to a crate and up on to the wall that ran along the back of the houses. Behind him he heard an angry roar from the garage owner.

After walking along the wall, slowly to keep his balance, he dropped down into the back garden of the Home. A postage stamp with weeds. Entering by the back door, he moved through the storage room and past the kitchen. He could hear voices. Preparations had started for the evening meal. Bolognese, judging by the smell. Mince and tins of processed tomatoes, seasoned with wedges of onion, ladled on to spaghetti. They'd had the same dish four nights ago. But it was a simple meal, and there were twenty of them to feed.

He came to the main hall. The air was stale and tinged with the smell of damp. The paint on the walls was dirty. From the outside the house had a certain grandeur, but inside everything was shabby and in need of repair. The front door faced him. Beside it was a noticeboard and a pile of coats and bags. To his left was the television room. The older children were watching motor racing while the younger ones shouted in vain for cartoons.

The front door was opening. Not wanting Susan to see him, he darted up the stairs to the first floor, a hall surrounded by bedrooms. Someone was listening to Duran Duran behind one of the doors. Another door opened and Mr Cook stepped out. He was one of the members of staff who lived on the premises. He smiled at Michael, his cherubic face, pale beard and bright red cardigan making him look like an oversized teddy bear. 'Did you say goodbye to Sean?'

'Yes.'

'You must be feeling sad. Do you want to talk?' His voice was warm, his expression friendly. Michael felt his skin crawl. Everyone knew what Mr Cook's friendship was all about. Scowling, he hurried up to the second floor.

His room was at the front of the house, buried in the eaves of the roof. It had a low ceiling, two beds and bare walls. When first he'd come here they had been allowed to hang posters, but not now. Something about damaging the paintwork. As if pieces of Blu Tack would make it any worse.

His own bed was a mess of sheets and blankets. What had been Sean's bed for the last year was now just a bare mattress. The bedding was at the laundry, being cleaned in preparation for the new occupant who would arrive next week. A boy of his own age whose name he couldn't remember, though Susan had told him. She had also told him that he must help the new arrival settle in. Show him the ropes. Just as he had done with Sean. He sat down on his bed, facing the window. His only view was of the council estate. The views at the rear were better. From Brian's room, over the rows of houses, you could see the tops of the skyscrapers of the City of London itself. The City. The magic square mile. The financial heart of the country, so Brian had told him, where unimaginable fortunes were won and lost every day.

Brian was fifteen. Soon he would be leaving the Home, going to make his own fortune. Brian boasted that he would be a millionaire by the time he was twenty-five, with a big house in the West End and a mansion in the country, a fleet of expensive cars, a wardrobe of designer clothes, and servants to carry out his every command. Brian was full of dreams. Perhaps they would come true. In spite of everything he had experienced, Michael still hung on to the belief that sometimes dreams did come true.

He gazed out of his window but saw nothing. In his head he imagined himself as Dick Whittington, walking through the City, dazzled by the glare of streets that were paved with gold.

He was still sitting there half an hour later when Susan came to hunt for Sean's photograph. His presence startled her. She hadn't realised that he'd returned.

'What happened to you?' she demanded.

He ignored her.

'You should have been there.'

A shrug of the shoulders.

'Sean was really hurt.'

'So?'

'So, you should have been there. You're his best friend.'

'I don't care.'

The sight of his back was annoying her. 'That was a wicked thing to do. Telling him all those lies about the Andersons.'

'They're not lies.' 'You really frightened him. You know he believes every word you tell him.'

'Not my fault. Stupid baby. Stupid fuckin' baby!'

A reprimand was called for but she didn't have the heart. She understood the reasons for his anger, even if there was nothing she could do to alleviate them.

'It doesn't have to be the end,' she said gently. 'You can still visit each other.'

'Oh sure! Canterbury's just down the road. I can walk there after school!'

He turned to look at her. She studied his face: the thatch of black hair, the harsh features that seemed too old for a boy of ten, and the accusatory blue eyes that always made her feel guilty. An angry face, with nothing that could be called attractive. Jenny, one of the social workers, believed that one day he would grow into his looks and be quite the lady-killer. She hoped so. Good looks were an advantage, and children like Michael needed all the advantages they could get.

It had gone six o'clock. Her own family would be waiting for her. 'I have to go. Will you be OK?'

He turned back to the window. 'Course.'

She didn't want to leave it like this. He needed her, in spite of the show of bravado. But so did her own family.

Where are they, she thought suddenly, all the barren couples searching for a child to take into their homes and pour their love upon? She knew they existed. But she also knew that most wanted a newborn baby or a sweet child like Sean who was still sufficiently undamaged to be able to respond to that love. Few wanted a child like Michael, a child who had somehow fallen through the cracks and who stared out at the world with eyes that were centuries old, full of suspicion and the dark shadows of neglect.

'I can stay a bit longer if you want.'

Another shrug.

She felt bad, but not as much as she would have done once. She had learned long ago not to care too much. It would just break her heart if she did.

'I'll be here tomorrow. We'll talk after school. You haven't lost him, Mike. Canterbury's not that far away.'

'Don't care.'

'Yes, you do.'

She left the room. He remained on the bed, facing the window.

That night, while the rest of the Home slept, he ran away.

After gathering together some clothes and those few possessions he wished to keep, he crept downstairs. As he slid through the dark, he could hear the occasional sigh of someone's breathing, but otherwise all was silence. The Home was always so full of noise. Sometimes he thought it would drive him mad, but now he found its absence eerie.

In the hallway he searched through the school bags and crammed his belongings into one that was bigger than his own. Then he began to move from room to room. The front and back doors would be locked. The windows were supposed to be locked too, but he knew that this was often overlooked. He found what he was looking for in the television room and climbed out into the night.

He walked through largely empty streets, the houses packed so tightly together that they looked as if they might burst. He passed the corner shop, from which he'd stolen sweets and comics, and the old church with the derelict graveyard that he had told Sean was haunted. His way was illuminated by the weak streetlamps and the occasional light from a window. The night was cold and still. The few people about were mostly returning from pubs and paid him no attention, though one middle-aged man, walking his dog, did turn and stare. He quickened his pace, hurrying away towards the light and noise of Mile End Road.

The road itself was quietening now, the huge thoroughfare empty save for the last of the evening's traffic making its way home to Essex or down into the City and on towards the late-night drinking clubs of the West End. The pavements, too, were emptying as the pubs and restaurants had closed. What life there was now congregated around a handful of takeaways and late-night cafés.

It started to rain. He went into one of the cafés, a small but cheerful place full of the smell of greasy food, with pictures of film stars on the wall and jazz music playing softly from a battered loudspeaker. The smell made him hungry. Though he had eaten nothing at supper, he wanted to conserve what money he had, so he bought only a coke and a packet of crisps before sitting at a table in the corner by the window, waiting for the rain to stop.

As soon as he returned from the kitchen, Joe Green noticed the boy sitting alone.

He nudged his nephew Sam, whose head was buried in a music magazine. 'Did that kid come on 'is own?'

'What kid?' asked Sam, without looking up.

'How many kids are there?'

Sam raise his head, nodded and returned to his magazine.

The boy had finished his crisps and was now sipping from his can. The sight of him troubled Joe. He shouldn't be out on his own. Not at this time of night.

The café was virtually empty, the only other customers two youths who were laughing as they tucked into pizza and chips. Joe assumed they were students from Queen Mary College, on their way back after a party. The boy's eyes were continually drawn to them. Joe guessed the reason why. He went back to the kitchen, piled chips on to a plate, then approached the table in the corner. The pavement outside was covered in litter and he made a mental note to sweep it away later.

He cleared his throat. 'Mind if I sit down?'

The boy stared at him with eyes that were suspicious and hostile. Joe smiled. 'Well?' No answer. Taking silence as consent, Joe sat down and pushed the plate towards the boy. 'My supper. Can't manage 'em all. Want some?'

The boy looked at the plate, then back at Joe. His eyes were still wary. Joe continued to smile. 'Go on. You'll enjoy 'em more than me.'

The boy reached for a chip. He ate it slowly and then reached for another. His eyes remained fixed on Joe. Unsettling eyes; troubled and full of anger. Joe gestured to the plate. 'Taste OK?'

The boy nodded.

'Don't want this place gettin' a bad name. Want ketchup?'

Another nod. Joe reached for the plastic tomato at the centre of the table and poured some sauce on to the side of the plate. 'What's your name?' he asked.

'What's yours?'

'Joe Green. To you, it's Joe sir.'

The eyes softened a little. 'Stupid name.'

'What's yours, then?'

No answer. 'The man with no name,' said Joe. 'Like Clint Eastwood. Where you goin', Clint?'

'Michael,' said the boy suddenly.

'Michael or Mike?'

'Don't mind.'

'Mike, then. Where you goin', Mike?'

The boy shrugged.

'Must be goin' somewhere. Gone midnight. No one's out this late 'less they're goin' somewhere.'

The boy lowered his eyes, reached for another chip and dipped it in the ketchup.

'Do your mum an' dad know you're 'ere?'

'Don't 'ave none.'

Joe whistled softly. 'Sorry about that, Mike. I really am.'

The boy gave another shrug. He had a spot of ketchup below his bottom lip. Joe fought an urge to reach across the table and wipe it away. 'It's late, Mike. Ain't you got somewhere to go?'

No answer.

'Shouldn't be out on your own. Not at your age. Ain't there somewhere you can go?'

'There's some people. The Andersons. They live in Canterbury. Got a big house with a garden.' The boy stared down at the table. 'Want me to live there. Said I can 'ave my own room and anythin' else I want. I could go there.'

'Sounds good.'

'I could go there,' repeated the boy. He swallowed. 'If I wanted to.'

'Bit late to go tonight, though,' suggested Joe.

A nod.

'So what you goin' to do, then? Wander round on your own?'

'Maybe.'

'Yeah, maybe.'

Joe sat back in his chair and looked out of the window. The pavement was empty now, save for a lone figure in a dirty coat, shuffling along on the other side of the road carrying a collection of bags. A tramp, judging by the state of him. Someone with no home and nowhere to go. Joe turned back to the boy. 'It's a rough world out there. Too rough for a kid like you. Ain't you got somewhere to go?'

No answer. Joe took the boy's chin in his hand and looked into his face.

'Listen, Mike. I don't know where you've come from. What you're runnin' from. If you don't want to tell me, then that's your business. But believe me, anything's got to be better than being out there on your own.' He paused, smiling gently. 'Don't you think?'

At first nothing. Then slowly the boy nodded.

'So,' continued Joe. 'You got somewhere to go?'

For a moment the eyes were filled with a desperate longing. Just for a moment. Then they became as blank as glass. Another nod.

The plate was empty. Joe looked at his watch. 'Still hungry?'

'Yeah.'

'We don't close for half an hour. Think we've some chocolate cake left. What d'you say I get you a piece, and then I'll run you back to where you've got to go. Shouldn't be walkin' round on your own. Not this time of night.'

The boy nodded.

'You sit there. Back in a minute.'

Joe went into the kitchen. There was some cake left. He cut a large slice.

But when he returned to the table

the boy was gone.

Michael let himself back into the Home through the window in the television room. He returned the bag to its place in the hall, then crept up the stairs.

He sat on his bed in the darkness of his room. In his hand was a small torch. He reached under his mattress, pulled out a small object and held it up to the light.

It was a shabby photograph of a much younger Sean, standing in a garden with his mother. She had been a tall, slender woman with the same blonde hair and gentle features as her son. She smiled for the camera, happy and healthy, before the cancer came and ate her alive.

Sean had had other pictures of his mother, but this had been his favourite, the one that could still make him cry. He had cried all the time in those first weeks. The other children, already conditioned to despise weakness, had victimised him. Sean, frightened and alone, had looked for protection from the person closest to him. The boy whose room he shared.

At first Michael had found Sean a nuisance. A shadow he couldn't shake. But as the weeks turned into months, annoyance had turned into affection. Sean had needed him to be strong and so he had been, burying his own fears and anxieties beneath a mask of confidence intended to reassure the younger boy, who rewarded him with an uncritical admiration he had never known before.

Now Sean was gone. Off to a new home and a new life. Sean had cried before he left, scared of what the future might hold. Sean had been a baby, always in need of protection. A millstone round his neck. He was glad to be rid of him.

He wondered what Sean was doing now. Perhaps the Andersons had locked him in a cellar, just as he had told Sean they would. He hoped so. He liked the idea of Sean in the dark, frightened and alone, with no one to care.

Just as he was now.

He stared at the photograph, Sean was terrified of its being lost. His hand tightened around it, ready to tear it into pieces.

But he couldn't do it.

Instead came the tears that he had been fighting against all day. He shed them in silence. Tears only mattered if there was someone to see, and there was no one here.

He returned the photograph to its place beneath his mattress. Tomorrow he would give it to Susan, tell her he had found it on the floor and ask her to send it to Canterbury.

Turning off the torch, he lay down on his bed and looked up into the darkness. In his head was a distant memory of someone in one of the countless foster homes telling him that he should never be afraid of the dark because God lived there.

He had been told a lot of stuff over the years. And all of it was crap.

In the still of his room he waited for sleep to come.

The next day he gave the photograph to Susan so she could send it on to Sean. But in the weeks that followed, when letters came from Canterbury, he tore them into shreds.

The City of London: 1999

Chapter One

'Which one of you two has more capacity?' demanded Graham Fletcher.

The two occupants of the cramped office looked at each other. Stuart's desk was bare, save for the acquisition agreement he had just received, two days later than promised and in need of urgent review. Though Michael's desk was covered with papers, he had spent much of the afternoon sending e-mails to his friend Tim. The prospect of what lay ahead was a powerful incentive to keep quiet, but in the end his conscience won out. He spoke up.

'I have.'

'Oh.' Graham looked disappointed. 'What are you doing, Stuart?'

'Project Rocket. The redraft's only just arrived and we have to get our comments to the client this evening.'

'I see. Michael, my office, two minutes. Bring a pad.'

'Lucky you,' said Stuart once Graham had left.

Michael sent a final e-mail and rose to his feet. 'My heart soars.'

Stuart smiled. He was older than Michael—over thirty—and had come into the legal profession after years as a physics lecturer. The two of them had qualified six months ago and had shared an office ever since. 'Sure you don't want me to volunteer?'

'No, thanks. You stick with Project Rocket.' Michael rolled his eyes. 'Project Rocket! God, who thinks up these names?' Picking up his notepad, he headed for the door.

'Watch the body language,' Stuart told him.

Michael gave him the finger. 'How about this?'

Stuart laughed. 'Good luck.'

Michael walked along the corridor towards Graham's office. Secretaries sat in booths outside the doors of the solicitors they worked for. The air was full of the tapping sound of fingers on keyboards, discussions of last night's television, complaints about illegible handwriting and the constant hiss of the air-conditioning. Solicitors kept emerging from their offices to give tapes to their secretaries, to visit colleagues for advice on technical issues, to delegate unwanted work or simply to chat.

He approached Graham's corner office. One of the partners, Jeff Speakman, stood over his secretary Donna, dictating orally. Donna's mouth was a thin line. She hated Jeff's habit of doing this. Michael gave her a conspiratorial smile as he passed.

A group of trainee solicitors lingered by the coffee point, complaining about a boring lunchtime lecture they'd been forced to attend. A few weeks ago they would have been more circumspect, but as the latest rumour was that the commercial department would not be recruiting in September, the desire to impress was fading.

As always, Graham's office was a mess, with open files covering every available surface. Graham was speaking fast into his hand-held Dictaphone, a cigarette clenched between his fingers. In the corner of the room,

Graham's trainee, Julia, worked quietly at her desk.

Sitting down, Michael gazed out of the window at the drab offices across the road. His friend Tim worked at Layton Spencer Black and had a panoramic view of the City. But, as Graham would have been quick to remind him, one came to Cox Stephens for the quality of its work, not its scenery. Graham finished dictating and bellowed the name of his secretary. No answer. He swore. 'Julia, track her down. Tell her I need this urgently.' Julia took the tape and left the room.

Graham stared at Michael. He was a tall, thin man of about forty, with thinning hair, sharp features and aggressive eyes. He was renowned as one of the biggest bullies in the firm, notorious for giving his underlings minimal support and then blaming them for all mistakes, including his own. 'So,' he said. 'Not busy, then?'

'Not especially, Graham.'

'Well, you're about to be.'

'Yes, Graham.'

'A new takeover's just come in.'

'Really, Graham.'

Graham's face darkened. Cox Stephens operated on a first-name basis. 'We don't stand on ceremony here,' the senior partner had announced to Michael and his fellow trainees on the day they joined. Michael knew that Graham considered this policy demeaning to his partnerial status, and consequently made it a point of honour to call him by his first name at every opportunity. Last Thursday, at their fortnightly department meeting, he had managed to use it four times in a single sentence, forcing Stuart to fabricate a coughing fit.

'We're acting for Digitron. Heard of them?'

'No, Graham.'

'They're a software company. One of Jack Bennett's clients, but as Jack's frantic I'll be in charge.'

Michael opened his pad and began to make notes. In the background he heard Julia return to her seat.

'Digitron produce operating systems for businesses. Small scale at the moment, but they're looking to expand their presence in the market and want to buy Pegasus, which is a subsidiary of Kinnetica. They're paying a fortune. The assets are worth bugger all, but the trump card is Pegasus's long-term software supply contract with Dial-a-Car. That's really what Digitron are paying the money for. You have heard of Dial-a-Car, I take it.'

'Yes, Graham.'

There was a knock on the door. Jack Bennett entered. 'Sorry to interrupt. I've just had Peter Webb at Digitron on the phone. He wants a conference call at 8.30 tomorrow morning. Is that possible?'

Graham nodded, then gestured across his desk. 'Michael's going to be helping me.'

Jack beamed. 'Well, I'm very grateful to both of you.' He was a short, stocky man with a rugby player's build and a jovial face. He had joined the firm six weeks ago, arriving from Benson Drake with a client list of computer companies that was the envy of most of the competition.

Still seeming to feel the new boy, he was extremely affable with everyone. As most of the partners had had to be forcibly restrained from shouting 'Hosanna!' when he arrived and covering the corridor with palm leaves, such behaviour seemed unnecessary. But it was an attractive trait.

Michael smiled back. 'No problem.'

'You can make the conference call?' asked Graham, once Jack had left.

'Yes, Graham.'

Graham took a drag on his cigarette. 'Of course,' he said slowly, 'I'll be doing all the talking.'

Michael understood the hidden meaning instantly. He nodded. 'OK.'

'In the circumstances, I think that would be best.'

Michael felt his shoulders tensing and tried to relax them. Rebecca was always warning him that what she called his 'sod off shoulders' were too much of a giveaway.

'These are important clients, after all. Don't want to get off on the wrong foot, do we?'

Graham kept staring at him, waiting for a reaction. He steeled himself, determined not to give him the satisfaction. 'Course not.' 'In the meantime I want you to organise company searches on Pegasus and Kinnetica. Review that acquisition agreement we did for Syncarta and identify the clauses we'll want in our document, and finally make a list of information we'll need Digitron to supply. And be sure to do it with reference to the client file. They won't be impressed if we ask for stuff we already have, and neither will I.' Graham raised an eyebrow. 'Think you can handle that?'

Still waiting. Well, you'll wait for ever, you little prick.

His body was as relaxed as if he'd just had a one-hour massage. He smiled sweetly, pouring all his contempt into his best fuck you eyes.

'Of course.' A pause. 'Graham.'

He closed his pad and made his way back to his own office.

He ordered the searches and began to skim through the Syncarta agreement. Stuart went to the staff shop and bought them both ice-creams. Rebecca phoned to tell him a joke that was doing the rounds.

Half-past five. Fetching the client file, he started on the questionnaire. The corridor was full of the sound of voices as the secretaries left for the evening. He worked quickly, as he was due to meet Rebecca at seven. As he did so, he sensed someone hovering. Julia stood in the doorway, looking anxious. 'I know you're busy, Mike, but could you look at these board minutes for me?'

'Sure. Hand them over.'

She stood and watched him. A quiet girl with mousy hair and nervous eyes. Less confident than the other trainees. He made one small correction then handed them back. 'These are great. Well done.'

Blushing, she lowered her eyes. He had long suspected that she fancied him. The idea seemed strange. Having spent most of his life accepting that he was ugly, it was still hard to believe that he was now far from that. He smiled at her. 'Surviving?'

crime time 3.2 181

'Barely.'

'You're doing fine. Everyone thinks so. Don't let Hitler's twin bully you.'

'Maybe I should take lessons from you.'

'It's easy. Just chant the word "Graham" as if it were a religious mantra. Then he'll have a heart attack and the curse will be lifted.' He gestured to his desk. 'Better get on. Take care, OK?'

She left. After spending a further ten minutes tidying up the questionnaire, he switched off his computer. The lift was stuck in the basement, so he used the stairs instead. He walked through reception, stopping briefly to chat with the security man before heading out on to the street. The April air was warm, and sticky from the rain that had fallen earlier in the day. He considered catching the tube but decided against. Having been in the office all day, he wanted to stretch his legs.

He made his way through Broadgate Circle and on past Liverpool Street Station, loosening his tie as he did so. The streets were solid with traffic, while hundreds of commuters with tired faces and determined expressions marched towards their trains. It seemed as if the whole world was wearing suits, and his lungs were full of the smell of petrol fumes.

A street vendor stood on the corner, selling the Evening Standard. He bought a copy as he passed by. Interest rates were expected to fall. A celebrity marriage was breaking up. Nothing out of the ordinary. Just another day.

Continuing down Cannon Street, he crossed Ludgate Circus and walked along Fleet Street towards the Strand. The ratio of tourists to locals increased. An American couple with rucksacks asked him directions to Covent Garden. In the distance pigeons dive-bombed Nelson's Column.

He reached Chatterton's bookshop and made his way downstairs to the non-fiction section. A jolly-looking woman of about thirty sat at the till. She beamed at him then pointed to the art and architecture section, where a girl with short blonde hair was helping an elderly woman choose a book. The woman seemed uncertain as to just what she wanted, so the girl was making suggestions, showing her volume after volume. As he stood and watched them, the girl sensed his presence and gave him a quick smile.

Eventually the woman made her selection and headed for the till. He went to take her place while the girl watched his approach. She was in her early twenties and beautiful. Slender and graceful with lively green eyes and a smile that always seemed on the point of toppling over into laughter.

'Hi, Beck,' he said.

'Hi, yourself.'

He kissed her. She smelled of soap and roses. 'I'm early. Want me to come back later?'

'No.' She gestured to a half-completed display of new books. 'Help me with this. Clare said I could go when I'd finished.'

They knelt together by the display.

He started passing her books, while glancing over at the till. 'Clare looks happy.'

'She is. The hunky sales rep has finally asked her out.'

'So your hints paid off?'

'Yes, and about time too. Now Clare's panicking about what to wear, so I'm being dragged out tomorrow lunchtime to help her choose a new outfit.'

They both laughed. 'How was your day?' she asked.

He told her about the new takeover. She looked delighted. 'They must be really pleased with you.'

That didn't necessarily follow, but it made her happy to believe it so he nodded in agreement. 'Guess so.'

She continued to smile, but a sadness came into her eyes. He touched her cheek. 'What is it?'

'Nothing.'

'Tell me.'

'Later.' 'Promise?'

'Promise. Let's get this done.'

They worked together in companionable silence. When they had finished, he waited as she fetched her bag. The shop was virtually empty now. He looked at the books that surrounded him. Thousands of them. A drop in the ocean of the world's knowledge.

He noticed a new book about the artist Millais and thought how much she would like it. An idea for her birthday, perhaps. It was months away, but already there was a long list of things he planned to give her.

The weather forecast for the rest of the week was good, and as he waited he decided to surprise her at lunchtime one day, bringing sandwiches so they could sit together in Trafalgar Square and feed the pigeons. Once, a million years ago, he would have despised feelings like this. But that had been in a different life, the memories of which were now kept in a locked room in the darkest corridor of his mind.

He went to chat with Clare, teasing her about her forthcoming date. Rebecca returned and they made their way up the stairs and out of the shop.

As they walked along the Strand, making their way towards Leicester Square and their dinner date in Gerrard Street, she pointed to a poster, promoting a new exhibition at a Piccadilly art gallery. 'Patrick Spencer. He was only one year ahead of me at St Martin's. Look at him now.'

Now he understood her sadness. 'Yeah,' he said quietly, 'look at him now.'

'I don't mind. He was good. He deserves it.'

'So do you.'

'Maybe.'

'Definitely. You'll have it too.'

'In my dreams.'

He stopped, put his arms around her and stared down into her face. 'You know what I reckon? That ten years from now, when Patrick Spencer is a big celebrity and in all the papers, the one question that every journalist will be asking him will be, "What was it like to be at college with Rebecca Blake? *The* Rebecca Blake. The biggest noise in the art world for decades." That's what I reckon.'

She smiled. 'Sure.'

'Sure. It's going to happen, Beck. Just you wait and see.'

They hugged each other, there on the street, with people jostling past them, all with their own destinations, their own lives, hopes and dreams. A middle-aged woman smiled at them as she passed. He smiled back and thought to himself: This is what love means. Wanting someone else's happiness even more than your own.

'Come on,' Rebecca told him. 'We'll be late.'

Arms draped round each other, they made their way towards Gerrard Street.

Dinner was not going well.

Mr and Mrs Blake adored Chinese food. On their frequent visits to London from Winchester they always insisted on having dinner at the Oriental Pearl in Gerrard Street. 'Wonderful stuff,' Mr Blake would proclaim as he tucked into his Peking duck. 'Why can't our national food taste like this?' Mrs Blake would nod her agreement and then observe that one day they really should make a trip to China itself. At this point Michael always had a vision of Mr Blake standing in the middle of the Forbidden City, that glorious monument to China's extraordinary history, haranguing a street vendor because his chop suey didn't taste the way it did in the Oriental Pearl. But as Mr and Mrs Blake were Rebecca's parents, he kept these thoughts to himself.

'And how are things at work, Michael?' asked Mrs Blake as she finished her soup.

'Fine, thanks.'

'He's just got involved in a really good project,' Rebecca told her mother. 'It only came in today, didn't it, Mike?' He nodded. The restaurant was crowded. A waiter was hovering, waiting to clear their plates. The others had finished their starters so he tucked into his final spare rib.

'Well, that's wonderful,' said Mrs Blake. She turned to her husband. 'Isn't it, John?'

'Let's see how it pans out before we start a standing ovation,' he replied caustically.

'Dad!' exclaimed Rebecca.

'Well, after what happened last month ...' began Mr Blake.

'That wasn't Mike's fault,' said Rebecca quickly.

Mr Blake wiped his mouth with his napkin. 'So whose fault was it?'

Rebecca looked annoyed. 'I thought we'd agreed not to talk about that.'

'Anyway,' added Michael, 'it won't happen again.'

Mr Blake snorted.

'Your father's just concerned, Becky,' said Mrs Blake. 'For both of you.' She smiled at Michael. 'I'm sure you'll do very well.'

He smiled back and found himself wondering, as he often did, which one of them he disliked more.

The table had been booked for five people. Rebecca's elder brother Robert had had to cancel at the last minute. 'An important meeting,' Mrs Blake had announced proudly. Robert was a surveyor, and doing staggeringly well if his parents were to be believed. Rebecca had been disappointed at the news. Michael had expressed disappointment, too, while taking it as proof that God had not yet forsaken him.

The waiter reappeared. Mr and Mrs Blake stared at Michael expectantly. Both had heavy, fleshy faces and the demanding eyes of those whose lives had held so little in the way of disappointments that the slightest setback could send them into a rage. They resembled each other in that strange way that so many long-married couples do. There was nothing of Rebecca in either of them. Her looks had been inherited from one of her grandmothers.

He still hadn't finished, but it was inhumane to expect Mr Blake to continue waiting for his Peking duck so he put the last rib back on his plate. A pool of juice had gathered there. He wanted to pick up the plate and lick it, just to see the shock on their faces. Instead he nodded to the waiter.

Mr Blake refilled their wine glasses. Rebecca nudged Michael's arm. 'Forgot to tell you. I think I've found us somewhere to live. It's only temporary, but it sounds really good.'

'Temporary? What do you mean?' The two of them were renting a small, furnished flat in Camberwell, but the lease was about to expire.

'It's another rental. Clare told me about it. Clare's my friend at work,' she explained to her parents. 'She has a friend called Alison. Alison's husband Neil works for one of the merchant banks. He's just been seconded to their Singapore office, and they have to leave in a couple of weeks. There's four months left on the lease of their flat, so they're looking for someone to take it over. It's fully furnished, so we wouldn't have to rush out and buy everything.'

'Where's the flat?' he asked her.

'South Kensington.'

'Jesus! We're supposed to be saving money. How much is that going to cost?'

'Not much more than we're paying now. The flat's very small, apparently, and the landlord is some work contact of Neil's father, so they're not paying the full market rate. But they are liable for the whole period.'

'South Ken!' exclaimed Mrs Blake. 'Oh, Becky, that would be wonderful!'

'But we're not looking for another rental,' Michael pointed out. 'We want to buy. Get settled in our own place before the wedding.'

'But our lease expires in a couple of weeks. We're not going to buy anywhere in that time, which means we'll have to extend for another six months. This way we're only committed for four. Most people wouldn't want such a short lease, but for us it's ideal.'

'And what fun to live in such a smart part of town,' added Mrs Blake.

'So how much extra rent are we talking?' demanded Michael.

'It would only be for four months.'

'How much?'

'I'm sure,' said Mrs Blake, 'that Becky's father would help out if it's a problem.'

Mr Blake smiled indulgently at his daughter. 'Of course I would, sweetheart, if that's what you want.'

'Yes,' said Mrs Blake. 'It would be lovely for you. But of course, if Michael is so set against it …'

'I didn't say I was against it,' Michael told her.

Mrs Blake sighed. Rebecca and her father were staring at him: Rebecca hopefully, Mr Blake coldly. He realised that Rebecca had not forgotten to tell him but had picked her moment carefully, knowing that her parents would back her up. He took a deep breath, trying to swallow down his anger. 'OK.'

Rebecca kissed him. 'We'll just go and look. We may not even like it.'

'I'm sure you will,' her mother told her.

'And if you need help with the rent …' her father began.

'We won't,' said Michael, more aggressively than he'd intended. He softened his tone. 'It's kind of you to offer, and I'm really grateful, but we can manage ourselves.'

The main courses arrived. The waiter stood over the table, preparing the Peking duck. Mr Blake's eyes were shining. 'That looks wonderful.' Mrs Blake asked Rebecca for news of their friend, Emily. Michael reached for his wine glass. The rest of the evening stretched before him like an assault course. Smiling at no one in particular, he waited for the food for which he had no appetite.

They left the restaurant at ten o'clock and headed towards Leicester Square. The streets were full of people and the heady smell of exotic food. They said their goodbyes, and Mr and Mrs Blake headed for the tube station and the train that would take them to Robert's flat in Clapham. Michael and Rebecca made their way to the bus stop on Regent Street. The bus arrived just as they did, ready to take them south, across the Thames and home to Camberwell.

Disembarking at Camberwell High Street, they walked up the hill, hand in hand. The air was cooler now, and Rebecca had no coat. He offered her his jacket. She said she was fine.

They reached the apartment block: a huge slab of red brick built at the end of the 1980s. Their flat was on the second floor: a functional unit of stone floors and neat surfaces. Michael walked into the kitchen and poured himself a glass of water. Rebecca stood watching him. 'You'll like the flat,' she said. 'I'm sure you will.'

'Yeah, I'm sure I will.'

'It's only for a few months. Just enough time to find somewhere to buy. A place that's really our own.'

He turned to face her. 'Why did you have to tell them?'

'Tell them what?'

'About work. What happened last month. They didn't need to know that.'

She lowered her eyes. Said nothing.

'Why?'

'Because I was worried. I wanted someone to talk to.'

'Why didn't you talk to me? It was our problem, not theirs.'

She sighed. 'They're part of my life, Mike. That doesn't stop because we're together.'

'I know it doesn't. But I'm your fiancée and this was between us. I told you there was no need to worry. Why didn't you believe me?' 'I did believe you.'

'No, you didn't. You told them.

Gave them more ammunition to use against me.'

'They're not against you. They're just protective.'

'You don't need protecting from me.'

'I know I don't. I didn't mean it like that.'

He put his glass down on the table. 'It doesn't matter. Let them hate me if they're so desperate to do so.'

'They don't hate you.'

'Like hell they don't.'

They stared at each other. She looked upset, and the sight made him feel ashamed. 'I'm sorry,' he said quickly. 'Don't take any notice of me. Today was hectic, and I'm just feeling strung out.'

Her face relaxed into a sympathetic smile. She walked up to him and began to massage his neck. 'Then why don't I make some hot chocolate? We can watch the rest of that Humphrey Bogart film and you can tell me all about it.'

He wanted to agree and make her happy. But the evening had left him full of nervous energy that he needed to dispel. 'Better if I go for a walk.' He kissed her cheek. 'You go to bed. I won't be long.'

But it was past midnight when he finally returned.

He crept into their bedroom. She was asleep, lying on her side, her breathing so soft that he could barely hear it.

She rolled on to her back. A piece of her hair stuck up like an exclamation mark. Gently he stroked it down.

She opened her eyes and smiled up at him. 'What are you doing?'

'Watching you sleep.'

'I'm not asleep now,' she said, reaching out and pulling him down to her.

After they had made love, they lay in each other's arms. Quickly she drifted into sleep. He remained awake, his mind leading him on a journey he did not want to take, across space and time, to a grey-stone house in Bow.

He had lived in that house for six years. It had been his home, his world. It had always been full of people, full of noise and life. He had never lacked for company. But he had always been alone.

All his life he had been alone.

Until now.

He tightened his hold on her, wrapping himself around her, as if trying to fuse the two of them into a single being that could never be parted.

Chapter Two

The following evening Michael saw his friend George for a drink.

It could only be a quick one. Rebecca had arranged for them to go and see the flat later. They met at a wine bar at St Paul's: an underground cellar with barrels for tables and sawdust on the floor. The wine bar gave free bowls of cheese crackers to its patrons, and when Michael arrived George was already sitting at a barrel in the corner, a wine glass in front of him, chewing furiously.

Michael sat down. The cracker bowl was virtually empty. 'Glad to see you eating. You need to build yourself up.'

George reached for more crackers. 'Frightening, isn't it? If I get any thinner I'll snap.' He had taken off his jacket, and his shirt struggled to contain his huge stomach. He was short and round, with a plump, babyish face. 'I got you a glass of white,' he said. 'Was that OK?'

Michael nodded. 'Thanks. How was your day?'

'More important, how was yours?'

'Don't ask.' A candle stood on the barrel between them. He moistened his finger and began to move it through the flame. George watched him. 'Are they still giving you a hard time?'

'Some of them, and it pisses me off. One mistake, that's all it was. It's typical of that place. You make a single slip and everyone forgets all the positive stuff. I'm good at my job. I'm the one that the trainees come to when they want help. People my own level too. I did that printing company acquisition virtually single-handedly, and it wasn't an easy one either. The client sent me champagne when it was done. Everyone was delighted, all looks wonderful, then one bloody phone call and it all goes pear-shaped.'

'It was a client,' said George awkwardly.

'So? It wasn't like I swore or called him an idiot or anything. I was just—' he paused, reaching for the right word '—a bit short. I was hassled. It happens. He didn't even sound that bothered. Then suddenly I'm hauled into the managing partner's office and given a formal warning, and now it feels like they're watching me all the time, waiting for me to mess up. A new merger's come in. I'm doing it with this wanker called Graham Fletcher who's going to dump all the work on me and try to get me fired if I make the slightest error.'

He stopped. His face was flushed, his breathing heavy. 'Sorry. You didn't come here for this. Rant over.'

George's expression was understanding. 'It doesn't matter.'

Michael leaned back in his chair and stared up at the ceiling. 'It just seems like I spend my whole life trying to fit in and not rock the boat for fear that all that's good in my life could be snatched away. Like last night. We had dinner with Becky's parents. Her father spends all evening looking at me like I'm dirt and her mother tries to cause friction and I just have to sit and smile and look like I'm happy to be there.' He took a deep breath. 'Sometimes I feel like I'm just going to explode.'

'Better at them than at work?' suggested George.

'Is it? Results could be catastrophic either way.'

His finger was hot from the flame. He sucked on it, downed his drink and managed a smile. 'Enough of my angst. You look mellow.'

'Naturally. We had a revision afternoon. Four hours reading the paper and *Loaded* magazine. You definitely picked the wrong profession.'

George was a trainee accountant with a small firm in the West End, trying and failing to pass his professional exams. Michael smiled. 'Are you saying that accountants are better than lawyers?'

'Of course. What are lawyers but

glorified penpushers? It's accountants who make things happen. We're the movers and shakers.'

'Is that right?'

'Absolutely. Accountancy is the new rock'n'roll. We're so hip it hurts.'

They both laughed. Michael had a sudden image of the two of them sitting in a classroom at school, arguing over whether Nirvana were as good as the Stone Roses.

'How's Becky?' asked George.

'Fine. She'd arranged to see our friend Emily or she would have come along. She says you must come for dinner soon.'

'You're lucky,' said George suddenly. 'Having someone like her. I know how tough it's been for you. You make me feel ashamed sometimes, when I think how I take my parents for granted. But you struck gold when you met her, and though I'm jealous as hell I'm happy for you too.'

Michael felt sudden affection for the plump young man who faced him. 'I'll get the next round. Some more crackers too. Can't risk you wasting away.'

Again they laughed. He made his way towards the bar.

He met Rebecca at eight o'clock at Embankment tube. She was poring over her battered London A to Z. 'I don't know which is the best station,' she told him. 'Let's go to High Street Ken and walk down.'

They passed through the ticket barrier and make their way down to the platform. There were delays on the Circle Line and the platform was crowded. 'How was George?' she asked as they waited for a train.

'Fine. How was Em?'

'Not too good, actually.'

He was concerned 'Why? What's happened?'

'Nothing in particular. She was just feeling a bit down about things. I felt bad about not being able to stay long, so I'm taking her out for lunch tomorrow. I know she'd like to see you. Will you come too?'

'Course I will.'

The platform continued to fill up with people, while the overhead display gave no indication of when the next train was due. The atmosphere was tense. They pushed their way through the crowds, towards the far end, trying to improve their chances of getting a seat when a train finally did arrive. 'Liz called me today,' she said.

'Liz from college?'

She nodded. 'Her new boyfriend's cousin owns a tiny gallery in Crouch End, and she suggested that a group of us put on an exhibition there and try to get some important journalists and dealers to come.'

'Sounds good.'

'You think?'

'It's a chance to get your stuff seen.'

'It won't be seen, though. Not by anyone who matters. Crouch End is hardly the centre of the art universe.'

'It might. We can phone around. Talk the show up.'

She sighed. 'We tried that for the show in Camberwell. A journalist from the *Guardian* promised to come but then didn't.'

'So? We try again and maybe this

time he will.' He stroked her cheek. 'No one said this was going to be easy. Nothing worth while ever is. But it's going to happen. You just have to keep believing.' Suddenly he laughed. 'God, listen to me. I sound like a self-help manual.' She laughed too. 'Just a bit.'

'All I'm saying, Beck, is that something good may come of it. So don't just say no, OK?'

'OK.'

They heard the sound of an approaching train. When it entered the station, everyone on the platform moved forward, only to see that the compartments were already packed. Groans of disappointment filled the air. The doors opened and a couple of passengers fought their way off. In the resulting confusion, Michael grabbed Rebecca's arm, elbowed his way through the people in front and into the resulting space. He heard someone shout abuse and smiled sweetly as the doors closed.

The train started to move. He grabbed a handrail, and Rebecca hung on to his neck. The air was hot and thick with the smell of bodies crammed against each other, sweat soured with vexation.

Half an hour later they walked out into the hum of Kensington High Street. It was nearly dark now. Rebecca studied her A to Z and led him down a side road. They wandered past tall, severe apartment blocks and smart white houses on quiet streets. The noise seemed to fall away behind them. The streets were wide and comfortable, with taxis and cars sliding smoothly along them. Peaceful but alive.

They made their way to Pelham Gardens, a large square, lined with sleek, four-storey houses of grey stone that had all been converted into flats. The houses, which had huge porches supported by pillars, all looked out on to a small walled garden at the centre of the square.

They reached number thirty-three. Rebecca pressed the intercom for flat six and they were buzzed in.

After crossing a tiled hallway they made their way up the staircase. The flat was on the second floor. A small, pale woman in her late twenties and the mid-stages of pregnancy stood in the doorway, smiling a greeting. 'I'm Alison. Come in.'

They walked into a small, carpeted hallway with a low ceiling. To their right was a sitting room that ran into a tiny but well-furnished kitchen. 'Neil sends his apologies,' explained Alison. 'Something's come up at work. Let me show you round.'

It didn't take long. At the end of the hallway was a good-sized bedroom. Next to it was a comfortable bathroom and a tiny boxroom, empty save for a couple of suitcases. 'I suppose it could be used as a spare bedroom,' observed Alison, 'but there wouldn't be room for much except a bed.'

They walked into the sitting room. Like the other rooms, its ceiling was low, but the effect was intimate rather than oppressive. The furniture was plain but comfortable. Alison pointed to the settee. 'That's a sofa bed,' she explained, 'so you can have people to stay.' A small dining table stood in a corner by the window. The curtains had not yet been drawn. Outside was a tiny balcony, looking out at a row of small but well-tended gardens and the backs of the houses that faced on to Cromwell Road. Though right in the centre of the metropolis, the atmosphere was surprisingly tranquil.

'It's a lovely flat,' said Rebecca.

Alison smiled. 'We've been happy here. Shame we have to leave, but it's a great opportunity for Neil.'

'What do you do?' asked Rebecca.

'I was in banking too,' Alison patted her stomach. 'But my career's on hold for a while.'

'What's the landlord like?' asked Michael.

'Mr Somerton? Very nice. At least I think so. I've never met him, though we've spoken on the phone a couple of times. He's a work contact of Neil's father, which is how we got the flat.'

'Will he want to meet us?' asked Rebecca.

'Doubt it. To be honest, I don't think he's that bothered. He's very wealthy, so this flat is small potatoes. I'm sure he'd have let us terminate the lease early, but we wanted to see if it could be of use to someone else.'

'Well, we really like it,' Rebecca told her. 'Don't we, Mike?' He nodded.

Alison beamed. 'Why don't I make some coffee and you can ask me any questions.'

Half an hour later they made their way back to the tube _ Gloucester Road Station this time, as Alison had told them it was nearer. They passed a huge Sainsbury's. 'That's handy,' observed Rebecca.

'Incredibly so. How can we live without Sainsbury's?'

'And there's a sofa bed.'

'I know. Your parents can book their train tickets now.'

'You hated it, didn't you?'

He shook his head. They had crossed Cromwell Road and were approaching the tube. A row of expensive grocery shops stood opposite. 'It just seems a bit upmarket for us.'

She looked anxious. 'It's only for a few months.'

He tried to scowl but couldn't manage it. 'OK. Let's take it. But I warn you: turn into a Sloane Ranger and it's all over between us.'

She kissed him. 'I won't.'

In the distance he could see a Mexican restaurant, all bright colours, full of noise and energy. He gestured towards it. 'I'm hungry. Let's eat out while we can still afford to.'

They moved in ten days later, on an overcast Sunday. Alison and Neil had already gone, flying out to a new life in Singapore. Alison had left a box of Thornton's chocolates and a card wishing them a happy stay and giving them a contact number for their new landlord.

They unpacked the basics, then went for a walk in Kensington Gardens, to watch parents help children sail boats on the pond and to hunt for the statue of Peter Pan that Rebecca had visited with her grandparents on a trip to London years earlier. The reality disappointed her. 'It's smaller than I remember.'

'You were only five,' Michael

pointed out. 'A Pekingese would have seemed like the Hound of the Baskervilles back then.'

He had brought his camera. A man took a picture of the two of them standing in front of the statue, arms round each other, smiling, happy to be together.

Later they phoned for a pizza. They ate it surrounded by their suitcases, listening to old tapes, sharing the memories resurrected by each song.

The following morning Michael was phoned by Alan Harris.

Alan worked at a law centre in Bethnal Green, providing free legal advice to people in the area. While at university, Michael had spent a summer at the centre as a volunteer, and occasionally Alan phoned him with emergency queries which he dealt with himself or referred to a handful of trusted allies scattered through the various departments of the firm. As Cox Stephens took an extremely dim view of its staff providing free advice, the whole thing had to be carried out in complete secrecy.

Alan explained that he was advising a distraught woman who was going to be evicted by her landlord that evening. 'The lease is only a couple of pages long. Could you have a look at it and see if there are any arguments we can raise to help her?'

'Sure. Fax it through right now. I'll go and stand by the machine.'

He arrived there only to find a fifty-page document coming through for one of the partners. As he waited he heard someone call his name and looked up to see Graham Fletcher striding down the corridor brandishing a huge document of his own.

'Michael, the revised acquisition agreement on the Digitron deal has just come through. Digitron want a meeting tomorrow morning to discuss it.'

'Tomorrow?' His heart sank.

'Is that a problem?'

'It doesn't leave us long to review it ourselves.' Behind him the fax machine whirred away. Graham frowned. 'You're the one who'll be reviewing it. I'm far too busy.'

That figured. He nodded, while the fax machine began to whine. Clearly it had jammed.

Graham handed him the document. 'The meeting is at their offices at eight.'

'I'll handle it. You don't have to worry about a thing.'

'I should hope not,' Graham retorted, before striding off towards the coffee machine. Hastily Michael fixed the jam, grabbed the lease and returned to his room.

He tried to phone Nick Randall in the property department only to be told that he was on an external course all day. That meant he would have to deal with the problem himself. He studied the lease, hoping for an easy solution, but one did not present itself.

Turning his attention to the acquisition agreement, he realised that it was completely different from the first version. Clearly the review was going to take hours, and he also had urgent work to do for a partner in the banking department. He considered phoning Alan and conceding defeat, but he knew a woman might end up homeless if he didn't come up with something. Picking up the lease, he headed for the library.

As Michael read up on landlord and tenant law, Rebecca continued unpacking.

She had taken a day off from the shop, determined to get the flat just how she wanted it. Chris de Burgh played as she worked. Michael loathed his music, but for her it was a guilty pleasure, and she took advantage of his absence to indulge.

Their framed movie posters now hung on the walls. Both of them adored old films. Rebecca's passion was the dramas of the 1930s and 1940s; Michael's the silent epics. On their first date he had taken her to see Abel Gance's 1927 masterpiece *Napoleon*, and she, eager to impress, had spent the whole time bombarding him with facts about Charlie Chaplin and other silent greats that she had read in a book that afternoon. The first present he had ever given her was a poster for Alfred Hitchcock's *Rebecca*. She hung it next to his *Napoleon* poster, both taking pride of place above the television.

Her cookery books were stored on a shelf in the kitchen. She had over a dozen, but *A Taste of India* was the only one she used regularly. Michael adored curry, and she made him one every Friday evening. After they had eaten, they would curl up together on the sofa and watch an old movie: a silent one week, a talkie the next. This Friday it was her turn to choose. She made a note to check out the local video stores.

The phone kept ringing. Her mother called to ask about the move, as did her brother and two of her aunts. She phoned Michael to inform him of her progress, but he sounded harassed and couldn't talk for long.

In the afternoon she went to the shops, introducing herself en route to an elderly man with a warm smile whom she met in the downstairs hallway: a retired pianist who lived in one of the ground-floor flats and who wished her a happy stay. On her return she discovered that a plant had been delivered: a house-warming present from Emily. She placed it on the table in the sitting room beside Alison's card.

The unpacking was virtually finished and already the flat was starting to feel like home. Picking up Alison's card, she reread the message inside. An impulse seized her. Walking into the hall she picked up the phone.

Quarter to nine. Michael returned home, the Digitron file clutched under his arm. Though he had managed to find a temporary solution for Alan's tenant, it had taken much of the afternoon and he was only halfway through his review of the agreement for the following day's meeting. He would have to finish it after supper.

He was greeted by the smell of chilli con carne. Rebecca appeared from the kitchen, smiling in welcome. 'Hope you're hungry.'

He nodded, rubbing his temples, feeling the first rumblings of a headache. In the background, U2 sang about a place where the streets had no name. 'Do I have time to change?'

'Not really.'

He walked into the sitting room and saw their possessions set out everywhere. She followed him in. 'What do you think?'

'Looks great.' He took off his jacket and sat at the tiny dining table. A bottle of wine, unfinished from the previous night, stood at its centre, next to a plant that had not been there that morning. 'Who's the plant from?' he asked.

'Em.'

'Oh, right. She called me today for a chat.'

'I hope you were nicer to her than you were to me.'

He smiled sheepishly. 'Sorry about that.'

She laughed. 'Doesn't matter.' After pouring them both some wine she sat beside him. 'Guess who I spoke to today?'

'Your mother?'

'Mr Somerton.'

The name didn't register. He waited expectantly.

'The landlord.'

'Why did he phone?'

'I called him. Wanted to say how much we liked the flat. He was really friendly, asking about us and what we did.'

She was starting to look guilty. 'And?' he prompted.

'I've invited him over for a drink tomorrow night.'

He groaned.

'It seemed like a good idea. I mean, this is his flat.'

'And we're paying him rent. He doesn't need the red-carpet treatment too.'

'He's not expecting that.'

He arched an eyebrow.

'He sounded really nice. I'm sure you'll like him.' 'Things are really hectic at work. I've got meetings tomorrow. They may run on.'

'He's not coming until nine. You'll be finished by then.' She smiled encouragingly. 'Please, Mike. We were really lucky to get this flat, and I just think it would be a nice thing to do.'

He exhaled. Managed a smile himself. 'OK.'

'Thanks. The food's ready. I'll bring it through.'

She walked back into the kitchen. He remembered the work he still had to do and his headache arrived with a vengeance.

For Michael, Tuesday proved to be a particularly bad day.

Most of it was spent at Digitron's offices in Docklands, sitting in a room with no windows, going over the revised agreement. It was surprisingly acceptable, and the meeting should have taken only a couple of hours. Unfortunately Digitron's financial director was in a bullish mood, complaining about virtually every provision, and it wasn't until four o'clock that a realistic list of objections had been compiled.

On returning to the office, Michael was cross-examined by Graham Fletcher, shouted at for not paying sufficient respect to Digitron's concerns, and told that three boxes of Pegasus contracts had just arrived and needed to be reviewed and reported on by Friday night. 'I'm not impressed with the way this deal is going,' Graham told him. 'You don't seem to be on top of things.' Michael was on the verge of replying that things would be going a damn sight better if Graham deigned to do some work himself, but managed to bite his tongue. He restricted himself to a cheerful, 'Yes, Graham. Of course, Graham. Don't worry about a thing, Graham,' before returning to his room.

He was met by his secretary Kim, full of apologies. 'You know I'm off to Greece tomorrow. Well, there's been a mix-up in the cover rota. I'm trying to fix something up, but I've got to go in five minutes.' He told her it didn't matter and wished her a happy holiday.

Sitting down at his desk, he began to wade through the contracts, checking them against the list Pegasus had sent. Two were missing. The covering letter was dated a week earlier. Graham had sat on it for days. He swallowed his resentment, established which departments should review which documents, then tried to call the relevant people, only to find that they had all left for the evening.

He located the all-important contract with Dial-a-Car and began to look through it. Digitron's financial director phoned. More objections to the agreement, all of them ridiculous. He spent a frustrating hour trying, as diplomatically as possible, to make him accept this.

As soon as he put the phone down, Jack Bennett charged in, looking stressed. 'We've just had new instructions. Computer maintenance company called Azteca, looking to sell a subsidiary. A rush job. I know you're stretched, but I really need your help. Can you do a meeting first thing tomorrow? Possibly all day.' Michael looked at the pile of contracts in front of him and managed a smile. 'Sure. Why not? Give me the details …'

When Jack had gone he looked at his watch. Eight o'clock. He needed to leave now if he was going to be home in time. Work lay piled up in front of him. When on earth was he going to get it done? The last thing he needed was a visit from the landlord.

For a moment he considered phoning Rebecca and telling her that he couldn't get away. It would be for the best. The mood he was in, it was doubtful he could go a whole evening without saying something he might regret.

But it was what she wanted. And he had agreed.

Switching off his computer, he made for the door.

Five to nine. Rebecca heard a key in the lock.

She had spent the first part of the evening making sure that the flat was spotless before showering and changing into a new dress. Now she was in the sitting room, pacing restlessly. Michael stood in the hall. 'Where have you been?' she demanded.

His face was flushed. He looked bad-tempered and irritable. 'Don't start,' he told her.

She ignored the warning. 'He'll be here in a minute. Go and get changed. I've ironed your blue shirt and it's on the bed. Wear it with the chinos.'

He smiled provokingly. 'And how was your day, dear?'

'Hurry up!'

The smile turned into a scowl. 'This was a bloody stupid idea!' He marched off to the bedroom. She removed the wine from the fridge. A Chardonnay. The man at the wine shop had assured her that it was delicious. It had better be at that price.

The buzzer went. Suddenly nervous, she pressed the entry button. In the last moments, as Mr Somerton made his way up the stairs, she checked, for the hundredth time, that everything was tidy.

There was a knock on the door. She took a deep breath and opened it.

The man who stood in the corridor was in his late forties, tall, like Michael, and well built, with light brown hair that was starting to grey, a strong face and shrewd dark eyes. He was dressed smartly but casually: wool jacket, dark shirt, cotton trousers, good shoes. He smiled at her. 'You must be Rebecca.'

She nodded. 'Mr Somerton?'

'Max, please.'

'And I'm Becky. Won't you come in?'

He walked into the hallway. 'Did you find it all right?' she asked politely.

'It was difficult, but I just about managed.'

She realised what she'd said and blushed. He laughed good-naturedly, moved into the sitting room and gestured around him. 'The flat looks wonderful,' he told her. 'Your possessions have made all the difference.'

He spoke slowly and easily. His voice was really beautiful: deep, rich and resonant. Like velvet. The telephone did not do it justice. She smiled shyly, liking him already. 'Thank you. Mike's just coming. Won't you sit down?'

There were footsteps behind them. Michael walked into the room. Her heart sank.

He was wearing jeans and a scruffy sweatshirt. His hair was uncombed, his smile unenthusiastic, his body language hostile. Max held out a hand. 'You must be Mike.'

He nodded, shook the outstretched hand. And then said, 'It's Michael, actually.'

For a split second a strange expression came into Max's face. Not anger exactly. Something Rebecca couldn't identify. She started to panic, convinced that the evening was ruined before it had even begun.

Then the expression was gone, replaced by a warm smile. 'Of course. A name is the most important badge we have to define ourselves. It shouldn't be shortened without permission. Forgive me.'

Michael had the grace to look embarrassed. 'Doesn't matter,' he said awkwardly.

They sat down, she and Michael on the sofa bed, Max on a chair facing them. Michael poured the wine. Max gazed about him as if looking for something. 'Do you mind if I smoke?' he asked.

'No. We don't, but please go ahead.' Rebecca fetched a saucer to be used as an ashtray. Max produced a silver case and removed a thin cigar. He lit it, inhaled, then blew a cloud of smoke into the air. The smell was strong but not unpleasant, making her think of the scent of trees after rain. She noticed he had a tiny cut on his neck, a shaving scar. He did not wear a wedding ring. 'We love the flat,' she told him.

Max sipped his wine. 'I hope it's not too small.'

'It's perfect, isn't it, Mike?' She hoped Michael would say something, but he just nodded. She wished she'd thought to put on a CD. They could use some background noise. She smiled nervously at Max. 'I'm glad you could come.'

'I'm delighted to have the chance to meet you both.' He tapped ash from his cigar and turned to Michael. 'Becky tells me that you're a lawyer.'

Again Michael nodded.

'Which firm are you with?'

'Cox Stephens.'

Max thought for a moment. 'Jack Bennett's just joined them, hasn't he?'

'You know him?'

'We've had a few dealings.' Max sipped his wine. 'This is delicious,' he told Rebecca. 'You have excellent taste.'

She felt relieved. 'Not me. The man at Oddbins. An exciting wine: unusual and challenging. Those were his words.'

'They always say that,' observed Michael, 'so they don't have people complaining when they realise they've spent a fortune on something that tastes like piss.'

Rebecca flinched. But Max looked amused. 'You weren't ripped off this time,' he reassured her. 'Quite the contrary.' Again he turned to Michael.

'I also understand,' he continued, 'that we hail from the same neck of the woods.'

'You're from Richmond?'

'Bow.'

The revelation took her by surprise. As it did Michael. 'I see,' he said.

'Bassett House to be precise. In Lexden Street. A Children's Home, which closed down soon after I left. Do you know Lexden Street?'

Michael turned to stare at Rebecca. She felt guilty, as if she had been disloyal. Max had been so easy to talk to on the phone that she must have said more than she'd intended. She gave Michael a nervous smile. 'Small world,' she said. He nodded.

'Where was the Home you stayed in?' Max asked him.

'Thorpe Street.' Max thought for a moment. 'There's a pub. What's it called? The Feathers?'

'The White Feather.'

'Yes, I remember the sign now. White feather against a black background.' Max smiled. His eyes remained fixed on Michael. 'Do you know Lexden Street?'

Michael nodded. 'There's a corner shop.' He didn't return Max's stare.

Rebecca, wishing she'd been more circumspect, tried to lighten the mood. 'Not the one you and your friends used to nick sweets from?'

Max smiled at her. 'I think we used to do that too.'

'It was a long time ago,' said Michael suddenly.

Rebecca decided it was time to change the subject. 'Where do you live?' she asked Max.

'Arundel Crescent. Do you know

it?'

She shook her head.

'The other side of the Old Brompton Road. Up towards Knightsbridge.' He laughed. 'Very handy for Harrods.'

'It sounds lovely,' she told him, then added: 'I don't know the area at all.'

'Then why not come and see it? I'm having a drinks party on Saturday night. Starts at seven. Quite informal.'

'That's very kind. Thank you.' She turned to Michael, not sure how to answer. 'Saturday night. We don't—'

Max came to her rescue. 'I'm sure you have plans already. But you'd both be welcome if, by any chance, you do find yourselves free.'

His glass was empty. Michael refilled it, while Max pointed to a painting that hung above their heads. Two ships in the moonlight. 'You mentioned that your degree was in fine art. Did you paint that?'

She shook her head. 'My grandmother did. My style is very different.'

'Have you always wanted to be an artist?' She nodded. He smiled encouragingly, so she began to tell him about her work and the factors that had influenced its development. Of her love for mythology and legend. Of her discovery of the Pre-Raphaelites whose works were steeped in those old stories, and her desire to become a painter herself. She found herself talking on and on. He was a good listener, possessing that rare gift of appearing totally focused on the words of another and inspiring confidences as a result. The smell of cigar smoke filled the room. It made her feel light-headed. As she spoke she was aware of Michael sitting beside her. She wished he'd contribute. But he said nothing.

Half-past ten. The wine bottle was empty. 'I've kept you long enough,' Max announced. 'Thank you for your hospitality. I must go.'

They rose to their feet. Shook hands again. 'Would you like us to call you a cab?' she asked.

'No, thank you. It's an easy walk.'

They stood by the door. 'Tell me,' Max said to Michael, 'have you been back?'

Rebecca didn't understand the question. Michael did. 'Yes,' he said. 'Once.'

'When?'

'Last year.'

'Visiting someone?'

'No. Just delivering some papers for work.'

'Was the corner shop still there?'

'Yes.'

'Did you nick a Mars bar? For old times' sake?'

For the first time that evening, Michael smiled. A rueful smile, meant more for himself than for the others. 'Something like that,' he replied.

Max kissed Rebecca's cheek. 'It's been a pleasure,' he said, giving her a card with his address.

Half an hour later she sat in bed. The overhead light was off. All illumination came from her bedside lamp.

A travel book on the South Pacific lay in her lap. As a child she had been enthralled by a novel about sailors who had been shipwrecked in the Fijian islands two hundred years ago, only to be mistaken for gods by the local cannibals. Since then she had always wanted to see the islands. Perhaps they would honeymoon there if funds permitted.

Michael appeared from the bathroom, naked save for his boxer shorts, and climbed into bed beside her. His dark hair, still damp from the shower, hung over his forehead. She brushed it back. 'I wonder if Sean has been back,' she said.

He didn't answer. Just looked thoughtful.

'You wonder too, don't you?'

'Maybe.'

'We could try to trace him.'

He shook his head.

'Don't you want to see him again? There was a time when he was the most important person in your life.'

'That was fifteen years ago.'

'But you still think about him. I'm sure he thinks about you too. And if you ever decide that you want to trace him, then I'll help you look. I'm sure that we can find him together.' Gently she stroked his cheek. 'I just wanted you to know that.'

He took her hand and kissed it. 'I do.'

'I'm sorry,' she told him.

'For what?'

'For telling Max about the Home. I didn't set out to. He'd been asking about me and then he started asking about you. I mentioned Bow. He asked if your family were cockneys, and it just came out. I didn't tell him anything else. Honestly.'

'Doesn't matter.' He put his arm around her. She leaned against him, feeling warm and safe. They sat together in silence. Comfortable. Familiar.

'I liked him,' she said eventually. 'Did you?' 'Yeah. He was OK.'

'We don't have to go to the party. Probably wouldn't be our sort of thing anyway.'

'Maybe we should, just to see the house. I know you'd like to, and it's not as if we'd have to stay long. I've got an early start tomorrow. Let's go to sleep.'

She put out the light. They lay together, she draped across his chest. His breathing was slow and deep. The darkness was strange to her: a new room in a new flat with its own sounds and shadows. Ten minutes passed. Twenty. Half an hour. She sensed he was still awake and whispered his name. He stroked her hair. Smiling, she allowed her eyes to close.

the verdict

The latest in books film and sound reviewed by people with time for crime

THE HARD DETECTIVE BY H R F KEATING, MACMILLAN, £16.99

After a lengthy and accomplished stint as one of the prime practitioners in the crime genre (not to mention one of its most astute commentators) H R F Keating appeared to have found the perfect niche with his highly entertaining Inspector Ghote books. But it's to his credit that Keating refused to rest on his laurels and inaugurated the series of which *The Hard Detective* is the most impressive yet. In earlier books such as *The Rich Detective* and *The Good Detective* Keating featured different detectives whose human weaknesses affected their crime fighting abilities. The focus this time is Detective Chief Inspector Harriet Martens who has acquired the nickname the 'hard detective' by cultivating a tough carapace to make her mark in a very masculine world. Her Stop the Rot campaign is having such a remarkable impact on local criminals, that she begins to suspect that the death of two of her officers within hours of each other may be connected to the campaign. And she further begins to realise that the circumstances of the deaths echo phrases from the Book of Exodus: Life for Life, Eye for Eye. It becomes grimly apparent that Harriet is facing four more deaths that will complete the quotation, beginning with Tooth for Tooth. With such a distinctive detective hero as Ghote to his credit, it is even more remarkable that Keating has achieved a similar feat with the distaff protagonist of the new book. If his grasp of modern idioms falters on occasion, few who pick up this latest offering from a master will be disappointed by the superior fare on offer here.

Barry Forshaw

A PERFECT CRIME BY PETER ABRAHAMS, PENGUIN, £5.99

It's not difficult to find Stephen King extolling the virtues of a particular book, but Peter Abrahams is the only writer he describes as his favourite American suspense novelist. And King is not alone in this assessment—more and more people are coming to appreciate the delicious meld of ingenious plot and pithily created characters that is Abrahams' speciality. This novel shows him at his best: an adulterous affair is disclosed, and a brilliant, twisted mind undertakes to inaugurate the perfect crime. Every aspect will be taken into account: opportunity, motive, suspects, alibis and so forth. The four people that Abrahams involves in this chilling narrative are each created with the kind of attention that has distinguished earlier books such as *The Fan* and *Lights Out*. Set against the wintry backdrop of an East Coast town, the sense of manipulation—both of the reader and the characters—provides just the kind of frisson mystery readers seek out eagerly.

Barry Forshaw

THE DISCRETE CHARM OF CHARLIE MONK BY DAVID AMBROSE, MACMILLAN, £10

David Ambrose has gleaned a considerable following for such powerful books as *Hollywood Lies* & *Superstition*, and this new tale of the dangers that may result from future science quickly establishes itself as a thriller of some distinction. Charlie Monk is, it seems, a heroic figure. He has no fear—but he has no conscience, or memory. Doctor Susan Flemyng has been working on a way to give him his memory back, and in a world where every aspect of reality is rigorously controlled, her gift is regarded as a dangerous one. While Ambrose defies category as a thriller writer (utilising elements from many genres) he remains a stylist of real achievement—and even if his prose is stripped down to the bare minimum, it functions perfectly in the context of his swift-moving narrative. Charlie is a highly unusual protagonist, and his relationship to Susan Flemyng is handled with intelligence and imagination.

Barry Forshaw

SAVING FAITH BY DAVID BALDACCI, SIMON & SCHUSTER, £9.99

Considerable attention is created by each new David Baldacci novel since the success of such mega-sellers as *The Simple Truth*. His speciality is the high-octane plot and a readability that brooks no interruptions, along with busy and involving plots set among the highest reaches of American society—but don't look for elegant writing. His protagonist this time is Danny Buchanan, a top Washington lobbyist who once earned a vast fortune serving the interests of giant corporations. But Danny has had a Damascan conversion caused by the appalling poverty he has witnessed on his global travels, and decides to use his political genius to help the world's poor. And Danny is prepared to bend the rules—something he's done for years. With the aid of his assistant Faith Lockhart, Danny begins to establish a secret network of politicians prepared to vote the way he wishes on international aid. But Robert Thornhill, a ruthless top ranking veteran of clandestine government activity, discovers the attorney's secret political influence, and blackmails him. The narrative moves toward an explosive clash between the CIA and the FBI, with Faith caught in the crossfire. While never forgetting the appeal of Machiavellian political infighting, Baldacci always delivers the palm-sweating thriller goods in a fashion that ensures few will be able to put this one down.

Brian Rittterspak

SECRET KINGDOM BY FRANCIS BENNETT, GOLLANCZ, £9.99

Francis Bennett's first novel *Making Enemies* demonstrated a remarkably sophisticated approach to the Cold War.

Bennett was able to demonstrate its effect on his characters with immense understanding and psychological penetration, and the acclaim that book gleaned raised hopes for the new one. If *Secret Kingdom* does not initially seem as involving, the reader is nevertheless inexorably drawn into a narrative that is every bit as complex and astringent as its predecessor. Taking place in the summer and autumn of 1956, in the months leading up to the Hungarian uprising, Bobby Martineau, the SIS man who was Bennett's protagonist in the first book, is posted to Budapest to report on the crisis. But he becomes aware that London is ignoring his warnings, and his sympathy for the Hungarians (risking their lives against the Soviet oppressors) is making him desperate to galvanise his colleagues. The situation is complicated by his relationship with Eva, a woman known to both the Russian and Hungarian security forces, who has her own forceful agenda. This is only a spy story in the same sense as Le Carré uses the genre to make telling and truthful points about human nature. A more than worthy successor to an excellent debut.

Judith Gray

THE MYSTERIOUS MR QUIN BY AGATHA CHRISTIE, HARPERCOLLINS, £4.99

Love her or hate her (and, God knows, many do), she remains the world's best-loved crime writer. Her books have been translated into every language, and despite the inevitable reaction against the distant world she describes, no-one has been able to unseat Agatha Christie as the Queen of Crime. *The Mysterious Mr Quin* is a collection of intricately plotted and atmospheric mysteries, with the marvellously beguiling conundrum in each one centred on the shadowy presence of Mr Harley Quin. Starting at a typical New Year's Eve house party, Christie takes us into world of dark psychology and desperate deeds. Mr Satterthwaite, noted observer of human behaviour, comes to feel that the evening has more to offer. A mysterious stranger arrives after this night. Who is this mysterious Mr Quin? And why does his presence have such a strong effect on Eleanor Portal, the woman with the dyed black hair? As always, Christie pays out the details of the ingeniously constructed narrative with a tantalising sense of precisely what will keep the reader riveted. Characterisation is basic, but absolutely perfect for this kind of page-turning narrative.

Eve Tan Gee

DARK HOLLOW BY JOHN CONNOLLY

To say that John Connolly enjoyed a remarkable success with his first book, *Every Dead Thing*, is to understate the case: this first thriller featuring Detective 'Bird' Parker was a highly unusual entry in the field, written in a raw, arresting style that transfixed all who were drawn to it. But is *Dark Hollow*, the second appearance of Connolly's fiery and inexorable investigator, equally gripping? Connolly himself has remarked that he wanted to give this new book a very sinister feel, rather than just a gruesome one. In this, he has succeeded triumphantly—and the latest novel builds on the considerable narrative achievements of its predecessor. This time, Bird (still recovering from murder of his family by The Travelling Man) returns to the scene of happier times, the wintry Maine of his childhood. But other memories are more threatening: another young woman is savagely killed along with a child, and Bird's previous encounter with the victims compels him to track down the murderer. There is an obvious suspect—but Bird, by putting himself into the extreme danger that is so often his lot, comes to believe that the real answer lies thirty years

Murder One for all the Pulp Fiction your heart desires.
Murder One where you can find all the Usual Suspects. If it's in Print, in English, we have it. If it's not in Print, we might well have it too. The **ultimate** mystery superstore.
Mail Order all over the world.
Catalogue on request.

Visit our spanking new, criminal website at www.murderone.co.uk **and** e-mail:106562.2021 @compuserve.com

Britain's Only Major Mystery Bookstore

murder one

71 -73 Charing Cross Rd, London WC2H 0AA, Tel 0171 734 3483 Fax 0171 734 3429

in the past. As the body count increases, it becomes apparent that someone else is hunting for Billy, the dead woman's ex-husband and chief suspect in the slaying. And this dangerous figure appears to know Bird intimately. Before long, the tormented detective is investigating the terrifying origins of a mythical killer: the psychopathic Caleb Kyle. Along with the kind of riveting storytelling skills we have come to expect from Connolly, the author has built into his narrative a superstructure of striking imagery: predatory nature and the cycle of the seasons feed into the darker corners of the plot and illuminate the grim psychopathology of the characters. Bird remains the most involving of protagonists—and by dovetailing his hero's troubled past into the search narrative, Connolly ensures the reader's total involvement. The author's way with disturbingly detailed prose remains as evocative as ever: *"'Nice car', he repeated, and a fat white hand emerged from one of his pockets, the fingers like a thick, pale slugs that had spent too long in dark places. He caressed the roof of the Mustang appreciatively, and it seemed as if the paint would corrode spontaneously beneath his fingers."*

Brian Ritterspak

THE SECRET OF ANNEXE 3 BY COLIN DEXTER, PAN, £5.99

Chief Inspector Morse, Colin Dexter's much-loved protagonist, featured in some of the most ingeniously plotted and richly atmospheric crime novels of the modern age. *The Secret of Annexe 3* is one of the most masterfully rendered. As usual, the lugubrious Morse is not allowing himself to be caught up in New Year celebrations. And a murder inquiry in a festive hotel has a certain appeal for him. It is a crime worthy of the season—the corpse is found in fancy dress. And among the guest list at the Haworth Hotel, few have registered under their own names. Utilising the format of the classic Christie manor house mystery, Dexter creates a plot engine of power and precision, with all the grim revelations falling satisfyingly into place. As usual, the by-play between Morse and his associates has a nicely acidic ring, and the cast of suspects is marshalled with aplomb. One of the finest Morse novels.

Judith Gray

BOY IN THE WATER BY STEPHEN DOBYNS, VIKING, £9.99

Authors set themselves a problem when they have a particularly well received novel to follow up. Stephen Dobyns' *The Church of Dead Girls* achieved such acclaim for its psychologically penetrating treatment of a terrifying situation that expectations were riding high for *Boy in the Water*. There's some suspense in the opening chapters as it becomes apparent that Dobyns is taking his time, but his strategy soon becomes clear, and the reader is treated to a new psychological thriller that is quite the equal of the earlier book. In the sylvan New Hampshire countryside, Bishops Hill academy and its new head Jim Hawthorne are in deep trouble. Dealing with the internecine squabbles of the staff (not to mention demons in his own past), Jim becomes aware that the school is harbouring a dark mystery. When the eponymous boy (a student) is found in the school pool, John finds himself in a steadily accelerating nightmare that is beyond his control. As before, Dobyns is particularly good at the delineation of conflict in the Groves of Academe. His protagonist is the perfect conduit for the reader in a tale that depends so much on slowly disclosed revelations. With the precision of a musician, Dobyns orchestrates his narrative to a truly powerful climax.

Barry Forshaw

THE SPIRIT DEATH BY DAVID DOCHERTY, SIMON & SCHUSTER, £16.99

From H G Wells and John Wyndham through more recent writers such as J G Ballard, the collapse of society has been a standard theme in novels and, if done well, it always guarantees a highly compelling read. Docherty's *The Spirit Death* has as its premise a tropical killer disease being released in London and creating terror and confusion. London's Centre for Infectious Diseases is soon under siege, and Docherty's hero Mike Davenport has his hands full with a crisis management situation. As Davenport comes closer and closer to the source of the deadly virus, he is also obliged to deal with a government putting its public relations agenda before the lives of its citizens. It's hardly surprising that this richly written book is currently being optioned for film and TV, as Docherty has a genuinely cinematic vision and his thriller sports a powerfully created panoply of catastrophe. Davenport is drawn without too much subtlety, but remains a strong protagonist.

Judith Gray

THE WILD ISLAND BY ANTONIA FRASER, MANDARIN, £5.99

Resist your impulse to groan at this one: Antonia Fraser has created one of the most enduring of female sleuths in Jemima Shore. With both economy and imagination, Fraser ensures that Jemima is one of the most believable protagonists in an over-crowded field, and this is one of her most assured outings. Taking a much-needed break from the stress of being a television reporter, Jemima heads for a remote Scottish island to find peace and isolation. But Charles Beauregard, who was to collect her, dies suddenly. And, needless to say, Jemima resolves to stay in the Highlands, only to find herself in the middle of a savage and bloody family feud between the Beauregard relatives and Beauregard Castle's new owner, Clementine, who claims to be a descendant of Bonnie Prince Charlie. Apart from the spot-on characterisation, the plotting here is as nimble and inventive as ever, while the Scottish atmosphere is conjured with maximum colour.

Eve Tan Gee

DEAD LONG ENOUGH BY JAMES HAWES, LITTLE, BROWN, £15.99

If you're one of the readers who resisted James Hawes' *A White Merc With Fins* and *Rancid Aluminium* despite all the brouhaha, now's the time for you to catch up with the most inventive and funny of British novelists. All the dazzling wordplay and deliriously inventive plotting that distinguished his first books are developed here in a beautifully constructive novel. Starting in a deceptively low key, Hawes introduces the reader to a group of people who meet on the same night once a year. They have an arrangement: all they carry is a toothbrush and some cash (and, of course, credit cards) and are primed for adventure—they have no idea where they'll end up that evening. And it could be anywhere in the world. The organiser is Harry—the man with the plan—but what begins as an adventure, for several deluded protagonists ends up in a manner that is both hilarious and disturbing. Apart from the manic plotting, the sardonic dialogue has a pungency that brings these characters vividly to life. And as *Rancid Aluminium* is soon to be filmed, the visual quality is of this diverting novel will probably ensure that it soon follows suit.

Judith Gray

BIRDMAN BY MO HAYDER, BANTAM, £9.99

It's easy to see why her publishers have such high hopes for Mo Hayder—*Birdman* is a really impressive debut. Neither Hayder nor her publishers make a secret of her debt to Thomas Harris—in fact, it's made into a positive virtue. But even those feeling we've all gone down the hyper-ingenious serial killer route just once too often should get on for the ride: Hayder's grisly epic really does the grab the reader by the throat. The London and Greenwich locales help escape the Harris overtones seeming too prominent: the Met's crack murder squad, AMIP, is called out by the CID to help in a gruesome case. Five young women have all been dispatched in ritualistic fashion, and young Inspector Jack Caffery realises he's up against a serial sex killer. What's worse, he has to take on board a disastrous case early in his career. And the bloodletting has only just begun.

Hayder has cannily realised that intelligent (and ever-surprising) plotting is the order of the day here, and effortlessly combines that with some sharply delineated characterisation for her hero. If the resolution of the mystery lacks Harris' aplomb, all the signs are that Hayder is getting there. And few will regret picking this one up—unless they're squeamish.

Brian Ritterspak

ARMS AND THE WOMEN BY REGINALD HILL, HARPERCOLLINS, £16.99

Readers await each new Dalziel and Pascoe novel from Reginald Hill with great anticipation—the more so since the author has inaugurated another series, the wonderful Joe Sixsmith books such as *Singing the Sadness*. There will be much rejoicing at the fact that the new outing for the uneasy duo, *Arms and the Women*, is absolutely vintage stuff: the pungently witty dialogue is in place, along with the highly intelligent and precise plotting that is so much Hill's hallmark. And after the massive success of *On Beulah Height*, Hill has introduced an innovation that ensures no-one could accuse him of resting on his laurels: the new novel is written in the book-within-a-book format, and the concept works (for the most part) successfully.

Ellie Pascoe has abandoned her career as a campaigner for the hard left, and is writing a book in her tiny study—the very book that (as readers of this narrative) we have access to. When Ellie finds her life being threatened, her friends assume it has to do with her marriage to a cop. But Ellie isn't so sure...and along with the involvement of the doughty duo of Dalziel and Pascoe, the three are dealing with Irish Republicans, Colombian drug-dealers and even bogus council officers. And Ellie's problems are shared with a strange assortment of other women, similarly in trouble: her middle-class friend Daphne, a vivacious South American money-launderer and a pushy female copper.

Is the target really her husband Peter? Needless to say, the narrative has enough twists and turns to pleasingly baffle the most astute reader, and each fresh revelation is both dramatic and unexpected.

As always, one of the greatest pleasures to be had from Hill's writing is the wonderfully non-PC characterisation of Fat Andy Dalziel, spraying out his northern prejudices and intolerance with nary a thought for the offence he causes: "'Waste of time,' said the Fat Man dismissively. 'The meeting 'ud be in aid of Women with Headaches or Underage Welsh Refugees with Acne...'"

Even without the pyrotechnics of plot,

Dalziel remains a highly entertaining monster, and Hill enthusiasts will feel that they are getting far more than their money's worth.

Brian Ritterspak

SINGING THE SADNESS BY REGINALD HILL, HARPERCOLLINS

There is an army of contenders for the title Queen of Crime, but (in the UK at least) many would consider the finest male practitioner of the genre to be the superlative Reginald Hill. His novels are crammed with atmospheric detail, richly ingenious plotting, and some of the sharpest characterisation in English writing—be that literary or crime novel. His detectives, Dalziel and Pascoe, have become among the best loved fixtures of the current crime scene. And *Singing the Sadness* is possibly his most beguiling entertainment yet— even though it's not a Dalziel and Pascoe book.

Recently, Hill has created a new character, Joe Sixsmith. Born in a short story, Hill so much enjoyed writing about Joe that he decided to give his redundant lathe operator-turned-private eye his own series of novels. As in the earlier Sixsmith books, *Blood Sympathy*, *Born Guilty* and *Killing the Lawyers*, Sixsmith proves to be a wonderfully laconic and winning personality: always up against it in both his personal and professional life, his half-haphazard, half-inspired piercing of some pretty sinister mysteries provides a very good time for the reader.

In the new book, Joe is going west— but only as far as Wales, where his local choir has been invited to compete in the Llanffugiol Choral Festival. Joe has agreed to accompany them—but soon discovers that no one seems to have heard of Llanffugiol. And instead of a welcome in the hillside, all that he finds is a burning house, with a mysterious woman trapped inside. Soon, Joe is dealing with a strange and suspicious group of characters: a drug-dealing student, a supercilious headmaster and a deeply antagonistic policeman. And that's not to mention the disaffected locals who have decided to sabotage the Festival, along with the caretaker's daughter who seems prepared to go to some remarkable lengths to take care of Joe. Amidst all the chaos, Joe finds himself (over the space of a single weekend) uncovering crimes that have been buried for years. And soon, as often before, his own life is on the line.

Written with all the sharp-edged humour and rich humanity that distinguishes his best work, this new development in Hill's much-acclaimed body of work bids fair to gain just as devoted a following as the Dalziel and Pascoe books, with Hill's prose style as keen as ever: *"she still regarded Joe's post-lathe career in private investigation as a symptom of stress-induced brain fever which marriage to a good woman, plus regular attendance at chapel and the job centre would soon cure. She'd reacted to the news that Joe had bought a mobile phone like a Sally Army captain catching a reformed drunk coming out of an off-licence with a brown paper parcel."*

Judith Gray

FAITH BY PETER JAMES, ORION, £16.99/£9.99

As a novelist, Peter James has always been able to call on two great strengths: his sheer panache as a storyteller, and his uncommon ability to deal in several different genres. Reading a new James novel, the reader is never really sure whether or not this is in the horror or science fiction genres—or is a straightforward thriller. In fact, this mixing of modes is precisely what makes his books so unique. If one is obliged to categorise this book, it probably falls into the medical thriller category. Ross Ransom, at the top of his profession as one of the most acclaimed (and wealthy) of plastic surgeons in the world, rejoices in an equally successful marriage—on the surface. His wife is perfect—but that's hardly surprising, considering that Ransom has spent many hours in surgery creating that perfection. But his wife becomes ill and rejects both conventional medicine and her unhappy marriage to Ransom. As she seeks help in the world of alternative medicine—and falls under the spell of a charismatic therapist—Ransom begins to feel a terrible sense of betrayal. And to re-establish the sense of order in his world, he begins a course of action that may be murderous, but in his eyes, is merely rational.

As always with James, characterisation is enjoyably functional rather than ground-breaking, but it is none the worse for that when the narrative demands of a thriller are so enjoyably accommodated. James admirers will enjoy this, but it has the capacity to make him many new friends.

Brian Ritterspak

JUPITER'S BONES BY FAYE KELLERMAN, HEADLINE, £5.99

Dr Emil Ganz was a remarkable man. As a physicist whose theories of cosmology entranced society, he vanished at the height of his fame to re-emerge as Jupiter, the leader of a bizarre sect that specialised in a mixture of mysticism and mathematics. Before his death, the sect was regarded as a dangerous magnet for the credulous and the damaged. But Ganz has committed suicide—or has he? The cult is on the brink of being destabilised, with a savage battle to succeed him underway. Lieutenant Peter Decker who is endeavouring to uncover exactly what happened to the scientist, realises that Ganz's death may lead to a holocaust of horrendous proportions. Kellerman is always adroit at channelling the current fears of society into a gripping thriller narrative, and her endeavours here are as successful as ever. Fascinating both as an investigative thriller and as a study of the psychopathology of cults, this is one to rank with such earlier Kellerman books as *Serpent's Tooth* and *Prayers for the Dead*.

Eve Tan Gee

DEATH BY DROWNING BY VINCENT LARDO, PIATKUS, £9.99

Michael Reo has witnessed a murder. But Michael has married money, and is prepared do anything to keep his privileged position. He has no intention of going to the police. Galen Miller, however, is a rebellious young man from a very different social background, desperate to preserve his stake in the family farm. These are the characters detective Eddy Evans finds himself investigating in Lardo's gritty thriller. And only one person seems know the truth behind the death—Galen Miller's ex-girlfriend. But she's not talking. Lardo's dynamically written thriller characterises its three very different principals with real assurance, and handles the ever-surprising plot with a highly attractive energy. Lardo's detective, Eddie, is a nicely judged creation, and we follow his dogged efforts with great interest. Populist and undemanding, this is still a diverting entry in the thriller stakes.

Brian Ritterspak

THE CUTTING EDGE OF BARNEY THOMSON BY DOUGLAS LINDSAY, PIATKUS, £6.99

Adjectives—all of them good—were flung at David Lindsay's *The Long Midnight of Barney Thomson*, a hilarious and mordant black comedy with several breathtaking set pieces. But can one of Scotland's most quirky and imaginative talents pull off the same trick again? *The Cutting Edge of Barney Thomson* manages to match the invention and hilarity of the earlier book with just as much vigour. If Lindsay seems to take a little time to get into his stride, the dividends are considerable in this tale of Scotland's most notorious—and misunderstood—serial killer, the eponymous Thomson. This time he's been accused of every crime since Jack the Ripper, and decides to hide out among the Holy Order of the Monks of Saint John. As Brother Jacob, he is quite a success as a barber. But his luck is running true to form: as the police close in on him, Brother Jacob realises that he has chosen the only monastery in Britain with its own selection of serial killers. This is a quite hilarious and diverting read, calculated to give offence to those outraged by its premise. The rest of us will be holding our sides.

Eve Tan Gee

THE SEA GARDEN BY SAM LLEWELLYN, HEADLINE, £9.99

The kind of acclaim that greeted Sam Llewellyn *The Shadow in the Sands* was of an enthusiasm usually granted to literary novels, and even though Llewellyn writes in the thriller genre, the acclaim is hardly surprising in view of the elegance and evocative power of his use of language. The new book, *The Sea Garden*, is a remarkable investigation of secrets: communal, familial and historical. Victoria and Guy Blakeney-Jones inherit the tiny Cornish Island of Trelise. At first everything is idyllic on the beautiful island with its friendly population. The couple begin their much-anticipated restoration of the sub tropical priory gardens to its former splendour. But as the restoration proceeds, Victoria realises that there are more than plants and philosophical notions hidden among the walls and terraces—such as the skeleton with a fractured skull. Soon the couple are discovering boxes of letters and diaries in the library, unopened since the death of their writers, and an incredible secret involving five generations of the Jones family unwinds. And a phantasmagoria of sex and death awaits. This rich, ambitious and intricate novel has immense appeal, and will please both lovers of the thriller and the serious novel.

Barry Forshaw

THE DETECTIVE WORE SILK DRAWERS BY PETER LOVESEY, ALLISON AND BUSBY, £5.99

Aficionados of the best crime fiction are fully aware that Peter Lovesey's Sergeant Cribb novels are a taste that is well worth acquiring. The elegant writing, the beautifully realised period atmosphere and (most of all), the characterisation of the laconic Cribb make this a series to treasure. *The Detective Wore Silk Drawers* is one of Lovesey's most celebrated outings for Cribb, with the detective investigating the world of 19th-century pugilism, and coming up against a ring promoting the illegal sport of bare-knuckle boxing. Cribb cannily dispatches Constable Jago, a police boxing champion, to act as undercover agent at the remote Radstock Hall, which he believes to be the gang's training centre. But the decapitated body of a pugilist has been found in the Thames, and Cribb has to move fast to ensure that Jago doesn't follow suit. This one is sheer delight, bringing to life the grim world of bare-knuckle boxing as vividly as it does the world of a 19th-century copper.

Brian Ritterspak

SOMETHING WICKED: NEW SCOTTISH CRIME FICTION EDITED BY SUSIE MAGUIRE & AMANDA HARGREAVES, POLYGON, £9.99

It's an interesting fact that crime writing in the English language has been largely derived from English and American culture: the polarity between the intellectual crime-solving of the sleuths of Conan Doyle and Dorothy Sayers contrasted with the hard-boiled gumshoe world of Raymond Chandler and Dashiell Hammett. But with the phenomenal success of such writers as Ian Rankin and Val McDermid, Scotland is fast becoming the home of cutting-edge crime writing. This first-ever collection of Scottish crime fiction demonstrates the quite remarkable range on offer (and that means from the sublime to the dull), with precisely the kind of gritty realism one might expect played against witty, entertaining scenarios and darkly Gothic tales. Alongside familiar names such as McDermid and Brookmyre, many newer writers vie for our attention, and this is an uneven but intriguing collection.

Eve Tan Gee

MURDER IN THE CENTRAL COMMITTEE / SOUTHERN SEAS BY MANUEL VASQUEZ MONTALBAN, PLUTO, £3.95 / SERPENT'S TAIL, £6.99

"Do you realise that we private eyes are the barometers of established morality? I tell you society is rotten. It doesn't believe anything." The words of Pepe Carvalho, the fat and cynical private eye of Manuel Vasquez Montalban's wonderfully atmospheric work perfectly encapsulates the moral climate in these seedy and atmospheric novels. Both *Southern Seas* and *Murder in the Central Committee* have established a devoted following through the sheer uniqueness of his dogged private investigator, who treads the mean streets of Barcelona. All PIs must have defining characteristics (along with the customary agile intelligence) and Pepe has a particularly persuasive manner, a taste for good cuisine and some dubious politics: links to the Spanish Communist Party and a stint in the CIA are also part of his resumé. In *Murder*, he investigates the murder of Fernando Garrido, the General Secretary of the Party, and Montalban is able to make several (and often very funny) comments on the changing face of Post-Cold War Europe. The colourful and exotic (as well as squalid and deprived) locales of Barcelona and Madrid are conjured up with fastidious skill, and Pepe's dislike for Madrid is nicely handled. In the equally adroit *Southern Seas*, Pepe's investigation of the murder of Stuart Pedrell, a powerful businessman (who has disappeared on his way to Polynesia in search of the visionary spirit of Paul Gauguin) uncovers a world of sex, politics and Nouvelle Cuisine. In this one, Montalban is particularly good on the class divisions of Spanish culture, with Pepe moving between the upper echelons and the lower depths in his usual persuasive manner. Two truly cherishable items from a master novelist.

Barry Forshaw

THE BLUE HOUR BY JEFFERSON PARKER

With books such as *Where Serpents Lie* and *Summer of Fear*, Jefferson Parker has very successfully strip-mined the grimly compelling Thomas Harris territory of serial killer pursuit. Parker's new book, *The Blue Hour*, consolidates the achievement of earlier work, while adding a finely-honed, lyrical finish to his prose that places the novel as much in the literary field as in that of the psycho-thriller.

Tim Hess is a detective who has had a dedication to the police that is second to none, but incipient cancer is giving him thoughts of mortality. Merci Rayborn, however, is at the start of her police career, with every intention of getting to the top—and at any price. The ill-matched duo are assigned to track down a brutal serial killer who has been abducting women from shopping malls. His victims are treated like animals, and all that is left after his horrific crimes is a signature to taunt the Orange County police: a purse full of entrails. But where are the bodies?

As Hess and Rayborn track down the Purse Snatcher, they find that dealing with a sickeningly disturbed mind is only one of their problems—their boss has a hidden agenda in assigning them to the case, and several false trails are allowing a monster to commit more atrocities. As his two protagonists close in on their prey, Parker is particularly adroit at revealing the growing obsession that unites them in their pursuit. In masterful fashion, he takes us into the grimmest recesses of the human soul, always balancing this with the humanity and resilience of his principals. While the book has all the mordant energy the genre demands, it is the carefully chosen, almost poetic prose that brilliantly set off the horrors and creates a highly unusual reading experience: *"Terrible sights. Hess had learned to forgive himself for them. Sometimes it made him sad to know he was like this. It was part of what made him good at what he did...but he could never unimagine what he saw."*

Eve Tan Gee

CRADLE AND ALL BY JAMES PATTERSON, HEADLINE, £16.99

Wisely avoiding the temptation to rest on his laurels, James Patterson has created a protagonist to rival the highly successful Alex Cross: Father Rosetti is the Vatican's chief and most trusted investigator. This new thriller has all the compulsive readability of Patterson's earlier work (including the famous brevity and concision), conjoined with a more supernatural atmosphere that frequently produces the requisite chills.

When a spate of supernatural events occurs, believed to be linked to the imminent fulfilment of the secret Fatima prophecies, Rosetti is the obvious choice to interpret their meaning. His considerable religious knowledge and vaunted mental agility are soon put to uses that he did not expect when he starts to believe that only a miracle can stop an unimaginable evil being unleashed on the world. Rosetti is a cleverly realised character, and this change of pace for a megaselling author is very welcome. Cross fans may miss their hero, but Patterson is likely to ensnare a whole new raft of readers.

Brian Ritterspak

DARK LADY BY RICHARD NORTH PATTERSON, HUTCHINSON, £15.99

Death has come to a struggling Midwestern city on the brink of an economic recovery. The two dead men, found within days of each other, are the general manager of the company building a new baseball stadium—the city's hope for the future—and an attorney with criminal connections. Both deaths are horrific—but are they both homicide? Stella Marz, Assistant County Prosecutor and head of the homicide division of the prosecutor's office is soon to discover that the deaths are (of course) connected in labyrinthine ways. As Stella descends deeper and deeper into a maze of corruption and murder, she finds herself investigating both the town's dark past along with disturbing issues in her own life. *No Safe Place* established Patterson as a thriller writer of considerable acumen, and this new book has the same fastidious attention to detail, built into an intriguing and carefully structured plot. Stella, too, is a heroine of powerful appeal.

Judith Gray

BACK FROM THE DEAD BY CHRIS PETIT

Chris Petit gleaned considerable acclaim for *The Psalm Killer*, a complex, hard-edged thriller reminiscent of both

Thomas Harris and Martin Cruz Smith, but absolutely individual in its achievement. With the remarkable *Back from the Dead*, Petit has created a haunting and atmospheric novel that is unlike anything else the reader is likely to have encountered: a disturbing and atmospheric book about people locked on a path of self-destruction.

McMahon, a rock star uncomfortably conscious of being past his best, is shocked to open a letter that appears to contain exactly the same declarations of love as those of an obsessed fan who wrote to him years ago. But Leah, the author of those letters, is dead—so how can these new letters contain things that only the dead girl could have known? As the employment of ex-coppers for celebrity security has become a necessary fashion accessory, McMahon's wife hires Youselli, an uncompromising and hard-nosed city cop in need some extra money, to look into this bizarre mystery. But soon Youselli is inexorably drawn into the decadent lifestyle of his substance-abusing employers. And as he digs deeper into the strange motives of the mysterious fan pursuing McMahon, he is plunged into a dark world of sexual obsession and manic love.

Petit is a novelist of real distinction, and the characterisation here is top drawer. We are as concerned with the insecure musician McMahon as we are with the down-on-his-luck Youselli, and the psychology of both characters is handled with a master's sure touch. The bizarre world of excess and indulgence that the rock star inhabits is conjured with a maximum sense of atmosphere: *"McMahon was making the best of appearing elegantly wasted, swigging a bottle of Jack Daniels from the neck, his eyes bulging and glittery with near obscene excitement, and looking several galaxies away. Youselli had to hand it him, he knew how to put on a party."*

Eve Tan Gee

A SLOW BURNING BY STANLEY POTTINGER, HODDER & STOUGHTON

The alert reader should be pre-disposed to like a novel that begins with a quote from Cole Porter, and it's a good augury here. Nat Hennessy saw his father battered to death by a drunken black looter in the Great Blackout of 1977. He's now a cop, with the chance that he has been waiting for: he can avenge the brutal murder, but only by compromising his integrity. Similarly, Cush Walker is obliged to live with the grim memory of seeing his father hanged by the Ku Klux Klan. Walker, now a surgeon, is attempting to alter the kind of bigotry that caused the death of his father. Pottinger's two protagonists in this controversial and hard-hitting medical thriller are linked by Camilla, engaged to one man and loved by the other. She, too, has a fateful incident in the past that shaped her life. But she is in a coma, and needs the technical skills of Cush to save her. Pottinger made a considerable impact with the scientific medical thriller *The Fourth Procedure*, and manages to import some serious points into this sheerly entertaining novel. All the protagonists are given the kind of solidity found in serious fiction, and the writing has a rugged and compelling vigour.

Judith Gray

REBUS: THE EARLY YEARS BY IAN RANKIN, ORION, £16.99

There is a consensus that Ian Rankin is now the most important crime fiction practitioner in Britain (never, of course, forgetting that his novels depict a brilliantly drawn Scottish milieu). And as

Introducing Inspector Kurt Wallander

FACELESS

drinks to much
works too hard
sleeps too little

KILLERS

police work wrecked his marriage
his errant daughter won't acknowledge him
his aging father barely tolerates him

but just now, he's too busy to do anything about all that...

FROM THE HARVILL PRESS
THE FIRST IN THE OUTSTANDING
SERIES OF WALLANDER MYSTERIES

FACELESS KILLERS is available from all good bookshops
in paperback, £9.99 and hardback, £16.99

H A R V I L L   C R I M E

John Hannah is shortly to incarnate Rankin's tough protagonist Rebus in a new television series, it's not hard to predict that the author's success will soon extend far beyond the literary. This cleverly conceived volume collects three of the early DI Rebus adventures, and it's salutary to see how fully formed all the aspects of Rankin's style were right from the start. The crackling dialogue, the hard-hitting characterisation and the brilliantly realised locales are present in all three books, with *Hide & Seek* being the most distinguished. In his customary laconic way, Rebus deals with the abduction and murder of two girls in *Knots & Crosses*, and a dark mystery that begins with the death of an Edinburgh junkie is the subject of *Hide & Seek*. Rebus is drafted to London for the compelling *Tooth & Nail*. Reading all three in succession, it's striking to note how rarely Rankin repeats himself: the plotting is always fresh and newly minted, with Rebus obliged to solve satisfyingly labyrinthine mysteries. If you've already read the later novels, this is the perfect chance to catch up on the early books. But if you realise that an introduction to Scotland's most intuitively brilliant copper is overdue, there's simply no better place to start than in this highly collectable volume.

Brian Ritterspak

STRIP JACK BY IAN RANKIN, ORION, £5.99

In one of Rankin's most sharply observed Inspector Rebus novels, the laconic DI is sympathetic to the dilemma of an MP that he finds himself involved with. Gregor Jack has been caught in an Edinburgh brothel with a publicity-conscious prostitute. As the media rounds on him, Jack depends on his friends to protect him. But some of wife's associates have extremely dubious backgrounds—and when the wife disappears, Rebus finds himself looking into the affairs of the young MP. As usual, dialogue and characterisation are effortlessly dispatched, and this one relies more on dynamic plotting than most. Rebus is involved in political scandals in several of Rankin's books, but his personal involvement here is particularly well drawn. The MP, Jack, is a carefully rounded character, with the reader allowed to make up his own mind about him.

Judith Gray

ONE FOR SORROW BY MARY REED & ERIC MAYER, POISONED PEN PRESS, $23.95

If you've been following the short stories featuring the investigations of John the Eunuch, Lord Chamberlain to the Byzantine Emperor Justinian, set in Constantinople in the sixth century AD, then you may already have rushed out to acquire this first full-length novel. If not, let me bring you up to speed. The stories are all set in the heyday of Justinian's long and powerful reign. Although Justinian is a Christian, his Chamberlain, John, is a pagan, worshipping Mithra, which itself introduces an element of tension. Justinian is, of course, all powerful, and could destroy John at any time he wishes, but he finds he can place a high degree of trust and faith in Justinian, as can his wife, the remarkable and feisty empress, Theodora. Trusting a eunuch has its advantages. It was Theodora whose strength and conviction saved Justinian during the Nika riots of 532AD, and it was following that uprising that Justinian was able to assert his absolute authority and take total command of the Byzantine Empire. That was where the first story in the series, *"A Byzantine Mystery"* (*Mammoth Book of Historical Whodunnits*, 1993), began, where John has to find a priceless relic lost during the riots. There have been four stories since then: *"A Mithraic Mystery"* (*Mam-*

moth Book of Historical Detectives, 1995), "Beauty More Stealthy" (Classical Whodunnits, 1997), 'Leap of Faith' (Ellery Queen's Mystery Magazine, November 1998) and, most recently, "A Lock of Hair for Proserpine" in Maxim Jakubowski's Chronicles of Crime (1999).

Now we have the delight of a complete novel. On the face of it the mystery is simple. Who murdered John's friend, Leukos, Justinian's Keeper of the Plate? At the start of the novel John, Leukos and others are at the Games in the city, although John's attention is somewhat distracted by one of the female bull-dancers, who reminds him of a girl he once knew in the days when he was still the sum of all his parts. But soon after, as John is returning home after other diversions, he stumbles across the body of Leukos in an alleyway. Justinian demands to know who committed the crime. And John has his work cut out for him as there are plenty of red herrings and distractions and devious developments. Perhaps the most fascinating is just who is the British knight Thomas who claims he is an emissary from the British King Arthur seeking the Holy Grail. And what does the Christian stylite know who sees so much but tells so little from his lofty site. And then there's that Egyptian brothel-keeper.

Byzantium comes alive in this novel and at last we begin to learn more (a lot more) about John the Eunuch, and his past. It bodes well for a long and interesting series. The sequel, Two for Sorrow, is already well under way.

Mike Ashley

CERTAIN PREY BY JOHN SANDFORD, HEADLINE, £5.99

In novels such as Rules of Prey and Shadow Prey, the American writer John Sandford has shown a commanding grasp of the thriller idiom, ensuring that his incident-packed narratives (while discursive) still move with express-train speed. This new one is as idiosyncratic and punchy as anything he has written. Clara Rinker is from the South: attractive and well turned out, she also happens to be one of the best hit women around. In her unspectacular fashion, she can always be relied upon to dispatch a victim with cool efficiency. But when she is hired for job in Minnesota by a crooked defence attorney, things start to go wrong. A witness survives and a cop called Davenport is on her tail, with no sign of giving up. The conflict between the ruthless anti-heroine and the dogged Davenport is handled with authority and skill, as Sandford juggles the demands of character and the mechanics of the thriller genre with a master touch. Setting the book in his native Minnesota allows him to pack in some utterly convincing local colour, and the only regret is that this is the 12th Sandford novel with the word 'prey' in the title—isn't it time for change?

Brian Ritterspak

FLORIDA STRAITS BY LAURENCE SHAMES, ORION, £5.99

Joey Goldman is a small-time New York hustler with ambitions above his station. How can he break into the higher echelons of Florida's ruthless gangster world? He has the cash—but he also has the complication of half-brother Gino, who turns up on the run from the Mob. Soon Joey's plans are in ruins, with his survival depending on a king's ransom of uncut emeralds owned by a much feared Mafioso. Laurence Shames is generally good at the frenzied cross-plotting of his vivid narrative, and if it's clear that Elmore Leonard is the model here (almost actionably so), this highly entertaining crime novel is none the worse for that, and its capricious energy is very winning. Joey, too, is a memorable anti-hero.

Eve Tan Gee

SPINOFF BY MICHAEL SHEA, HARPERCOLLINS, £16.99

Michael Shea won considerable approval for *Spin Doctor*, a witty and inventive novel utilising his knowledge of political intrigue as a career diplomat. *Spinoff* represents a development on that book and his other earlier work by again delivering an entrée into the world of politics, but dovetailing a smooth and involving thriller plot into his narrative. American scientist Harper Guthrie is invited to be a guest researcher at an important Edinburgh laboratory. He is pleased by the prospect of furthering his research into the spread of deadly viruses, but soon finds himself deep in an international crisis. Shea's other principal protagonist, Lyle Thane, is Downing Street's most important spin doctor. But when PM Peter Morgan begins behaving very strangely, Thane notices that other powerful men in Britain are falling ill. And soon both he and Guthrie are in a search for the cause of a major new disease. The characterisation here is razor sharp, but it's Shea's adroit way with his compelling narrative(despite plotting hiccups) that ensures maximum reader attention.

Brian Ritterspak

SHADOW WALK BY JANE WATERHOUSE, PIATKUS, £5.99

Two teenage girls, Garner Quinn and Lara Spangler, have made a vow to be friends forever. But the teenage friendship is brutally severed when 16-year-old Lara is savagely killed (along with her whole family) by her outwardly quiet father Stanley. He vanishes without a trace, and Garner becomes a best-selling true crime writer. But she never forgets the Spangler family. And when a journalist friend gives her a lead to the vanished murderer, she decides to bring the case to closure. But then the journalist is murdered.

This is thriller writing without a wasted word. Although Waterhouse is careful to ensure that the psychology of her characters always rings true, her plotting is a tad pedestrian, and this compromises some adroit characterisation.

Barry Forshaw

LOSING THE PLOT BY PAUL WHEELER, PHOENIX, £6.99

Black comedy is so much a staple of the novel these days, that it's sometimes forgotten that some of the finest writing in the genre extends back to Evelyn Waugh and books such as *Vile Bodies*. Wheeler's sharp and funny novel synthesises the best of The Master's mordant wit with a very modern sensibility in this tale of screenwriter Alan Tate, spending his life wishing that he had written the classic movie comedies (and watching his career collapse about his ears). An encounter with a pushy German producer seems to suggest that he is about to make movie that he has always wanted to—after a little research. Investigating the sexy world of high finance, Alan finds himself mixed up in a high-tech bank robbery, with the police looking at his screenplay as some kind of a blueprint. And then people start to die. The manic plotting never undercuts the sense of solid crime writing craft so essential to point up the humour – but , finally, the reader is left with the feeling that the era of Waugh's scalpel-like incisions is past.

Brian Ritterspak

MANNER OF DEATH BY STEPHEN WHITE, PENGUIN, £5.99

In the competitive field of the thriller, Stephen White has produced a highly individual body of work, with his novels featuring the clinical psychologist Alan Gregory (*Harm's Way*, *Remote Control* and *Critical Conditions*) demonstrating elegant storytelling skill and a gift for vigorous characterisation. Of course, White's own background in medicine provides that essential underpinning of verisimilitude that makes his novels quite as convincing as they are engaging. It is winter in Colorado, and Gregory is obliged to attend the funeral of an old colleague. But the death, which at first appeared to be a tragic climbing accident, takes on the appearance of something more sinister. Gregory encounters two retired FBI investigators, who force him to revisit painful memories and conclude that there is something sinister behind the deaths of old friends. White's narrative has his usual bitter skill, and when a meticulous and relentless killer puts Gregory's name on the list, the tension is ratcheted up even more.

Barry Forshaw

THE LAST KABBALIST OF LISBON BY RICHARD ZIMLER, ARCADIA, £11.99

Many books have attempted to pull off the remarkable trick that Umberto Eco achieved so memorably in *The Name of the Rose*: embedding a highly compulsive historical thriller within the context of a serious literary novel. But Richard Zimler's *The Last Kabbalist of Lisbon* is, at best, a mixed success in its contribution to this fascinating sub-genre. Set among Jewish communities living clandestinely in Lisbon in the 16th century, Zimler begins his narrative with Abraham Zarco found dead with a naked girl by his side. Zarco is a renowned Kabbalist, a practitioner of the arcane mysteries of the Jewish tradition at a time when the Jews of Lisbon were forced to convert to Christianity. And Zimler's unlikely protagonist, forced to investigate his uncle's murder, is Berekiah, a talented young manuscript illuminator. As Berekah discovers in the Kabbalah clues that lead him into the labyrinth of secrets in which the Jews sought to hide from their persecutors, his own life is threatened in terrible ways. Functioning principally as a compelling and atmospheric thriller, Zimler's novel is also a stinging study of intolerance, couched in prose of elegance and gritty strength that overcomes some warmed-over elements.

Eve Tan Gee

THE BEEKEEPER'S APPRENTICE BY LAURIER R KING, HARPERCOLLINS, £6.99

When I was writing my *Murder Done To Death* I found there were more than one thousand parodies and pastiches of Sherlock Holmes. It seems Cox's and King's Bank, sadly now moved from its historic offices, must have had a strongroom bulging with battered trunks marked *"Private—Dr John H Watson"*. The earliest parodies appeared within one year of the first Holmes story in 1891. Pastiches take two main forms. One is to reconstruct every case mentioned casually in the Canon. The other is to match Holmes with literary figures, like Dr Fu Manchu or Jack the Ripper, or to set him solving murders on the Titanic, at Greyfriars School and Harry Houdini's stage show.

Mrs King's approach is to take the Holmes story on to his retirement to the Sussex Downs in 1915. (Remember the Casebook appeared in 1927). A fifteen-year-old American-Jewish girl, Mary Russell, meets him and becomes an apprentice sleuth. Several short cases start the book, which is quite lengthy at 347 pages of smallish print. With the Doyle and Agatha Christie short stories you look forward to the next, and this happens here, but the last adventure of 197 pages is a book in itself. The style is a trifle leisurely and not always congruous with a fifteen-year-old about to become what Wodehouse would term an Oxford undergraduate. Some descriptions ring rather modern but the speech rhythms of Holmes are accurate. At times one ponders the misogynistic 54-year-old Holmes submitting to strictures from a girl young enough to be his grand-daughter.

John Kennedy Melling

PHREAK BY DENISE DANKS, ORION, £5.99

In two areas at least, Denise Danks can claim to be among the foremost female crime fiction practitioners in the UK: she is probably the premier noir writer, with a very personal dark and sinister universe as the scene of some terrifying crimes and ruthless criminals. And she is probably the only computer crime writer, specialising in the new arena of technocrime . Her computer journalist heroine Georgina Powers was introduced in *The Pizza House Crash*, and this hard-edged female investigator with a taste for rough sex is one of the most memorable protagonists in current crime writing.

Phreak is probably Danks'most eye opening thriller yet. Georgina is investigating a phone scam in the East End of London: phreaking involves the cloning of mobile phones. But her contact, Abdul Malik, a leading scam artist in the phone field (and someone with whom Georgina has been enjoying some vigorous couplings) is murdered and dumped in a skip. His neck has been broken, and lipstick smeared on his T-shirt. Georgina's hacker friend Chronic, a local drug dealer, is missing, and she finds herself under suspicion by the police. But that's not her only problem: a Bengali protection gang is interested in knowing how Abdul was killed, and Georgina is forced to enlist an old friend, East End villain and ex-boxer Tony Levi to help her crack the mystery and save her skin in the middle of a gang war that covers both the mean streets of London and cyberspace.

As in such powerful thrillers as *Better Off Dead* and the remarkable *Torso*, Danks has few equals in conjuring up a dangerous and atmospheric world for her amoral, hard-living heroine. Georgina is a brilliantly created figure, with her messy sex life, ill-advised substance abuse and mastery of the technocrime that is her beat making for a truly memorable and unique heroine. The gags, as usual, are delivered with impeccable timing, and the fusion of the violent world of East End gang culture and cyberspace is handled with real aplomb. Danks also has few equals in creating some of the most indelible images in current crime fiction: *"To the left, to the right, his shoulders jolted with the imaginary force of a recoiling machine-gun. Long red flares of burning tobacco streamed out behind him like the tails of a night kite while his body jerked back and forth and his hair fell over his face. He raised his no-show Kalashnikov aloft, pumping his arms in triumph and then he stopped, just like that, and turned to me, his eyes all craziness and confusion. He waited one speechless moment before he legged it, leaving me alone with the dead body of Abdul Malik."*

Brian Ritterspak

THE OFFICE OF THE DEAD BY ANDREW TAYLOR, HARPERCOLLINS, £16.99

There are thrillers in which the use of language is pared down and functional to ensure the swiftest possible movement of the plot. But some writers have demonstrated that it is possible to utilise prose of the most elegant and sophisticated variety without sacrificing one iota of the riveting narrative quality that all the best thrillers have. Andrew Taylor is one of the finest stylists in the genre, and remarkable pieces of work such as *The Barred Window* have made his books essential reading for the most discerning of crime

"...I exclude knives, razors or any other sharp instrument which would involve both an appropriate knowledge of human anatomy and a very steady hand, qualities I do not possess..."

SINGLEMINDED
by Hélène de Monaghan

Available from all good bookshops or by post from CT Publishing, Dept CT32) PO Box 5880, Edgbaston, Birmingham, B16 9BJ (Postage and Packing free) - or buy on the web from www.crimetime.co.uk

ISBN: 1 902002- 13- XPrice: £6.99 Paperback

CT PUBLISHING, PO BOX 5880, BIRMINGHAM B16 8JF.

enthusiasts. But his Roth trilogy (of which the first two books were *The Four Last Things* and *The Judgement of Strangers*) has elevated his considerable art to a genuinely rarefied area of achievement. The final book of the trilogy, *The Office of The Dead*, is both a perfect conclusion to this unique sequence and an individual thriller quite unlike anything the reader is likely to encounter. Taylor has created each book to be read on its own as a self-contained story, and although they are designed to work together, they may be read in any order.

Dealing with the linked histories of two families, the Appleyards and the Byfields, Taylor has fashioned a remarkable panoply that is both a picture of British society in all its strata and a complex crime narrative that delivers all the requisite suspense of the genre. The new book is set in 1958, with Taylor's protagonist Wendy Appleyard in deep trouble: untrained for any work, without funds and facing divorce. She looks to her oldest friend, Janet Byfield, for assistance. Unlike Wendy, Janet appears to be enjoying everything that life can offer: a good-looking husband, a loving daughter and an exquisite home in the Cathedral Close of Rosington. Her husband is an ambitious young clergyman, on the verge of promotion. But there is the worm in the bud: sins of the past begin to make a devastating claim on the present, and death comes to the Close, along with a mystery that reaches back to the previous century and an ill-fated poet priest and opium addict called Francis Youlgreave.

Wendy, as the outsider in this close-knit community, begins to suspect the truth about the dark secrets around her, and finds herself having to unlock a double mystery stretching back to the turn of the century in time to prevent catastrophic events in the present.

Taylor's skills at characterisation are considerable, and he possesses the unique gift of rendering a highly complex narrative in a fashion that gives the reader just as much information as is necessary to either second guess the author or wait breathlessly for the next revelation. Taylor's theme, as in so much serious literature, is the inexorable hold that the past has over the present, and this is rendered in language of the most thoughtful and exuberant kind: *"My mother thought Hillgard House would make me a lady. My father thought it would get me out of the way for most of the year. He was right and she was wrong. We didn't learn to be young ladies at Hillgard House—we learnt to be little savages in a jungle presided over by remote predators."*

Brian Ritterspak

THE NEW ADVENTURES OF SHERLOCK HOLMES, EDITED BY MARTIN H GREENBERG ET AL., ROBINSON, £8.99

Further outings for Conan Doyle's definitive sleuth written by other hands can hardly be called a cottage industry any more, as their number overtook all the official stories in the canon some time ago. For those addicted to these new Holmes adventures (as the great detective was to the needle), it's something of a lottery to pick up such a volume. Authors such as Nicholas Meyer created brilliantly inventive riffs on the classic tropes, while others merely reheated the formula without adding an iota. This volume, originally published to celebrate the centennial of the appearance in 1887 of *The Speckled Band*, the first case for Baker Street's immortal denizen, has been newly updated, along with new stories by a truly mouth-watering list of authors. If you want to see what Stephen King, Peter Lovesey, Anne Perry and John Gard-

We bow to no-one in our admiration for Steven Saylor's Gordianus novels. so we asked him for a few words on the new book, Rubicon (Constable Robinson)...

EVEN AT THE HEIGHT of Rome's empire, many countries lay beyond the rule of Rome, and yet a fascination with things Roman reached even as far as Finland...and still does. Certainly the reach of Rome never extended to America, and Texas (where I was born), and yet even there, 2000 years after Caesar, I grew up with a boyhood fascination for chariot races, fire-catapults and the sensuous delights of the Roman baths. To those fascinations, as I grew older, came an even greater fascination with the intrigues of Roman politics and the drama of Roman justice. The result are my novels of *"Roma Sub Rosa"*—a secret history of Rome, or a history of Rome's secrets, as seen through the eyes of my hero, Gordianus the Finder. That these books now find their way from America to even Finland delights me, for Gordianus has gone where no Caesar ever conquered!

And Judith Gray looks at the new Gordianus outing...

RUBICON BY STEVEN SAYLOR, ROBINSON CONSTABLE, £6.99

Some day, there will be a battle royal between Lindsey Davis and Stephen Saylor to decide who writes the most brilliantly plotted Roman sleuth thrillers. It really is impossible to say who does it best, as each successive novel by both writers has one marvelling at the continuing levels of freshness and inspiration. The new Saylor is one of his finest yet, taking his protagonist Gordianus the Finder into ever more sinister levels of Roman society, where corruption stretches from the senatorial bathhouses to the stinking gutters. Pompey commands Gordianus to find the killer of the Emperor's favourite cousin, and this time Saylor's slippery hero find himself projected into the thick of war. As usual, the scholarship is as assured as the characterisation, and the sleight of hand whereby a modern consciousness is projected into an ancient hero is achieved seamlessly. One day, perhaps, Saylor may be forced to repeat himself, but on the evidence of *Rubicon*, that day is some considerable time in the future.

Judith Gray

ner (author of the wonderful Moriarty novels) can do with Holmes and his doughty chronicler Watson, then this entertaining but inconsistent compendium is essential. Needless to say, not all the stories aspire to the Master's untouchable heights, but there isn't a fully fledged dud in the pack, and the finest stories will have most readers adjusting the antimacassar and reaching for their meerschaum pipes.

Brian Ritterspak

SILVERMEADOW BY BARRY MAITLAND, ORION, £9.99

With the detective duos outnumbering the criminals these days, it's an inventive author indeed who can inaugurate something fresh in this department. Barry Maitland's Brock and Kolla series has done just that in books such as *The Marx Sisters* and *All My Enemies*, shaking up familiar ingredients and creating really memorable protagonists in the rumpled but brilliant Inspector Brock and his coolly efficient colleague Kathy Kolla. Maitland's utilisation of standard police procedural themes is not innovative, but so superbly plotted (particularly so in this fifth outing for the duo) that readers quickly realise they are in for a highly satisfying diversion. Silvermeadow is a massive new shopping complex, all glittering surfaces and high tech surveillance, owing not a little to Bluewater. All is hunky-dory for the retailers until a sinister (and very violent) criminal brings the Centre close to collapse. Brock and Kolla are called in when several disappearances take place (quickly achieving a sinister significance among both customers and retailers) and before long the first body is found. Is Brock dealing with some kind of insurance shakedown, or something more complex and dangerous? And is the first major suspect who comes to light too obvious a choice? As Brock and Kolla cut deeper into the heart of the mystery, violent death is only one of the ingredients in a baffling investigation.

Maitland's duo is as authoritatively characterised as ever, while the cogency and dash of his plotting are consolidated from book to book. If there's a caveat, it is that something more innovative may be required in future volumes to avoid a loss of freshness, the besetting sin of so many detective series.

Brian Ritterspak

ICE STATION BY MATTHEW REILLY, PAN, £5.99

If you're looking for Indiana Jones concepts built into a blockbusting novel, search no further: Reilly's massive thriller ceratinly finds no room for subtlety of characterisation in its 700 pages, but delivers the requisite kinetic action and outrageous plotting necessary to keep the pages turning very quickly indeed. In a remote US ice station in Antarctica, a remarkable discovery has been made by a cadre of scientists. Deep beneath the surface and encased in layers of ice, there is an object millions of years old. But it's made of metal, and defies scientific logic. Soon men are killing for this amazing discovery, with Reilly's tough protagonist Lieutenant Shane Schofield leading a crack team of US marines to make a play for the object in the teeth of other nations' murderous ploys. The object itself (which it would be cruel to name here) is the perfect fulcrum for all the exhilarating bloodletting that Reilly delivers with such panache – but don't look for nuances.

Eve Tan Gee

THE LAST DANCE BY ED McBAIN, HODDER & STOUGHTON, £16.99

It's inevitable that any review of Ed McBain begins with an expression of disbelief about his continued productivity: this is his 50th novel set in the 87th Precinct; his Matthew Hope series, begun some 22 years later, already stands at 13 and counting. He has written another six books as McBain, and twenty more novels under his real name, Evan Hunter. I suppose 87 novels of the 87th Precinct is probably out of the question.

In the novel under question, the reasons for McBain's continued popularity are apparent. He is a master of quick characterisation, and revealing dialogue. He builds his characters as they advance the action, and uses their lives to add muscle and tension to what are usually reasonably simple plots, often revolving around the kind of twist more common in parlour mysteries than tales of cops in the streets. The twist in this one may be far fetched, at least to anyone who actually lives in London, but that's not the point.

The Last Dance revolves around the rights to a long-lost musical, and the book upon which it was based. The battle for rights, and the authenticity of the claims, give just enough fodder for the plot, and the characters within the precinct provide the rest. This is really where Hill Street and NYPD have their origins. One thing we also need to ask, is what did John Connolly do to irritate McBain so? In *Every Dead Thing* Connolly had a character named Fat Ollie Weeks, an evident hommage to McBain's detective Fat Ollie Watts. In *The Last Dance* McBain's Ollie is told about this and gets irritated: *"He's writing a book about cops and he never heard of me?"* Meyer tries to calm him down: *"This is just another Thomas Harris rip-off serial killer novel. I wouldn't worry about it."* Let's hope McBain, through Meyer, is talking tongue in cheek!

Michael Carlson

THE VISITOR BY LEE CHILD, BANTAM, £9.99

Within a relatively short space of time, Lee Child has gleaned the kind of recognition for his tautly written thrillers that is the envy of other practitioners. The assured *Die Trying* won the W H Smith Thumping Good Read Award, and this latest thriller featuring his tough and likeable protagonist Jack Reacher is another powerful entry. With more casual panache than in even the previous Reacher adventures, Child dispatches a cannily written narrative which has his protagonist (as usual) in mortal danger by chapter two. Two high-flying army career women are found dead in their houses, naked in baths filled with army camouflage paint. Both have been victims of sexual harassment by their superiors, and forced to resign from the service. Reacher, an ex-US military cop, knew both of them. But can he work with the spiky agent Blake, who is in charge of the case? Blake has his sights fixed on a drifter who is party to some dark secret involving the murdered women. As before, the English author shows a consummate grasp of America idioms (something Child takes great pride in) and his tale will ensure many a train stop is missed.

Eve Tan Gee

THE ASPHALT JUNGLE BY W R BURNETT, PRION, £5.99

William Riley Burnett authored some thirty-six gangster novels, including the classics *Little Caesar* (1929) and *High Sierra* (1940). *The Asphalt Jungle*, first published in 1949, tells the story of a half-million dollar jewellery heist which develops complications. In forty short chapters spanning 230 pages, the novel develops over a series of atmospheric scenes. Despite its huge cast of characters, the reader is drawn into the story of Emmerich, Reimenschneider, Gus, Schemer and Dix.

Reimenschneider, just released from prison, has plans for a heist, but needs the financial backing of Emmerich, a rich and powerful lawyer. Emmerich, however, has troubles of his own, which he seeks to resolve with the help of a crooked private detective. The muscle is provided by Dix, *"an out of work heavy"* who despises the grubby city and his city-girl, Doll, and yearns to go home to the country. Schemer, who dreams of a settled home life with his innocent wife and their baby son, will perform the break-in. Gus, a hamburger flipper, who is *"A Number 1 with all the big boys"* and knows enough of what's going on in the city *"to blow the whole administration out of City Hall"*, is the driver.

Tensions develop as preparations are made for a robbery that each member of the gang hopes will change his fortunes. The planning unfolds against a backdrop of rumour, suspicion and double dealing. When things don't go according to plan, each man must find his own way of escaping.

Eddie Duggan

PLOUGHING POTTER'S FIELD BY PHIL LOVESEY, HARPERCOLLINS, £5.99

Frank Rattigan tortures a woman to death over a three day period, reducing the body to 'porridge'. There isn't much left for the pathologists to work on, so the police only know what Rattigan tells them about what he did and why he did it. Sentenced to an indeterminate term in a secure institution, Rattigan, *"The Beast of East 16"*, becomes the object of investigation for forensic psychiatry student Adrian Rawlins. Whilst Rawlins questions Rattigan as part of a national offender-profile database project, he is also seeking to uncover Rattigan's motive for the killing for his own doctoral dissertation, seeking to replace the notion of 'evil' with a more rational, psychologically based explanation of motive.

Rawlins is a failed advertising copywriter turned alcoholic, who has reinvented himself as a forensic psychiatrist after a psychology degree at Essex University. His investigation of Rattigan triggers an introspective turn in Rawlins as Rattigan begins to engage Rawlins in a series of mind games. Rawlins records in his journal: *"I, Adrian Rawlins, imminent Doctor of Forensic Psychiatry, would 'solve' Rattigan. I would find the missing motive which had baffled the experts for so long."* Will he uncover more about Rattigan or himself than he's bargained for? Can you guess? Read it and see if you were right.

Eddie Duggan

KILLER'S PAYOFF BY ED MCBAIN, ALLISON AND BUSBY, £6.99

The first time I realised I was into crime writing—this was back in '84 or '85—was when I looked up at my bookshelf and realised I would have to make space for some more McBain's. At that point I think I had at least ten 87th Precinct books. Now I've got around 35 and I recently bought *The Big Bad City,* the very latest. Having neglected the series for a while I loved it. It was like meeting an old friend unexpectedly and having a great time as a result—there is no finer pleasure. And then this re-issue of an early 87th dropped on the doormat. Re-reading these two brought back a lot memories from those early days; Carella and his wife (God, she is beautiful), The Deaf Man, the bomb in the squad room, Detective Kling finding his girlfriend murdered, the guy who got skinned alive at the end of one (which one was that?), *"The city in these pages is imaginary"* (when, of course it's not—Isola is New York 'flipped over'). Oh, I could go on, but I won't. It was great reading this again. I don't remember reading it the first time—which is OK because I got to enjoy it all over again.

I offer you these ramblings because nothing I can say will add to the greatness that is Ed McBain. The 87th Precinct books are one of the truly enduring monuments of crime writing. If you know what I mean you'll nod your heads. If there is any one out there who doesn't know McBain, well here is as good a place to start as any (although the series starts with *Cop Hater*, first published, amazingly, in 1956).

Peter Walker

LA REQUIEM BY ROBERT CRAIS, ORION, £5.99

LA Requiem is Robert Crais's eighth Elvis Cole novel. Here, Crais combines the LA Private Eye novel with the LA Police Procedural and produces a big league work. Crais also provides plenty of background on Joe Pike, Cole's shadowy sidekick. When former gang-banger turned tortilla magnate Frank Garcia's daughter goes missing, the LAPD shows little interest. However, the daughter's former boyfriend just happens to be Joe Pike, ex-LAPD and partner to PI Elvis Cole. Frank Garcia calls on Joe Pike for help because the LAPD seems to be dragging its feet. Things get interesting when the daughter turns up dead—interesting enough for the LAPD's Hollywood division to be pulled off the case, and interesting enough for the Robbery-Homicide division to take over, and for the FBI to become involved.

Joe Pike and Elvis Cole are tested to the limit in Crais's latest work. Cole's relationship with Lucy Chenier is also developed and tested as she is caught up in the case. *LA Requiem* is a big novel, and Crais is a big hitter.

Eddie Duggan

A MATTER OF HONOR BY EUGENE IZZI, AVON (USA), $6.99

This was the first of Izzi's posthumously published novels, and there is still no sign of a British release on the horizon. It contains many of Izzi's familiar themes: a cop married into a higher-class family (which was such an important feature of the Nick Gaitano books), the sweltering city of Chicago, on the edge of full-scale in the summer heat, and the sharp contrast of political corruption and individual honesty.

If the book harbours the massive ambitions of scale which drove Izzi, it also reflects the obvious haste with which it was written: it follows a schematic outline and rushes along, trying to propel itself from one incident to the next, with Izzi often riffing, as it were, in free-form association, using his characters to vent his own substantial anger.

Believe it or not, this works. The struggles of individuals, even of partners to keep their friendship in the face of racial conflict, of honest men to work within a dishonest system, of career opportunists to finally do something right, are all laid out and effected as part of the most intricate plot Izzi had bothered with in some time. It gets a bit obvious in its resolution of the main character's dilemma, but Marshall del Greco is one of Izzi's better main characters. The supporting cast is strong, including the ever-controversial Reverend Afrikaan. This is like *Hill Street Blues* for real, blown up onto a grand scale. Izzi tried this once before, in *Bulletin from the Street*, in which many of the same characters appear, and to which this could be read as a sequel, summer to that book's winter.

In America, *A Matter of Honor* received far more reviews than usual for an Izzi novel, but that was because his death had generated massive publicity. Most of the mainstream critics, sniffing at reality TV perhaps, were not kind, looking at it as a sort of 'flabby docudrama'. Yes, the writing does let the story down at times, but at other times it is as angry and powerful as anything

Izzi ever wrote. Not the best place to start with this writer, necessarily, but a good place to pick up, if you've encountered Izzi before. And you should have done so by now.

Michael Carlson

INFIDELITY BY PAUL FERRIS, HARPERCOLLINS, £5.99

Ferris's *Infidelity* is based on the true story of George Shotton, who bigamously married in 1918. Shotton, a marine surveyor, is exempt from military service. His work involves travel around the country which keeps him frequently away from home, and from his frigid wife, May. Mamie Stuart is an independent young woman who shares a house with other girls. George soon begins a double life, conducting an affair with Mamie, whose *"dirty remarks [...] closely resemble a man's dirty thoughts."* 1918 being a time when special marriage licenses are issued readily to allow service men to marry sweethearts while on leave, Mamie wants more of a commitment from George: fearing he might lose Mamie, the inevitable happens. Shotton carefully arranges his travels, zigzagging between wives and shipyards. He communicates with them via telegram, like a primitive form of email. A life of deception soon takes its toll: despite George telling himself that *"Lying came from the heart; it was only a complicated way of being honest"*, a query arises concerning the whereabouts of a certain Mrs Shotton.

The story as Ferris tells it is captivating, and he captures a feel for the language, mores and morality of the period. Less appealing is the framing device Ferris employs, setting the story within a 1960s investigation, which offers a trite doubling of the Shotton story. Ultimately, Shotton learns that *"two lives are better than one"*—until they collide.

Eddie Duggan

MORTAL REMAINS BY GREGORY HALL, HARPERCOLLINS, £5.99

The most interesting thing about this novel is the alternating narration by Liz and Jack Armitage, brother and sister, whose father abandoned them in their youth and was implicated in scandals both personal and governmental. Jack is a ne'er do well, charming but insubstantial, and after killing his fiancée in a car crash, abandoned contact with his family. Liz is a spinster schoolteacher, whose promising tennis career was ruined in that same crash, and who lives in the huge family house looking after her senile mother. When Jack loses his job at a London museum not a million miles away from the V&A, he returns to Oxfordshire, begins an archaeological dig he worked on as a child, and discovers a skeleton which turns out to be his father's.

Hall handles the dual narrations convincingly, playing with flashbacks not only to reveal the backstory but to show how it has shaped the perceptions of the narrator. Liz's narration is the more impressive; her internal feelings are delineated more clearly. Jack, as the more shallow of the two, makes that harder to do. But their narrative voices are clear and that works well. The story, mired in the past, is also constructed cleverly, with Jack and Liz's personal histories constantly reverberating with effects on the crimes which are uncovered. The same applies to the village of Crowcester (despite the presence of the obligatory West Country sub-Fred West character), whose boundaries seem to tighten around Jack in particular, as his past comes back to face him. It is exactly here that the book starts to become something else indeed.

Jack's ex-wife pops in from the US for a visit. You know she's American because all Americans say 'honey', even if her next line: *"he sounded a proper English gentleman"* would never be spoken by an American. For Americans to sound is to make a noise and when one noise resembles something they would say 'sounded like'. Her presence is necessary only to get Jack to find a photo and to convince him of his love for the village shopkeeper, neither of which is crucial at that point. But she serves as a sort of catalyst, for as soon as she leaves, *Mortal Remains* transforms itself into a piece of Agatha Christie stagecraft, complete with a Feydeau-style bell ringing and door being opened in the middle of a shooting, and a rush of wooden explanatory dialogue like this: *"Yes, and it was a good thing you kept calm and used your first aid, when Fran and I were useless with shock."* Liz's final confrontation with the villain, whose identity has been obvious, is set up by a plot device so hoary and obvious I won't give it away, and his doom is sealed by another trick which leads us to believe the villain never watched a single cop show on TV.

It's a shame, because Hall created two intriguing characters and a fascinating story, built the two together through a nice literary device, and then lets it all go careering off through a maze of cliché before a couple of shoot-outs sort it all out. And at different points along the way both Liz and Jack actually faint! Really! All this revelation is just so very difficult to bear.

Michael Carlson

THE WATCHMEN BY MATTHEW LYNN, ARROW, £5.99

John Buchan still casts a shadow over thriller writers in the new century, and this cannily written piece transplants the *Thirty Nine Steps* chase motif into a fast-moving tale of double-edged danger, with Lynn's hero and heroine on the run from ruthless professionals. Harry Lamb is sacked from his job at a top city stockbroking firm—but is the sacking connected to research he's undertaking on a massive broadcasting and telecom company? At the same time, Julia Porter is seconded to the Serious Fraud Office—where she stumbles on a major City insider dealing ring. Soon, both are on the run, trying to prove themselves innocent, not to mention simply surviving. Lynn is as sharp on the action set-pieces as he is on the more prosaic narrative passages—Harry's embarrassing dismissal is handled with real skill. If at times, the reader has to swallow some implausible plotting, the dividends are many in a lively and cynical adventure that rarely allows pause for breath.

Judith Gray

THE SKULL MANTRA BY ELIOT PATTISON, CENTURY, £10

"At 1600 hours on the fifteenth a body was discovered. Five hundred feet above the Dragon Throat Bridge. The unidentified victim was dressed expensively, in cashmere and Western denim. Two surgical scars on his abdomen. No other identifying marks."

Identifying, like a head. Cashmere and denim. Western denim. He could be an American. But this is not America. This is Tibet.

Discovered on a remote mountainside by a work gang, the gulag's Buddhist monks down tools, fearing the handiwork of a 'hungry ghost' and regional big-wig Tan is forced to enlist the help of Shan Tao Yun in his search. But Shan—for now and the foreseeable—is part of that prison gang himself; sentenced for embarrassing the Beijing Party.

Comparisons to Ecco's *The Name of The Rose* are a little fatuous. For all its apparent exoticism—occupying Chinese forces, Tibetan sorcerers, Buddhist resistance fighters—there's a mundane 'literary' thriller at the heart of all this. Murders, as Shan points out, are usually, *"the* result of one of two underlying forces. Passion. Or politics." The Skull Mantra, sadly, is an idea in search of a plot. Just because you can transplant criminal shenanigans to an alien land doesn't mean you should. (Further evidence: Martin Limon's pitiful *Jade Lady Burning*.)

Eliot Pattison is the non-fiction author of numerous works on *"international policy"* and it shows. His prose is adequate but dry, dialogue little more than functional. Put the emphasis on thriller, not literary. You'll probably like it. I didn't.

Gerald Houghton

THE CRIMSON TWINS BY FRANCISCO GARCIA PAVON, ALLISON AND BUSBY, £9.99

The Pelaez sisters have never married, and live a quiet life in Madrid. Both are in their sixties, and notable only for their bright red hair. But after a mysterious telephone call, both sisters leave the house, call a taxi and vanish, never to be seen again. This is the starting point for a satisfyingly labyrinthine case for Manuel Gonzalez, better known as Plinio, chief of the Tomelloso police force. Strange clues are found in the apartment: a foetus preserved in a specimen jar, a room full of dolls and other enigmatic objects points Plinio and his Watson Don Lotario on a trail that leads to a disturbed philatelist and a malignant widow. Before long, Plinio is finding his own life on the line as he struggles to crack the mystery. The celebrity enjoyed in Spain by Pavon for his crime novels is fully deserved on the evidence of this intelligently plotted and atmospheric novel. Plinio is a well-rounded and unusual protagonist, and the novelty of the setting will make this a highly attractive proposition for non-Spanish readers.

Barry Forshaw

CANDLELAND BY MARTYN WAITES, ALLISON AND BUSBY, £16.99

No-one ever stayed poor from underestimating the huddled masses. Sitting comfortably? Good, then let's check the signifiers. Cover's all paint-smear stop lights, *"malformed and unfinished in the sodium-etched dawn"*. That means British. Three parts, great slabs of italics. Moody chapter headings. Serious physical stuff, like we're not the only ones with a tick-list. Rules followed. Genre obeyed.

And rules obeyed here too, so listen: Edinburgh kid ran away. Pappy's a cop who knows she went to London. Drugs? Check. Kiddie prostitution? Check. Gangsters? Check, check, check. Throw in some watch-words—trawl, underworld—and all you have to do is play Scrabble for 254 pages. This reads like bad TV, alright. But wait, things can get worse: Waites has negotiated a cameo from Detective Inspector Christy Kennedy, star of those laughably inept Paul Charles novels. Be still my beating heart.

This should not stand. We have a right to expect better: British crime writing that is not itself criminal. No wit, imagination, or love of form or language. Stodge that's at best moribund, very likely pernicious.

This need not be. Where's the British Woodrell? Pelecanos? A misanthrope like Willeford? An historicist like Mosley? The lyricism of Gifford and Sallis? Our very own Elmore Leonard? There's John Harvey and the brilliant Resnick, I suppose. Humane, intelligent writing that really understands contemporary Britain. Waites, Charles and their sad, sorry underlings are but pale imitations of his craft. Just say no. And keep saying it until somebody bloody listens.

Gerald Houghton

DAY OF RECKONING BY JACK HIGGINS, HARPERCOLLINS, £16.99

Sean Dillon makes his eighth appearance in this return-to-form thriller by an accomplished novelist who had seemed to be writing on autopilot all too often recently. Dillon and his clandestine intelligence colleagues endeavour to help an American White House security insider, Blake Johnson, avenge the murder of his ex-wife. Johnson's wife has been killed in pursuit of a strikingly sensational gangland story. As in the best of his earlier work, Higgins shifts the action with practised ease between London, Beirut and Ireland as his former IRA terrorist-turned-government-enforcer protagonist takes on the machinations of Jack Fox, the face of the new Mafia, and his equally dangerous colleagues. The innovations of *The Eagle Has Landed* may be behind Higgins now, but the assurance with which he handles familiar formulae is deeply satisfying when he goes for the jugular (as he does here). Forget the recent below par offerings, this is Higgins as we like him to be.

Eve Tan Gee

HAPPY NOW BY CHARLES HIGSON, ABACUS, £6.99

Charlie Higson's dual career as a TV comic actor and novelist of real skill continues apace with this typically tense offering. Written in a fastidiously cool style, Higson details how violence lurks beneath the surface of an otherwise settled middle-England milieu. Tom Kendall has decided to stop attending his anger-management therapy sessions. While leading a normal, blameless life, he has had to struggle with the white hot anger that is always at the edges of his consciousness. Meanwhile, Will Summers believes that he has the kind of life he has been looking for. This involves breaking into people's houses—and when Tom Kendall discovers Will's diary, he embarks on a bizarre course of action that means risking everything—including his sanity. The developments of the ever-surprising plot are handled in a chilling and restrained fashion, with the tension sharply orchestrated. Perhaps this one is a little slower exerting its grip than previous Higson novels such as *Full Whack*, but it nevertheless builds to a masterful climax.

Eve Tan Gee

FLYING BLIND BY MAX ALLAN COLLINS, SIGNET (US), $5.99

Max Collins' Nate Heller novels occupy a small genre all their own, historical mysteries set very much within the most fascinating era of American criminal history. *Flying Blind* is the tenth in the series, and historically one of the most fascinating, as Heller winds up solving the disappearance of the famed aviatrix Amelia Earhart. The theory that Earhart (and her co-pilot Fred Noonan) were actually on an intelligence mission for the American government is not a new one, but in Collins' hands it becomes exceedingly credible. This is because he's done such an excellent job at setting the scene, both in characterising Earhart (and other important players like her promoter/husband G P Putnam) and in explaining the strange mix of bravery and bunkum that was her career. We tend to think of hype as a modern invention, but if there's one facet of history in which Collins excels, it's in conveying the sense of the way the public figures of the early part of this century achieved and coped with their fame. Our perception of Earhart's fame has been eclipsed today by the mystery of her disappearance, but Collins manages to persuade the reader of both her standing as a celebrity and of her own motivations for the things she did. In an age where every person who accomplishes anything seems to attract sponsors, particularly if they're attractive females, this carries a particular resonance. I admit that I'm a sucker for the 1930s, and have been since I listened to *Gunsmoke* on the radio as a child, and to my grandfather and mother explaining the great radio shows of the era to me. My own theory is that we've been living through the early 1930s for the past few years: Jimmy Carter was America's Woodrow Wilson, Ronald Reagan the new improved version of the corrupt and incompetent Warren Harding, George Bush the taciturn Calvin Coolidge come to life, and now we're sitting on the verge of something big. I also like cyclical theories of history, which might not appeal so much to Heller. But don't get the idea this is some sort of history lesson. There's somewhat less action, because the focus is on what happens to Heller as a result of meeting Earhart, as much as what happens to her. In that sense, it's a transitional volume, but the mystery of Earhart's disappearance is as compelling as any of the cases Nate has tackled. And teaming with Earhart shows us a softer side of Heller, and he has to stretch credibility a bit to get Heller into the book's climax. Series fans who recall Heller's change of character beginning in the third book in the series *The Million Dollar Wound*, will be happy to let this be the starting point. It's a dangerous area for Collins, because the books are written out of sequence, and internal contradictions always threaten to be a problem. As he's indicated (see his interview in Crime Time 2.7) that he's about at the halfway point with Heller, he'll have to be careful. Meanwhile, someone in Britain should get these books back into print. There hasn't been a British Heller since the lovely illustrated Sphere edition of the first one, *True Detective*. It's about time that mistake was rectified.

Michael Carlson

REVENGE OF THE HOUND BY MICHAEL HARDWICKE, IBOOKS, £9.99

This idiosyncratic and entertaining pastiche has enjoyed a considerable reputation since its first appearance, and this spanking new edition, graced by a striking cover and interior paintings by the legendary illustrator Jim Steranko, presents it in its best incarnation yet. Riffs on Conan Doyle are ten a penny, and most sorely lack the spark that the Master brought to the exploits of 221b Baker Street's most famous resident. But the supernatural shenanigans here, while nowhere near as clever as Nick Meyer's outings, often aspire to the spine-chilling magic of *Hound of the Baskervilles*, with a sense of atmosphere and narrative integrity that is truly satisfying. The tone is just right as well—never lapsing into parody, and always acknowledging that the Great Detective's feats of deductive legerdemain already verge on self-parody without needing to be pushed any further. The supernatural events are handled with just the right beguiling touch, and while no one (least of all, one suspects, Hardwicke) would claim that this is in the Conan Doyle class, it's nevertheless a fitfully entertaining piece.

Eve Tan Gee

WHOEVER HAS THE HEART BY JENNIE MELVILLE, ALLISON AND BUSBY, £6.99

Sherlock Holmes said the countryside holds as many crimes and horrors as the slums of London, and Jennie Melville takes this to heart in this tale of brutal murder in aristocratic Windsor. As the inventor of the womens' police procedural her detective in this series is Charmian Daniels. Interesting in that this is written in the first person, a tricky approach that Miss Melville achieves brilliantly. From this we learn of Charmian's views on food, clothes, criminals, crime and the cathartic effect on her of what first seemed a normal murder and dismembering of an attractive, amoral girl. Later there is another straightforward killing of a man with a secret—but is this the start of the saga? Why was a family of three mysteriously wiped out some time before Charmian takes over a cottage in this beautiful but ominous village? Why did the second victim's wife commit suicide because of these three deaths? What is the secret of the family of the Lord of the Manor? Is there a coven of witches practising here? Charmian traces and faces the killer who drives to death as she escapes.

Authors have either the eye or the ear. Miss Melville amazingly has both. Her descriptions of buildings, lunches, conferences, ring so true you feel they must be real. Her knowledge of psychology makes all her characters live, behave as you know they must be real, be they aristocrats, police, professional men, actresses, witches or villagers. The murders are more vicious than the usual hard-boiled story but always described dispassionately, an effect which hits the reader very much harder.

Ken W Ferris

LOST BY LUCY WADHAM, FABER, £9.99

When young widow Alice Aron arrives with two young sons on the island where her husband was born, she is closely scrutinised by Mickey da Cruz, a small time criminal. Alice soon discovers that this is anything but an island paradise: despite the ever-present sun, the land is barren and the people brought low by governmental corruption, longing for an elusive independence. When Alice's seven-year-old, Sam, disappears, a blanket of silence descends. Only the unpopular detective Antoine Stuart offers a lifeline—but is he more interested in nailing the crime on a violent criminal on the island whom he loathes? Lucy Wadham's remarkable novel functions both as a thriller and a literary novel in the style of such writers as Graham Greene. Her particular speciality is a nicely understanding way with characterisation, the protagonists created with a minimum of superfluous description. The plot itself is secondary to the sultry atmosphere of distrust and fear, but there is never a sense that Wadham is a listless storyteller: when the narrative needs to move forward, it does so in no uncertain terms.

Barry Forshaw

SOMETHING FOR THE WEEKEND BY PAULINE MCLYNN, HEADLINE, £9.99

Is Pauline McLynn's *Something for the Weekend* a comic novel? Or an off-kilter detective story? Actually, it's both—and within the first few pages, McLynn has demonstrated that she is in the great tradition of Irish humorous writers stretching right back to Flann O'Brien. Heroine Leo Street is greeting her thirtieth birthday with dismay, stuck in a rainy Dublin with her job as a private investigator bringing in nothing but unsettled bills. And then there is Barry, her permanently resting actor boyfriend who takes advantage of her at every opportunity. But when a particularly unpleasant client sends her to County Kildare to spy on his cheating wife, she chooses as her cover to become a member of a cookery course. And this is only the start of Leo's problems—for, as a culinary expert, she's the kind of person who has difficulty boiling water. Along with the kind of larger-than-life, wry characterisation that is clearly a pre-requisite for such a tale, McLynn is quite as good at the elements of mystery necessary to the plot. And as the layers of marital infidelity are stripped away, Leo finds herself dealing with far more sinister matters than bread-making. This is a comic voice to watch for.

Barry Forshaw

CUBA BY STEPHEN COONTS, ORION, £5.99

Fidel Castro is dead, and Cuba is suddenly on the brink of war. Castro's Minister of Security, Alejo Vargas, is planning to release biological warheads at Amer-

"HIGGINS IS MY FAVOURITE. NO, HE DOESN'T LEARN FROM ME, I LEARN FROM HIM." - ELMORE LEONARD

THE AGENT
GEORGE V. HIGGINS

SUPER SPORTS AGENT Alexander Drouhin, a handsome, ruthless, slick lawyer, and his motley support team inhabit a cut-throat world obsessed with money, fame, and power, so when Drouhin is found with a couple of .44 slugs in his head, there is no shortage of suspects. By the time Lt Francis Clay arrives at the crime scene, it appears that everyone has an alibi and no one has a clue.

More than a detective story, The Agent, is an unrelenting examination of a world in which no outrageous amount of money is ever enough and there is more to the game than just scoring points. George V Higgins, master of the literary thriller, turns his eye for detail and ear for dialogue to the seamy underside of the high powered, high dollar world of sports agenting.

Available from all good bookshops or by post from No Exit Press, (Dept CT32) 18 Coleswood Rd, Harpenden, Herts, AL5 1EQ (Postage and Packing free) - or buy on the web at www.noexit.co.uk

PRICE: £6.99 PAPERBACK

there is.... *NO EXIT*

ica, and it is up to the US armed forces, spearheaded by Rear Admiral Jake Grafton, to save the day.

Therein lie the bare bones of the plot, to which Stephen Coonts attempts to add flesh. And he does, for the first three-quarters of the novel. But then he finally gets the chance to do what he obviously wanted to all along—describe in painstaking detail US air attacks on Cuba. A former aviator, he has little trouble convincing the reader of the veracity of these scenes, but sometimes their strict adherence to technical detail obfuscates the narrative drive. Certainly, by the book's end I was sick to death of TLAs (Three Letter Acronyms).

Cuba is the seventh in a series featuring hero Jake Grafton, yet his involvement in the plot is minimal. Of more interest is CIA agent Tommy Carmellini, whose ruthless quest for revenge makes more of an impact than Grafton's 'gung-ho' patriotism.

If your favourite film is *Rambo*, then this novel, with its casual regard for human life, will be up your street. Similarly, if your penchant is for such unusual names as Toad Tarkington or Tater Totton, you too will be satisfied. Otherwise, steer clear.

Mark Campbell

THE AGENT BY GEORGE V HIGGINS, NO EXIT PRESS, £6.99

When *The Agent* was published last year in America it received lukewarm reviews. Some critics were put off by its erstwhile subject matter, the business of a sports agency, while others seemed to find Higgins' dialogue-driven narrative too much work. Times do change, as Higgins' previous novel, *A Change of Gravity*, had suggested, and kinder, gentler crime fiction is all the rage is some quarters, while stylishly violent stuff dominates others. I mention the other critical response only because it's ironic that *The Agent* would be Higgins' last book published before his untimely death, and that its tweakings of his own formulae would go virtually unnoticed. This is something that should cause us considerable regret.

Higgins' subject matter was always the grey areas where society's workings were influenced by (in fact depended on) corruption. The villains in Higgins' work were not just hardened career criminals, they were lawyers, politicians, cops, real estate speculators, and other 'respectable' people. So it should have been no surprise that sports agents, who in America at least tend to start out as lawyers anyway, should eventually have become grist for Higgins' mill. And he gets the business down well. I spent a lot of time working at the hard end of the sports' industry, and Higgins' Alexandre Drouhin (who seems loosely based on Boston agent Bob Woolf, with a dash of Mark McCormick tossed in) is a well-drawn character, and his business dealings are dissected with autopsy-like precision. Strangely, the only errors are the kind of sports mistakes any fan might make, but none of them affect the story.

What is fascinating about *The Agent* is not the business, but the way Higgins uses a triptych model for the story. In the first small section he introduces you to Drouhin, shows you the basics of how the man operates, and even once or twice slips into narration to get the points across. But the two major dialogues in this section, between Drouhin and first, his junior partner, and then with a local cop who has arrested one of Drouhin's clients, are Higgins at his absolute best. The inverted commas stack up like dominoes, as a speaker quotes another quoting a third.

The second, main, section follows State Police Lieutenant Francis Clay as he investigates Drouhin's murder, interviewing people first at Drouhin's mansion and then at his firm. Higgins can fill in backstory, build characters, even create or destroy suspicion, all through dialogue. And the beauty of this is that it puts the reader in the investigator's shoes. Which is why the third part of the triptych is so fascinating, because Higgins turns into Agatha Christie. Clay has all the materials he needs to solve the crime, and the reader ought to have them as well. I was concerned at this point, because some of Higgins' novels have functioned, in effect, as shaggy-dog stories, and the punch line was not always worthy of the build up, though at least once, in *Defending Billy Ryan* it provided a magnificent, powerful ending. But here, it's no shaggy-dog tale; literally without warning you discover you're in a classic who-dunit, and when Higgins delivers, he does so with gusto. It was a fascinating, brave thing to do at that stage of his career, and, best of all, it works.

A final Higgins' novel *At End Of Day* will be published posthumously in America this year. We can hope No Exit will repeat the coup of bringing it into print in this country.

Michael Carlson

EVANS ABOVE BY BY RHYS BOWEN, ALLISON AND BUSBY, £5.99

Journeying to Wales and Scotland has been likened to going abroad without getting seasick. A crime story set in North Wales has the advantage of the Welsh dialect and speech rhythm—although the 20th century philosopher Sir Walter Raleigh did say, *"The Welsh are so damn Welsh it sounds like affectation"*.

Evans is a likeable, well-educated, young police constable in the village of Llanfair. Missing children, a returned paedophile, and two climbers found dead on nearby Snowdon give him the intrigue and crime he thought he had left behind in the Swansea force. Evans is intelligent and brave, and ultimately proves his worth by capturing both the rather shadowy multiple murderer (after a third body is found on the mountain) and a harmless but threatening lunatic.

Bowen's first book in Britain has several plus marks and one or two minuses. It is written with humour—one lady even says 'look you'. Evans is the target of various young women especially the attractive schoolteacher and the pneumatic barmaid, and there are cunning red herrings to divert him. The minus marks can be erased by a trifle more research in Britain or better proof-reading, and can be explained by the fact that the author currently lives in San Francisco. For example, someone asks why Scotland Yard hasn't been called in (which hasn't happened for years), and Evans cautions the murderer making the same mistake Agatha Christie made of saying his words could be used against him (oh no, they couldn't). Another very good bonus point is that Alison & Busby have dropped the imitation Penguin plain cover in favour of graphic illustrations, which, if you look closely, give a clue to the mystery (as did those beautiful Agatha Christie paperback covers).

A worthy new recruit to the classic ranks.

John Kennedy Melling

SQUIRE THROWLEIGH'S HEIR BY MICHAEL JECKS, HEADLINE, £5.99

Michael Jecks's seventh historical novel once again features the fourteenth century detective duo of knight turned medieval super-sleuth, Sir Baldwin Furnshill and his partner, Bailiff Simon Puttock. The pair investigate the death of a five-year-old boy, Herbert, who only days before had inherited a title and great wealth following his father's death (by natural causes). Initially, the boy's tragic death appears to be the result of a hit and

Are you a fan of pulp & vintage fiction?

Do you like writers such as John Creasy, Edgar Wallace, Rex Stout or J D MacDonald?

Or characters such as the Saint, Doc Savage, Dan Turner or the Shadow?

Then check out ThrillerUK...

...a bi-monthly fan magazine that plans to bring you brand new pulp stories as well as articles on pulp & vintage fiction

First issue out now at £2.95*
*price includes postage & packaging

ThrillerUK is only available by mail order from:
ThrillerUK, 1A, 15 Wilbury Road, Brighton BN3 3JJ

Please make cheques/postal orders payable to: T Fountain

check out our website at: www.thrilleruk.fsnet.co.uk

run medieval road traffic accident(!) but as the dust settles, information comes to light which would seem to indicate that something far more insidious is afoot. The perspicacious Sir Baldwin and his sidekick accrue all the evidence and sift the wheat from the proverbial chaff in an attempt to illuminate the dark ages with their powers of deduction. An engaging, well-written book, *Squire Throwleigh's Heir* is packed full of fascinating, well-researched historical detail, vivid, full-bodied characters and possesses a teasing, labyrinthine plot that keeps the reader guessing until the very end.

Charles Waring

H.M.S.UNSEEN BY PATRICK ROBINSON, ARROW, £5.99

When a British submarine goes missing on a routine training exercise (the appositely named H.M.S.Unseen), little do the Western powers realise that the vessel has in fact been stolen by a nefarious Iraqi terrorist, Benjamin Adnam. Adnam is a master submariner trained by the Royal Navy, who, despite his loyalty and diligent service in the cause of his mother country, was visited by assassins at the behest of Saddam Hussein (apparently Saddam's usual way of saying 'thank you'). Fleeing his native country for neighbouring Iran, the terrorist is hired by Tehran and plans a series of cunning attacks on the West which will mistakenly be attributed to his old employer, one Mr Hussein of Baghdad. Using the stolen sub as a missile launch platform, Adnam begins a series of stealthy attacks on western passenger aircraft crossing the Atlantic. Although the wily Adnam holds the initiative for much of the book, he meets an equally tenacious opponent in the bullish, irascible figure of Admiral Arnold Morgan of the US Navy, whose task it is to flush the terrorist into the open. With its corkscrew plot, pacy narrative and convincing characterisation, Patrick Robinson's third novel proves to be an exciting, edge-of-the-seat, techno-yarn.

Charles Waring

THE CRIMSON TWINS BY FRANCISCO GARCÍA PAVÓN, ALLISON AND BUSBY, £9.99

Writing about Cuban crime writer José Latour recently I commented that Cuban crime writing was a closed world to most of us. It occurs to me, in reviewing this, that this is also true of Spanish crime writing in general. Which is strange really, given the rich and varied traditions of Spanish literature dating back to the Spanish 'picaresque' novels of the 16th and 17th centuries with their emphasis on 'realism', daily life and the underclass. In many ways these books (such as the classic *Gil Blas* by Alian-René Lesage) helped define a nation in the way they take the form of a travelogue. Certainly, for our more modern purposes, they obviously taper into crime writing. More recently writers such as Felipe Alfau—in the amazing *Locos*—and Borges (an Argentinean but also a Spanish writer) have combined the notion of 'picaresque' with the 'fantastic' to focus on the book itself as detection—to read it is to solve the mystery (thus laying the foundations for contemporary writers like Eco).

For those of you who are not at all interested in my thesis on Spanish literature—indeed all literature—and the Gramscian notion of 'sedimentation' (there may be one or two of you) then let me put it another way: there is more to Spanish crime writing than Vasquez Montalban (although Montalban's Catalan hero and culinary wizard makes for an interesting comparison with the essentially Castilion heros of this book). García Pavón was, in fact, one of Spain's most celebrated and popular crime writers (he died in Madrid in 1989). For this reason alone this new (and excellent) translation is to be welcomed.

In brief the story centres around the disappearance of the Paláez twins and, when called to Madrid to investigate, Chief Pilinio and his assistant Don Lotario find the twins' flat full of intriguing, puzzling and extraordinary clues. It's all hugely enjoyable and surprising and well worth your attention. Perhaps the 'mystery' as to why more books like this aren't available to us is, simply, the added cost of translating them.

Peter Walker

GOD IS A BULLET BY BOSTON TERAN, MACMILLAN, £10

Imagine *The Searchers* with the Manson family replacing the Indians, and the John Wayne role going to a runaway cult member trying to kick a heroin habit, and you'll have some idea of the emotional intensity which is packed into this powerful first novel. But unlike *The Searchers,* where there is safety behind the doors of the family home and society, *God Is A Bullet* works on the assumption that there is no real safety for the people cult leader Cyrus and his desert rats call 'sheep'.

The seemingly random ritual rape and murder of a man and woman, and kidnapping of the woman's daughter, soon turns out to have deeper causes, and the ties between Cyrus and the local police are much closer than anyone would suspect. But the girl's father, a cop himself, determines to find and rescue her, as much, it would seem, to validate his own existence as anything else. That search will lead Bob Hightower (whose allegorical name soon becomes Bob Whatever), the Jeffrey Hunter, initiate figure, into dark worlds of violence and depravity, with Case (another wonderful allegorical name) the ex-junkie cult member as his guide.

But first, the two have to come to grips with each other. Each takes on the journey for different reasons, some of which they can't, or won't, even admit to themselves. But the great beauty of this novel is Boston Teran's ability to reveal characters within their own terms of existence. Neither Bob nor Case actually understand what the other is saying, or doing, and what Teran does is let us understand each in their own terms, without filtering them through a third sensibility. This is direct, and powerful, writing.

The force of this novel isn't in the graphic violence, nor the sense of dread which Teran conjures up so easily. In fact, the most evil character in the book, the cop in league with Cyrus, is offstage for far more time that one might have expected. The real impact comes from the characterisations, and the desert setting in which those characters exist: a hellish nightmare landscape, which seems ready to swallow up the areas of so-called civilisation which have been carved out of it. Teran plays on the mythological force of it all; there are even explicit references to *Moby Dick*. But none of it seems artificial or forced, even if I still can't figure out why ouroboros, the snake which eats it own tail, is misspelled throughout. In the end, I don't care; this book will get a lot of attention because it is a violent and nihilistic story, the sort of bleak desert romp that neo-Tarantinos will latch on to for its vengeful style. Which is fine, what gives it that style, and what should attract attention, is the quality of the writing. Keep your eye on Teran.

Michael Carlson

BLACK DOG BY STEPHEN BOOTH, HARPERCOLLINS, £9.99

The 'black dog' is depression, but readers are more likely to be disappointed. Everyone seems hot and sweaty in this tale of the murder of a teenage girl in the Peak District. Using dark deeds in a rural setting with rival policemen gives it a soap-like quality: *"Inspector Morse reads Mrs Dales Diary at Peak Practice"*. It lacks an unusual or new feature to get it out of cliché town. As it is, the plot seems very contrived and too full of holes to float. Over description clutters the pages: the dog does not just lie on a paper but on the Eden Valley Times, Sports Section. The trainer is not just on another piece of newspaper but on the Buxton Advertiser, on pages advertising a Cantonese restaurant and the births, weddings and deaths!

When the characters are not biblical-like, saints or whores, they are stereotypes. PC Diane Fry is such an eager careerist that she not only moves from the town to the country, where outlets are fewer, but seems to view every occasion as a promotion opportunity. Worst of all is the lame dialogue. Famous writers are often quoted because their words are pregnant with meaning and subtext. Throughout this book people are only saying what they mean to say and answer what is asked. The result is flat and lacks pace, conflict and development.

Most will find the ending disappointing with a hefty bit of *"one thing I still don't understand inspector"* thrown in after the villain is discovered. But even if this were properly foreshadowed it would still not convince.

Martin Spellman

FRIENDS IN HIGH PLACES BY DONNA LEON, HEINEMANN, £15.99

Sometimes you strike a rich vein and Donna Leon's ninth book is one of those enjoyable events. Comissario Guido Brunetti, of the Venice police, has disturbing news and, after a deceptively easy start, begins investigating drug abuse and loan-sharking. The title is a reminder of Italian corruption, which is immediately obvious. Leon only began her fiction-writing career as a joke, back in 1992. A friend had slagged off a conductor at a concert, saying *"Why don't we kill him?"* and they plotted a scenario, which was the inspiration for her first book, *La Fenice*, named after the Venetian theatre. There are strong parallels between Leon, who is American, and Michael Dibdin. Both are teachers of English at higher education level; have lived abroad for most of their lives and write about Italy—Dibdin's Aurelio Zen being no stranger to Venice either.

This was my first (but not my last) Leon book, although I have read most of Dibdin's. Both are intelligent and witty writers apart from being good storytellers. Why aren't they more popular? Perhaps it is because of their choice of Italian setting, which might seem unfamiliar and remote to fans of crime fiction set in metropolitan England or the USA. Or is it the commercial hype given to other writers? Little, Brown, part of the Time-Warner empire, has just announced a four month, £400,000 campaign for Patricia Cornwell's latest *Black Notice* and *The Last Precinct* and the relaunch of the nine Scarpetta backlist titles. Does the world, or even Patricia Cornwell, really need this? Putting resources into such writers, plus old best sellers like Christie, starves the lesser-known and up-and-coming writers of opportunities.

Martin Spellman

DARKNESS PEERING BY ALICE BLANCHARD, BANTAM PRESS, £9.99

Maine Police Chief Nalen Storrow discovers the body of a Down's syndrome girl on the edge of a pond, whose death may have been caused by his own son, Billy. He can't cope with the thought of this, and blows his brains out. Flash forward eighteen years and Storrow's own daughter, Rachel, herself a cop now, is faced with another death—with the finger of suspicion again pointing at Billy.

Darkness Peering is a fine début novel. Alice Blanchard fills the narrative with startling, poetic imagery that raises the book to the top strata of the crime genre. The characters are real people, with real backgrounds and relationships, and when death strikes it is a shock for all concerned—a tragic and momentous event, not just another twist in a formulaic plot. The manner in which the second victim dies is particularly harrowing, and made doubly poignant when the blind children she taught have to face the reality of her murder. Leads are followed, suspects questioned, and the final dénouement is as gripping as any I have read.

Detective Rachel Storrow is a believable character with a troubled, guilt-filled childhood and plenty of personal issues that have yet to be resolved. Her future seems unclear at the end of the novel, but she's far too good a creation to be allowed to fade away. I for one hope Blanchard brings her back for another chillingly absorbing case like this one.

Mark Campbell

CLUTCH OF PHANTOMS BY CLARE LAYTON

Those who follow the impeccable thrillers of Natasha Cooper will be intrigued by the inauguration of a new nom de plume, Claire Layton. The first Layton book is *Clutch of Phantoms*, described by her publishers as a psychological thriller. But this is no schematic division along the lines of Ruth Rendell / Barbara Vine (even though Vine's name is invoked on the jacket)—Cooper could not help but write a novel overflowing with psychological acuity under any name, although it has to be said that the thought processes of the characters are certainly more detailed in this one. The book is certainly tougher than any of the novels under the Cooper moniker (except, perhaps, the grim *Fault Lines*), and this may account for Ian Rankin's imprimatur (which *Clutch of Phantoms* has already acquired). The book is concerned with the genesis of violence and the possibilities of change in the lives of Layton's protagonists. Cass Evesham is that rarity in the City: a woman trader. Having undergone a weekend of hell, with her lover dumping her in a cruel fashion, she finds the press besieging her with news about the grandmother she thought dead. And when her grandmother has finished serving a prison term for violence, Cass finds the experience of meeting her both disturbing and intriguing: although she can relate to her, her relative is nevertheless a very strange woman. And soon a remark said half-admiringly to Cass in the City (where she is described as a psychopath in her business dealings) comes to have a threatening significance: how much is Cass a victim of her genetic inheritance?

Another player in the drama is Julia Gainsborough, the actress daughter of a famous diva who has died in her prime. Julia, who is attempting to kickstart her career by starring in a cycle of revenge plays, becomes a key factor in Layton's dark drama. And as this brilliantly orchestrated piece moves towards its sombre finale, the reader is both beguiled by an intense novel of character and obliged to confront the myths and realities of how much we are in thrall to genetic inheritance. This is no whodunit, but Layton's skills at riveting the reader are firmly in place: *"She bent down for her bag and stood up with it dangling from the left hand. There was no point sitting for an hour or more, looking at food she'd never be able to eat. 'Ten per cent do you?' Alan asked, glancing up. He looked evil. 'Cheap at the price, really, for six months' fun. A decent hooker would've been much more.' Cass wasn't aware that her right hand had moved until the back of it crunched into the side of his head with the full weight of her body behind it. Alan swayed in his chair swearing, and grabbed for a handhold. There was nothing. Cass couldn't move. She watched him overbalance and crash into the next table as glasses broke*

around him and cutlery rained down."
Eve Tan Gee

REPRISAL BY MITCHELL SMITH, HEADLINE, £5.99

Loaded down with the enthusiastic approval of such fellow practitioners as Jeffrey Deaver and Clive Cussler, Mitchell Smith's energetic thriller really delivers the goods. When his protagonist Joanna Reed spends time in her family's summer retreat, an idyllic Massachusetts coastal town, she soon finds herself in the middle of a nightmare. Her husband and father both die in quick succession in accidents that appear to defy explanation, and her attempts to convince the police that they were murdered come to nothing. She is vulnerable, and in this state someone comes into her life who makes all the grim events of the recent past seem mild compared to a new nightmare. As in the best thrillers, plot and characterisation mesh in a piece of bravura storytelling that moves with considerable speed, despite some familiar plot conventions.

Eve Tan Gee

WHILE I WAS GONE BY SUE MILLER, BLOOMSBURY, £6.99

Jo Becker's adult life has been shaped by a murder. In her twenties, she was confused and selfish, on the run from a comfortable, if loveless marriage. She finds friendship and discovers her true self in a communal lifestyle. Now a successful professional with a family and a devoted husband, she appears to have everything. But when someone from her past settles in her home town, she begins a relationship that threatens all that she values in life.

The murder, although presaged earlier is in the novel, is slow in coming. The intervening pages and chapters build to it, and when it does happen, it is sudden and shocking, but this richly imagined novel is as much about living with violent death as about the murder itself. The period detail, rather than force-feeding us on sixties kitsch, deftly evokes the mood of the time and leaves the reader's imagination (or memory) to fill in the rest.

If you like a teasing puzzle, with plenty of neatly dovetailing plot lines, then *While I Was Gone* may not be for you. It is, however, a beautifully written novel of love, betrayal and loss.

Margaret Murphy

RUN BY DOUGLAS E WINTER, CANONGATE, £10

I am tempted to write this review in a single sentence, to illustrate *Run*'s extraordinarily furious prose style. But I won't. I couldn't. Douglas E Winter I am not, you'll be glad to hear. *Run* is like James Joyce on acid. It reminded me of last year's breakneck speed-trip *The Ultimate Rush* by Joe Quirk, another helter-skelter ride through the underbelly of American organised crime written in a dazzlingly confident prose style. *Run* is—if possible—even faster and harder than Quirk's debut, but perhaps loses the former's clarity and humour in an escalating series of bluffs and double crosses. Burdon Lane is a gun runner with a conscience (but not much of one) who gets caught in a gig that goes very badly wrong. Fleeing from one death-trap to the next, Lane's extravagant exploits take him deeper and deeper into the raked-over ashes of Conspiracy Territory with only the mysterious Jinx and his trusty Glock for company. For the first 100 pages, the style seems terrifically fresh. But then the plot disengages from reality, and you suddenly feel like you're running on the spot. There's a dénouement at a church wedding that goes on for too long, and by the time you hit the final sentence you're desperate for air. This may well be Winter's intention, but in burying the warp and weft of what could've been a decent plot under industrial-strength adrenaline-soaked prose, he's ultimately produced a gun-lover's wet dream that's rather less than the sum of its parts.

Mark Campbell

WALKIN' THE DOG BY WALTER MOSLEY, SERPENT'S TAIL, £14.99

Socrates Fortlow represents the kind of three-dimensional character that nowadays is so hard to find in mainstream fiction. The black ex-con first featured in *Always Outnumbered, Always Outgunned*, and now he's back in more stable surroundings with all the surface attributes of freedom—home, job, lover and a two-legged pet dog called Killer. But as the leisurely prose unwinds, it becomes obvious that he still has plenty more battles to fight. Mosley is a master storyteller, spinning a totally believable tale about a flawed man trying to do the right thing in a world that seems more prison-like than the jail he left nine years ago. And yet it's much more than that—the themes of free will and responsibility Mosley sets down, although informed by the race issue, go far beyond it. Characters' motivations are as shifting as windswept sand; fables illuminate the here and now; and the narrative has that authentic ring of truth about it. The dialogue is blisteringly sharp, the small details just right, the smell of LA hovering on the brink of war pungent as sulphur in the nostrils. Socrates may not be on the side of the angels, but he's trying hard. He has a wisdom born of experience and a moral code that lifts him above the rest, even if he can't shake the habits of a lifetime. And when he speaks, it's like he's giving you his heart and soul on a plate. You have to listen.

Mark Campbell

audio crime
barry forshaw

TWO OF THE MOST sheerly entertaining audio books of recent months are in the Isis catalogue: a bleak and expressive rendering of Ian Rankin's *The Hanging Garden* by Joe Dunlop, and Christopher Scott's reading of one of Lindsey Davis' finest Falco mysteries, *Shadows in Bronze*. The Rankin is a particular pleasure: this is the one in which Rebus, buried under a pile of paperwork generated by his investigations into a suspected war criminal, becomes involved in escalating dispute between upstart Tommy Telford and the head of a local gang. But however familiar we are with the narrative (cleverly utilising illegal Chechen refugees in its richly plotted texture), it's the casually expressive reading that Dunlop achieves that is the real pleasure here. Nothing in Dunlop's otherwise workaday TV appearances conveys the skill he displays here—but then anyone judging Judi Dench or Patricia Routledge on their dismal TV sitcoms would be similarly misguided.

Christopher Scott brings just the right sardonic edge to *Shadows in Bronze*, taking us into the highly atmospheric Rome that we know and love from Davis' consistently brilliant thrillers. Falco, now Imperial Agent to the Emperor, becomes involved in a plot to usurp the purple robes of power, and both treason and a senator's daughter present even more headaches than usual.

Trying to recreate the excitement and enthusiasm of entertainment from an earlier, simpler age is a very difficult task (Steven Spielberg triumphantly recreated the Saturday afternoon serials of the Forties in the Indiana Jones series), and although humour needs to be present, it has to be balanced by a certain sense of reality. We may smile at the naiveté of earlier eras, but recreations can't be simple send-ups. *The Thriller Playhouse* (BBC) is an ill-judged attempt to recreate the thrills and spills of the Dick Barton Golden era of radio thrillers. Trying unsuccessfully to work as both a homage and an affectionate guying of these days of eccentric detectives and master villains, the series treads the line between parody and celebration with an uneasy balance. Of course, when one is creating Max Carrados, the famous blind detective with the ability to shoot a villain by aiming at the sound his beating heart, or Norman Conquest (alias 1066), who always has a quip ready while dusting off the heavies, actors of a rare stamp are required, and the series has them in spades. With no less than Simon Callow, Lionel Jeffries and Christopher Cazenove in the cast, the best is done with the hit-or-miss material.

From Macmillan, Brett Easton Ellis' *Glamorama* comes with a warning about the explicit sexual material to be found therein. Suitably hooked, CT found itself enjoying the book for far more in Dexter Fletcher's sassy reading than any encounter with the printed page had been. Similarly Sean Barrett's reading of James Herbert's *The Dark* (from the same company) genuinely adds a new dimension to Herbert's otherwise quotidian thriller. Barrett is adroit at ratcheting up the tension, and this is almost a calling card for the audio book medium.

As is the unabridged reading (on ten well-filled cassettes) from Isis of Harris' highly controversial Hannibal. We've rehearsed the merits and de-merits of the book in these pages: suffice it to say that Daniel Gerroll's reading will have the effect of making any listener consider this much awaited sequel anew. Gerroll's achievement is all the more impressive in the context of a totally unabridged reading, in which the listener's attention is never over stretched. If you were one of the naysayers about the book, this may change your mind.

Another company with a copper-bottomed commitment to bring out the very best crime and thrillers in the audio book format is Macmillan. At the moment, a rich selection is available (such as the two listed above), of which a high point has to be Stephen Pacey's reading of Martin Cruz Smith's latest Renko book, *Havana Bay*. This wonderfully detailed return to form by Cruz Smith has Renko as a fish out of water in Cuba, dealing with the death of another Russian. Pacey has absolutely the right approach to the text and renders it as rivetingly in his reading of the novel. The abridgement is skilfully done, as it is with two Wilbur Smith titles, *Power of the Sword* and *Burning Shore*. As so often with Smith, these novels are difficult to categorise—but who cares? They remain remarkably compelling, particularly when delivered by one of the finest actors in this country, Tim Piggott-Smith. The actor's voice has all the colour and nuance one could wish for, in these two highly attractive tapes.

With *10 Classic Detective Tales* (CSA), we have a promising idea—take ten classic detective tales, stretching from the golden era up to the present, and chose to render them the subtle voice of Edward Hardwicke. If using the finest of all Watsons (to Jeremy Brett's Holmes) may smack of opportunism, that's to disregard his massive accomplishment as an actor—it's impossible to imagine these gripping tales being read with more character and imagination than here. And what a selection: from the inevitable Conan Doyle (*The Dying Detective*) and GK Chesterton (*The Man in the Passage*), through such sterling fare as Nicholas Blake's *The Assassin's Club* and Muriel Spark's deliciously grim *Chimes*, up to Colin Dexter's Morse and *The Burglar*. All the tales are given very specific individual identities in the readings, and such is Hardwicke's way with the texts that even writers not of the first rank (such as Edgar Wallace) seem to belong in this august company. A perfect justification for the audiobook medium.

writing crime
natasha cooper

WHITHER CRIME FICTION?

Spending the millennial weekend surrounded by whitewash and ladders in the Villa Crusoe, a ravishing eccentric pink house on an estuary in the West Country, I found myself wondering where crime fiction is going. I had a bundle of books to read and re-read in between wet walks and champagne-and-oyster indulgence on New Year's Day. One made the oysters churn in my stomach. It was, of course, Mo Hayder's *Birdman*. As most Crime Time readers will already know, the novel is about the police hunt for a serial killer, who turns out to be a necrophiliac. He kidnaps women, hacks them about while they are still alive, then kills them in order to have sex with their dead bodies. And so on

The descriptions of what he does to the women while they are still alive are revolting and leave us all with the question of where else writers can – or will— go. If they want to go on shocking readers (pleasurably or otherwise), writers will have to ratchet up the violence with every novel, making the descriptions of torture and mutilation more explicit each time. There are many problems with this: one is the obvious risk of diminishing returns; another is that crime may turn into a subcategory of horror.

There is a subplot in Mo Hayder's novel that strikes me as being rather more interesting than the gory serial-killer theme, on which I can't see that there can be much more to be said. The police hero, Jack Caffrey, lives in the house he inherited from his parents. Inhabiting one opposite, and continually taunting our hero, is the man Caffrey suspects of having murdered his brother years earlier. Hayder suggests throughout that she is going to allow Caffrey to discover his brother's remains, but it doesn't happen. Perhaps she's keeping that for the next book. Caffrey is a character with potential and his relationship with the girlfriend he no longer loves is both bleak and well realised. It will be interesting to see where Hayder takes him and whether she resists the temptation to pile torture on agony and blood and faeces on decomposing corpses next time.

Pushing back the boundaries of any genre gets a writer noticed, and there is no doubt that horrifically explicit violence does appeal to large numbers of the reading public. It also makes some commentators treat a novel more seriously, which continues to surprise me.

Reginald Hill has been pushing back rather different boundaries with his latest novel, *Arms and the Women*. Exploring ways of making crime fiction more literary, he plays with Homeric, Arthurian and Shakespearean themes, inserting into his narrative parallel texts 'written' by his characters. He uses archaisms to defamiliarize the reader at one moment, then offers the cadences of a well-known pop song ('Eleanor Soper/married a cop, had a kid, didn't march any more/what was it for?') at the next. It is always a pleasure to read one of Hill's novels, but in this one I kept feeling that the prose was full of little aliens dancing about and shrieking 'Geddit?' at me.

It is no surprise that writers who have been living with murder, corruption and every sort of emotional and physical cruelty for a long series of novels should want to do something different. Val McDermid is one writer who switches from series to series. Having started out with lesbian private-eye Lindsay Gordon, and given us the warmth and jokes of her Kate Brannigan series, McDermid won the CWA/The Macallan Gold Dagger for the first of her ferociously violent Tony Hill novels. Then last summer, she produced something quite different in *Place of Execution* and showed that a big novel doesn't have to contain explicit descriptions of cruelty and murder. Judith Cutler is another writer of distinct series. Her first, featuring amateur detective Sophie Rivers, consists of attractive, light-hearted novels that follow the well-established tracks of the amateur sleuth. The second series is rather different. Consisting of only two novels so far, it could best be described as feminist police procedural. The leading character is Sergeant Kate Powers, a woman whose strength never compromises either her warmth or her humanity. Full of serious political points about the position of women in society, racial bullying, and the unacceptability of the profit-loving bourgeoisie, the latest novel, *Staying Power*, is crime fiction as social comment. It whisks readers from scene to scene, realistically piling up different cases until Kate's life becomes a blur of competing demands. The cruelty in this novel is primarily emotional and all inflicted on women by men, just like the physical variety in most serial-killer thrillers.

Andrew Taylor is one of the few who has created a female psychopath. Having written his *Roth Trilogy* from end to beginning, he has been able to show how she developed, and his take on the subject is much more interesting than the usual diagnosis of 'unable to form relationships, inadequate, emotionally and/or sexually abused by the opposite-sex parent'. The Angel of the 1990s instalment of the trilogy is a truly chilling creation. With her emotional torture of one of the men she hates, Taylor has shown how writers can produce shuddering horror in their readers without any description of the actual perpetration of physical cruelty. That takes great skill. As I stood on that muddy Devon foreshore on New Year's Eve, watching our party's two millennial fireworks and the bursts of sparkly colour from much more lavish displays up and down the coast, I wondered why so many of us want to read novels that make us shudder. Is it because our lives have become so safe that we need to scare ourselves? Or do we want our worst nightmares brought into the light by someone else's imagination to make them seem less real? Could reading about anger and hatred exploding into violence give us vicarious satisfaction and so allow us to appease our own furies without damaging anyone else? I couldn't decide. My only certainty was – and is –that all crime writers have to expand their range. Otherwise they risk joining the rest of the embalmed bodies in the great unvisited library of the past. I came back from the Villa Crusoe not much wiser, but a great deal more thoughtful than I had gone. And that was no bad thing for the start of a new millennium.

CT prides itself on the number of top crime writers who are happy to write for these pages – and here's Natasha Cooper, regularly to be found as reviewee at the back of CT for her HarperCollins Trish Maguire crime treats, talking about the crime writers life...

the trio

capsule comments by three key ct reviewers (eve tan gee, brian ritterspak & judith gray)

HALF MOON STREET BY ANNE PERRY, HEADLINE, £17.99

A body lies reclining in a punt, clothed in a torn dress. But it's a male body: and soon Perry's sleuth Pitt is deep in London's Bohemia where playwrights are fighting against censorship. Smoothly written and compelling in Perry's distinctive style. ETG

RAVELLING BY PETER MOORE SMITH, HUTCHINSON, £10

At her parents' party, little Fiona Airie goes missing, and a family is torn apart. Her brother Pilot is tormented by schizophrenia, apparently triggered by childhood tragedy. Smith's marshalling of a complex plot shows real skill, and this is pretty well unputdownable, although the characterisation is conventional. ETG

LOST BY LUCY WADHAM, FABER, £9.99

Concentrating on the emotional impact of crime, this is a novel of some distinction, dealing with the heroine's agonised response to the possible kidnapping of her son. JG

KILLING ME SOFTLY BY NICCI FRENCH, PENGUIN, £5.99

You may think you're tired of the dark erotic thriller, but this is one of the most accomplished entries in genre, and French is as good at dealing with obsession as anyone you're likely to encounter. BR

LILIES THAT FESTER BY HAZEL HOLT, MACMILLAN, £16.99

For those not for alienated by the Christie-esque mystery, this is a confidently handled entry in the Sheila Malory series, Holt's eleventh. Perhaps not as compelling as some previous entries, but pretty diverting nevertheless. ETG

THE MAN AT THE WINDOW BY BETTY ROWLANDS, HODDER & STOUGHTON, £16.99

I make no apologies for being a devoted fan of the cosy, and this is one of the smoothest contemporary outings, with Melissa Craig a well handled heroine. Mark Timlin would hate it, but that might be reason to pick it up. ETG

THE DISORDER OF YOUR NAME BY JUAN JOSE MILLAS, ALISON AND BUSBY, £9.99

Many of us are finding foreign crime fiction a particularly fertile field, well worth investigating. I don't believe the name of the translator here (Rod Usher!), but he's done a very atmospheric job on a remarkable dark thriller. JG

DR MORTIMER AND THE ALDGATE MYSTERY BY GERARD WILLIAMS, CONSTABLE, £16.99

The first in a new Victorian series featuring the young physician Dr James Mortimer and his partner Doctor Violet Branscombe. Engaging and colourfully drawn (if familiar territory), with two winning protagonists—a series to watch. BR

THE SLEEP OF BIRDS BY SARAH MACDONALD, HEADLINE, £5.99

Set against the rugged coastline of Cornwall and the bleak spaces of Dartmoor, this is a haunting tale of damage and distress that may take a little time to engage the reader but more than pays dividend. ETG

A PLACE OF EXECUTION BY VAL MCDERMID, HARPERCOLLINS, £6.99.

What more needs to be said, other than this is the paperback issue of McDermid's most compelling book in years. Unmissable. JG

THE TEMPEST BY JUAN MANUEL DE PRADA, SCEPTRE, £14.99

Winner of a prestigious literary prize in Spain, this is a sophisticated and elegantly written literary thriller by a young Spanish writer set in present-day Venice. Sensuous and involving. BR

RED FLOWERS FOR LADY BLUE BY DONALD THOMAS, MACMILLAN, £16.99.

London in the Thirties: the streets are still clouded with Holmesian fog, and the seedy underworld still exerts an insidious grip in Thomas' complex novel. Some of his villains are a touch larger-than-life (more subtlety might have been advisable) but this is still a highly compulsive read. BR

BENEATH THE BLONDE BY STELLA DUFFY, SERPENTS TAIL, £6.99

Of the younger crime writers, Duffy is in a class by herself: the use of language, her canny plotting and (most of all), her wise-cracking heroine Saz Martin make each new entry de rigeur – even a journeyman entry such as this. ETG

THE VANISHED CHILD BY SARAH SMITH, ARROW, £5.99

New England 1887: an eight-year-old boy sees his grandfather murdered. He is kidnapped and presumably, murdered too. But 20 years later, a man shows up in Boston who looks like the vanished child. Taut, professionally written psychological mystery with some novel twists. JG

HEAD WOUNDS BY VALERIE KERSHAW, CONSTABLE, £16.99

Swift moving, funny and idiomatic: Kershaw may have been a newspaper and radio journalist, but don't let that put you off this highly entertaining thriller. BR

UNDERTOW BY LESLIE GRANT-ADAMSON, NEL, £5.99

It becomes harder and harder to turn out something new in the field of psychological suspense, but Grant-Adamson shows she still knows how to do it in this elegantly written novel, set in the Somerset of her Patterns in the Dust. JG

POWERDOWN BY PETER TONKIN, HEADLINE, £5.99

A Nasa astronaut is dying on the Antarctic ice shelf. Tonkin's hero Richard Mariner becomes involved in a desperate rescue attempt. Powerfully written FBI thriller: there's little that's new here, but plenty of page-turning nous. BR

SEA FEVER BY ANN CLEEVES, ALISON AND BUSBY, £6.99

Amateur sleuth George Palmer-Jones joins a band of bird watchers, but bloodshed rather than avian delights soon becomes the order of the day. The writing here is basic, but nevertheless engaging and colourful. ETG

INK BY JOHN PRESTON, BLACK SWAN, £6.99

Mordantly written and full of canny observation, this is a literate and involving second novel about the nature of identity. BR

KILL THE WITCH BY JUDITH COOK, HEADLINE, £5.99

Cook's Elizabethan series demonstrate the usual intelligent research and sense of period; this fourth entry is not the strongest, but is still an essential purchase for anyone who's enjoyed the earlier books. BR

SHIFTS BY ADAM THORPE, CAPE, £14.99.

The writing here is of a very special order indeed, and Thorpe shows that Ulverton was not a one-off. Utterly compelling. JG

QUINN BY SEAMUS SMYTH, FLAME, £6.99

With a devious modern day Moriarty at the centre of his thriller, Smyth offers a tasty and macabre piece of work that grips pretty comprehensively despite the odd misstep. ETG

THIN ICE BY JOYCE HOLMS, HEADLINE, £5.99

The kidnapping of a small boy gives lawyer Tam Buchanan an unlooked-for problem in the week before Christmas. Witty and adroit, this is well up to Holms' usual high standard. JG

THE WATCHMAN BY MATTHEW LYNN, ARROW, £5.99

Long after John Buchan, Lynn proves that it's still possible to pull off the first-rate chase novel, although Hannay never had to cope with CCTV cameras. This one move with some considerable speed. BR

NIGHT WORK BY LAURIE KING, HARPERCOLLINS, £16.99

I've always been a great promoter of King, and this new book will do nothing to alter that enthusiasm. The plotting is the thing with King, and it's as assured as ever in this latest outing. ETG

ABSOLUTE MEASURES BY HUMPHREY HAWKSLEY, HEADLINE, £5.

The experienced journalist shows with his third novel that he has made the transition to thriller writer with great skill. The political dimensions of the book are (unsurprisingly) as solid as its thriller credentials. JG

THE OTHER DAUGHTER BY LISA GARDNER, ORION, £19.99

A dark tale of malign intentions, which builds on the success of the accomplished Perfect Husband. Cryptic messages and hatred fuel this intense narrative. BR

GOD IS BULLET BY BOSTON TERRAN, MACMILLAN, £10

A wild ride into a savage subculture of cult violence, with a bloodthirsty devil-worshipping tribe called The Left-handed Path. Scattershot stuff, but a debut of real accomplishment. JG

film

milennial movies:

crime time picks the favourite crime movies of the past 1000 years... yes, we know they only made films for 100 or so of them...

CRIME TIME asked a distinguished and eclectic panel of 14, plus two of our own, to choose their 10 favourite crime movies of the past Millennium, in any order (or none) with appropriate explanations, justifications, or no comment at all. We asked for favourite, rather than 'best', because we were looking to identify the movies that stick with us, that we enjoy the most, that we remember quickest, rather than those that are necessarily the 'key' movies in the genre. We also left the very definition of a crime movie to each individual: it drove some people crazy! Two of the panel deliberately avoided letting a single director (Hitchcock in one case, Scorsese in another) dominate their choices. The usual pattern was that the first five or six or eight films came to mind quickly, but cutting the list off at ten was difficult...in fact, impossible for a number of people, myself included! All the movies chosen came from the 20th Century (just kidding, in fact, only one person chose a film from the silent era!) The contributors are listed in alphabetical order, and the results are fascinating, as I'm sure you'll agree ...

PHIL ABRAHAM

(Director of Photography, *The Sopranos*)

"Just off the top of my head (and in no particular order)":

The Killing (Stanley Kubrick) *High Sierra* (Raoul Walsh) *Gun Crazy* (Joseph H Lewis) *Criss Cross* (Robert Siodmak) *Key Lar*GO (John Huston) *Out Of The Past* (Jacques Tourneur) *Where The Sidewalk Ends* (Otto Preminger) *Elevator To The Gallows* (Louis Malle) *The Parallax View* (Alan Pakula) *Heat* (Michael Mann)

"Hey, that was fun!"

michael carlson

JEANINE BASINGER

(Author of *The Silents; A Woman's View; The World War II Combat Film; Anthony Mann: A Critical Analysis* and many more; Professor of film studies at Wesleyan University):

Criss Cross (Robert Siodmak) *Lady From Shanghai* (Orson Welles) *Pickup On South Street* (Sam Fuller) *In A Lonely Place* (Nicholas Ray) *Kiss Me Deadly* (Robert Aldrich) *Big Heat* (Fritz Lang) *Laura* (Otto Preminger) *Moonrise* (Frank Borzage) *Gun Crazy* (Joseph H Lewis) *The Locket* (John Brahm) *Out Of The Past* (Jacques Tourneur) *The Big Combo* (Joseph H Lewis) ... and many more: *Double Indemnity, Raw Deal* (Mann, not Arnold), *Border Incident, Pitfall, The Enforcer* (Bogart, not Clint), *The Killing, Private Hell 36*.

MICHAEL CARLSON

(film editor, *Crime Time*):

"I confess a fondness for small, perfectly formed caper movies."

The Big Sleep (Howard Hawks) *Chinatown* (Roman Polanski) *Double Indemnity* (Billy Wilder) *The Friends Of Eddie Coyle* (Peter Yates) *The Godfather* (Francis Ford Coppola) *The Big Heat* (Fritz Lang) *The Big Combo* (Joseph H Lewis) *The Killing* (Stanley Kubrick) *The Outfit* (John Flynn) *Gun Crazy* (Joseph H Lewis) or *The Asphalt Jungle* (John Huston) or *Knife In The Head* (Reinhard Hauff) or *The Front Page* (Lewis Milestone) or *The Getaway* (Sam Peckinpah) or *Once Upon A Time In America* (Sergio Leone) or *Miller's Crossing* (Coen Bros.) or *The Picture Snatcher* (Lloyd Bacon) or *Manhunter* (Michael Mann) or *Charley Varrick* (Don Siegel)

HARLAN COBEN

(Whose latest Myron Bolitar novel is *The Final Detail*)

"I keep drawing a major blank. Is that weird or what? That said, in no particular order:"

Strangers On A Train—my favourite Hitchcock film (I could fill this list with just Hitchcock films) and if pressed, I'd list this as my numero uno. Yowza. Check out Robert Walker watching Farley Granger play tennis. Subtle creepy. *Marathon Man*—Is it safe? Nope. Loved the book, loved the movie. *Usual Suspects*—Okay, so the big surprise ending is hardly a surprise. You got the goods here. Plus Keyser Soze, perhaps the best name in crime moviedom. *Maltese Falcon*—Bogie. What I love most about this movie is that the hero is far from likeable. I have a reproduction of the *Maltese Falcon* sitting on my desk. I stare at it while I write. But it never tells me anything. *The Godfather*—Okay, this one is too obvious. Boring pick. *Fargo*—Coen brothers. Delightful in so many ways. *Shawshank Redemption*—I don't know if this fits under the category. One of the most underrated movies of all time. I loved it. *Witness For The Prosecution* — Twists and turns galore, plus Marlene Dietrich and the always-great Charles Laughton. Go for it. *Breaker Morant*—my favorite court martial film. My favorite legal thriller. A must, must see. *Body Heat*—Sacrilege but I liked this even better than the original *Double Indemnity*.

MICHAEL CONNELLY

(Author of the Harry Bosch novels, *Blood Work*, and, most recently, *Void Moon*)

1. *Chinatown* 2. Robert Altman's *The Long Goodbye* (which most diehard Chandler fans consider an abomination but I love for other reasons.) and then in no particular order: *Farewell My Lovely* with Mitchum. *Bullitt* with McQueen. The best sound effects for a car chase ever. McQueen's Mustang sounded like pure testosterone. *The Third Man* (which I only recently watched for the first time at the urging of Otto Penzler who put it at the top of his list of 100 best crime movies ever.) *The Silence Of The Lambs. Blade Runner* (if it can be deemed a crime film) *The French Connection. Magnum Force.*

"As you can tell, I lean heavily on the recent contemporary and for the most part these choices are based on their inspirational value to me in my formation as a writer of crime stories. As films some are probably considered mediocre by the critics and scholars, but they used basic constructs of the loner cop going against the odds, a storyline though often repeated was very stirring to me as a young person who wanted to become a writer. It's not in my top 10 but you ought to check out a small film of a few years ago called Hard Eight."

JOHN CONNOLLY
(Author, *Every Dead Thing, Dark Hollow*)

"I've been mulling over the movies all week and here, in no particular order, are my current faves":

Harper, Diva, The Big Sleep (Bogie, not Mitchum) *The Long Goodbye, North By Northwest, The French Connection, The Maltese Falcon, Manhunter, The Friends Of Eddie Coyle, LA Confidential, Chinatown*

"Yes, I know that makes eleven!"

BARRY FORSHAW
(Editor, Crime Time)

The Big Sleep, Les Diaboliques, Psycho, The Big Heat, The Godfather. Vertigo, Point Blank, Dirty Harry, Bonnie & Clyde, Kiss Me Deadly

ANTHONY FREWIN
(Author of three crime novels and several non-fiction works, and assistant director on many films, most notably for Stanley Kubrick. He is currently working on a screenplay of his first novel, the excellent *London Blues*, and on a documentary about Kubrick):

"Top Ten? Well, Top twenty was the best I could do and there are some, I'm sure, I've left out. But then, what is a crime film? How about, for example, Blade Runner? Because it is set in the future is it primarily considered a science fiction film, but it is about crimes...so I made it the twentieth title. I guess this isn't the place to get into the taxonomy and such of film genres. In chronological order":

Double Indemnity Billy Wilder, USA, 1944 *Force Of Evil* Abraham Polonsky, USA, 1948 *White Heat* Raoul Walsh, USA, 1949 *Night And The City* Jules Dassin, USA/GB, 1950 *The Blue Lamp* Basil Dearden, GB, 1950 *D.O.A.* Rudolp Maté, USA, 1950 *Strangers On A Train* Alfred Hitchcock, USA, 1951 *Kiss Me Deadly* Robert Aldrich, USA 1955 *Les Diaboliques* Henri-Georges Clouzot, France, 1955 *The Killing* Stanley Kubrick, USA, 1956 *The Long Arm* Charles Frend, GB, 1956 *Le Trou* Jacques Becker, France, 1960 *Robbery* Peter Yates, GB, 1967 *Bullitt* Peter Yates, USA, 1968 *Get Carter* Mike Hodges, GB, 1971 *Villain* Michael Tuchner, GB, 1971 *The Godfather* Francis Ford

Coppola, USA, 1972 *Blade Runner* Ridley Scott USA 1982 *Once Upon A Time In America* Sergio Leone, Italy/USA, 1984 *Goodfellas* Martin Scorsese, USA, 1990

MICHAEL GOLDFARB
(critic, *Front Row* (BBC R4) *Meridian* (World Service))

Godfather's I & II (Coppolla) *The Killing* (Kubrick) *Charley Varrick* (Siegel) *The French Connection* (Friedkin) *North By Northwest* (Hitchcock) *Public Enemy* (Wellman) *High Sierra* (Walsh) *The Set Up* (Wise) *The Getaway* (Peckinpah) *Goodfellas* (Scorsese)

JOHN HARVEY
(Editor, Publisher, Poet and Western author who occasionally writes crime novels, including a series set in Nottingham featuring Charley Resnick, which has been reasonably successful in print and on BBC television):

"As of today, and in roughly chronological clusters:"

The Maltese Falcon, The Big Sleep, Out Of The Past ***, *Psycho, Vertigo* ***, *Point Blank, The Godfather 1 & 2, Chinatown* ***, *Cutter's Way* (Ivan Passer), *In The Line Of Fire* (Wolfgang Petersen), *Seven* (David Fincher).

MIKE HODGES
(Director, whose crime films include the classic *Get Carter, Pulp, and Croupier*):

Asphalt Jungle John Huston, *Le Boucher* Claude Chabrol, *Brighton Rock* John Boulting, *Godfather I* Francis Ford Coppolla, *King Of Comedy* Martin Scorsese ("*it is about a kidnapping, after all*"), *Kiss Me Deadly* Robert Aldrich, *Odd Man Out* Carol Reed, *Le Samourai* Jean-Pierre Melville, *Strangers On A Train* Alfred Hitchcock, *The Third Man* Carol Reed, 11. *Cape Fear* J Lee Thompson (the original, just misses the list.)

"*I've listed them in alphabetical order, though in fairness, Asphalt Jungle was actually the first that came to mind, and Brighton Rock the next.*"

MAXIM JAKUBOWSKI
(Author, editor, film programmer, and founder of Murder One)

"*Blame all the French films to a wasted youth spent on the Cinematheque steps in Paris. In no order then*"

Vertigo Hitchcock, *Detour* Edgar Ulmer, *La Sirene Du Mississipi* Truffaut, *Caught* Robert M. Young (rarely seen but likely to be at the NFT in July), *Point Blank* John Boorman, *Liebestraum* Mike Figgis, *LA Confidential* Curtis Hanson, *Ascenseur Pour L'echafaud* Louis Malle, *Hammett* Wim Wenders, *Heat* Michael Mann, *Coup De Torchon* Bertrand Tavernier, *Miller's Crossing* Coen Bros (the best film inspired by, though not credited, to, *Hammett*).

"*Yes, I know that makes twelve!*"

STEPHEN KALLAUGHER
(Screenwriter whose credits include *The Force, Dead Flowers* (aka *Verfuhrt)*, and *Click,* currently in preproduction from Trajan Films)

"*Ever since Oedipus and Medea, the bulk of drama is made up of crime stories of one sort of another. What better form for exploring notions of morality and justice? What better way to hook an audience than by flirting with and/or breaking taboos of violence (and sex, since they go—you'll forgive me—hand in hand.) And even that's just a fancy way of saying that one of the prime attractions of crime stories is that they give you the vicarious rocks of enjoying the company of people who get to do things you don't have the nerve to. That said, we also get to enjoy the bad guys getting their just desserts, which makes crime stories fundamentally socially conservative. I sometimes wonder whether the happiness we feel upon seeing the wicked punished reaches deeper—like to the Idea of Justice—because it is so universal, and so satisfying. It's a rare piece that can allow the bad guys to get away with it and not leave me feeling cheated and somewhat soiled. "So, my choices, in no particular order. Not many surprises here: There's a reason that the canon is the canon. When I started reaching deep into my memory for, say, that Sterling Hayden movie about the heist, I found I could remember only scenes, or characters. They just didn't stick."*

Chinatown—stands as an exception to the above rule. A crime movie (like the one below) that captures the emotional zeitgeist of its time perfectly. This was the feeling of the early 70s: the omnipresent corruption of every institution from family to government, and the impossibility of the individual to effect any change, or any improvement, however small. Not to mention great performances, one indelibly classic scene (My sister! My daughter!), a hero with his face bandaged for half the movie, a perfect closing line, and the shocking creepiness of seeing Roman Polanski—in his first movie since his wife was butchered—sticking a knife in someone. *Bonnie & Clyde*—oh, what 60s! The glamour of rebellion, crime as freedom, the sympathetic treatment of the wounded, romantic, doomed outsiders whose only crimes are against the property of the Establishment. Plus the proto-stoner quality of Michael Pollard, more bandaged faces, the treachery of the solid citizenry and the balletic dance of death to make sure we enjoy every pornographic moment. *M*—If part of the artist's job is to create our myths (and thereby contribute to their reality), then props to Lang for possibilty the first explication of what has become our modern demon: the faceless, anonymous, everyman serial killer. Props also to Peter Lorre's pathetic performance, the expressionist dislocation of the mise-en-scene (you knew I had to get that in somewhere, didn't you?), and the ambiguity of the criminal's court. *Goodfellas*—Speaking of expressionist dislocation, let's hear it for the cocaine-crazed camerawork and editing, the utter banality of the criminal life, and the anti-Dylanesque world in which there is indeed no honor amongst thieves. *Body Heat*—makes the list simply for the greatest, hottest, wettest femme fatale in film history. I still say you straight guys are crazy, but at least Kathleen Turner makes me understand the attraction. *White Heat*—More than just a family business, here's crime as the glue of family love, and insanity as a genetic bond. Not one, but two unforgettable scenes—the prison lunchroom and the ending—top one of the handful of classic performances in movie history, a performance as over-the-top as it is pitch-perfect. Cagney is as ferocious, unforgiving and frightening as anything before or—even given the continual jacking up of explicit violence—since. Plus another closing line for all time. *The Maltese Falcon*—featuring the definitive dick with the dick's definitive code of honour and all the scars to show for it; the whiff of perversion and decay contributed by Lorre & Greenstreet; the comic relief of Elijah Cook Jr.; a genuine puzzle for the mystery buffs; crackling dialogue. All this and a broken heart brought on by a spider woman. What more can you want? What more is there? I'll tell you what more: another one of those great closing lines. Honourable mention to *The Big Sleep* which almost makes it for the character of Baby (*Martha Vickers as Carmen Sternwood, -editor*), but misses out on plot incoherence. *Psycho*—two, two, two movies in one, with two crime stories. See where straying from the path of righteousness leads you? Straight into Norman's shower. Taking all those 'White Heat' themes one step beyond, Hitchcock succeeds in doing one thing most crime movies are too detached, too cool, too outside of the material to accomplish: he terrorises us with the evil everywhere around us. He makes the violence as real as we can stand. Scorsese may by the sociologist of crime, but Hitchcock is the psychoanalyst. Ultimately, I chose this one over any of several others for the shower scene. Forget about the sheer dazzling technique, which is as good as any scene ever put on film: When a piece of art/entertainment enters our national nightmares and becomes a cultural touchstone the way that scene, that music has, it's reached somewhere primal. *Les Diaboliques*—Hooray for Sebastian Japrisot, the most underrated of crime writers. Hooray for whoever directed it. Hooray for poor, seduced Simone Signoret. For a plot that keeps you guessing. And let's not forget the bathtub. *The Big Clock*—Probably I could put any of the honorable mentions in this spot, but I choose this as a sentimental favorite and neglected piece of wonderfulness. Charles Laughton and Elsa Lanchester steal it, as they usually did whenever they appeared. Great net-tightening around Ray Milland as an innocent man trying to evade capture and expose his dastardly boss. Excellent adaptation work from the novella. Good plotting, which is a prime directive in my book. Nine Honourable Mentions (and Joan Crawford!):*Apartment Zero* (only misses because of the too-blatant *Pyscho* rip-off), *Manhunter*, *Topkapi*, *Beat The Devil*, *Public Enemy*, *Scarface*, *Lethal Weapon II*, *Z*, *I Am A Fugitive From A Chain Gang*, *Mildred Pierce*.

KIM NEWMAN

(author of *Life's Lottery*, *Millennial Movies* and *Dracula Cha Cha Cha*)

The Roaring Twenties, *Get Carter*, *Night And The City* (Dassin), *Hell Drivers*, *Double Indemnity*, *The Big Sleep* (Hawks), *Murder My Sweet*, *Mean Streets*, *King Of New York*, *The Ladykillers*

JAMES SALLIS

(Whose most recent Lew Griffin novel was *Bluebottle*. Forthcoming books include a biography of Chester Himes, two major collections of poems, another of essays, and *Time's Hammers*, his collected stories.):

1. *The Big Sleep* Howard Hawks 2.

Chinatown Roman Polanski 3. *Night Zoo* Jean-Claude Lauzon (1987, Canada) 4. *Alphaville* Jean-Luc Godard *Romeo Is Bleeding* Gary Oldman *The Usual Suspects* Bryan Singer 7. *Cotton Comes To Harlem* Ossie Davis 8. *Coup De Torchon* Bertrand Tavernier 9. *Dark Passage* Delmer Daves *American Beauty* Sam Mendes

JUDITH WILLIAMSON

(Critic, whose film writing was collected in *Deadline at Dawn*(Marion Boyars) and who presented the BBC Film Noir series *Fatal Attractions*):

This list includes not just 'crime genre' films, but also some of other genres that nevertheless are about crime or centre on a criminal act. It is in alphabetical order, not order of preference.

The Big Heat (Fritz Lang 1953 US) One of the most compelling and disturbing films noirs, where the boundaries between goodie and baddie disintegrate as an honest cop and family man finds himself drawn into the world of crime he investigates. *Blackmail* (Alfred Hitchcock 1929 UK) Hitchcock made both a sound and a silent version of this, but the silent one works more potently in its harrowing investigation of guilt when a policeman's sweetheart commits a murder in self-defence and (initially) lets a witness take the rap. *Casino* (Martin Scorsese 1995 US) I would have liked to put more Scorsese films on this list, because he has to be the filmmaker of our time who understands crime both as American culture, and as a profoundly macho culture, better than anyone. *Casino* is about much more than crime: it shows—through crime—the structure of a whole society. *Chinatown* (Roman Polanski 1974 US) This is an all-time classic movie about the uncovering of crime, an unravelling of criminal acts which ultimately links the spheres of public-political and municipal crimes—and private—highly intimate crimes. *Dog Day Afternoon* (Sidney Lumet 1975 US) An extraordinarily radical film about a crime—bank robbery—which goes absurdly wrong, with both comic and, finally, sad results. The detail—a hostage bankteller's husband phoning in to ask what he can eat for supper -is fantastic, and the unhurried pace gives space to the emotional drama that unfolds. *The Lavender Hill Mob* (Charles Crichton 1951 UK) One of the most insane crime comedy films ever made, with gold bullion Eiffel Towers and an incredible chase sequence with schoolgirls milling around in classic Ealing fashion. It is also, though, a kind of meditation on class as the gang spans a range of accents and stereotypes. *Lucky Luciano* (Francesco Rosi 1973 Italy) This is the true 'godfather' story—Rosi's dark and forceful movie tracks the ins and outs of Mafioso Luciano in a very precise context of social and political power, making *The Godfather* look almost sloppy by comparison. *Pickpocket* (Robert Bresson 1959 France) A dreamlike yet lucid story of crime and redemption, this film centres on a crime not just as a symbol, but as its very material, becoming almost a catalogue of pickpocketing methods as hands slip in and out of pockets with a sensual skill. The crime is both physical and spiritual, and as always with Bresson these dimensions are inseparable. *Touchez Pas Au Grisbi* (Jacques Becker 1953 France) This is often seen as the classic French gangster film, with Jean Gabin as the criminal trying to 'retire' and instead becoming embroiled unwillingly in gangster conflicts. It portrays an almost nostalgic world of 'decent' crime with its own rules and warmth, hence the English title used, *Honour Among Thieves*. *White Heat* (Raoul Walsh 1949 US) A film which focuses on the pathology of the criminal himself, with Cagney as the all-time Mommy's boy, famously shouting *"Top of the World, Ma"* as he goes up in flames in the climactic scene on top of an oil refinery. The sheer energy of the gangster comes across in this movie superbly.

ADRIAN WOOTTON
(Director, London Film Festival, Programmer National Film Theatre)

Having already listed six films in his five favourites for his interview in CT2.7, Adrian had only four to go. But it wasn't easy!

"In no particular order:"

In A Lonely Place Ray, *Shoot The Piano Player* Truffaut, *Out Of Sight* Soderbergh, *The Big Sleep* Hawks, *The Big Heat* Lang, *The Third Man* Reed, *Point Blank* Boorman, *After Dark My Sweet* Vertigo Hitchcock *Heat*

("Did I already say *Heat*?"

"No, that was The Big Heat"

"I want to include the Michael Mann Heat, *the long* Heat. *You could almost call it* The Long Heat—*there's a title no one's used yet!*")

FINAL NOTES

I hope, like me, you were amazed at the variety of choices: each of the 16 contributors had more than one film no one else chose, making a 'short list' of over 100 films. Which suggests some more viewing is in order. The films selected most often (in order of love) were:

Godfather
Chinatown
The Big Sleep
The Big Heat
The Killing
Kiss Me Deadly
The Maltese Falcon
Point Blank
Vertigo

That's a pretty impressive top 9: you can fill in the tenth yourselves. A vote for *The Godfather* automatically included both I and II and automatically excluded III unless otherwise stated. There are, as John Connolly reminded us, two versions of *The Big Sleep*, one's a great movie and the other's directed by Michael Winner. All the votes were for the Hawks version (did I need to tell you that?). And personally, no offense to Steve Kallaugher, in the race for hottest film, I was glad to see *White Heat* and *The Big Heat* outpolled *Body Heat!* Gloria Grahame with half her face scalded can still steam the adhesive right off Kathleen Turner!

michael carlson
films in review

THE LIMEY

Directed by Stephen Soderbergh written by Lem Dobbs starring Terence Stamp, Leslie Ann Warren, Peter Fonda, Luis Guzmain, Barry Newman

You wouldn't've thought, just a few years ago, that Steven Soderbergh would have swung so naturally into crime movies, and done them so well. There is a sense in which the traditional storytelling values which previous generations of directors had absorbed from books and theatre, and other movies, were lost to those who grew up with TV and videos, and they were doomed to inward-focused and self-referential work (cf *Sex Lies And Videotape*). But given the relatively tight framework of crime stories, directors as different as Tarantino and Soderbergh have been able to find a form which allows them to express themselves through Not that *The Limey* isn't referential, using clips from Terence Stamp in Ken Loach's *Poor Cow* to illustrate the Limey, Wilson's, wide boy years. This isn't anything new; it was used by Don Siegel in *The Shootist*, it was even used in a made for TV movie a few years back, but what's interesting is the way the scenes from the past not only illuminate Stamp's character, but heighten the contrast between what we now recall as 'the Sixties' and its somewhat less glamorous reality, and even more the contrast between that time and what we're living in now. Of course, that's where Peter Fonda comes in. As the music producer, Valentine, who may have been responsible for the death of Wilson's daughter, Fonda is at his most unctuous, half mellow to the point of vegetation, half reptilian. The most interesting character, however, may be Barry Newman, as Fonda's security man. He gets to reprise his driving scenes from Vanishing Point, but he also seems to be the one character who doesn't need to marshal his resources, who is what he is, to the point that you wonder why he's still hanging around Fonda. Then you realise, it's for the money, and for all the counter-culture posing, money is what has got Fonda to where he is, kept him there, and involved him in the business that resulted in Wilson's daughter's death.. Cultural contrast is what made *The Limey* so popular. Almost no one in LA understands what Stamp is saying (the gimmick turns into a classic line, when Bill Duke, playing a DEA agent says *"There's only one thing I don't understand: every word you've just said"*) and Wilson too has his problems with cultural adjustment (he thinks parking valets are hired muscle). But Stamp's performance resonates beyond California Kray. At first, some of the more powerful moments (a shootout, the scenes with Duke) seemed to be an actor doing his *Hale & Pace* East End tough guy, but soon you realise that what Stamp is doing is showing Wilson gathering his forces about him; stepping into his own role. The strongest point of *The Limey* is the way Soderbergh plays with memory, with time, and how this winds up being reflected in the story, as the springboard for his daughter's demise is a misunderstanding that goes back to her English childhood. The most poignant scenes of the movies as memory are with Stamp's infant daughter. It seems to me that for Soderbergh she, even as a corpse, is *The Limey*'s most important character. She is someone who has been let down by Stamp, Fonda and the rest of the 'survivors' of the 60s, maybe her whole generation, which includes Soderbergh, has. This feeling is heightened by the way Wilson in effect walks away from his revenge, as if seeing himself reflected in Valentine. Two icons of a past which turns out to have been hollow. And as Stamp sits in his airplane seat, you (and maybe he) literally don't know whether he is coming or going.

BRINGING OUT THE DEAD

Directed by Martin Scorsese screenplay by Paul Schrader based on the novel by Joe Connelly, starring Nicholas Cage, Patricia Arquette, John Goodman, Ving Rhames, Tom Sizemore

This reunion of Scorsese and Schrader (*Taxi Driver*, *Raging Bull*, *Last Temptation Of Christ*) is high concept in the extreme: call it *Return To The Mean Streets*, or *Ambulance Driver*, or *Leaving Hell's Kitchen*. It's *ER* meets the dark side of New York, as Cage with his most hangdog, suffering El Greco face (Martyr Scorsese?) spends three nights on ambulance duty with three different partners, and three days chasing down the troubles in the life of a woman whose father is lingering on after cardiac arrest. The woman is played by Patricia Arquette, looking mighty well-fed for a recovering junkie, but she is not a delusional 12 year old needing a rescuer, as Jodie Foster was in *Taxi Driver*. Here she is someone simply worn down by life, but more accepting of it than Cage's Frank Pierce (whose name echoes both Frank Burns and Hawkeye Pierce from *MASH*, while also suggesting his vulnerability). Pierce drives through the netherworld of New York, literally haunted by the ghost of a girl he failed to save. He speaks to the dead, or the nearly-dead, hearing the unvoiced pleas of Arquette's father as he lies on the hospital bed, unable to die. But the focus of the film is on that treacherous and narrow space between the two worlds that are pulling Pierce apart, that is, the 'real' world. Despite the high concept, the three bravura performances by Goodman, Rhames, and Sizemore sharing of the portmanteau segments, the lively soundtrack and beautiful gritty nighttime shooting of New York are really all just flashy disguises for what is a sombre and tired movie, about taking stock of lives and surviving the everyday brutality of existence. It is a movie about coming to grips, and it comes to grips with itself in an understated way that is strong enough to overpower the undeniable flash that goes before it. It's a case of there being less than meets the eye going on here, and sometimes, less is more.

THE BONE COLLECTOR

Directed by Philip Noyce screenplay by Jeremy Iacone based on the novel by Jeffrey Deaver, starring Denzel Washington, Angelina Jolie, Michael Rooker, Luis Guzmain

Let's start with what's good about *The Bone Collector*. It has one of the most impressive blendings of sound editing with camera work that I've seen in a long time: beautiful shots of New York from angles which suggest a beautiful geometric structure, a work of logic, are contrasted with an underground City which steams like the third circle of Hell. Off-screen, rain water drips insistently, like the creeping threat of things about to fall apart. Contrasted with all of this is Denzel Washington's flat, in which his character, Lincoln Rhyme, is trapped after being paralyzed while working as a forensic investigator. This New York is more atmospheric and affecting, in its way, than Scorsese's, and just as manipulative. Lincoln Rhyme is a great name for an investigator, and if Washington plays him with a bit too much insouciance, he does better than Richard Dreyfuss in a similar situation. Rooker gives his now-usual turn as a big-headed blowhard, Guzmain, who is now Hollywood's leading all-purpose Latino, has his usual fun with a character role, and Ed O'Neil (of *Married With Children* infamy) looks born to play a New York cop. Now let's get to what isn't do good about this movie, which is just about everything else, and it's a shame so much was wasted on this crap. Rhyme, the first actually 'nero' Nero Wolfe winds up with Angelina Jolie (model turned cop, really!) as his Archie Goodwin when she exhibits good forensic instincts upon discovering what turns out to be a serial murder with clues left to track down further killings. Jolie is the world's smallest cop since Holly Hunter. After her fetishistic donning of her full patrolperson's rig early in the film, she moves as easily as Neil Armstrong on the Sea of Tranquility. With everyday clothes on, it's all hip shaking wiggle, two steps sideways for every one forward. Jolie's arms are thinner than the glasses she drinks from; at one point she takes a distasteful nibble at a pushcart pretzel; the most unconvincing bite of junk food since Cameron Diaz winced while trying to pretend to eat a hot dog in *Something About Mary*. All of this would be no problem if Jolie could actually act, but the only part of her with any expressiveness is her lips, and all they do is quiver, as if they had their own life-support system, similar to the one Rhyme is kept alive on. When Jolie dons a Maddona-mike to crash a crime scene while Denzel guides her by remote control, it's like someone glued Carly Simon's beestungs on Skinny Spice. This is what the new PC feminist Weed will look like this when Bill and Ben the Flowerpot Men make their return to British TV. Imagine someone only slightly bigger than Martin Amis sporting Mick Jagger's lips and you'll get the idea.

Though even that makes more sense than the story, which creaks so badly I'll bring a can of oil if I ever try to slog through one of Deaver's novels. Here's Link Rhyme, cop, teacher, lecturer, and we are told more than once, famed author of a best-seller about the most gruesome murders in New York's history. So when he finally deciphers the serial killer's helpful clues, he sends Jolie out to find a *"turn of the century"* book, which turns out to be a paperback (only paperbacks weren't invented until the 1930s) detailing, uh, some of the most gruesome killings in New York's history. Only Link has gone Missing; he hasn't recognised any of those murders, not a one. Then it turns out the killer has been harbouring a grudge for years against Rhyme. Yet he's had any number of opportunities to kill Link, but passed them by, in order to kill a few people and go one up on Rhyme first. Jeez. At least this time they let Denzel end up with the skinny white girl with blubber lips. Remember how the relationship with Julia Roberts in *The Pelican Brief* stayed Platonic? Well, I guess in Hollywood's eyes it's OK to let him suffer Jolie liplock, because since he's paralyzed below the neck, the audience won't have to go home worried there might be some actual miscegenation in store. We could only hope. Paralyzed from the neck down? Well, Jolie's giant lips HAVE to be good for something!

the cops

tv

charles waring

THEY SNORT COCAINE, smoke pot and swear a lot. But that's not all: they lie, cheat, eat lots of chips, drink lots of beer, plant contraband and then beat up innocent people. If you think these are the bad guys, think again: for these are *The Cops*.

Ever since the advent of commercial television in this country during the 1950s, the work of the police has always figured highly as the subject of small-screen drama. But periodically, the accepted cop show format has received a rude awakening at the hands of a mould-breaking new series which alters the way that society's law enforcers are portrayed. During the era of *Dixon Of Dock Green* (a 1950's show which ran for twenty years about a paternalistic, superannuated beat bobbie, George "Evenin' all" Dixon), the approachable British copper was someone the public could trust and look up to. Perceptions about the hitherto unquestioned moral probity of the nation's crime-fighters changed somewhat when the BBC launched a gritty, warts-and-all series about brusque Northern coppers called *Z Cars* in the early 1960s. *Z Cars* was the first British cop show to depict the police as normal human beings rather than one-dimensional moral crusaders. After *Z Cars*, British crime shows tended to be more realistic but received another slap-in-the-face wake-up-call in the mid-1970s when the scruffy, vulgar, loud-mouthed, beer-swilling, bird-pulling members of London's Flying Squad, Regan and Carter, screeched onto the screen in a souped-up, shit-brown Ford Granada. That was, of course, *The Sweeney*, arguably the best indigenous British crime show to hit the small screen. But since those halcyon days of loutish, politically incorrect cops, British crime drama has proved a profound disappointment, characterised by dull, formulaic and ultimately forgettable shows. Although the long-running police soap opera, The Bill, has had a few decent moments in the 1990s, it rarely makes consistently arresting viewing. In 1998, however, we Brits finally had a show to write home about. That was *The Cops*, a BAFTA Award winning series which recently returned to BBC2 for a second ten week season. So, what makes *The Cops* any different from any other routine police drama we've been served up since the laddish antics of Regan and Carter were banished from our TV screens? Well, for starters, *The Cops* looks different. True, on purely aesthetic grounds, the show wouldn't win any glittering prizes—it's gritty, grimy and dominated by camerawork that's so unsteady it's likely to induce an attack of nausea in some viewers. Indeed, at first glance, *The Cops* would appear amateurish and crudely made but that is a key component in the strength of its appeal and an integral part of its clever, calculated deception. The series is consummately skilful in the way it masquerades as a rough-hewn, voyeuristic documentary. Hand-held cameras wobble feverishly and strain to maintain focus on the action while the seemingly slap-dash, cut-and-shut editing often results in truncated dialogue and the sense that the viewer has stumbled across events just as they are unfolding. The conspicuous absence of a music soundtrack and the fact that the show lacks production artifice and orthodox camera direction, emphasises the programme's palpable cinema verite, feel as does the casting of relatively unknown actors. An unsuspecting channel surfer who dropped in part way through *The Cops* would very likely assume that the show is a bona fide fly-on-the-wall documentary about the state of the nation's police force. According to the show's creator and producer, Tony Garnett, the primary aim of *The Cops* was to avoid jaded formulas and approach the cop show format from a new angle. Authenticity was paramount for Garnett and to achieve the programme's powerful sense of verisimilitude he insisted that intensive background research should include the show's writers spending a minimum of a fortnight working with the police—in addition, another of Garnett's prerequisites before embarking on filming was that all of the show's cast had to train to be police officers. *The Cops* depicts both the professional and off-duty lives of a group of police officers based at Stanton Police Station in an fictionalised part of Greater Manchester. For the uninitiated, it's an insightful, if slightly unsettling experience. The programme pulls no punches in its graphic delineation of a police force whose individual members lead lives almost as troubled and tortuous as those they arrest out on Lancashire's mean streets. The main recipients of the Police Station's attention are the impoverished residents of the nearby crime-riven Skeetsmoor Estate (who are somewhat pejoratively referred to as the "scrotes"). The notorious estate (in the main populated by smack heads, wife-beaters, prostitutes and assorted low-lives) witnessed a riot at the climax of the show's first series as the result of public protest against the death of man in police custody. The second series kicks off with the aftermath of that event with Stanton police attempting to rebuild shattered public trust by instituting a community policing programme. Although *The Cops* scrutinises in some detail the ambivalent relationship between the police and the public (who do they really protect and serve?), its other main focus is the internal workings of the police force. While there are many compelling storylines concerning problems confronting twenty first century urban Britain (drug-dealing, racism, domestic violence and juvenile vandalism), the human chemistry and inter-personal relationship between each member of the force is equally riveting and crackles with a fierce intensity. Not only is there daily confrontation with the residents of Skeetsmoor but also within the Police station itself. Conflict and tense rivalries manifest themselves in various guises: between males and females, black and white officers, hardened veterans and callow probationers, CID and the uniformed coppers. Ultimately, this conflict can be distilled into a battle between idealism and reality, between Inspector Newland's politically correct jargonistic soundbites and the grim certainties of the beat copper's prosaic everyday tasks. Between these two polarities is an abyss-like grey area of unfathomable complexity. Traditionally in TV crime drama, conflict's harsh, discordant note is harmoniously resolved at the denouement, with the criminals ending up dead or going to jail, thus allowing the world to rest easy once again. None of us, however, live in a perfect world and the police don't have all the answers to the problems they face. *The Cops* doesn't shirk its responsibilities towards veracity and steadfastly refuses to invest in this hackneyed happy ending scenario. With a conviction or arrest, a battle may have been won, but the war goes on relentlessly. The emphasis on three-dimensional characterisation is undoubtedly the show's forte— there's a full-bodied complexity and depth to each character which contributes to the show's believability. These cops are no angels but ordinary people burdened with the flaws and foibles that each and every one of us carry around with us every day. Some of what we witness is not pleasant viewing and at times it seems difficult to single out a character who is a decent and likeable human being. If *The Cops* does have a flaw, it's an apparent lack of pathos resulting from its slightly jaundiced perspective of humanity. Or at least it appears that way. With the exception, perhaps, of a couple of characters, the occupiers of Stanton Police Station aren't the sort of people most of us would wish to be associated with. For some observers (including the Greater Manchester Constabulary, who withdrew their support and co-operation after the tabloid furore that the first series engendered regarding PC Mel Draper's penchant for Bolivian marching powder!), *The Cops*' naturalism is much too close for comfort. Certainly, as a candid portrait of a modern police force, the show presents a disturbing picture for those with orthodox views on the unquestionable moral rectitude of the police. One thing's for certain, *The Cops* is unlikely to function as an effective advert for a career in the police force. The best British cop show since *The Sweeney*, *The Cops* has injected an element of risk-taking back into a television genre that had become as plodding and infirm as old George Dixon himself. For those who missed *The Cops* (shame on you!), the first series is available on video while a third season is planned for later this year. If Tony Garnett and his crew stay true to their principles, I, for one, can't wait. In the meantime, it's back to the same old fuzz fodder—A Touch Of Frost, The Bill, Taggart et al.

THE COPS—THE RAP SHEET

PC NATALIE METCALF
(CLAIRE MCGLINN)

An ambitious, coldly efficient female officer who started out as a sociology graduate working at the housing department before being prompted to join the force after being the victim of a vicious attack. Metcalf's unsmiling, adamantine exterior actually conceals an idealistic nature and truly altruistic motives for becoming a police officer (she harbours a genuine desire to help society's vulnerable people). Her Achilles heel is her involvement in a somewhat turbulent relationship with the manipulative, obnoxious D.S. Alan Wakefield.

PC MEL DRAPER
(KATY CAVANAGH)

Draper's coke-snorting exploits came to the fore in the first series but now she's a little more responsible, having graduated from probationer to community officer assigned to the Skeetsmoor Estate. Mel's close working liaison with the follically-challenged community worker, Darryl Stone, leads to an ill-judged romantic involvement.

PC ROY BRAMELL
(JOHN HENSHAW)

A rotund, plain-speaking old-school copper whose twenty years of experience and knowledge has led to a scathing cynicism of police modernisation and the cultivation of his own, often right-wing, personal doctrines. Frequently at loggerheads with the station's new sergeant, Roy, takes the impetuous young copper, Dean Wishaw, under his wing. His long-established diet of chips and beer results in serious repercussions for his health. Despite having no compunction in planting drugs on a suspect and organising the beating-up of a young Asian man, Roy is a character who elicits sympathy.

SERGEANT EDWARD GIFFEN
(ROB DIXON)

Recently transferred to Stanton, Giffen, is burdened with a terminally ill mother who takes up most of his time outside of work hours. Diligent, honest but essentially lonely, Giffen is falsely accused of sexual assault by a young black probationer.

PC DEAN WISHAW

Wildly impetuous and confrontational, Wishaw is blonde-haired live-wire whose youthful enthusiasm for aggravation resulted in the riot on Skeetsmore Estate in the first series' grand finale. Wishaw has no qualms in arresting his own father (a sponger and ne'er do well with a criminal record) for stealing money from his mother's handbag. Sometimes intoxicated by his power as a policeman, Wishaw lacks diplomacy and maturity.

PC MIKE THOMSON
(STEVE JACKSON)

A good cop whose marriage to his teenage sweetheart has irrevocably collapsed and leads him to question the direction his life is going. He volunteers to take the rap for a juvenile prank that goes wrong (handcuffing black probationer, PC Kennett, to some railings) and decides to quit the force.

PC COLIN JELLICOE
(STEVE GARTI)

A deep-thinking, loquacious loner, Jellicoe is regarded as something of an old woman by the rest of his colleagues. An open-minded, compassionate copper who's a bit of an anorak when it comes to Quiz Night at the local pub. His new job as Schools Liaison Officer leads to a tip-off about a parent who's growing marijuana—when Jellicoe discovers it's an MS sufferer who gains relief from cannabis tea, he turns a blind eye.

PC AMANDA KENNETT
(PAULETTE WILLIAMS)

The jewel in Newland's crown, but this ambitious, arrogant black graduate is an unpopular figure at the station. Brought down a peg or two when humiliated by being hand-cuffed to a railing by some of her colleagues. Falsely accuses Sgt Giffen of sexual harassment.

CHIEF INSPECTOR NEWLAND
(MARK CHATTERTON)

Institutes "Problem Orientated Policing" after edicts from on high. An aloof, soundbite politician more concerned with the issuing of "mission statements" than everyday police matters.

PC JAZ CHUNDARA
(PARVEZ QUADIR)

Asian copper who aspires to climb the chain of command: becomes a community officer as a stepping stone to CID but fiscal problems lead him to moonlight as a taxi driver at Hassan cabs.

DS ALAN WAKEFIELD
(DAVID CRELLIN)

A repugnant character who attempts to blackmail Mel Draper after he finds drugs in her flat: he'll keep quiet in exchange for sexual favours.

music

musical mugshots: john barry
charles waring

WHO CAN PRETEND TO understand the vagaries of fashion? One minute you're hot, the next you're not, with no apparent logic dictating this change in fortune. So, when the soothsaying style-gurus employed by glossy Sunday supplement fashion bibles inform their readers that John Barry is back, should you believe them? Suddenly, the 66 year-old composer is a hip cultural figure again, championed by in-the-know music pundits and even by contemporary musicians who cite him as a seminal influence. Record companies jump the bandwagon and begin releasing material that hasn't seen the light of day since it was first issued many, many moons ago. The whole shebang smacks of a cynical marketing ploy because in truth, Barry's never been away and in Hollywood, he's always been considered 'hot' (he's worked on several movies a year for the last three decades).

Barry's sudden elevation to a British cultural icon may be due to the growing interest in 60's kitsch, including lounge music, with which, Barry (quite erroneously, in my opinion) seems to be associated. The growth in the film soundtrack market has also enhanced Barry's status as a composer and a venerable grandee of British popular music. However, if there was one event that catapulted Barry's name back into the orbit of popular consciousness it was the Guinness company using the song *We Have All The Time In The World* in an advert to promote their black and tan nectar. The song, written by Barry and Don Black, featured the inimitable Louis Armstrong on vocals and was culled from the 1969 Bond movie *On Her Majesty's Secret Service*. That was 1996, and since then the public have evinced a genuine appetite for all things Barry. Or so we're told. John Barry burst on the film soundtrack scene like an exploding supernova back in the early sixties. Although the British composer, Monty Norman, scored the first James Bond movie, *Dr No*, in 1963, Barry was engaged by the film's producers to spice-up Norman's Bond theme with a contemporary edge. The rest, they say, is history. Barry was born in York in 1933 as John

Barry Prendergast. As an aspiring musician who wanted to become a household name, Barry considered his surname a bit of a mouthful and abbreviated it to his first two Christian names, thereby giving it a snappy, showbiz ring.

The Yorkshire composer's interest in the cinema began at a very young age. His father, in fact, was the proprietor of several local cinemas in York and by the time that Barry was a teenager, he was already assisting in the projection booth.

Barry's musical inclinations were encouraged at an early age (he began playing the piano at the age of 9) and his teachers included Dr. Francis Jackson of York Minster and the jazz player, Bill Russo, from the renowned Stan Kenton orchestra. Even before he was eligible to leave school, John Barry was determined to pursue a career as a film composer. He began his professional career playing in a jazz big band and when sufficiently seasoned, formed his own outfit (in 1957, at the height of the rock'n'roll era), The John Barry Seven. Barry's group soon rose to fame through live performances and television appearances. Barry and his group collaborated with an up-and-coming young cockney singer, Adam Faith, a creative liaison that resulted in Faith's first major chart record, *What Do You Want?* Faith, whose singing style sounded akin to musical hiccups, jumped at the chance to play the lead role in a low-budget film called *Beat Girl* (1959), and Barry, who was Faith's arranger, was asked to contribute the score. News of Barry's talent spread fast and with only a couple of scores under his belt, the Yorkshireman was approached to supply all the music to accompany the second cinematic adventure of Ian Fleming's suave, playboy spy, James Bond.

Barry not only was responsible for the incidental background music but also wrote the music to the signature songs that opened and closed each Bond movie (he would often use the lyricist Don Black, who collaborated with Barry on many Bond songs). The combination of Bond's glamorous espionage exploits and Barry's almost brash, overly dramatic orchestral score worked well and established a creative template that would remain in place for the first seven of Harry Saltzman's and Cubby Broccoli's 007 series (just like Sean Connery, Barry would return later on in the series). Barry's penchant for jazz nuances coloured his bright, inventive scores and seemed the perfect musical accompaniment to Sean Connery's on-screen exploits. Although the famous Bond theme of the opening titles belonged to Monty Norman, Barry's distinctive orchestral sonorities and exciting use of twanging electric guitar (a stylistic throwback to his rock'n'roll days) gave the tune a flavour all its own. The composer's penchant in the midsixties seemed to be for moody, minor key themes that suited crime and espionage thrillers (the theme to *The Ipcress File* with its continental, European flavour is a quintessential piece of midsixties Barry with an arrangement that is echoed in the composer's marvellous piece *Vendetta*).

Versatility sums up John Barry's musical style and despite working on ten Bond titles, he has not been restricted to macho action dramas. Barry's range as a composer is astonishingly varied: he's scored movies as diverse as *Midnight Cowboy*, *King Kong*, *Howard The Duck* and *Peggy Sue Got Married!* He received an Academy award for his song to the African-based wildlife drama, *Born Free* (1965), and was critically lauded for the sombre grandeur of his score to the historical tale, *The Lion In Winter*; moreover, without breaking into a sweat, Barry's talents can extend to faithfully creating a pastiche of Victorian waltz music (in the black comedy, *The Wrong Box*, 1966) scoring a western (Monty Walsh, 1970) and producing steamy saxophone jazz for the noirish thriller *Body Heat* (1981) starring William Hurt and Kathleen Turner. Barry received two further Academy Awards, one each for *Out Of Africa* and *Dances With Wolves*.

In 35 highly industrious years, Barry (recently made an OBE) has produced over 90 film scores and the superlative compilation below gives a value-for-money selection from many of his significant film oeuvres.

THEMEOLOGY: THE BEST OF JOHN BARRY, COLUMBIA 488582-2

First released in 1997, *Themeology* remains the perfect introduction to John Barry's music. It's a marvellous, mid-price 23 track compilation which spans three decades, beginning with the composer's early 1960's rock'n'roll excursions (*Beat For Beatniks*) progressing to the haunting score he produced to accompany Kevin Costner's Oscar-winning 1990 epic western, *Dances With Wolves*. Eight tunes are culled from Barry's long and successful association with James Bond, including his dramatic treatment of Monty Norman's famous James Bond Theme with its propulsive lead guitar and boisterous brass section, the brooding *Space March* from *You Only Live Twice* and the main title songs -performed by the inimitable Cardiff song-siren, Shirley Bassey - from *Goldfinger* and *Diamonds Are Forever*. In addition to his sterling contributions to James Bond, this collection includes Barry's memorable themes for sixties movies like *The Knack*, *The Ipcress File* (the famous Len Deighton espionage thriller starring Michael Caine as Harry Palmer), *The Quiller Memorandum* and *Midnight Cowboy*. Also included are some Barry TV themes, including his distinctive tune for *The Persuaders*, a popular early 70s programme starring Roger Moore and Tony Curtis. Highly recommended as a delectable entrée, to the inimitable Barry sound.

THE CLASSIC JOHN BARRY, THE CITY OF PRAGUE PHILHARMONIC, SILVA SCREEN RECORDS FILMCD 141

Also worth investigating is this recently recorded orchestral compilation of Barry filmscores. Although Barry's seminal Bond work is excluded, what we have instead is an enthralling set that focuses on memorable music from *Zulu*, *The Lion In Winter*, *Body Heat*, *Dances With Wolves* and less well-known pieces like *Chaplin*, *Somewhere In Time*, *Raise The Titanic* and *Hanover Street*.

Some of these latter films may not have been memorable but Barry's scores are always engaging. A well-rounded collection.

RAISE THE TITANIC: THE COMPLETE FILM SCORE
BY JOHN BARRY
SILVA SCREEN FILMCD 319

Although the 1980 film starring Alec Guiness and Jason Robards (based incidentally on the book by Clive Cussler) suffered the same ignominious fate as the ocean-going behemoth that inspired it and sank without trace, John Barry's evocative score has gained near Holy Grail status amongst his legion of fans. Apparently the original recording of the score has never been commercially available, having been mislaid. Enter Barry's longtime associate and orchestrator, Nic Raine, who has sedulously attempted to reconstruct the original music in all its detail. Now, thanks to those dedicated soundtrack buffs at Silva Screen Records, we can hear the versatile City Of Prague Philharmonic sail effortlessly through the complete 50 minute score. Barry's score is majestic. The music's brooding symphonic elegance conjures up the darker, more contemplative side of his early James Bond work and paints vivid sound pictures of the deep sea quest for the doomed ship. Barry's opulent score evinces great pathos and sentiment but never descends into sentimentality. Under Raine's direction, the City Of Prague Philharmonic produce a superlative performance, their interpretation wringing out every nuance of expressive detail from the score. A haunting, grandiloquent piece of music which fully justifies its lofty elevation in the John Barry canon.

cd reviews
charles waring

**CT ALBUM OF THE MONTH
CITIZEN KANE: THE ESSENTIAL
BERNARD HERRMANN FILM
MUSIC COLLECTION (2CDS)
SILVA SCREEN FILMXCD 308**

If you ever wanted to know why Bernard Herrmann is the greatest film composer of all time, here's the compelling evidence, all 110 minutes of it. This double set functions as an excellent introduction to the man's music, containing all the key moments from seven famous Hitchcock films, including *North By Northwest* (the whirlwind fandango), *Marnie*, *Psycho* (that gruesome shower scene where Janet Leigh is stabbed by...violins!) and my own favourite, *Vertigo*. This compilation also includes extracts from *Torn Curtain*, Herrmann's final but doomed collaboration with Hitch: the corpulent British director was pressurised by Universal into discarding Herrmann's nerve-jangling score in favour of a more commercial one for a run-of-the-mill espionage thriller which paired Paul Newman with the unlikely Julie Andrews. Aside from the inspired liaisons with Hitch, other Herrmann music here comes from *Cape Fear*, the sci-fi classic *The Day The Earth Stood Still*, *On Dangerous Ground*, Orson Welles' monumental *Citizen Kane* and the jazz-inflected music for Scorsese's 70's masterpiece, *Taxi Driver*. Herrmann's versatility is reflected in his inventive music for the fantasy films *Jason And The Argonauts*, *The Seventh Voyage Of Sinbad* and *Mysterious Island*. A unique and peerless figure in film scoring, Herrmann approached his task with all the seriousness and zeal of a classical composer. He repudiated melody in favour of fragmented motifs and unusual orchestral textures which lent his scores a highly-charged, heightened dramatic emphasis. He has been much parodied but remains much loved. If you only had to buy one soundtrack album in your entire life, I would be compelled to recommend this one. Pure genius! (For an in-depth appraisal of Herrmann's art, refer to CT1.11)

**RUN LOLA RUN, ORIGINAL
SOUNDTRACK BMG 74321 60477-2**

The low-budget German movie which spawned this soundtrack has been attracting much press attention. It has even been hailed in some quarters as a teutonic Trainspotting, garnering good reviews at the 1999 Edinburgh film festival. Set in Berlin, Lola, the movie's heroine (a punk with dayglo orange hair, reminiscent of Toyah Wilcox circa 1980!) is given an ultimatum by an angry mob boss: she has just 20 minutes to locate 100,000 marks or else her boyfriend gets it (apparently he's in debt to the gangster). Aside from its breakneck pace, hand-held videocam feel, cut and shut editing and three alternative story endings, the film boasts this adrenaline-inducing soundtrack composed largely by the team of Johnny Klimek, Tom Twyker (also the film's director) and Reinhold Heil. Not household names, then, but I'm pretty sure that this cult movie's soundtrack will soon become an in-demand item for dyed-in-the-wool dance music fans. The music is throbbing, electronic techno, dominated by pulsing beats and metallic, ambient textures. It works well outside of its cinematic context. The film's eponymous star, played by überbabe, Franka Potente, also contributes a spoken lead vocal to the song *Believe* that opens the album. Members of the chemical generation who enjoy pounding dancefloor Panzer beats will lap this up. An exciting, high-tempo score but not recommended for people fitted with a pacemaker!

THE GENERAL'S DAUGHTER, ORIGINAL SOUNDTRACK MILAN/BMG 69474-2

If you're a regular cinema-goer, you've probably already witnessed John Travolta's mesmerising, somewhat OTT performance as a military investigator gathering information on the death of a high-ranking army general's daughter in America's deep south. The majority of this attractive score consists of music composed by Carter Burwell. Although Burwell supplied music to *Wayne's World 2* and last year's Mel Gibson thriller, *Conspiracy Theory*, it's the composer's work with the Coen brothers that has attracted attention (in particular his haunting score to the Coen's crowning cinematic achievement, *Fargo*). Burwell supplies a grandiose, brooding and elegiac score full of rich orchestral sonorities. A recurring musical motif is voiced by an evocative slide guitar, imbuing the score with a sultry, deep southern flavour. The soundtrack also includes four songs which demonstrate the wonders of modern technology: several authentic accapella African-American folk songs recorded over 60 years ago are given contemporary backings. The most effective of these is *She Began To Lie* which contains portions of the bluesy folk song *Sea Lion Woman* performed many moons ago by Christine and Katherine Shipp. The result is extraordinarily evocative. Given the military context of this film, it's refreshing not to find some clichéd rolling of martial snare drums in the score.

FIGHT CLUB, THE DUST BROTHERS RESTLESS/BMG 70173-2

Fight Club is a movie that unites Hollywood heart-throb, Brad Pitt, with director David Fincher. The two previously worked together on the ingenious, claustrophobic thriller *Se7en* a couple of years back. This movie has already stoked fierce controversy with its focus on two disenchanted men who inject meaning into their lives by setting up a club where young men can ease their existential frustrations by indulging in gory pugilistic combat. The soundtrack is the work of the dynamic dance duo, Michael Simpson and John King, otherwise known as The Dust Brothers. The Dust Brothers are not your average "here today gone tomorrow" one-hit-wonder dance outfit. In fact, this highly-regarded duo have spread their creative wings beyond the somewhat restrictive parameters of the dance milieu to work with veteran rock icons, The Rolling Stones. This tenebrous, hypnotic score encapsulates The Dust Brothers edgy, cut'n'paste approach to music: *Fight Club* boasts a sampledelic patchwork of mutant beats, electronic bleeps, buzzsaw synthesisers and ricocheting echoes, all of which packs an almost visceral punch. Moody synthscapes are contrasted with pugilistic groove mantras that complement the film's bruising action sequences. The music is intense and mesmeric but lacks sensitivity (mind you, considering the movie's storyline, this comes as no surprise). A potent soundtrack album which will sell well simply on the strength of the Dust Brothers' illustrious reputation. The BBC Radiophonic Workshop has a lot to answer for!

A SIMPLE PLAN, MUSIC BY DANNY ELFMAN, SILVA SCREEN FILM CD 310

Danny Elfman is one of the finest soundtrack composers currently working in the film medium. It was Elfman's partnership with director Tim Burton that established his reputation as a particularly imaginative film scorer: *Beetlejuice*, *Batman*, *Edward Scissorhands*, *The Night Before Christmas* and *Mars Attacks* have all been enhanced by Elfman's evocative, compelling music. Elfman's dynamic style is the musical equivalent of a match being thrown in a box of fireworks: his scores snap, crackle and pop with vibrant orchestral colour and boundless invention. In Elfman's music, the humorous and sinister live side by side. If one piece of music summed up the quintessence of Elfman's art it's his marvellous theme to *The Simpsons*. However, Elfman's music for Sam Raimi's rendering of Scott B.Smith's bestselling novel, *A Simple Plan* (starring Bill Paxton and Billy Bob Thornton as two brothers whose lives are complicated when they stumble upon a cache of stolen money) is more subdued. Here, Elfman mutes his trademark pyrotechnics in favour of a darkly atmospheric, less extravagant score. Although his sombre, slow-moving orchestral textures lack the vitality and immediacy of his most well-known work, *A Simple Plan* demonstrates the composer's growing maturity. A lugubrious almost funereal score, maybe, but one which effectively complement's the movie's bleak, snowbound setting.

BOND: BACK IN ACTION FILM CD 317

Silva Screen's soundtrack stalwarts, The City Of Prague Philharmonic, find themselves under the baton of conductor Nic Raine for this latest Bond bonanza. Raine, in fact, is more qualified than most to present an interpretation of classic Bond scores: for more than a decade he has been John Barry's orchestrator and worked in tandem with the composer on 1985's *A View To A Kill*. Presented in an attractive Ferrari-red case with an informative booklet, *Bond Back In Action* features seven orchestral suites composed of music from *Dr. No, From Russia With Love, Goldfinger, Thunderball, You Only Live Twice, On Her Majesty's Secret Service* and culminating with *Diamonds Are Forever*. Apart from the music for *Dr No* (some of which is recorded here for the first time) and the immortal Bond theme (both of which were penned by Monty Norman), the lion's share of *Bond Back In Action* stems from the imaginative pen of John Barry. Barry's Bond themes are marvellously recreated here with all the verve and panache you would associate with 007 (and in vivid Dolby Surround Sound too!). One of the undoubted highlights for Bond aficionados will be the guest appearance of guitarist Vic Flick, an ex-John Barry Seven member and player on the original version of the Bond theme. Flick (also a film composer in his own right) reprises his role as lead guitarist on Nic Raine's robust rendering of the 007 signature tune. Make yourself a big Martini (shaken not stirred, of course!) then sit back and wallow in the soundtrack feast that is *Bond Back In Action*. Suave, sophisticated and sexy. And that's just the music!

8MM, ORIGINAL MOTION PICTURE SOUNDTRACK BY MYCHAEL DANNA

Canadian-born Mychael Danna is best known for his several collaborations with the Armenian film director, Atom Ergoyan, including 1994's Cannes prize winner, Exotica and more recently, the Academy Award nominated, *The Sweet Hereafter*. Danna's intriguing, unusual soundtracks often contain elements of middle eastern music and the composer's music for Joel Schumacher's controversial thriller, *8mm*, is no exception. The film stars Nicholas Cage as a small-time PI who obsessively tracks down the makers of a snuff-movie. Danna expertly captures the dark, sinister atmosphere of the film, frequently using a snaking, Arabic flute over static string structures. The tension and unease is almost palpable. An insidiously seductive score but not recommended for the faint-hearted.

DEATH WISH OST, HERBIE HANCOCK, COLUMBIA 491981-2

If truth be told, it's tantamount to a death wish if you're a resteraunteur who opens his or her doors to Michael Winner, the rotund film director turned Sunday supplement culinary critic. Winner's assaults on the food industry are almost as vicious as Charles Bronson's attacks on muggers in the British film director's most famous movie. That was, of course, *Death Wish*, a controversial urban fable of vigilante payback which caused quite a furore back in the seventies. While Winner has descended from Hollywood heights to tabloid journalism, Herbie Hancock, the composer of *Death Wish*'s soundtrack, has gone from strength to strength, confirming his status as a living legend in black music. For the first time ever in the UK, Hancock's re-mastered *Death Wish* receives a long overdue release. Recorded in 1974, *Death Wish* represented Hancock's second foray into movie scoring (his first had been Antonioni's *Blow Up* in 1966). Issued a year after he cut his seminal jazz-funk classic, *Headhunters*, Hancock's *Death Wish* features the combined talents of the jazz-maestro's *Headhunters* ensemble. The outstanding track is the extended theme tune, a brooding masterpiece of funk fusion augmented by shimmering strings and woodwind. *Joanna's Theme* is a stately mid-tempo ballad with Hancock's eloquent piano lines floating against a dramatic orchestral backdrop. The remainder of the music on the soundtrack is less commercial and more abstract. *Do A Thing*, for example, has keening strings and resounding piano bass notes punctuating tense, metronomic hi-hat configurations while *Paint Her Mouth* has a varied orchestral palette consisting of *Psycho*-esque string stabs, some weird and wonderful wailing synthesisers and eerie percussion effects. Scary stuff! Don't expect any airy-fairy cocktail-lounge tunes here. The title cut is excellent but the remainder of the music, while unusual, does not quite work without the movie's visual images to support it.

THE THOMAS CROWN AFFAIR SOUNDTRACK, RYKODISC/MGM RCD10719

In 1968, Steve McQueen starred in two classic movies. *Bullitt*, the groundbreaking cops and killers thriller was one, while this was the other, Norman Jewison's attractive, likeable crime-caper, *The Thomas Crown Affair* (recently re-made with Pierce Brosnan in the title role). In this movie, McQueen played the affluent, high-flying financier, Thomas Crown, who masterminds a daring bank robbery simply to amuse himself and beat the system (even in an uncharacteristic white-collar role, McQueen played a rebel). With Norman Jewison's dazzling visuals and multiple, split-screen imagery, the film engraved an indelible impression on many who saw it. The hypnotic effect was enhanced by Michel Legrand's symphonic jazz score, which not only gave the movie a strong musical identity but also lent a subtle cohesion to the overall feel of the film. *The Thomas Crown Affair*, has, in its time, experienced as many detractors as extollers of its virtues. The further the 1960s have receded from the horizon, the more vociferous its opponents have been. Generally, the film is regarded (somewhat erroneously, in my opinion) as an inconsequential, indulgent movie and a product of 1960's hubris. It's often dismissed by contemporary critics as an irrelevant slice of eye-candy. Legrand's music, too, is undervalued, merely perceived as superficial musical candyfloss bereft of true substance. I couldn't disagree more. Having watched the film recently from DVD, I was surprised to find that it hadn't dated as badly as I had been led to imagine. From a purely musical perspective, and as this superbly remastered deluxe CD illustrates, Legrand's bewitching score works in an amazing symbiosis with Jewison's film, complementing cinematic images in a way that has never been repeated. Admittedly, the film's theme song (Noel Harrison crooning the MOR ballad, *The Windmills Of Your Mind*) sounds a tad twee but the rest of the score contains some wonderful pieces, notably *A Man's Castle*, the frenetic *Playing The Field* (accompanying the scene where Crown plays polo) and the superb finale, *The Crowning Touch*, boasting an almost baroque sonic architecture of descending piano chords with rich orchestration. One of the film's most famous scenes, *The Chess Game*, where McQueen and Faye Dunaway play an erotically suggestive game of chess, has some wonderfully evocative music to accompany it, enhanced by Legrand's striking use of percussion and orchestral effects. As a bonus for fans of the film, the music is interspersed with some movie dialogue while the music CD also doubles as a CD ROM featuring the film's original cinema trailer. An accompanying booklet also encloses an informative essay and some photographic stills from the film. Thirty-two years down the line, Michel Legrand's score still sounds fine. Crime has never been so attractive!

MUSIC FROM THE MOTION PICTURE OUT OF SIGHT, JERSEY RECORDS MCD11799

Elmore Leonard and Hollywood have not always had an easy marriage. Up until 1995's *Get Shorty*, no one had successfully adapted a Leonard book, not even the author himself (who over the years has produced several screenplays of his own work). Hot on the heels of that film was Tarantino's much-touted rendering of the novel, *Rum Punch*, re-christened *Jackie Brown*. Even better was 1998's *Out Of Sight*, starring ER heart-throb, George Clooney and perfectly-derriered Latino actress-cum-chanteuse, Jennifer Lopez, whose palpable onscreen chemistry approached thermonuclear meltdown. The director was Steven Soderbergh, a talented, innovative film-maker who had found success with *Sex, Lies And Videotape* 10 years earlier but not much else since. In addition to scintillating direction and magnetic onscreen performances, *Out Of Sight* also yielded an engagingly funky soundtrack. Belfast-born David Holmes created the movie's excellent incidental music, supplying some muscular funk grooves and dreamy ambient soundscapes, notably the shimmering *Tub Scene* and final, poignant, *No More Time Outs*. Interspersed between Holmes' original score are some classic uptempo tunes, including two from the soulful Isley Brothers (the infectious *It's Your Thing* and *Fight The Power*) and some hispanic dancefloor workouts by the likes of Mongo Santamaria (*Watermelon Man*) and Willie Bobo (*Spanish Grease*). Even the booze-sozzled lounge crooner, Dean Martin, adds a Vegas cocktail bar twist with his laid-back rendition of *Ain't That A Kick In The Head*. Although the inclusion of chunks of relevant film dialogue gives the music a cinematic context, this excellent soundtrack works well in its own right. Fine musical accompaniment to a superlative film.

crime and history
gwendoline butler

While writing her own highly acclaimed crime novels for HarperCollins and CT Publishing, we're glad to say that Gwendoline Butler finds time to take her regular look at recent historical crime novels for CT...

When it is your pleasure and your duty to read a number of crime stories in a relatively short time then you soon see that they fall into groups. The mind likes order.

First, let me group together two brilliant, high quality books: *The Electrical Field*; Kerri Sakamoto (Macmillan, £7.99), and *A Time to Pray*; Stephanie Churchill (Citron Press, £7.99): these two books have nothing in common except their brilliance. Kerrie Sakamoto's book is forceful, elegant and compelling: in some ways, a sad book. *A Time to Pray* is quite different but equally powerful. I salute these two books.

Deserving of a place with them is *The Crimes of Charlotte Bronte* : James Tully (Robinson, £7.99), which is an enjoyable if not totally believable tale. The letters of Charlotte to Mrs Gaskell and the replies do not suggest a killer. Charlotte of the letters was above all a realist, and the Charlotte that James Tully depicts is not. But this is an original and enjoyable read. Another clutch of books that constitutes the Anne Perry group: namely, *Bedford Square* (Headline, £5.99), *Brunswick Gardens* (HarperCollins, £16.99), and *The Twisted Root* (Headline, £17.99). The first two stories are Inspector Pitt investigations, with Pitt helped by his wife Charlotte and sometimes by her well-married sisters. The casual reader might think that the two women do most of the work. Pitt is a dull fellow, but he grows on you as you read. The sense of period is not subtle: London squares, London rain, and heavy boots for Inspector Pitt (with a good deal of laundry, ironing and kitchen work for his wife). William Monk is the detective hero of The Twisted Root. He is a private investigator. A strong plot here, with a powerful final curtain. Monk, toohas the support of his wife. These two books offer a picture of a mid-Victorian world but not, perhaps, one that Queen Victoria would have recognised.

The next group look back to an earlier world. *The Foxes of Warwick*: Edward Marsh, (Headline, £7.99) is set in an Anglo-Norman world with the Domesday Commissioners playing a part. Interesting and amusing but suspend judgement as a view of a past world.

Fortune like the Moon by Alys Clare(NEL, £5.99) is a diverting and persuasive read. These are perfect books for when you want to go back to another world.

I want to end up by drawing your attention to two straight detective stories : *Dying to Score* by Judith Cutler (Headline): a highly enjoyable read to refresh you after the intellectual effort the medieval tales may demand. And finally, another from the series that delights so many: *The Cat Who Robbed a Bank* by Lilian Jackson Braun, (Headline, £17.99). This is one for the addicts. Don't miss *The Horus Killings* (Paul Doherty, HarperCollins, £9.90); or *Death and the Peerless Pool* (Deryn Lake, Hodder, £16.99) and *Death in White Satin* (Michelle Spring, Orion, £9.99).

a personal view
mark timlin

AS USUAL, I was stuck for what to write for this piece until *Crime Time* 3.1 popped though the letterbox and I read the piece *Eddie Bunker: Life Goes On by Mark Campbell*. Towards the end Mark asks the following question:

"Your criminal record has given your books a certain credibility. Do you sometimes read other crime writers, and think they haven't got the details right?"

To which Bunker replies:

"Yes. Unless they've been there, they wouldn't understand. What they have is a myth they've got from some other source or they take it from movies. What else do they have?"

Now wait a minute Eddie. To say that statement is spurious and doesn't hold water is to put it mildly. In fact, with all due respect to the man, or any man for that matter who wanders about, and I quote again from the piece: 'Heavily armed', it's utter bollocks.

Think about it for a minute. Did William Shakespeare go to Scotland? It would have been a long trip in his time. Or Denmark? Even longer. If he didn't then he should never have written Macbeth or Hamlet. And frankly, The Tempest would be out of the question. And was Arthur Conan Doyle a junkie? I don't know and frankly I don't care. But Sherlock Holmes's seven-percent-solution of cocaine gives the great detective a certain frisson that would otherwise leave him just too good to be true. And a whole literary genre, namely Science Fiction could not exist. No Jules Verne, No Ray Bradbury. No *Martian Chronicles* as just one example, because no one on Earth has been to Mars no one is allowed to write about the experience. See what I mean? The theory just ain't on.

Now don't think I haven't given this argument some thought during my writing career. I dish up novels of extreme ultra-violence set in London, where quite honestly my hero would be dead or in jail long ago if he really acted like he does. But they're just stories for God's sake. They come out of my head. And the one of the few saving graces of the human race from what I can see is what happens between our ears. Our imagination. And no one, not even an icon like Eddie Bunker should try and take it away from us.

Now, although I have fired guns and even owned some, I've never actually shot at anybody. Just paper targets. And everyone knows that targets don't shoot back. But I wanted to know what it was like to actually use one of the weapons that Nick Sharman totes about the badlands of south London. And whether or not, as some writers seem to think that the recoil will knock you on your arse. And no, it doesn't.

And I've only been at the wrong end of a gun barrel once, in East Germany as it was then, when I was driving a band from Berlin to Bonn and got on the wrong side of a border guard with a machine gun, and believe me it was no fun. The expression: 'His bowels turned to water' certainly has the ring of truth to it as I can testify.

But I reckon I write good violence, even though I haven't had a fight since 1987 and that was just girlie enough for me to vow never to again. However, I've been in a few situations since when things could've gone off, and I managed to bluff my way out, without any blood being spilled, by simply acting the way Sharman would a one of my books. And, I've been in a couple of situations where things were definitely going to go off and I just kept my big trap shut and managed to get away unscathed. Because as I get older and I hope a little wiser I know that the human body is made up of brittle bone, bruisable meat and jelly, and I want to live long enough to collect the private pension that almost breaks the bank every month.

And because I'm so scared of getting hurt I think that is why I do write good punch-ups. It's back to that old imagination thing again.

NOW, LIKE I SAID last time, I rejoined the CWA this year, and I'm glad I did, because the first thing that happened was that I found the publisher of large print titles for libraries name and e-mail address in *Red Herrings* (That's the private and secret magazine of the association if you don't know) and blasted off so many e-mails to her that she finally relented and made an offer for the last Sharman novel.

Not such good news was the first meeting I attended at the New Cavendish Club in London's swinging West End. Blimey, if that's the *New* Cavendish Club, I'd hate to see the old one! The few members who didn't flee before the meeting started were entertained in the corner of the dining room, where, believe me you wouldn't want to stay for a late supper, redolent as the place was of institutional cooking and reminded me of my old school canteen, which is one memory that sits uneasily with me.

But all was not lost. After the meeting finished a bunch of us dived into a cab, laughing hysterically, and were transported down the road to Soho where we enjoyed a fine Italian meal, and later a few drinks in a club of my acquaintance.

Then, my pal Denise Danks organised a London chapter meeting at the same restaurant and club a few weeks later, which was a great success. Almost thirty people showed up, no one fell out, everyone paid the very reasonable tariff and a good time was had by all.

I've just heard a rumour that the CWA might move the meeting venue to the Soho House (very up market) which will be a huge improvement.

More on that later.

TIMLIN'S TOP TIPS FOR 2000 II
The Blue Hour by Jefferson Parker
Void Moon by Michael Connelly
Layer Cake by JJ Connolly (Highly recommended)
Black Mountain by Les Standiford,
Endgame by James Elliott
Burnt Sienna by David Morrell
The Defense by D.W. Buffa

the view from murder one
maxim jakubowski

His own books have earned him the sobriquet King of the Erotic Thriller; he's one of the genre's premier editors, and he runs the UK's leading crime bookshop, Murder One in Charing Cross Road. From the pages of The Guardian we bring you...Maxim Jakubowski.

For years now, a touch of noir has been the perfect accessory for all hip crime writers. We've had country noir, blue-collar noir, New York and L.A. noir (as well as most other US cities or States), girlie noir, London noir (guilty, m'lord!) and my own novels appear to have inadvertently opened up a hornet's test of erotica noir—don't blame me, it's just the way I write them... Since the death of Derek Raymond, however, I can only think of James Ellroy whose books actually deserve the epithet amongst contemporary crime authors. Until now. *God is a Bullet* by Boston Teran (Macmillan 10.00) assigns its author to the pantheon of darkness in one effortless swoop. If you read a bleaker book this year, I'd be surprised. This searing debut novel is set in the feral wasteland of the Southern California desert and the badlands of Mexico and grips like a nightmare gone bad. The kidnapping of a fourteen-year-old girl by a satanic cult led by the murderous Cyrus who makes Charles Manson look like a school truant, and the massacre of her mother and stepfather, set Bob Hightower, the girl's father and a cop, on their trail. His only hope is Case Hardin, a female ex-drug addict and cult member, whom he is reluctant to trust. Their quest turns both surreal and savage and becomes a gripping headlong immersion into the hard bitten world of junkies, child pornography rings and ritualistic violence. To be cleansed of all sin, you have to wallow through the dirt and accept the worse the world can throw at you, and both Hightower and Case soon have to face dreadful torments and trauma. It's a roller coaster of an experience, noir as a purging metaphysical experience that will take your breath away and wallop your brain cells with an acid-dripping machete. Needless to say I relished every dark page, but fans of genteel, cosy crime should read this haunting offspring of Sam Peckinpah and Jim Thompson with caution.

Equally frenetic, but for a very different reason is *Motherless Brooklyn* by Jonathan Lethem (Faber & Faber 9.99) where the involuntary sleuth, Lionel Essrog A.K.A. the Human Freakshow suffers from Tourette's Syndrome, which results in an uncontrollable urge to shout out nonsense, touch every surface in reach, rearrange objects, etc... Spurning drugs which could dim his perception, and finding that his appearance is an invisible disguise, Lionel is drawn into investigating the case of the mysterious death of Frank Minna. Frank was Lionel's saviour from an orphanage and the case is very personal indeed. Lethem had previously established a reputation in the science fiction field and his venture into the mystery genre is assured, witty, a love song to his native Brooklyn and full of sparkling dialogue and plot twists. But what impresses most is his affection for his highly fallible characters. A fascinating adventure, already on its way to the screen where Edward Norton plans to direct and star as the hapless Lionel. *Afterburn* by Colin Harrison (Bloomsbury 9.99) tells the tale of a Vietnam survivor in his late fifties, whose family has imploded and is looking for a woman to bear his child. Enter the voluptuous and obligatory femme fatale with dangerous links to the mob. Soon, a relentless plot is in motion racing from Wall Street and Hong Kong high finance to the criminal underworld, highlighting a fascinating set of characters under pressure and high octane drama. An impeccably literate thriller by the author of *Manhattan Nocturne* and still a much underrated talent.

Eliot Patison's *The Skull Mantra* (Century 10.00) blends a headless corpse, a disgraced investigator and a conspiracy of silence into a cocktail of action adventure set in Tibet. Political and religious intrigue, sorcerers, corrupt Chinese officials, American mining industrialists and evocative landscapes crowd the pages in what is unambitiously just a great read, in the tradition of Lionel Davidson's classic Rose of Tibet. Perfect entertainment.

Hailed by Muriel Spark, *Corpsing* by Toby Litt (Hamish Hamilton 9.99) sees a young British mainstream novelist try his hand at the criminous and pull off a remarkable achievement. Following the path of a bullet in two directions—one into the body it enters and the other back into the gun barrel into the motivation of the person who fired it, Corpsing manages to be both suspense-filled and full of literary conceits. Fetishistic a la Cornwell in its systematic analysis of bullet penetration and autopsy and hard-edged in its x-ray of modern relationships, this has all the hallmarks of a future cult book. The boy done good. While Toby Litt ingeniously reinvents the crime genre, Reginald Hill is a comfortable veteran of the traditional British police procedural with a sting in the tail and the latest Dalziel and Pascoe, *Arms and the Women* (HarperCollins 16.99) focuses on Ellie, Pascoe's wife, and an attempt to kidnap her. As ever, the roots of the case lie in the past and Hill orchestrates the whole thing with inch-like precision and sly wit. Maybe not his best, but Dalziel and Pascoe are always great company.

...and finally

SHORT STORIES

Crime short stories appear in unexpected places. Hosting a Hitchcock Evening for the Westcliffe Film & Video Club in Rochford, Essex I met an old friend, former policeman-turned-author, Ken Westall. He publishes *Stories From Seven Pens* (Seven Pens Press, £3.99) as each volume comprises from seven Essex writers. Volume 2 had three by Ken himself *Museum Piece*, *Prometheus Denied* and *Nothing Is As It Seems*. The first told of a former Anti-Terrorist chief, now a Museum Curator who finds himself taking part in an occult time-warp police raid, realising that the officer whose uniform he has put on is about to be shot. The details of the raid and the Museum are completely credible.

The second is the minute by minute account of the convict who, believing himself superior to all men carefully plans to explode the floor below his cell so he can escape. The explosion succeeds, but not how he planned it.

Another very short book is *The Case of The Uppingha Emeralds*, a clever Holmes pastiche by Roy Andrews. A useful book to keep.

COMMENT COMPRENDRE....?

An American critic asked why I don't translate French quotations in my books. The reason is that I will not put my interpretation on a French author's words. I have specialised in *polars* and *romans policieres* for some years from when I corresponded with the courteous and helpful Georges Simenon for my *Murder Done To Death*. How do you find the answers to research queries, titles, translations, et al? des Litteratures Policieres, part of the organisation of the Mayor of Paris, in his Direction des Affaires Culturelles. Ask a question—get the answer. I sent a fax about a Simenon translation title at 9 am—and got the faxed reply at 11 am! They were sponsors of a recent Convention. The office is at 48-50, Rue du Cardinal Lemoine in the Fifth Arrondisement of Paris, 75005, the telephone number is 42 34 93 00, fax 40 51 81 23. Comment comprendre ? How to Understand—we don't have the like in Britain. The Detec-

john kennedy melling

tion Club has a library somewhere, the C W A fields some queries—but this doesn't help librarians, scholars or readers. Europe has an excellent French magazine Le Nouveau Detective published every Wednesday, 32 pages of true crimes throughout the world, but more detailed and dispassionate than the American and English "troodick" journals. BILIPO has copies from 1928 to date, so invaluable when checking on any particular murder case. There is an association in France called 8 1 3, after the 1910 title of Maurice Leblanc (1864-1941) who created Arsène Lupin. It publishes a large, well-written, glossy journal, holds conferences—and admits crime <u>readers</u> unlike all the other associations!

ASSOCIATIONS—DISJOINTED

I wonder why the various crime writers' organisations have had such sad problems lately? First, Mystery Writers of America. They have an excellent office in Manhattan, which I have seen for myself. Their Presidents include all the great names from Ellery Queen onwards including the Belgian Georges Simenon. They award a Grand Master only when they feel it appropriate and they have a prestigious annual dinner and conference in New York when the Edgars are presented. BUT in the last few years acrimonious arguments have erupted over the continental Chapters—are they too big for their boots ? Are they doing enough ? Should they be abolished ? Then the bitter row over the role of the Executive Director, as a result a new Director had been elected whose name in the Magazine seems to be in smaller type. The Crime Writers' Association of Britain founded forty years or more ago by the prolific John Creasey (600 books under 17 names).Good sponsorship, strong membership, Gold and Silver Dagger Awards, Annual Dinners and Conferences, Regional Chapters.... BUT—sharp arguments over whether the C W A should be a Trade Union—yes, a Trade Union—how could it have worked ? Then the acid battle over morality, Baroness James, a religious woman and member of the Prayer Book Society, uttered the obvious truth in a broadcast that the better you are educated the more choices you have of evil. Yes, this is clearly stated in the Bible. Could you expect the unlettered tribes of Africa to pronounce on computer hacking, or the average American or English farm labourer to hold forth on insider trading ? (I did see recently a young schoolgirl show her mother how to use her office computer!). This argument actually raises the standard and standing of crime writing, sorely needed when compared with earlier decades. Earlier Decades—the Detection Club was founded in 1931 by the <u>creme de la creme de la dreme</u> as Miss Brodie would say—Chesterton, Bailey, Berkeley, Christie, Sayers, Rhode, Simpson. When I was first taken to one of their regular Dinners I was enthralled to meet the witty Michael Gilbert, the elegant Josephine Bell and the charismatic Christianna Brand, with whom I was to dine in Fleet Street after C W A meetings. When Dame Agatha died, what a choice of Heirs Apparent, plus Eric Ambler, Michael Innes (not Leslie Charteris, he never got elected to this self-perpetuating body).Were they asked ? Did they refuse ? If so, why ? The choice came rather downmarket to Julian Symons (pronounced Simmons he insisted) the brother of the more famed A. J. A. Symons of Quest for Corvo glory. I am prejudiced for two reasons. First Symons was extremely rude to me when I was editing the Black Dagger Series for the C W A and one of the organisers of the Christie Centenary—so much so that I failed to finalise the contract to publish a Symons book! Secondly, when fellow columnist Gwendoline Butler was made Hon. Secretary it was agreed I do the bookwork as Hon. Auditor. At the first Dinner we organised there were several catering mistakes, necessitating my rushing into the kitchens to correct them for Gwendoline. The Chef didn't mind because he knew I have a catering qualification—but the then President received three letters asking why Melling behaved as if he were a member of the Club! Years ago the Club members collaborated on several detective stories written by a team of half a dozen greats—The Floating Admiral, Behind The Screen, etc.— when each writer constructed a chapter using another writer's sleuth, so ingeniously that they have all been reprinted in recent years. What a friendship, courtesy and fun. I did enjoy three years on the C W A Committee but I don't belong to any associations!

THE OXFORD COMPANION

In 1989 I edited the *Crime Writers' Practical Handbook* published by the Crime Writers' Association for sale to members; I contributed the Chapter on Forgery. I received a Special Award—a genuine red herring—it was a fossilised fish from the mountains of America, at the 1989 Dinner. As a result a year or so later I was asked to write the Chapter on Forgery for the *Oxford Companion to Crime and Mystery Writing*. When I was in New York in 1993 I rang to enquire the position. Slow progress, I was told. During the next five years letters arrived reporting progress, sending proofs, suggesting fees—and in 1999 it finally appeared. As I bought my contributor's copy this cannot be a review, but it is such a useful book for crime writers, readers, librarians, booksellers and University professors. It is not like 20th. Century Crime and Mystery Writers to whose Third Edition I also contributed two chapters: this was a list of hundreds of authors with explanatory essays and complete lists of every book and short story they ever wrote, with one or two errors. The Companion is more like an encyclopaedia, like all the other Companions, for example Theatre has been an invaluable reference for me for forty years, and the only time I met editor Phyllis Hartnoll was in New York Public Library in 1957. C&MW has chapters on crime writers, plots, characters, sleuths (aristocrats, police' criminals, crimes, milieus (country houses, Universities, etc.), satire, private eyes, organisations—almost any heading you can think of is therein, well-written with gargantuan cross-references and further recommended readings. I must say I am delighted to be part of it and to find my own book as recommended reading.

John Kennedy Melling is a critic, public speaker, and all round good chap, whose book Murder Done To Death *(Scarecrow Press) is required reading for lovers of the parody and pastiche in detective fiction.*

new crime fiction
adrian muller

JANUARY

David Ambrose—*The Discrete Charm of Charlie Monk*. Macmillan, £10.00

David Baldacci—*Saving Faith*. Simon & Schuster, £9.99 D.W.

Buffa—*The Prosecution*. No-Exit-Press, £10.00 Michael

Collins—*The Keeper of Truth*. Weidenfeld, £9.99/£16.99

John Connolly—*Dark Hollow*. Hodder & Stoughton, £10.00

David Craig—*Bay City* (Brade & Jenkins). Constable, £16.99

Clare Curzon—*Guilty Knowledge*. Virago, £5.99

Nelson DeMille—*The Lion's Game*. Little, Brown, £10.00

Bret Easton Ellis—*Glamorama*. Picador, £6.99

Raymond Flynn—*Over My Dead Body* (an Eddathorpe mystery). Hodder & Stoughton, £16.99

Colin Forbes—*Sinister Tide*. Macmillan, £16.99

J.M. Gregson—*A Turbulent Priest*. Severn House, £17.99

Paula Gosling—*Underneath Every Stone* (Blackwater Bay). Little, Brown, £16.99

Richard Haley—*Fear of Violence*. Robert Hale, £16.99

Colin Harrison—*Afterburn*. Bloomsbury, £9.99

Mo Hayder—*Birdman* (debut crime novel). Bantam, £9.99

Geprge V. Higgins—*The Agent*. No-Exit-Press, 6.99

Lilian Jackson Braun—*The Cat Who Robbed a Bank* (Cat mysteries). Headline, £17.99

H.R.F. Keating—*The Hard Detective*. Macmillan, £16.99

Max Kinnings—*Hitman* (debut crime novel). Flame, £10.00

Jonathan Letham—*Motherless Brooklyn*. Faber & Faber, £9.99

Sam Llewellyn—*The Sea Garden*. Headline, £9.99

James Long—*Knowing Max*. HarperCollins, £9.99

Edward Marston—*The Owls of Gloucester* (Domesday series). Headline, £17.99

Steve Martini—*The Attorney*. Headline, £17.99

Peter May—*The Fourth Sacrifice* (Li Yan & Campbell). Hodder & Stoughton, £16.99

Ed McBain—*The Last Dance* (87th Precinct). Hodder & Stoughton, £16.99

Scott McBain—*The Mastership Game*. HarperCollins, £12.99

Michael McGarrity—*Hermit's Peak* (Kevin Kerney). Robert Hale, £16.99

Jennie Melville—*Dead Again* (Charmian Daniels). Macmillan, £16.99

Richard North Patterson—*Dark Lady*. William Heineman, £15.99

Jefferson Parker—*The Blue Hour*. HarperCollins. £9.99

George P. Pelecanos—*Shame the Devil*. Gollancz, £9.99/£16.99

John Ridley—*Everybody Smokes in Hell*. Bantam, £9.99

Norman Russell—*The Dark Kingdom*. Robert Hale, £16.99

Andrew Taylor—*The Office of the Dead* (Roth Trilogy). HarperCollins, £16.99

M.J. Trow—*Maxwell's Ride* (Peter Maxwell). Hodder & Stoughton, £16.99

FEBRUARY

Pauline Bell—Stalker (Benny Mitchell). Constable, £16.99

John Binias—Rene Quite's Theory of Flesh. Macmillan, £9.99

Ethan Black—Irresistible. Headline, £17.99

Alice Blanchard—Darkness Peering (debut crime novel). Bantam, £9.99

Janie Bolitho—Betrayed in Cornwall (Jack Pearce). Constable, £16.99

Hillary Bonner—A Deep Deceit. William Heineman, £10.00/£16.99

Simon Brett—The Body on the Beach (new series). Macmillan, £16.99

Jennifer Crusie—Crazy For You. Pan, £5.99

Patrick Dixon—The Island of Bolay (debut crime novel). HarperCollins, £5.99

David Docherty—The Spirit Death (debut crime novel). Simon & Schuster, £16.99

Jack Ehrlich—Command Influence. Robert Hale, 16.99

Malcolm Forsyth—Only Living Witness. Severn House, 17.99

Simon Gandolfini—Aftermath. Orion, £9.99/£16.99

Jane Goldman—Dreamsworld. HarperCollins, £9.99

Eileen Goudge—One Last Dance. Orion, £9.99/£16.99

Iris Gower—When Night Closes In. Corgi, £5.99

Alex Graham—The Shaft. Piatkus, £5.99

John Grisham—The Brethren. Century, £16.99

Gerald Hammond—Dead Weight. Macmillan, £16.99

Janis Harrison—Roots of Murder (debut crime novel). Robert Hale, £16.99

Ellen Hart—Hunting the Witch (Jane Lawless). The Women's Press, £6.99

Jack Higgins—Day of Reckoning (Sean Dillon). HarperCollins, £16.99

Reginald Hill—Arms and the Women (Dalziel & Pascoe). HarperCollins, £16.99

Linda Howard—All the Queen's Men. Pocket, £5.99/£16.99

Greg Iles—The Quiet Game. Hodder & Stoughton, £10.00

Jonathan Kellerman—Monster (Alex Delware). Little, Brown, £15.99

Roy Lewis—An Assumption of Death (Arnold Landon). Constable, £16.99

Bernard Knight—The Awful Secret (Crowner John). Simon & Schuster, £16.99

Vincent Lardo—Death by Drowning (debut crime novel). Piatkus, £9.99.

Michael Larsen—The Snake in Sydney. Sceptre, £10.00

Dennis Lehane—A Drink Before the War. Severn House, 17.99

Douglas Lindsay—The Cutting Edge of Barney Thomson (Barney Thomson). Piatkus, £6.99

Toby Litt—Corpsing. Hamish Hamilton, £9.99

Joan Lock—Dead Image (debut crime novel). Robert Hale, £16.99

Gregg Main—Every Trace (debut crime novel). Robert Hale, £16.99

Elizabeth McGregor—The Wrong House. Macmillan, £16.99

Gretta Mulrooney—Marble Heart. HarperCollins, £10.99

Eliot Pattison—The Skull Mantra (debut crime novel). Century, £10.00

Otto Penzler (Editor)—Criminal Records (story collection). Orion, £10.99/£17.99

Elizabeth Peters—Curse of the Pharaohs (Amelia Peabody). Robinson, £6.99

Ann Quinton—Put Out the Light. Severn House, 17.99

Ian Rankin—Set in Darkness (John Rebus). Orion, £16.99

Michael Ridpath—Final Venture. Michael Joseph, £9.99

Rosemary Rowe—A Pattern of Blood (Libertus). Headline, £17.99

Rob Ryan—Nine Mil. Headline, £9.99

Steven Saylor—Rubicon (Gordianus the Finder). Robinson, £6.99

Sarah Smith—The Vanished Child. Arrow, £5.99

Doug Swanson—Umbrella Man. No-Exit-

Press, 6.99
Boston Teran—God is a Bullet. Macmillan, £10.00
Donald Thomas—Red Flowers for Lady Blue (Sonny Tarrant). Macmillan, £16.99
Gerard Williams—Dr Mortimer and the Aldgate Mystery (debut crime novel—new series). Constable, £16.99

MARCH

Campell Armstrong—Deadline. Doubleday, £9.99
Catherine Arnold—Class Action (Karen Perry-Mondori). Hodder & Stoughton, £16.99
Marian Babson—A Tealeaf in the Mouse. Constable, £16.99
Toni Cade Bambara—Those Bones Are Not My Child. The Women's Press, £12.99
Gareth Creer—Cradle to Grave. Anchor, £6.99
Murray Davies—The Sampson Option. HarperCollins, £5.99
Juan Manuel De Prada—The Tempest. Sceptre, £14.99
Nick Duerden—Sidewalking. Flame, £10.00
Hodder & Stoughton, £16.99
Quintin Jardine—Screen Savers (Oz Blackstone). Headline, £17.99
John Kelly—The Little Hammer. Jonathan Cape, £10.00
Valerie Kershaw—Head Wounds (Mitch Mitchell). Constable, £16.99
Paul Kilduff—The Dealer. Hodder & Stoughton, £9.99
Laurie R. King—Night Work (Kate Martinelli). HarperCollins, £9.99
Jayne Ann Krentz—Eye of the Beholder. Robert Hale, £16.99
Frank Lean—Boiling Point (Dave Cunane). William Heineman, £16.99
E.A. MacDonald—The Keeper. Simon & Schuster. £16.99
Barry Maitland—Silver Meadow (Brock & Kolla). Orion, £9.99/£16.99

Hannah March—A Distinction of Blood (Robert Fairfax). Headline, £17.99
Ken McClure—Tangled Web. Simon & Schuster, £16.99
David Michie—Conflict of Interest. Little, Brown, £10.00
Bill Murphy—Tin Kickers. Hodder & Stoughton, £16.99
Bill Napier—Revelation. Headline, £16.99
Yang-May Ooi—Mindgame. Hodder & Stoughton, £16.99
Maureen Peters—Valentine (new series). Robert Hale, £16.99
Mike Phillips—A Shadow of Myself. HarperCollins, £16.99
Nicholas Rhea—A Well-Pressed Shroud (Montague Pluke). Constable, £16.99
Betty Rowlands—The Man at the Window (Melissa Craig). Hodder & Stoughton, £16.99
Emma Sinclair—The Path Through the Woods. Piatkus, £5.99
Andrew Taylor—Where Roses Fade (Lydmouth). Hodder & Stoughton, £16.99
Peter Tremayne—Hemlock at Vespers (Sister Fidelma). Headline, £17.99
Martyn Waites—Candleland. Allison & Busby, £16.99
Julia Wallis Martin—The Long Close Call. Hodder & Stoughton, £10.00
Gillian White—The Witch's Cradle. Bantam, £9.99
Douglas Wynn—The Crime Writer's Sourcebook (reference). Allison & Busby, £8.99

APRIL

Phil Andrews—Goodnigh Vienna (Steve Strong). Flame, £10.00
Lisa Appignanesi—Sanctuary. Bantam, £9.99
Nick Barlay—Crumple Zone (Cee Harper). Sceptre, £10.00
Dave Barry—Big Trouble. Piatkus, £9.99
Marc Behm—Afraid to Death. No-Exit-

Press, 6.99
Michael Bond—Monsieur Pamplemouse on Probation (Monsieur Pamplemouse). Allison & Busby, £6.99
Lynda Chater—Makeover. Pocket, £5.99
Lee Child—Visitor (Jack Reacher). Bantam, £9.99
Elizabeth Corley—Fatal Legacy (Andrew Fenwick). Headline, £17.99
Ellen Crosby—Moscow Nights (debut crime novel). Piatkus, £17.99
Joolz Denby—Stone Baby (debut crime novel). HarperCollins, £9.99
Paul Doherty—The Treason of Ghosts (Hugh Corbett). Headline, £9.99
Ruth Dudley Edwards—The Anglo-Irish Murders (Amiss & Troutbeck). HarperCollins, £16.99
David H. Hackworth—The Price of Honour. HarperCollins, £10.00
Julia Hamilton—Other People's Rules. HarperCollins, £16.99
Sparkle Hayter—The Chelsea Girl Murders. No-Exit-Press, £6.99/£14.99
Juliet Hebden—Pel and Death of a Detective (Pel). Constable, £16.99
David Hewson—Native Rites. HarperCollins, £6.99
David Hood—Fatal Climate. Gollancz, £9.99/£16.99
Simon Ings—Painkillers (debut crime novel). Bloomsbury, £9.99
Kazuo Ishiguro—When We Were Orphans. Faber & Faber, £16.99
Peter James—Faith. Orion, £9.99/£16.99
Alison Joseph—The Night Watch (Sister Agnes). Headline, £17.99
Mim Latt—Ultimate Justice. Robert Hale, £16.99
Gay Longworth—Wicked Peace. Pan, £5.99
Phil Lovesey—When the Ashes Burn. HarperCollins, £16.99
Jim Lusby—Crazy Man Michael (DI McFadden). Gollancz, £16.99
Anthony Masters—Murder is a Pretty Business (Daniel Boyd). Constable, £16.99
Viviane Moore—Blue Blood (new series). Gollancz, £9.99
Peter Moore Smith—Ravelling (debut crime novel). Hutchinson, £10.00
Jane Morell—Bloodlines. Robert Hale, £16.99
David Morrell—Burnt Siennna. Headline, £17.99
Walter Mosley—Walkin' the Dog (Socrates Fortlow). Serpent's Tail, £14.99
James Patterson—Cradle and All. Headline, £9.99
Anne Perry—Half Moon Street (Thomas and Charlotte Pitt). Headline, £17.99
Anne Perry—Paragon Walk (Thomas and Charlotte Pitt). HarperCollins, £5.99
John Preston—Ink. Black Swan, £6.99
Andrew Pyper—Lost Girls. Macmillan, £12.00
Nora Roberts—River's End. Piatkus, £5.99
Nora Roberts—Carolina Moon. Piatkus, £17.99
Peter Robinson—In a Dry Season (Alan Banks). Macmillan, £16.99
Denise Ryan—Dead Keen. Piatkus, £17.99
Mary Scott—Murder on Wheels. Allison & Busby, £16.99
Frank Tallis—Sensing Others. Hamish Hamilton, £9.99
Rebecca Tope—Death of a Friend. Piatkus, £17.99
Lucy Wadham—Lost. Faber & Faber, £9.99

Sources

For further information on the above titles, or to find books mentioned in this issue contact:

Crime in Store, 14 Bedford Street, Covent Garden, London WC2E 9HE.
Tel: +44-171-379-3795, fax: +44-171-379-8988.
email: CrimeBks@aol.com
www.ndirect.co.uk/~ecorrigan/cis/crimeinstore.htm

Murder One, 71-73 Charing Cross Road, London WC2H 0AA.
Tel: 0171-734-3483, fax: +44-171-734-3429.
email: 106562.2021@compuserve.com
www.murderone.co.uk

Post Mortem Books, 58 Stanford Avenue, Hassocks, Sussex BN6 8JH.
Tel: 01273-843066, fax: 00-44-1273-845090.
email: ralph@pmbooks.demon.co.uk
www.postmortembooks.co.uk

Blackbird Books, James and Loretta Lay, 24 Grampian Gardens, London, NW2 1JG. Texl 0181 455 3069

Richard Platt, 16 Bramhope Lane, Near Blackheath, London, SE7 7DY
email: richardplatt.books@btinternet.com
www.abebooks.com/home/richardplatt

Zardoz Books, 20 Whitecroft, Dilton Marsh, Westbury, Wiltshire, BA13 4DJ, UK
email: mflanagan@zardozbooks.co.uk
www.zardozbooks.co.uk

USEFUL WEBSITES

If you're trying to locate copies of some of the books mentioned in CT these sites may be of help:

www.crimetime.co.uk
Yes, it's our own site, with lots of links to online bookstores, reviews, features and much more.

www.thebigbookshop.com
Has all the current books mentioned in the latest CT in stock at an average 20% discount.

www.abebooks.com
The Advanced Book Exchange is used by book dealers internationally as is...

www.bibliofind.com
As with the ABE this site lets you search or browse the stock of hundreds of bookdealers around the world.

If anyone else would like their site/shop mentioned email the details in the format above to ct@crimetime.co.uk and we'll list it next issue.

back issues

Crime Time 1 Our debut issue contains interviews with John Harvey, Martina Cole, Derek Raymond, Andrew Klavan (*True Crime*). Plus, features on *Cracker*, Colin Wilson, Griff, Dannie M Martin, and our notorious reviews section.

Crime Time 2 Sorry, sold out.

Crime Time 3 We interview Robert Rodriguez (*Desperado*) and Michael Mann (*Heat*), investigate the transvestite hitman fiction of Ed Wood Jr, talk the talk with Elizabeth George, Elliott Leyton, and Lawrence Block, give the low-down on German crime fiction, and feature an article by Booker prize nominee Julian Rathbone.

Crime Time 4 'The Violence Issue' Reservoir Dog, ex-con and writer Edward Bunker tells us how it is, Ben Elton takes the piss out of it, Joe Eszterhas exploits it, Morgan Freeman abhors it. Plus *Mission: Impossible*, *Heaven's Prisoners* (Phil Joanou), *Curdled*, Kinky Friedman, *The Bill* and *The Verdict*!.

Crime Time 5 Female Trouble! Interviews with Patricia Cornwell, Michael Dibdin, James Sallis and William Gibson. *Feisty Femmes And Two-Fisted Totty* gives the lowdown on women PIs, Ed Gorman talks about Gold Medal books of the Fifties, Hong Kong filmmakers Wong Kar-Wai & Christopher Doyle discuss *Fallen Angels*, and Michael Mann (*Heat*) is examined.

Crime Time 6 The Mean Streets issue contains interviews with writers James Ellroy, Gwendoline Butler, Sara Paretsky and Joseph Hansen, and film directors George Sluizer and Andrew Davis. Articles include Post-War Paperback Art, Batman, Crime Time: The Movie, and Steve Holland's excellent Pulp Fictions.

Crime Time 7 Val McDermid, Hong Kong Cinema, Phillip Margolin, Molly Brown, Ian Rankin, Michael Connelly, Daniel Woodrell and a cast of 1000s in this special 96 page issue!

Crime Time 8 Fantastic! Homicide, Faye and Jonathan Kellerman, Mark Timlin, Anthony Frewin, Gerald Kersh, Gwendoline Butler, Chandler on Celluloid, James Sallis on Chester Himes, The Payback Press and the biggest review section yet!

Crime Time 9 We *Got Carter*, with *Get Carter!* director Mike Hodges writing about making the film and Paul Duncan profiling the man who wrote *Jack's Return Home*. This plus scads of good stuff and the inimitable review section...

Crime Time 10 *Sin City*, Ed Gorman interviewed, Lawrence Block in the Library, Stella Duffy, Lauren Henderson, Sean Hughes, Denise Danks, Jerome Charyn and a cast of squillions...

Crime Time 11 Shut It!!! *The Sweeney* cover feature with those cheeky chappies Regan and Carter, Colin Dexter, Sparkle Hayter, David Williams, Gary Phillips, Janwillem Van De Wetering and the Great Grandam of kid's crime Enid Blyton.

Crime Time 12 The Last Time! (In floppy format anyway!) Joe R Lansdale, Simon Brett, Jay Russell, Steve Lopez, James Patterson, *Black Mask* magazine and the late Derek Raymond on Ted Lewis.

Crime Time 2.1 We re-invent ourselves in shorter, thicker trade paperback format, with interviews with features and fiction including James Sallis, Mark Timlin, Gwendoline Butler, Colin Dexter, Alan Moore, Jerry Sykes, Edward Bunker and more! 288 pages of sheer crime pleasure

Crime Time 2.2 Ed McBain, Mark Timlin, Steve Aylett, Fred Willard, Gary Phillips, Jason Starr, Russell James, Neil Jordan, Stuart Dawson, Paul Duncan and a host of others make this the most enjoyable 288 pages since the last issue of *Crime Time*.

Crime Time 2.3: Loads of stuff, just take our word for it. Oh, OK. Reg H ill, John Milne, Sharky the Sharkdog (just checking to see you're awake), Mark Timlin, Simon Clark. Much too much to list here.

Crime Time 2.4: NYPD Blue

Crime Time 2.5: Payback and all the usual stuff

Crime Time 2.6: The Sopranos, amongst other things...

Crime Time 3.1: Eddie Bunker arouses Mark Timlin's ire...

Each issue up till number 12 is £3.00 post paid in the UK (please add £3.00 p&p per order overseas and Southern Ireland). Issues 2.1 to 2.6 are £5.00 each. Make cheques payable to 'Crime Time' and send your orders to: Back Issues (Dept CT32) Crime Time, 18 Coleswood Rd, Harpenden, Herts AL5 1EQ.